ROSES IN THE NIGHT

Books by Malcolm Bell

The Turkey Shoot: Tracking the Attica Cover-up (Grove Press 1985),
updated and reissued as

The Attica Turkey Shoot: Carnage, Cover-up and the Pursuit of Justice,
(Skyhorse Publishing, 2017, paperback 2022)

Praise for Roses in the Night

From the quetzal's first observations in its role as Greek Chorus to the final ponderings about torture and survival, Malcolm Bell has woven the Mayan theme of resistance during the years of civil war in Guatemala and El Salvador into the warp and weft of his historical novel, *Roses in the Night*. Unrelenting fear, terror and horror funded by their governments and the complicity of ours provide the weft, but the stronger warp threads of hope, perseverance, great courage and love predominate to create an unforgettable novel.

> —Gail Mott, longtime human rights activist, former member of the Sanctuary Movement, and co-publisher of *Interconnect*, a quarterly of the U.S.-Latin America solidarity community.

In *Roses in the Night*, Malcolm Bell has spun a tale of love and admiration for the courageous survivors and martyrs of Guatemala's Mayan genocide. He deftly weaves together two worlds: a Mayan village in Western Guatemala in the 1980s and the beautiful, mountainous terrain of Vermont, home to Mayan refugees displaced by the violence. Full of revelations about US foreign policy toward Central America, the Sanctuary Movement, and the special needs of survivors of torture, this is a story that needs to be told and needs to be read by all who value the courageous opposition mounted to one of the United States' most violent and devastating interventions. Most of all, this is a tale of love in its various modalities, including the latticework of solidarity between those oppressed and brutalized with the help of the US government and those who risk their own safety to walk with them and help them to heal. The stories in *Roses in the Night* are not easy to forget, and this is all the better; they need to be remembered.

> — Patricia Davis, author, longtime human rights activist, Board President of the Guatemala Human Rights Commission/USA, co-author of Sister Diana Ortiz's memoir *The Blindfold's Eyes: My Journey from Torture to Truth.*

With compassion and candor, Malcolm Bell has captured a story that opens hearts and minds to better understand the depth of desperation that drives those who undertake enormous risks to enter a strange land, simply to find the same kind of safe and peaceful life that most of us take for granted.

> —Christine Christopher, Emmy Award-winning film producer, Sundance, Documentary Film Institute grantee

With searing detail, Malcolm Bell tells a story of brutality and terror, also of remarkable humanity, during Guatemala's civil war (1960–1996). The U.S. helped engineer a 1954 military coup d'etat that put in place a dictatorship that became one of the most brutal in Latin America's history, one that lasted for more than four decades. These stories are part of that history. With keen insight into the human nature of both soldiers trained in brutal counterinsurgency tactics and their victims, and then his account of the U.S. Sanctuary Movement in which he participated, he bears witness to realities about which all Americans need to know. While this is a work of fiction, all the stories narrated here are of events that actually took place.

—Margaret Swedish, former director of the
Religious Task Force on Central America & Mexico

Bravo! I just finished your book, and I am so glad I read it. At times, it was hard to put down. I think you depicted torture thoroughly and accurately, as sad and tragic as it is. Your character development was excellent in that I felt I knew most of the characters well. I loved María's courage, irreverence, and vigorous relationship with her family and community. You also effectively emphasized the centrality of spirituality in the culture. Also, using the Quetzal as the observer was brilliant—I even felt attached to the bird.

Brenda's journey and torture story are quite detailed and an important aspect of the book. Her remarkable resilience shines through, as it does with so many survivors. Charlie was a great character and a testament to sensitive men in the world. You did a great job with how denial can unfold and how post-traumatic stress symptoms can occur when the walls of denial start to fall.

Admittedly, I did not know the full history of Guatemala and El Salvador, and I am thankful for the knowledge I've gained through the book. Although I've worked with survivors of torture from over thirty other countries of origin who resettled in Vermont, your book gave me further insights into the horrific humanitarian crises of these countries.

— Karen M. Fondacaro, Ph.D. Professor Emerita, Licensed Clinical Psychologist,
Director, Connecting Cultures, Director, New England Survivors of Torture and
Trauma, University of Vermont

The 1980's Sanctuary Movement in North America provided protection and accompaniment for refugees fleeing the death squads, torture, and massacre of hundreds of Maya villages in Guatemala. The refugees found a safe place in over 600 churches and synagogues to speak publicly about the U.S.-backed slaughter of the Mayan people. This relationship in Sanctuaries became transformative for North Americans.

Now, *Roses in the Night* invites the reader into the same journey through the stories of two Maya women trying to understand and survive the tragic violence as it swept over them. This fine novel will lead a reader into the culture and history of the Maya, providing the strength for these women to endure and survive. Their story will transform the reader just as the stories of the refugees transformed so many North Americans in the 1980's.

—Rev. John Fife, Co-founder of Sanctuary Movement,
Pastor Emeritus of Southside Presbyterian Church, Tucson

This is a story that we are happy to ignore but that is, I fear, more common than we like to admit. The first part has the power of an ancient folk tale, or Greek tragedy. The second part is fascinating on many levels. I am impressed by your compassion for the villagers and even for the soldiers. The characters all seemed absolutely real. I find it amazing that a Vermont Yankee could describe the life of a Guatemalan village and a refugee's progress towards becoming a U.S. citizen with such empathy and accuracy.

—Richard Dougherty, longtime provider of food and education
to impoverished children in Cuernavaca, Mexico

Roses in the Night gives the reader a story which is by turns intimate, endearing, and horrifying. Provocative and sure to be put in the "banned books" category by some, it is necessary reading for those who have the guts to look at the U.S.'s past crimes squarely in the face.

—Suzanne Greene McLone, Social Epidemiologist

ROSES IN THE NIGHT

Mayan Sisters Confront CIA-Backed Terror

MALCOLM BELL

Roses in the Night
Mayan Sisters Confront CIA-Backed Terror

Malcolm Bell

Fresh Look Press
Randolph Center, Vermont

freshlookpress.com

Author's photograph by Bob Aldrich
Photographs from public domain sources.
Quetzal on back cover: Zdeněk Macháček via Unsplash

Book and cover design: RSBPress, Waitsfield, Vermont

Library of Congress Control Number: 2023917622

ISBN 979-8-9889080-0-5 tradepaper
ISBN 979-8-9889080-1-2 ebook

This book is dedicated to the Maya of Guatemala,
to those who recently survived more than
four decades of terror and to the more than
200,000 souls who did not survive.

The character of Brenda, who is one of the Roses
in the title of this fact-based novel, is modeled on
a trilingual Mayan friend. Other friends survived
torture by several U.S.-backed regimes in Latin
America. I wrote the book for them, for the
voiceless millions on the receiving end of
ill-considered U.S. power, and for my
beloved country, which can do better.

"For the United States, it is important that I state clearly that support for military and intelligence units which engaged in violence and widespread repression was wrong, and the United States must not repeat that mistake."

—President Bill Clinton in Guatemala, March 1999

In the U.S., for people like me who are privileged…, it was so amazing to meet people who could not read, but who were really well-educated about their human rights out of necessity…. [I]n the case of traditional women living in the mountains…, I made this profound discovery that these people are so similar to me even though the context is so different.

— Jessica Fujan, March 2010
Peace Brigades International volunteer

During that whole time it was so fascinating to see the [Sanctuary] Movement spread throughout the country—to many different congregations, faith traditions, even some cities. There truly was no leader directing it! Except the Spirit of God. It was like the veil falling off our faces—to see the truth of what was happening to these people in their countries at the hands of soldiers we had trained. In torture. And tactics. And that our tax dollars financed it. I'll never forget the look of terror on the face of one of the immigrant women the day she saw an army helicopter landing outside the window of the hospital where we were. She said they had fled helicopters into the mountains the day they left their village in Guatemala.

— Sister Judy Stephens

Not everything that is faced can be changed, but nothing can be changed until it is faced.

— James Baldwin

Contents

Book One: María's Courage

I   The Jaguars Prowl

Chapter 1

I am a quetzal. To some of you North Americans I am only a speechless parrot that rhymes with pretzel, but for the Maya of Guatemala, I am their bird of freedom. They honor my kind, and we watch over them. My likeness adorns their blue and white flag, much like the image of a fierce and graceful eagle that I saw on your embassy. As you may know, my people say my name *ket-SAL*.

I am a bit larger than one of your footballs, and my tail flows behind me for more than a meter. People call my highland home the land of eternal spring. I eat termites and wasps whose stings you North Americans fear and I do not. My plumes are brilliant green except where scarlet floods back from my breast. Resplendent as I am, people seldom see me. I am often surprised by what people do not see.

Nor is it true that we cannot speak. Rather, we do not choose to speak. I have never heard that a quetzal said a word to any person. Why, then, do I break the silence of my kind? I would betray my people if I failed to offer you North Americans what I witnessed today.

It is morning. I am flying above the great forest. No rain, no soft nurturing fog. The breeze is fresh and the high sky, blue and white. Above the mountains, the slopes of two volcanoes climb into the air like mighty cones about which my world revolves. Off to the left I notice a twisting pillar of smoke that casts coiling shadows across the green. I have seen such smoke too often. Even as I fly towards it, it weakens into wispy tendrils. The huts of the Maya burn fast.

By the time I arrive, it is over. Blackened circles where huts stood are still smoking. Red still oozes into the earth from dogs, chickens, pigs, goats, and people that sprawl where a village bustled when I passed over at the first light of this day. The smell of burning wood mingles with the stench of burnt flesh. Violent death is part of life, but these dead, many of them children, shout unheard against nature. Though I did not know this village well, my heart scalds within my blazing breast. Does no one remain to grieve for those forms frozen on the ground?

I see three naked women alive on a grassy mound upwind of the smoke.

One lies on her back, her black hair splayed about her head, her legs apart, one arm across her eyes, the other outstretched, her fingers clutching again and again at the grass beside her. Another woman sits with her face pressed against a drawn-up knee. She seems to shake with sobs. The third is picking up skirts and blouses, theirs I suppose, which are gaily colored and badly ripped.

I have seen all I can bear. I circle higher, wanting neither to stay nor to leave, while the black scars and twisted forms grow smaller amid the rippling green below. As I fly off, black dots grow larger in the sky. We quetzals often go hungry. The vultures seldom miss a meal.

In my grief I fear for the lives of Sara and her niece and virtual daughter, María, the two human beings I care most about. I fly between green mountains through the warm breeze towards the village where they live. Should trouble arise, I am probably as helpless as a ghost, but I feel that somehow things may go better if I watch over them.

As I skim the valley to their village, a ball of dust swirls out of the foliage ahead. Two trucks, their beds open, jolt a cargo of men dressed in blotchy green and brown along the rutted road. The thin black barrels of weapons slung on their backs point upwards. I rise and pass well above them as the snarl of these iron jaguars shatters the peace. My wings beat faster to speed me up the valley. Farther on, two more trucks sit off the road around the bend from Sara and María's village. No soldiers in sight.

Their village brims with life as the smoking ruin brimmed but hours ago. Children play among the huts, which are made of sticks plastered with dried mud and capped by cones of gray thatch. Here and there a woman works at her rainbow weaving on a back-strap loom that she has tied to a doorpost of her hut. Others cook at little ovens that send pure wood smoke up to greet me. Out in the fields, men and boys toil among their corn and beans. Some fields slant steeply. Stonewalls terrace them into the slope, and rows of ridges run across them to keep the rain from washing off the topsoil. Now and then a man falls off his field, but usually he is not hurt and the others laugh as he picks himself up.

I glide closer and hear mingled voices of people and animals. They seem to have enough food for now, and their life remains good under the sun. Its warmth draws me down. Though I come to this village often and know much about its people, Sara is the only one who has ever seen me and that, only once. I find her now with María and Ana, who was once María's close friend, on an open plot of short grass and a few trees that are surrounded by several thatch-roofed huts. The hill drops steeply off behind the last huts, where a well-trod trail winds down among the bushes to a spring that gurgles beside the rutted road.

I alight in a tree where I can hear the women talk but they are not likely to notice me. Of all the Mayan languages, only theirs sings in my head. Their language, which is called Mam, does not sound like Spanish but more like some German tourists I once heard talking beside Lake Atitlán, where tall volcanoes painted themselves upside down on the blue of the lake.

All three women wear the colorful *huipil* and *corte* of the Maya, bright and neat and of patterns different from the torn garments of the other three. Sara and Ana are kneeling on woven mats on the grass near my tree. Each of them is grinding corn with a stone arm which looks like a roller but is too flat-sided to roll. Each of them presses the arm back and forth across a ka, which is a concave stone rectangle that slopes away from her on stubby legs.

Earthenware surrounds them. From a large jar Sara dips handfuls of kernels, which are bloated from soaking in a slurry of water and lime. Wide bowls at the low end of the kas receive the whitish mash that the women push into them. Between the women sits a bowl of water that their corny fingers have clouded. On Ana's other side, another large jar receives the twice-ground corn. María and Ana look like the friends they used to be. I am glad.

Sara and Ana's wrists rock the stone arms across the corn on the kas, crushing it, mushing it, ridging it, pushing it. They pause only to dip water and wet the arms, the kas, and the quickly flattened kernels before they rock tirelessly on. Thus my people have ground corn for centuries, though usually inside their huts. Thus, the three women who were violated and others who lie dead ground corn this morning on kas now blackened.

Fire and delight fill María. She dances about on the grass, holding her skirt out from her thighs, her feet never grazing the bowls or jars. Or she sits swaying on a rock that is as big as a goat and has tufts of green brushing its base. She is the tallest of the three and slender, with thick black brows, a broad face that may turn stormy in a flash, and cheekbones that many Maya share with the men from China whom I have seen training local soldiers. Her piquant energy enchanted me when she was a little girl. It does today. I think of the trucks and pray it will tomorrow.

Silver lights the black through Sara's hair, and sometimes her joints creak like tree limbs rubbing in the wind. Life has left her gently bitter, though her heart remains clear. She is older than forty, and it was she who birthed María and Ana. Perhaps because she lost her only child, she takes special delight in pulling other women's babies into the world, head first and sometimes feet first. Perhaps this, too, is why she takes such joy in María, half her daughter, half a dear friend, and barely a niece at all. María's mother, who is Sara's sister, does not mind, and María showers her sunlight on both women—light that María hid so long behind gray clouds of sorrow that flicker across her brow even today.

Ana's cheeks, breasts, and hips are pleasingly round, and she smiles most often of the three. She works hard to care for her children and usually for her husband. Her words are almost always harmless. Like many people, she prefers to believe that the way things are is good and only fools look for trouble. You may call her the salt of the earth.

Another woman rises from the trail and trudges onto the bare brown path beneath me, a water jug teetering on her head. They greet as she passes into the village. It soothes me to see these three so peaceful and contented, oblivious of what happened to the village where a black ka and crumbled clay dimple each smoldering rectangle that, hours ago, was a family's home. Those three women on the grassy mound will soon grind corn again if they are to live, though tears may dampen their mash. Perhaps they will bear babies of the soldiers who raped them.

Chapter 2

The voices of these three remind me of the village marimba, which is festooned with weavings as brilliant as the women's clothes and needs three people standing behind it to play. One hammers out the high notes, another the mid-range, and a third the vibrating bass. Just so, Ana's voice plays as brightly as a chime, María's flows like dark honey though sometimes it stings like a bee, and Sara's rumbles like the pebbles in a mountain freshet.

"Please let me help you," María says gazing down at the other two, her feet apart, grass between her toes, her fists on her hips.

"Not today." A white smile glistens across Ana's brown face. "Not the bride!"

"Surely I can help you to help Ernesto's parents," says María.

"You'll be grinding again tomorrow," Sara tells her niece mordantly, though light dances in her eyes.

So María is about to marry at last! My heart swells with joy. I had hoped it would be soon. Often when I have flown here, I have seen her and Ernesto walk like lovers, finally free from the bondage of their sorrows. Custom calls for the parents of the groom to provide the corn for the first fiesta of the wedding, and I am not surprised that Sara and Ana are helping them today. Five years have passed since María's beloved Luis vanished. Her tragedy would have doubled if her grief had outlasted her youth.

This is María's day! She is so vibrant, has recovered so well from the loss that made her eyes older than Ana's though they entered the world during the same summer. People say a broken bone heals stronger than it was. Thus did the cleft where Luis was torn from María's heart heal at last. After he disappeared, she was desolate, living out her days and weeping at night in her parents' hut while the steel within her, time, and the warmth of her family and friends—every friend but Ana—and finally Ernesto restored her. Now she will share her life and children with him, if God permits and soldiers from those trucks do not intervene.

It is good to see María and Ana chatting amiably, as I have not seen them since the day Luis and María were to marry—since the first day of their marriage, I should say, since a Maya wedding lasts through three fiestas, with days or even weeks between. María waited for Luis on this very spot, as radiant as she looks below me now. But the road remained empty all that afternoon while her joy turned to worry and then to fear. No Luis. As if a volcano had sucked him down its fiery throat. Or the beast named Terror.

María, shouting afterwards inside her family's hut in the quiet of the night, denounced the beast. I think most of the villagers blamed it, too, though I never heard one dare to say so. But Ana refused. She has the wish, or the need, to believe that the powerful people around her—her parents, Old Pablo, the men with guns—mean well and are never fierce without just cause. Where Terror rules, many people get along by going along. I do not fault Ana for avoiding María during that bygone time, or else smiling and prattling to her as though things were not terribly wrong. That's the way Ana is. You may criticize her, but softly please. She did what many of us would have done in her place.

Neither do I fault María for speaking bitterly to her parent and her sister Brenda about the ways Ana had deserted her. Time heals many things, sometimes even broken friendships. María's anger at Ana may not have outlived her grief for Luis, but even today her directness will clash with Ana's denial over matters small and great.

Whenever I have seen the Terror fall like the lightning from the sky, I have hastened to watch over Sara and our sprightly niece, and indeed the whole village. So far the Terror has passed them by, as I pray it will today, except for a bomb from a plane that killed Ernesto's wife and children a few years ago. Perhaps those trucks in the valley mean nothing for the village.

"Oh, Ernesto! I was so afraid this day would never come!" María clasps her hands below me, yet fear sounds through her joy like the sadness that tints the gayest melodies of the marimba.

"In a few hours it begins," Ana burbles, not hearing María's fear.

Yes, Ana, many things may begin. Only a woman like María would not care that her wedding to Ernesto is to begin on the same day as her wedding to Luis. Her strength will become her as a matriarch if she lives that long.

"At least let me grind the portion for the women who are pregnant." María swoops down to take Sara's stones, but Sara shakes her head and keeps on pushing the stone arm across her ka.

"How many are pregnant now?" Ana asks, her teeth sparkling.

"Three." As if she has answered too quickly, María adds, "I think."

"See how she keeps track," Sara teases.

A rosy glow fills María's cheeks. "I'm such an old lady."

"At twenty-one?" Sara raises her eyebrows.

"You're no older than I am." Ana pouts, as if María has called her old too.

The light fades from María's eyes as she gazes across the valley. "The army made me a widow before I was a bride."

"I've asked you not to talk like that," Ana snaps. She rocks a ragged sheet of mash off her ka, and her fingers brush the last white bits into the bowl at the end. Since they are preparing for a wedding fiesta, there are no black or yellow kernels in the mash, which will be wrapped in cornhusks along with chicken and salsa to make the tamales. Sara balls up the mash piled up in her own bowl and slaps it hard onto Ana's ka for the second grinding.

"Praise the Virgin María!" Sara often says these words for the mother of Jesus, but this time they raise a lovely red through her niece's cheeks once again. "When you waited so long for Luis to return, I was afraid you'd wait forever."

"How long has it been?" Ana asks. María turns to her with a look of surprise.

"Five years. Remember? My fiestas were to begin soon after you married Byron."

"I was so happy then. And so sad for you." Ana shudders as María and Sara exchange glances. "I try not to think about what may have happened to Luis."

"I know you don't." María's voice is as hard as a ka.

"No one likes to think of torture," Sara says.

"You can't know this!"

"Only one who is blind..." Sara begins, as though to a child.

"Please! Not today," María says half to herself, half to God.

"Happiness," says Sara, "depends on where you aren't and what you don't know."

The distant snarl of the iron jaguars, softer than the voices of the birds on the hillside, drifts upwards on the breeze. I feel a sudden chill but the women do not hear it. It stops, or perhaps the breeze carries it another way.

"We have discussed this before," Ana explains to Sara. "She said, 'The army took him.' I said, 'Don't say dangerous things when you don't have proof.'"

"So now we avoid the subject and remain friends." María's words drop like dry pebbles on sand.

"Does your friendship depend on what you can't talk about?" Sara's tone probes deeper than her words.

"It's not a problem," Ana answers lightly, as she shoves more mash off the end of her ka. Like humans I have listened to in many places, Ana skims through the air above the rocks of reality upon a mat woven out of dreams.

"So far." María sounds somber as she picks at a nub of clay on the wall of a hut. She shakes her head as if to dislodge a gnat or a dried-up scrap of anger.

"I never told you," Ana gushes, heedless of María's mood, "how much I admired you for waiting so long for Luis to return."

"She had other chances," Sara confides.

"María! You never told me!" Ana sounds hurt. María steps behind her and brushes her fingers across Ana's glossy black hair. Ana, ducking, is not diverted. "Well?"

"Well…" María hesitates, like one who is about to reveal something long withheld. "My father opened the door for two others, both fine men. You'll agree if you guess their names, which I'm not going to tell you. One has become a father since then. Both times I found chores to do around the hut while the candle flickered and those men talked with my parents about trivial things, nothing that usually makes people visit in the middle of the night. I didn't like to disappoint them, but…"

"They got the message."

"Four men have chosen you! In such a small village!" Ana sounds impressed.

"Our María is a prize!" Pride fills Sara's voice.

"Ernesto is the prize," María says. "He provided well for his wife and their children. And I knew deep things about him. I was hoping he would find me worthy."

Ana's face darkens. "I hope *he* doesn't say dangerous things."

"*We* talk about everything." The rebuke in María's voice seems lost on Ana.

"And…" Sara teases like a child poking a frog to make it hop. "There's another reason your father opened the door so quickly for Ernesto." María's softly hollowed cheeks flush once again from light brown to lovely crimson as Sara adds, "He was afraid he had an old maid on his hands."

"He needn't have worried…unless she chose to be one!" It warms me to hear Ana defend María.

"But I don't!" María says. She is standing on the rock. Arms aloft, she jumps off, rippling her heavy, brilliant skirt above her calves. "I choose Ernesto. He chooses me!"

I watched them all grow up—María, her older sister Brenda who was still unmarried the last time we saw her, Luis, Ana, Byron who is Ana's husband, Ernesto who is a few years older than the others, and his wife who was killed. Though María frolicked with them all, Luis was always her special friend. They played tricks on each other or explored up the mountain when they were supposed to go no farther than they had to to gather firewood. When they entered puberty, she first, he played tricks on her were not so nice, and one day I saw her punch him. As they grew used to their new selves, they came together again, and I would see them standing on the edge of this spot gazing across the valley and talking about their shining world and what its future would hold. Most Maya are virgins when they marry, perhaps because they marry young. Among the romances I have seen, María and Luis's was a common story and very beautiful. I was as happy for them then as I am for her and Ernesto today.

Though I flew here to watch over these women, it is I who soak up comfort from their prattle. I can almost shut away the smoky ruin and dead Maya that burned into my brain but an hour ago, almost forget those snarling trucks. Perhaps this village is not where they are headed.

"I wonder if Ernesto is thinking about you out in the fields." Stars, or perhaps the dreams that Ana thrives on, light her smile.

"Actually he's out in the forest." María's brows knit. "On civil patrol."

"These patrols are so stupid." Ana sounds impatient. "There aren't any guerrillas around here."

"Guerrillas aren't the point." María scuffs the grass with the ball of her foot. "The army uses the patrols to turn us into ants—always good, never free."

"María!"

Though Ana spoke loudly, María did not hear her. She is staring across the lost years of her womanhood, as I have seen her stare many times from this spot after the army disappeared Luis. Again she speaks to herself and to God. "Nothing must go wrong today! Nothing!"

"It won't," Ana says brightly, still reveling in the banter that has nearly died, snapping María back to the moment.

Sara scowls down at her grinding. María notices. "What's the matter?"

"Nothing."

"Yes there is."

"If something happens so your fiesta must wait a few days…."

"Nothing will happen," María cuts in as if to convince herself, "once Ernesto returns."

It is good that I cannot warn the women on the grass below me about the other village. If soldiers don't come here, telling them would dash their happiness for nothing. If soldiers do come, my experiences tell me that there may be nothing they can do to save themselves. Best they chatter in the sunshine as long as they can.

"I hope no one will be superstitious." Sara decides to share her news. "I saw soldiers in the valley this morning."

María's face drains paler than the mash. Her hand flies to her mouth.

"Soldiers protect villages," Ana chirps.

"When they don't destroy them," Sara retorts. Her eyes stab in vain to pierce the younger woman's illusions.

"They only attack villages that help the Communists," Ana recites as if from a catechism.

"They will take him!" María croaks, too alarmed to hear Ana. She paces rapidly back and forth on the grass.

Sara lays the stone arm across her ka, pushes herself stiffly to her feet, and puts her hands gently on María's shoulders, stopping her in mid-course. "They're probably going into the mountains to chase guerrillas."

"If they take him… It's too horrible to think about!"

"Old Pablo went with him." Sara's calm, deep voice soothes María like a firm hand on a jumpy cat. "They're both good at staying away from trouble."

"If they *do* meet soldiers"—Ana sounds sympathetic at last—"they'll wave their flag of Guatemala, and everything will be all right."

"We can't stop our lives every time the army comes around," Sara says. "I warned Old Pablo about them before he left."

"I *am* superstitious." María half smiles. Her shoulders relax beneath her aunt's mash-flecked hands, and her fear trots off like an old dog that has learned when to wait outside.

Sara releases María and sits against the rock, her hands pressing her motley skirt to her short, thick thighs. Joy mixed with pain bursts from her. "It's so beautiful that you marry in the tradition of our people!" She tugs at a sleeve of her *huipil*. "Like the beauty of our weavings, the music of our marimbas. Our culture will live no matter what."

María catches Sara's spirit and turns to Ana. "Do you remember what the bride vows about bearing children?"

"I…Sort of."

"Say it with me!"

"Her first fiesta has not come," Sara grunts as she lowers herself stiffly, knuckles on the grass, to her mat. "Already she knows the vow for the third one."

Ana hesitates. "You lead."

They chant the familiar words, María smiling, Ana following. Sara smiles, too, as the gentle harmony of the younger women brings tears to her wrinkled eyes.

"I will be a mother," their voices blend, "I will suffer, my children will suffer, many of my children will die young because of the circumstances created for us by white men. It will be hard for me to accept my children's death, but I will bear it because our ancestors bore it without giving up. We, too, will not give up."

They cease, and for a long moment no one speaks.

"It sounds so sad." A frown banishes María's smile. "Some of my children may die."

"We must always hope for the best."

"You lost Carlitos," María replies.

Sorrow withers Ana's smile as her turn comes to face her loss. "My poor Carlitos. His helpless eyes and bulging belly, little arms around my neck until he grew too weak…" She falters, her eyes overflowing.

"So many of us went so hungry then."

"Were you Ana's midwife?" María asks.

The happier memory stanches Ana's tears, as Sara nods. "One in eight babies that I pull into the world never sees its fifth birthday. Sometimes one in four!"

"Padre López told me that's common among us Maya," María says. She looks at Ana, who is rubbing her nose with her wrist.

"I don't like to think about that."

"But it's true," María snaps. Ana pouts at her mash and rocks the stone arm over her left thumb. She shakes off the pain, showering the grass with flecks of corn.

"They're like the children I don't have," Sara says, "They bring me such happiness, so often grief."

Shadows splash on the grass like silent bombs around María, but she remains in the sunshine. "My children will be my joy even if some of them are only with me a few years."

"I hope you still think like that if one of them dies," Sara mutters.

"Was it always like this," Ana turns to Sara, "that so many of our children do not live very long?"

"Our life has been hard for seventeen generations, though it's much harder now than when I was a girl."

"What happened?"

"Things I'm supposed to tell the bride and groom at the serious part tonight."

"When you're my grandmother!"

"She's only your aunt," Ana says with the faint condescension that someone who knows the rituals may show to someone who doesn't.

"You know my grandparents are dead. Tonight we're making her an old lady." María leaps behind Sara and tries to tousle her hair, which is wound up in a colorful *nestor*. Sara ducks, knocking her ka and gripping it to keep the unflattened kernels from rolling off. The stone arm bumps to the grass. She scoops up water in her hand to rinse any dirt off it, then wipes her hand on a red and blue striped napkin and resumes grinding.

"You will tell them not to let their children drink Coca-Cola because it's bad for their teeth," says Ana, the good pupil and mother.

"It's also bad for our culture," Sara says.

"What else will you tell them?"

"You don't remember from your own fiestas," María asks, "and all the others you've been to?"

"I was only sixteen at mine." Ana, intent on her work and her excuse, does not see María and Sara nod to each other.

María hesitates, as though uncertain how to vent her annoyance without dousing their fun. "Then do not close your ears to what Sara says tonight."

"For rich *ladinos*," Sara mutters, "we are fit only to work and to die."

"You remember about Coca-Cola, which comes at us like piss from a goat, but not the history of our people." María's scorn seeps out like steam from the lid of a pot that has been simmering too long. Ana, for whom triviality is a refuge, ignores it.

Perhaps you are surprised that a person as intelligent as Ana does not remember what has befallen her friend, her village, and her people. But to see how much she denies is to understand that when the Terror roams the land, his fiery breath sears far beyond the bodies he devours. Is it strange that Ana puts from her mind what her mind cannot bear? I have known many people like her, and perhaps you have, too. Perhaps there's a bit of her in you and me.

"Maybe I'm not as ignorant as you think. Why don't you test me?" I wonder whether it's good or bad that Ana accepts María's challenge.

"All right," María says. "Who was the first Spaniard to oppress out people?"

"Pedro Alvarado arrived from Mexico almost five centuries ago and conquered many of our villages."

"But not all of them. Who overthrew Guatemala's democracy in 1954 and even today tells the army which of us to torture and kill?"

"I... I don't know."

"The CIA, dummy! Every Maya should know that?"

"Most of us do," Sara mutters, "but she's not a dummy, just careful not to know too much."

"Thank you, Sara," Ana huffs in vindication.

The Lord in his mercy hides the future. These three, and I clutching my limb, could not know how the old dispute that twists aimlessly between María and Ana like a snake already dead, may soon determine who among them will live and who will not. Nor can we know the choices that María will make as she struggles to save this village from ending like the other one before the sun, so warm above us now, flames red behind the mountains. Yet as I bask in the radiant triviality below me—nothing that lives is trivial—the wind of fear chills the feathers on my neck. I long to stop the sun in the sky and hold these three in this moment, smiling Ana, creaky Sara, and María burning bright.

Chapter 3

The roar of a heavy truck surging into gear shatters the peace. Fear flickers across the women's faces. Their bodies tense, as the birds continue of chirp and voices to filter from the village.

"What's that?" cries María.

"What?" asks Ana, though the fear in her voice says she heard it too.

A second truck roars into harsh harmony with the first.

"Oh, God!" María covers her mouth with both hands.

Sara puts aside her grinding, hobbles stiff-legged between the last two huts to the top of the trail, and peers down. There are shrubs and grass on the steep slope to the valley, then short trees where the ground flattens out, and grass where the road runs at an angle past the hillside. Sara reports matter-of-factly, "Two trucks are driving around the bend. Soldiers scurry in the road, like ants when you kick their hill."

"I stood where you are standing." María's tone is empty. "I saw Luis where you see soldiers. He waved and I waved. He turned and I never saw his face again."

"They're coming into the trees." Sara is still calm.

María returns to the moment, as does her fear. "Where?"

"On our side."

"No!"

"To rest probably," Ana says. "The shade is on our side."

"So it is." Sara sounds impressed.

María shakes her head, as if trying to reassemble the shards of peace that the soldiers have smashed like an earthen jug at her feet. "You're probably right." Her face falls and her fingers twist together. "I have an awful feeling about today."

"A bride can be superstitious," says Sara.

"I wasn't meant to be so happy!"

"Of course you were." Ana's teeth are so white in the tan of her face.

"I wish our men would return," says Sara.

"I feel better that you're worried too." María stands behind Sara and rubs the nape beneath her colorfully wound hair. Sara always liked to be massaged, more since age has stiffened her neck. She peers back into the valley. "Nothing. Only dust hanging in the sunlight. Quite beautiful if you forget about those monkeys in the trees." She walks around María and lowers herself to the mat, knuckles first.

"You mustn't worry about Ernesto. Germán is late, too, but I'm not worried," Ana says reassuringly.

"Where's Germán?" Sara sounds surprised.

"In Quetzaltenango. His mother's sick. We expected him back last night... But maybe he stayed over," she adds brightly.

I should tell you that my people follow the Spanish custom of saying Germán's name *hair-MAN.*

"Their children, too, are mine," Sara says.

"Is Lourdes upset?" María asks Ana.

"This morning I heard her in their hut. She said, 'I'm sure Papa will come home soon unless he has to stay with Grandmama.'"

"She seemed very quiet while we were grinding inside," Sara muses.

"Everyone grinding but me," María murmurs.

"She's nearly always quiet when other people are talking," Ana says. "That's part of what I like about her."

"I never suspected she was worried," Sara says.

"Please, God, let them all return!" María presses her fingers to her temples.

"They will," Ana assures her. "I'm so happy for you. But sad to think that we don't talk any more the way we used to."

Once again María shakes off her fear. "You were starting a family, so it's natural we talked less then."

Ana's brow furrows. "I'm hurt that you never told me about those men who came to your door."

"You built a wall between us," María says evenly. "I can't worry what you'll let me tell you and what you won't."

"How can you say that!" Dropping the stone arm in her lap, Ana strikes the grass with her fists. "We talk of many things."

"Safe little things."

"Endless gossip."

"Exactly." Now María's voice sounds harsh, as the steam has finally toppled the lid off the pot. "My heart broke when Luis was taken. You wouldn't let me talk about it."

"Your grief made you crazy against the army." Ana sounds as if tears tiptoe behind her eyes.

"I would have killed the soldiers who took him."

"What if someone denounces you, *us*, when you talk like that?" Ana asks in a strained hush. "There are soldiers down there. They may be very close." She puts the oblong arm back on the ka and guiltily brushes some stray white flakes off the red, violet, orange, and indigo of her *corte*.

"It must be more painful than I can imagine to lose the man you love on the first day of your wedding." Sara speaks with the edge of one who has also held her peace too long. "You open your hearts to each other. Suddenly he is gone…" Seeing pain cross Ana's face, Sara softens. "I will listen to my friend when her heart lies like a jug you smash on a rock. I will listen to her, danger or no danger."

Children chirp in the village, and birds talk in the forest as Sara's gaze follows her words into the heart of the younger woman. Ana's eyes dart back and forth as if seeking a way to escape, though her body does not move. At last her lips compress, and her chin begins to quiver.

"You're right!" Tears stream from her eyes once again as she turns to María. "You needed me and I didn't listen! I'm sorry, so sorry."

María and Sara look at each other in surprise.

"It's good you see this the first time you hear it," Sara says, nodding her approval. "And very unusual. Many people will dance on glowing coals before they'll admit they were wrong."

But María was too hurt for too long to relent at once. "You don't face things—what the army did, why Carlitos died, where our friendship went. What do you face?"

María's anger draws anger from Ana through her tears. "Today I face many things! All right?"

María softens. "All right."

"I was too busy learning to be a wife to see your sorrow!" No longer under attack, Ana lets her remorse flow. Perhaps she, too, has been holding things under a lid, afraid to discuss María's pain, fearing they'd quarrel if she challenged María's certainty that the army caused it, or guilty that her silence was adding to it.

"But it was more than that," she continued. "I was too careful to speak only of things that don't frighten me, the safe little things, the gossip you threw in my face just now. I hid behind my smile and gossip when I must have known your heart had broken and I might have comforted you. Can you forgive me?"

"Of course." María kneels and grips Ana's shoulders. Ana's hands fly up to cover María's knuckles, smearing them with white paste.

"A perfect day for friendship," Sara says. Like me, Sara has waited five years for these two friends to say what matters. Now it is happening more easily than I had expected, as when you humans pick off an old scab and the skin beneath has already healed. Their love for each other returns, however far apart their beliefs about life and the Terror.

"I'm so glad we really are friends again. You complete my happiness." María wields her forgiveness like a broom to sweep dead cinders out the door. She pulls the shorter woman to her feet and hugs her off balance and upsetting the ka. Ana regains her footing and sits down. They right the ka, which is on its side, and cup up as much mash as they can off the grass without mixing dirt or bugs into it. Their heads nearly bump, like children playing with a beetle.

"I was in my own little cave." Ana wipes tears from her cheek with her wrist. "What can I do?"

"About what?"

"To make up for hurting you."

"Nothing. There's no need."

"We must talk about everything. As you and Ernesto talk."

"Even about Luis?" María sounds doubtful.

"Now?" Sara sounds apprehensive.

"My grief is long past and I love you again," María says. "Isn't that enough?"

"We must clear away all that stands between us. I did not know a wall was there. Now I feel it still is. I know I don't always face what I should..." Ana's voice trails off.

"Can't you save it until after the fiestas?" Sara shrugs and gives up.

María gives up and begins. "You know what happened to him."

"He disappeared right before the first fiesta of your wedding. How?"

"You and I told him goodbye right here. I waved to him right over there. You don't remember?"

"That was five years ago!"

María's lips tighten, but she continues. "His parents didn't have enough corn for the tamales. Some of his cousins made them in their village down the valley." María gestures to her right. "They watched him carry off a heavy load of them. He said they were warm against his back—his last words. No one ever saw him again."

"How painful!" Ana says. "I must have known all that."

María stares at her feet. "Your father and mine, Old Pablo, and other men went looking for him, all the way to the other village. They came back late that night, stumbling along even though it was the dark of the moon, because they knew how worried we were."

"He just disappeared?" Ana says.

"The army took him!"

"It could have been the guerrillas. Or a jaguar."

"There are no jaguars around here," Sara mutters.

"At the first light, the men went back to look for him again. An old woman they met on the road told them that she had seen a truck the day before with soldiers in the back and a man tied up with a blindfold across his face. We think he was Luis."

"When a young man disappears, it nearly always means the army has taken him, either to draft him—if they did that, we would have seen him quite soon—or to kill him." Sara arches an eyebrow at Ana. "This happens often. I'm surprised you find it hard to believe."

"What had he done?"

"Nothing."

"They never tell you."

"Forgive me, my friend. There's another reason I didn't want to talk about this before." A warning in Ana's voice draws their eyes. "Do you blame the army so you won't have to think that maybe Luis ran away from you?"

Fire leaps in María. "You *can't* blame the army, can you?"

"Now that you're friends again," Sara says soothingly, "you're free to fight."

María's anger flickers lower. "If you hide these suspicions inside yourself, it's no wonder we aren't so close."

"I *am* trying…"

"Believe me, Ana, I found it as hard as you do to accept that the army took his life."

"She used to tell us, 'If the army killed him, show me his grave,'" Sara says. They are pausing more often in the grinding now as their talk cuts deeper. Sara reaches into her jar and scoops out more bloated kernels.

"Did you dare to go to them?"

María nods yes, bringing a little gasp from Ana. "The soldiers told me, 'We don't have him. Maybe it's the police.'"

"You see!"

"But his father had already gone to the police. A soldier also told me, 'Maybe he ran off with another woman.'"

Ana's back straightens. "I hope that soldier was punished!"

"That's almost what *you* said just now," Sara says.

"I didn't say another woman!"

"The other soldiers laughed, and I walked away. Weeks went by. Then years. Everyone gave up but me. At last I faced my life. I even thought of becoming a nun."

Ana's jaw drops, showing the two big front teeth, but she does not speak. The glow quickens across María's cheeks. "But now you are grinding the corn for Ernesto and me." Suddenly she shudders as if the ghost of Luis is dancing before her eyes. "Nothing must stop us! Nothing!"

"It won't," Ana says cheerily.

How quickly the anguish drops from María's eyes, as if into a well that has no bottom. "After they took Luis," she says matter-of-factly, "I used to wake up screaming. I dreamt that soldiers had come for me too. I always fought them, but they held my arms and legs…They did things to me."

Ana looks puzzled, then gasps as she realizes what María is saying. María continues, recalling yet again the hours that her tragedy began.

"I wept all night the day he vanished. I wept many nights and kept as busy as I could from first light to sundown. Sometimes hope would come. A man who looked like him would be seen in another village. You don't remember those reports?"

Ana half smiles and shakes her head.

María's mouth turns bitter, like the empty cup of the waning moon. "Finally even my hope for Luis turned into pain. My hope gnawed at my heart like a hungry rat, and…" Her features twist. "And I drove it off! No more hope for my beloved Luis! What else could I do?"

Again Ana looks puzzled. María turns again to gaze across the valley. "Lovely dear Ernesto. If I lose you, I will die!"

Chapter 4

During a famine that befell the village about two years after Luis was disappeared, María lost her older sister, Brenda, to separation, not starvation. The rains did not come, the harvest was meager, everyone went hungry, and two babies died, Ana's Carlitos and another one. Padre López was able to arrange for a single family, which turned out to be María's, to have one less mouth to feed. Since Brenda knew more Spanish, because she loved learning it, than any youth in the village except Frida, the padre offered to send her to El Salvador where a priest he knew could get her a job as a housemaid. Her parents very sadly accepted Padre López's offer, Brenda very sadly left their home, and María missed her terribly. Now, though, none of them went so hungry and Brenda actually had enough to eat. She had long hours of work, three spoiled children to manage, and almost no pay.

One evening well after the famine ended, I happened to be perched atop the family hut and heard, through the smoke-hole in the thatch, María's parents telling her the happy news from Padre López that Brenda had now taught herself to write Spanish so well, by tediously copying words out of a Bible during her meager spare time, that she was able to land a job as a clerk with a small accounting firm in the city of San Salvador. As you see, Brenda is what you may call an intellectual. In their teens, María grew taller than she, but when she spoke, her voice was firm; and while she lived at home, María lived in her shadow. Much as they all missed Brenda, María blossomed after she left. Brenda's hard-earned good fortune, which allowed María to come into her own, may serve the village well on this day of prowling jaguars.

Since Luis vanished five years ago, I have seen many tragedies. That village this morning was only the latest. Perhaps this is why it feels so good to bathe in the warmth of these women as they prepare the food for María's first special night. I do not mind their disputes and tears today because that's how humans are. This is life as it should be, what people in a hurry call nothing happening.

"This is the time I fear," says Sara. "The lovers walk hand in hand, but evil crouches by the trail like a jaguar ready to pounce. The village must protect your love, like the fragile egg of a quetzal."

Ana's face brightens. "The quetzal!"

"Our bird of life," María says.

"Isn't it the bird of freedom?" Ana asks tidily.

"Same thing," Sara says.

"I've never seen one," Ana says. "Have you?"

María shakes her head.

Sara gazes into the years. "Once, after Tomás died. I was sitting in the forest remembering how I would wake up beside him in the dark. A large quetzal flew towards me. So green. The brightest scarlet you can believe. He passed above me as silent as a dream. I felt he was Tomás."

Yes, Sara, it was me.

The stones mash the corn. Birds talk among the trees. Snapping sounds, like the cracking of dry sticks, whisper from the forest above them, but the women do not notice. Children chirp and a goat bleats in the village. Sara picks up her jar and pours the last fat kernels onto her ka. Hearing her talk like this, I ache with longing for the life that was and can never be again.

"The blood of the martyr shines scarlet on his breast," Ana says at last. "Is it true that he cannot live in a cage?"

"I never heard of one being captured," Sara says.

"Life in a cage isn't life." María says sourly.

Yes, Ana, it's true. For me at least, a cage would soon kill me.

A woman in her early twenties walks briskly towards them from among the huts. It is Lourdes, the wife of Germán. Her blouse is white, and her skirt is brilliant. A green, purple, and yellow *liston*, long and narrow if it were unrolled, binds up her hair. She looks too small and wiry to have borne two babies.

"You may stop now," Lourdes says. "We have enough." She glances at the bowl below Ana's ka and into the large jar beside her. "More than enough."

"You have the leaves and salsa," Ana says, as she clumps the mash from her bowl into the jar. "The chicken has been plucked. Will it be safe to go down for more water?"

"I fetched a jug at first light," María says. "That's my only contribution."

"Why wouldn't it be safe to go down for water?" Lourdes asks nervously.

"Some soldiers are running around down there," Ana says as she pats down the ragged peak of the mash in her jar.

Lourdes's hands go to her mouth. "My God! They have Germán!"

"That's not likely." Sara's voice is calm. "They didn't arrive until this morning."

Ana puts an arm around Lourdes's slender shoulders, hugging her. "Most likely his mother's still sick and he stayed in the city to care for her."

"Even if she's better," María adds. "You know how seldom he gets to see her."

"This is what I told the children." Lourdes's voice is faltering. "I kept repeating it to myself at the grinding all during the palaver that's usually so pleasant. When you three went outside, I wanted to come with you, right on down the trail and down the road, all the way to Quetzaltenango. I'd tell him, 'Germán, I know you have to stay, and Mother Culán I'm so glad you're better. I'll hurry home and tell the children that everything's all right.'"

Sobbing, she paws at Ana's shoulder, her little fingers curled, while Ana holds her, rubbing her back until she turns free and shakes her head like a wet dog. "I worry too easily. It's almost certain that he's safe."

"What reason could the army have to detain him?" Ana asks.

"They don't need reasons, Ana," Lourdes says. The tightness leaves her brow. "But, since they don't have one, maybe they haven't taken him."

"Are the children upset?" Sara asks.

"Julio isn't." Lourdes laughs, chasing the last tears down her cheeks. "He said, 'No one can hurt my Papa, he's too strong.' I looked into the hut just now and found Juanita at her little ka making tortillas. She said, 'If I make them for Papa's lunch, he must come home to eat them.'"

"I hope she's right," Ana says. Sara's face is turned from the others. She stares stolidly at the grass.

"Then I'd better make some tortillas to bring Ernesto back," María says with a short laugh.

"Where is he?" Lourdes sounds surprised.

"On civil patrol with Old Pablo."

"Then we'll worry together about our men," Lourdes says, "but not too much."

"Who'll worry about Old Pablo?" Ana asks.

"I will," Sara says, "but not too much."

Up the hill the bushes thrash, as though a bull is plunging through them. Fear tightens Ana's face and Lourdes's as the women turn towards it. The thrashing grows louder. María takes a few steps towards the noise and plants her feet, hands on hips, confronting the noise as if to protect the others. Sara, seeing her niece's bold stance, shakes her head.

The bushes part. A boy of about nine struggles out, his back bent beneath a bundle of sticks. Pepe has been gathering firewood for his mother. The women laugh. They tell him the bundle is bigger than he is and ask him how he could pull it through the forest without getting stuck. María tousles his hair as he staggers past.

Lourdes puts her hands on María's shoulders. "You fear what I fear. We tell ourselves that our fears are foolish, but they scurry through our heads like mice across the floor."

María embraces her. "May this day end well for everybody!"

Sara trundles over and puts her arms around them in a three-sided embrace. "God forbid that the army has any of them!"

"I wish I could ease your minds," Ana says.

"I feel better. I must take this back." Lourdes says. Sara hands her the red and blue striped napkin. She folds it into a *yagual*, puts it on her head, hoists up the large jar of mash with a woman's ease that always surprises me, and teeters into the village, as top-heavy as Pepe or the woman who brought water from the valley before the soldiers came.

"What a shadow those soldiers cast across the day," María says in disgust once Lourdes is out of earshot.

"Our village is lucky because we don't make trouble." Ana says, then reflects. "Only that bomb three years ago…"

María cuts in. "Which killed Ernesto's wife and children!"

"How stupid of me to forget!"

"If he hadn't gone to the fields before first light," María says bitterly, "he too would have been blasted into bloody chunks."

"It must have been awful for Ernesto to see them like that, then never again." Ana considers. "You said you learned some deep things about him. How? When did you have a chance? Were you alone with him? Did your parents know?"

"At our Christian base community…" María ponders. "Someone who can read reads us a scripture."

"It's dangerous to have a Bible."

"We keep it buried inside three plastic bags. After the reading, we reflect, and each one says what he thinks those old words mean for us right here and right now."

"The army is correct," Sara says. "The Bible is subversive if you take it seriously."

"Doesn't Padre López teach you?"

"Usually he isn't there. Even when he is, each person has a say. We're as equal to each other as we are to God."

"Are women equal to men?" Ana asks dubiously.

"Of course."

Ana's face darkens, then lights up as she turns to María, who is sitting on the rock again. "That's why you speak so boldly when men are with us."

"This one," Sara nods towards María, "speaks boldly when she feels like it. As she has ever since Brenda left."

"The talk leads us to do things," María says. "Doing things gives us ideas for more talk, which leads to more action, and so on."

"What actions have you done?"

"For example…" María looks at Sara. "Shall I tell her about the GAM?"

"No."

"So tell me one deep thing that Ernesto has said to you?"

María, standing now, puts one foot up on the rock, pulling her *corte* tight against her leg, and leans a slender brown forearm across her knee. "After his family was killed…" She pauses. "We were discussing the part where Jesus says you should turn the other cheek when someone strikes you. Before Ernesto came to peace with his grief, he talked about joining the guerrillas. Even though he thinks they can't win…"

"If they can't win," Ana interrupts, "why would he join?"

"He's a man of principle." María gives a quick laugh as she continues. "He even made a crazy plan to go to North America and shoot their President, which people sometimes do there."

"Their President?" Ana sounds mystified.

"Who do you think sent the bomb that blew up his family," Sara says wearily, "and the plane it fell from?"

"It's good the soldiers don't know he thinks like this," Ana says.

"He doesn't anymore," María says. "As he reflected, he saw that killing people makes things worse."

"How surprised you were!" Sara says to María.

"Then *I* reflected, and was glad he said this. I stopped wanting to kill the soldiers who took Luis."

"In your heart?" Sara looks hard into her eyes.

María turns and gazes down the valley, but her eyes are warm and a smile begins to form like a new moon. "Sometimes I feel more fire inside me than I know what to do with. Ernesto is the only one who calms me."

"I hope so." Sara does not sound convinced.

"If those soldiers come up here," Ana says, "you could make trouble."

"Don't worry yourself," Sara says. "She did something better…"

"Wait!" Ana cocks her head and walks over to the top of the trail. "What's that?"

Sara listens. "What?"

"Behind that hut." Ana gestures.

"I don't hear anything," María says. She peers into the valley, then walks over and looks down the trail.

Ana goes to the edge to see for herself into the valley. Sara joins her as María paces back and forth behind them.

"It seems all right," Sara says after a moment.

"Do you think someone's here?"

"No," María says, then more firmly, "No."

"All those soldiers," Sara reflects. "Now, nothing."

"If they're hiding behind these huts," Ana says, "we wouldn't know it."

"You go round this hut," María tells Sara, startling her and Ana. "I'll go round that one."

"Isn't it safer if we only talk about safe things?" Ana says in a loud whisper. "Then it won't matter if they overhear us."

"Scream if they grab you," María says, laughing.

"Probably one of us may be able to scream." Sara sounds doubtful.

"I'll stay here to spread the alarm," Ana says, and backs up behind the rock.

"Well." Sara hesitates. "I don't think anyone's there."

"Come on!" María disappears around the hut by the trail. Sara, shaking her head, hunches around the other one. Ana, alone in the sunny clearing, turns anxiously from one empty hut to the other.

Chapter 5

Soon Sara emerges. She and Ana exchange worried looks just as María strides out from behind the other hut. She grasps Sara in a hug that lifts her off her feet. In all my visits to villages, I have never before seen a woman hold another woman off the ground. "No soldiers today," she chants from behind Sara's startled face. "No soldiers today!"

She sets her puffing aunt softly down. "Why doesn't Ernesto get back here?"

"You're such a lovely child," Ana says, smiling to herself. The others don't hear.

"Any moment," Sara says.

"Now that we know the soldiers aren't listening"—Ana is so persistent—"what did María do?"

"Well..." Sara looks at María.

"We talk about everything now," María says, smiling at Ana.

"Do you know what the GAM is?" Sara begins.

"Only that it's what you wouldn't let her talk about just now." Ana's brows knit. "I've heard of it."

"It's a mutual support group for a lot of people, mostly women, whose loved ones have been disappeared. Two of its leaders were horribly killed for denouncing the disappearances."

"They held a blow torch to the mouth of one," María breaks in, causing Ana to shudder. "The undertaker stuffed his mouth with cotton so the people at his funeral wouldn't vomit when they saw him. We think that the ones who took them made the woman watch while they pulled the fingernails out of her boy, who was two years old. They killed both of them too, and also her brother, who was twenty-one."

"Mother of God!"

"This did not stop the GAM." Sara says. "They marched in Guatemala City. About a thousand, mostly us Maya. It was very dangerous to be seen there..."

"So we tied bandannas across our faces," María says with an impish smile.

"You!" Ana looks as though her worst fears are confirmed.

"It was all right. Sara went with me."

"I had no idea!" Ana says.

"Please don't tell anyone," María gently warns Ana.

"We told people we were going to a big American hotel in Guatemala City to sell weavings to the tourists," Sara says.

"Which we also did." María shrugs, with the same impish smile.

"You're very brave!"

"Sometimes too brave for her own good," Sara says.

"I don't feel brave today."

"You fear for your beloved," Sara says. "That's different."

"I never saw this part of you!" Ana's admiration sounds uneasy, as though she has discovered a deep arroyo where she thought that only level grass lay between herself and her friend.

"You won't run and tell the soldiers," María jokes.

Ana sounds serious as she replies, "Of course not! But perhaps I shouldn't hear any more about dangerous things."

"You would hear many things," Sara says, "if you came to our Christian base community."

"Dangerous things. I'll stay with the traditional church."

"The Old Church locks God up in a big cathedral in the sky," Sara says. "If you don't make trouble, maybe when you die you can stay with him inside it. But don't worry today while people take your land, your labor, and your life on Earth."

"We say God is everywhere," María says. "They say, not in politics."

Uncomfortable as this talk makes Ana, she holds her ground. "I believe that God wants us to stay out of politics so we can lead normal lives and raise our children."

"The ones that live," Sara says.

"Do you believe that Jesus loved the poor?" María's tone is innocent.

"I think so." Ana senses a trap.

"People have been killed for saying that." María's mouth bows in a little smile.

"Four thousand catechists," Sara says.

"Dead?"

"Dead," Sara assures her.

"Then isn't it safer not to say it? In case you're right?"

María swings her foot across a tuft of grass, her hands clasped behind her. "They would disappear Jesus himself if he preached the Gospel in Guatemala."

Sara nods. "The tortures he'd suffer here are worse than the ones he suffered on the cross. They didn't use electrodes in those days or pull his fingernails off with pliers or stuff his head into a *capucha*."

Ana shudders. "Don't joke about our Lord." Her brows are pinched, her tone, offended.

"You'll understand what we're trying to tell you," María says, "if you understand we're not joking."

"One day that you probably didn't hear about," Sara tells Ana, "the colonel called Padre López and the other priests to his office. He told them, 'I have the power of life and death in this district. You will not teach that Jesus loved the poor. It is not true. It is Communism.'"

"Again you say subversive things!" Again Ana sounds upset.

"The colonel's own words are subversive?" Again Sara arches an eyebrow.

"You don't join our Christian base community." There is more disappointment than anger in María's voice. "You're never in Mario Tzul's hut when '*Voz Popular*' comes on the radio. It's no wonder you don't know what's happening."

"I don't take chances that can't do anybody any good." Ana tilts her face defiantly, as if she cannot see herself ever taking a chance.

"So you don't worry while three men are late and soldiers are in those trees." Sara regards them with a tight smile.

María shakes her head. "Worry never made the water boil."

"I'm pretty sure they're all right," Sara says.

"Germán must be safe because he doesn't take chances." Ana's voice sounds less sure than her words.

María smiles happily and hugs Ana. "It's a perfect day! Jesus said, 'Know the truth, and the truth will make you free'!"

"Or dead," Sara mutters.

"Unfortunately," María agrees. She picks up a pebble and sidearms it sharply down the trail. She throws harder than the few women I have ever seen throw a stone.

"You put your life in my hands!" Ana looks more upset. "What if I denounce you?"

"Don't joke like that," Sara snaps.

"Dear Ana," María says, putting her hands gently on Ana's shoulders from behind. "We're not trying to upset you."

Ana rubs her chin affectionately across María's fingers, but her face shows pain. "In all the hours we've talked, you've never talked like this."

"Until today you were good little Ana. The army protects us. María and

Luis live happily together. Their children play with yours." María's hands remain gently on Ana, but her voice is bitter as she gazes off at the mountains. Ana starts to weep, and again María speaks tenderly. "You are walking across thorns to come to me, and this is how I talk to you!"

"It's not easy being friends again." Ana sniffles and smiles. "But it's worth it."

"Instead of wanting to take lives," Sara answers María, "you and Ernesto will make lives."

"You're supposed to speak about that tonight," María says, releasing Ana and running her hand over Sara's hair, causing her aunt's gaily colored *liston* to fall loose across her shoulders and her black and gray hair to fan out across her back.

Sara rewinds her hair and tucks it in above her nape as the women talk. "Also at your third and fourth ceremonies."

"I only had three ceremonies!" Ana's face darkens as if she had broken a rule.

"We count the open door as the first ceremony," María explains. "The first fiesta is the second. Then two more fiestas."

"Then I am properly married." Ana's face goes smooth again.

"Of course," María says.

"I'd better go check on Miguelito," Ana says. "I'll be right back."

"Is he sick?" Sara asks.

"Diarrhea all night. He lost *so* much water."

"Would he drink?" Sara continues.

"A little, after we greeted the sun."

"Poor little thing." María's voice sounds like a mother's.

"Mama's watching him sleep." Ana passes beneath me and disappears among the clustered huts.

"I worry most about my children," Sara says.

"Did you birth Miguelito?"

Sara nods. "And Gloria. I like to catch the babies for whole families."

"I hope you'll catch mine."

"I hoped you'd ask me."

"Who else could I ask?" María walks briskly to the top of the trail. "I'll go down and see if I can see any soldiers."

"No!"

"I'll be careful." Her bare feet crunch on the gravel as she starts to drop from sight.

"You know what they may do to a woman."

She turns. "Not to me! That door will open only for Ernesto!"

I worry as much as Sara does about María. Every village needs a María or two, but too many spirits like hers would break it apart. Seeing that she cannot make María fear for her own safety, Sara tries guile. "You want to be here when he returns, don't you?"

"Well…" María turns, hesitates, and walks slowly back to the rock. "If the soldiers are coming, I wish they'd hurry."

"I hope they never come. So do you."

"That's true," María says. "I'm touched that Ana wants to be close to me again."

Sara nods. "Ana loves you more than she fears the truth. This is exceptional. Are you still angry with her?"

María droops a shoulder and with her thumb rubs a spot on the rock. "Anger filled me like water fills a jug, and perhaps I was too careful not to spill it. Now Ana and I are open again, the jug feels lighter on my head, but I can't tell if it's empty."

"It's probably not."

María shrugs. "She wanted to get away from us just now."

"With the soldiers so close."

María's mouth forms an incredulous O. "She'd never…"

"Do you know if Miguelito is really sick?"

"Sara!"

"He probably is."

"My poor friend. She's so gentle and afraid."

"If she shuts her eyes so tight, perhaps we're wrong to pry them open."

"She's not stupid," María fumes, "but look what she forgets. How Luis was disappeared. That the family the bomb killed was Ernesto's. The history of our people. Is that normal?"

"What is normal in a time of Terror?"

"Pretending things are fine makes them worse!"

"Many people," Sara says more warmly, "maybe most people, find it better to live in a dream than wake up to a nightmare."

"So maybe they wake up dead!"

"If she does what most people do about the Terror, then what she does cannot be so bad."

"It can destroy the village!"

"Most people don't climb the hill to our Christian base community," Sara says, "or go to Mario Tzul's hut to listen to the guerrilla radio station."

"They hide from reality until reality finds them!" María subsides. "Besides,

I don't think that most of them trust the army as much as she does."

Ana, who has been standing unnoticed between the huts, walks up and says primly, "You don't have me to quarrel with, so you quarrel between yourselves."

Sara glances at Ana and continues, "Perhaps those soldiers will give us a chance to find out who in the village trusts them."

"Sickness took Uncle Tomás," María answers. "Since the army didn't kill him, you can't feel what I feel about them."

"Tomás died for want of a medicine that many people have but we could not afford. The way-things-are killed him too."

"It's dangerous to say that," María tells Sara with a grim smile.

"But it's true."

"I…" Ana rises uncertainly. "I'll come back when you talk of other things."

"You needn't leave," Sara says.

"You see!" María puts her hands on Ana's shoulders and pushes so that Ana loses her balance and sits down hard on the rock. "We trust you. For most people, we wouldn't say what we think."

"Don't say that," Sara teases. "She'll think we *are* subversives."

"But it's true!" María smiles in triumph.

"I've heard enough for the first day of your wedding. You can tell me other dangerous things at your second fiesta."

"How's Miguelito?" Sara asks.

"Still asleep. So's Mama."

"Pray God he gets better," María says.

"He's taking water. He probably will," Sara says, reassuring at least María.

"The sun is bright! My beloved comes! No more talk of hard things."

"You're my dear friend again." Ana hugs María.

A scream rises like a jagged line of lightning from the valley. María draws back. Ana's arms fall to her sides. Sara slowly shakes her head.

"What's that!" María's fists tremble before her shoulders. Her eyes grow wide and lips pull tight in a flat smile of fear.

"An animal?" Ana, too, sounds fearful.

Another scream rises on the warm breeze, trailing into a moan that disappears beneath the shouts of the children playing in the village.

"I cannot chatter anymore! Not until Ernesto returns." María paces rapidly back and forth, bruising the grass in front of the rock.

"It could be anybody." Though Sara tries to hide it, she sounds nearly as frightened as María.

"Or an animal or a bird," Ana says.

"Pray God nothing is happening to Ernesto or any of them!"

"He'll be here any moment," Ana says.

"The Lord in his mercy hides the future."

"Really, Sara." Ana sounds exasperated.

"Some man is in great pain," María says, in control of herself again. She adds with a snort, "Maybe a soldier stepped in a hole and broke his ankle."

"Both ankles," Sara says. "He screamed twice."

"I worry about Germán." María shakes her head in frustration. "But more about Ernesto."

"No one worries about Old Pablo," Sara says to the void over the valley.

María stands, feet apart, her eyes shut so tight that her nose wrinkles. "What can I do! God, oh God, what can I do?"

Like María, I worry today about Germán but more about Ernesto. Germán is a good person, and Lourdes and their children are dear. But the Terror has yet to touch them as it has Ernesto and María, who paces below me, driven I'm sure by the screams from the valley and inside her heart. Her fears are my fears.

Chapter 6

The screams from the valley have stopped. María is pacing back and forth scuffing the grass beneath me while fear and anger flicker across the hollows of her face. Ana, at a loss for comforting words, sits against the rock gazing at her empty ka. Sara, at the edge, looks now to the mountains, now at the trees and road below. Nothing is happening except the turmoil I sense within these women.

"I don't want to make you more upset," Ana tells María, finally breaking the silence, "but we must talk of one more thing…"

"Perhaps it will take my mind off Ernesto."

"In case the soldiers do come up here." Ana begins to speak with the intensity of a person who will remember later what she is saying now. "Our mothers taught us to make tortillas together when we were little. I'm so glad we're open with each other again, but I'm also thinking, who is inside my friend? Will she bring trouble to my family? María, you frighten me."

María goes to her knees and opens her hands to the shorter woman. "Oh, Ana. I did not mean to…"

"You must finish this later," Sara interrupts, glancing towards the trail. The gravel crunches.

"It's me, Ana. It's still me." María rises quickly, pats Ana's shoulder, and turns to the trail. Her face is alert, almost eager. Fear fills Ana's eyes.

"This is not a good way to leave this," Sara mutters to the grinding stones. Her face shows nothing.

A stocky man, not old but with white hair flaring out from beneath his white straw hat, rounds the first hut. His shirt, trousers, and boots are plain. His right fist clutches a machete and a stick from which flutters a shiny blue and white plastic rectangle with my likeness in its center. Close behind him walks a younger, taller man wearing a white shirt, no hat, and carrying a slender rifle that bears deep scratches on its brown wooden stock. Smiles break across the women's faces.

"Ernesto!" Dodging round Old Pablo, María seizes him and presses her cheek to his chest. He closes his free arm around her. "I was so worried." His shoulder muffles her words.

"The corn is ground for the tamales," Ana chirps, as the bride and groom release each other. "María made us finish out here."

"That's very kind of you women," Ernesto says.

"It's nothing," Sara and Ana say together.

Old Pablo glances at the kas and bowls. "You never see women grinding corn outside. Very rarely."

"It's easier to stand at the grinding table, much easier in the hut," Sara explains. "The other women stayed inside and finished sooner, but María thought it would be fun to grind on our knees out here."

"Who needs smoky gloom?" says María. "This is a day for sunlight!"

"My parents will be very grateful." Ernesto leans the rifle against the hut that is closer to the trail.

"Is that safe?" Ana sounds alarmed.

"He keeps the bullets in his pocket," María says. Ernesto pulls out a few cartridges, wiggles them at Ana, and thrusts them back.

"Is that all of them?"

Patiently he takes up the rifle, slips out the bolt, and holds the weapon aloft. "See the sky, Ana?"

With her fingertips she steadies the brown stock and squints up the serpent-black barrel. "Yes! What good is a gun with no bullets in it?" she teases as he returns the bolt to the rifle and it to the wall. "What if you meet a snake?"

"I killed a snake this morning," Old Pablo says, brandishing the machete with a fierce scowl and smiling eyes.

"That's why I let him lead the way," Ernesto says. María smiles, as does Ana a moment later.

Old Pablo lays the machete and flag on the dirt by the rifle. "Something's going on."

"Some soldiers have a prisoner," Ernesto says. "We couldn't see his face."

"Germán Culán was due back from Quetzaltenango last night," María says. "He hasn't returned yet."

"I didn't know that." Old Pablo's tone says that he expects to be told such things. He shares with Ana a strong sense of how things are supposed to be done.

"He left here two days ago." At last Ana sounds worried. "His mother's sick. Lourdes and the children are upset. I hope nothing's happened to him."

"I wish she hadn't moved away." Sara's voice betrays her longing for her old friend.

"Wait a minute!" Alarm enters Old Pablo's voice. "Mateo Mendez came back from Quetzaltenango last night. He saw her yesterday morning. She asked him why Germán hadn't arrived yet."

They look at each other. Ana says, "Whatever delayed him may not be bad."

"Going to his mother when she's sick?" Disbelief fills Sara's voice.

"Why don't you men go look for him?" Ana's tone tells them it's their place to take the risk.

"That would be dangerous while the soldiers are near." Sara says with a snort that tells Ana to forget her little rules and return to earth.

"I'll talk with Lourdes before I leave for the fields," Old Pablo says. "If she's worried, we'll go look for him."

"All the way to Quetzaltenango?" Sara asks.

Old Pablo shrugs. "If the soldiers ask what we're doing, we'll tell them."

"Is anyone else missing?" Ernesto asks.

"Not that anybody's told me," Old Pablo sounds cross that nobody told him about Germán's venture.

"They could have captured a man from another village," Ana chirps.

"Or a guerrilla they're torturing for information," Sara says.

"Those screams. Because he refuses to betray his *compañeros*." María uses the Spanish word that means comrades who will take risks for one another. If she were a guerrilla, she would probably have shortened it to *compas*.

"It may be best if we never know...." Old Pablo's voice trails off.

"As long as Germán returns," Sara finishes his thought. A pleasant tension seems to play between them.

"The man they have..." Ana begins to tremble. The others regard her strangely shining face. "It couldn't be..."

"What, Ana?" María coaxes.

"It couldn't be...Luis!"

"After five years? Not likely." Old Pablo sounds dismissive.

Sara reproves him with a glance and turns to Ana. "It's not likely to be Luis."

"A little while ago we upset her," María tells the men.

"We were talking about the day that Luis was disappeared."

María takes Ernesto's arm. "I'm not letting you out of my sight till the roosters crow to end the fiesta."

"They make us prowl around with these stupid weapons." Old Pablo gestures to their puny arsenal. "But they're not above shooting us for carrying them—by mistake of course."

"I can't think why they'd come up here," Ana says.

María's fear breaks through again. "Nothing must stop our fiesta!"

"It's not likely," Ernesto assures her. The fear leaves her face.

"It's lucky you keep the rifle unloaded. If a soldier stumbles up here, I might shoot him."

"María!" Ernesto turns to his bride as one betrayed.

"They tortured someone, not half an hour ago, not two hundred meters from here!"

"She jokes," Sara says, adding to María, "When he takes you from the last fiesta, *then* you can say what you like."

"And make him bring me back?" María flashes a coquette's smile.

Ernesto, ever pleasant, ever serious, declines to flirt. "María and I have discussed violence. On this subject we may never agree."

"Your way is right"—María does not sound subservient—"but when I think what they do to our people... It's good I have you to calm me down."

"If Ernesto can forgive them, maybe you can too," Ana says.

Sara turns on her. "Can you forgive them for keeping things-as-they-are, which killed your dear Carlitos?"

"That wasn't their fault!"

"And my Tomás and María's Luis and Ernesto's whole family were not their fault," Sara says. María glances anxiously at Ana, who wears a strange little smile.

"It's not so much that I forgive them..." Ernesto reflects. "Those days in the fields that I spent hating the soldiers were long and hard. Time turned sweeter and passed faster when I thought about Nora and the children, even while tears filled my eyes so I could not tell the corn sprouts from weeds. The dogs of hatred ran off when I stopped feeding them with dreams of revenge." A warm current draws María closer to him though they do not move. "Now I think about our life together and the hours fly."

"Joyful day! Isn't it wonderful!" María hugs Sara instead of Ernesto.

"On that happy note, I'd better grab some tortillas and head for the fields. It's bad enough the morning's gone," Old Pablo says, and turns to trudge off.

I have heard some of you North Americans say you wonder where someone is coming from. I think we all come from our past. Now that Ernesto and Old Pablo have safely evaded the soldiers and only Germán remains unaccounted for, let me lead you on the wings of words back to several bygone events you have already heard fragments of—the oppression of my people, the disappearance of Luis, the march of the GAM, the secret religious gatherings that brought María and Ernesto together—that have done much to shape the ways in which our friends will respond to the fatal challenge that the army is about to force upon them. For ghosts of the past hold harsh dominion over this sunny day.

II The Past Returns

Chapter 7

The first fiesta of Ana's wedding to Byron came shortly before Luis was disappeared. I perch in the dark on the thatch of a hut where I can see into the village plaza. Below me Sara, María and her sister Brenda, their friend Frida, and their parents sit on mats among the other villagers around a bonfire that sends sparks into the air and crackling through the night. Nearby, Germán and his wife Lourdes and Ernesto and his wife Nora are sitting among their children. Everyone is eating tamales and the adults are drinking strong *guaro* from glazed earthen cups while three young men standing at the village's marimba hammer out poignant melodies that chase each other across the dark valley. Many voices blur together so that I catch only an occasional word or two.

Now Ana and Byron kneel for prayers as the fire burns lower, the happy chatter stops, and I hear only the night sounds of the forest. Ana's father's father, who is not very old, stands.

"Our people are the Maya," he proclaims in a deep voice filled with pride and pain. "We were once a great civilization, skilled with crops and mathematics and the courses of the stars. The calendar of the Maya was more accurate back then than the North Americans' is today. Our forebears worked their rich, lowland fields for only a few months each year in order to grow food ample for all. Sometimes they fought bloody wars, which they paused during the times for planting and harvesting the corn and beans. On altars atop their steep stone pyramids, they made bloody human sacrifices which cannot compare in numbers or ferocity to the human sacrifices that the army is making to different gods today.

"Then came the Spanish with guns, germs, and Christianity, bringing pestilence, slavery, and much early death to our people. After three hundred years, the Spanish were thrown out, but a few *ladino* families, protected by the army and the Church, kept the best land for growing indigo and coffee; and life for our people was hard. In the Christian year 1944, the last dictator was also thrown out, and democracy arrived, but it lasted only ten short years. The Colossus of the North decided that our President Jacobo Arbenz was a Communist, which was not a crime and was not true. All the same, their CIA overthrew the government of Guatemala. Then more coups and elections, but always the soldiers have done what they wanted and killed whom they chose. Rich *ladinos* and the army said they were saving us from Communism, but they took even more of our land. They grow coffee, bananas, sugar, and cotton which they sell to North Americans, and they all grow rich and richer, while we labor all year yet sometimes starve. Many Maya die needlessly, little children and others."

Ana's grandfather talks, too, about the Terror, which was worse a few years ago than it is today but still takes many lives. After he finishes, the chatter sounds soft and sad. I watch mothers take their children off to bed. Everyone else drinks more *guaro* probably to help digest the bitter words they have heard tonight and already know.

You may be surprised that these humble Indians who live in simple huts know much about their history and present reality. People like Ana see that anyone who tries to improve the lives of the Maya—or who object when their starving children's bellies bulge like pregnant dolls—is called a Communist and killed or disappeared; so they do and say nothing to attract the army's attention. Thus the Terror thrives.

To be *disappeared* means to be killed, usually in agony but also in secret so people like Ana and killers, who find the truth inconvenient, can say that the person may still be alive. Many thousands of my people have shared the fate of Luis and the grief of María. What torture she must have endured, knowing her beloved would have longed for death before it came!

Ladinos, incidentally, are Guatemalans, about a third of the population, who are not Mayas. *Ladinos* usually run things, though many of them are also poor; and their skins are usually lighter, which many people think important. Having green and red feathers side by side on my body, I cannot take seriously the differences among human skins that merely range between brown and pink.

Chapter 8

For reasons that I have never understood, some people think that virginity and innocence go hand in hand. The disappearance of Luis kept María a virgin, but it ended her innocence. I remember well the day he vanished five years ago, shortly after Ana and Byron were married.

That day was as sunny and warm as today. I did not see Sara as I glided above the village, so I alighted in this same tree so I could soak up the village beyond before I sought her further. I have always paid close attention to Sara's life, and I planned to be an unseen guest at María and Luis's fiesta that night as I was at Ana and Byron's. María's mother's mother and her father's father were to recite the history of my people that Sara is supposed to tell us tonight.

Sara had become a second mother to María during the years after she lost her own precious Paz—our little girl—who was eight years old. The reason that María's mother never minded sharing her daughter with Sara is because this is the way of the Maya and Sara is her beloved sister. For Sara, Paz lived and flourished through her blossoming niece. When María hurt, Sara felt pain. As Sara felt about Paz, I felt about Paz. About María too, Sara and I came to feel the same.

Below me on that far off day María stood at the edge, gazing into the valley. Beside her, Ana. Just like today. "He's on the road already," María cries out. She reaches to the sky, pulling her bare brown heels off the ground, and waves her hand like a tiny, spiny flag.

Ana waves too, her elbow bent and feet firm. Since no one else is there to notice me, I fly upwards and see below me Luis in a white shirt and the familiar straw hat that looks like the hats that men from Texas wear. Walking backwards, he sweeps his arm in a high arc.

"Goodbye, Luis," María shouts.

"He can't hear you," Ana says.

María shouts louder, *"Vaya con Dios!"*

He waves again, his teeth bright in the distance, turns and disappears. Before the young women turn away from the road, I alight on the same limb I clutch today.

"What does that mean?" Ana asks. "Is it another Mayan language?"

"Go with God. It's almost the only Spanish I know. Someday I'll learn more."

"It sounds so serious."

"I always want him to go with God, all right? Often when he leaves me, even if it's only to work in the fields, I think, what if I never see him again? Today especially, I won't rest until he's back."

"You saw how fast he's walking." Ana puts an arm around María's shoulder. "He'll be back sooner than you think."

María walks out from under Ana's arm, her head down, her hands clasped behind her. "I've always loved this spot. It's so quiet, no matter how crazy it gets in there." She nods towards the other huts, where children's laughter and threads of blue smoke are rising above the gray thatched roofs. "You can see more mountains from here."

Ana laughs. "Remember how we used to come here when we were little? We'd chase each other round the rock."

María lifts her head. "Let's do it."

"We're too tall. I can almost step across it."

"Not if we're on our knees. Come on!"

"I'll tear my *corte*. It took so long to weave it."

"Hike it up to your armpits. If your kneecaps tear, they'll grow back."

Looking doubtful, Ana untucks her blouse and work her skirt up beneath it as high as it will go.

"See!" María says. "Your breasts hold it up." María hiked up her own skirt, but having shallow breasts, she has to press her elbows to her sides to keep it from falling. Ana laughs.

They stand on their knees with the rock between them. One starts one way, the other hobbled the other. They feint and bob. Ana can't reach María across the rock, and when María reaches out an arm, her skirt falls crooked. They laugh and say, "Ow, ow," when tufts of grass sear their flesh or a pebble digs into a knee. They do not hear the footsteps on the trail.

"What's this?" says Sara. Startled, they turn. She is standing at the top with a jug on her head. "The new bride and the not-so-new bride are children again."

María bounds up and prances around Sara, her skirt dropping to her hips, her hands brushing round the jug to steady it. "It takes a child to make a child," she tells her laughing aunt. "I'll soon be on my way."

María's headlong words about such intimate matters bring a shadow of disapproval across her aunt's face and a blush to Ana's. Ana slaps the dirt from her knees, tucks her blouse into her many-colored skirt, and says to Sara as one matron to another. "It's her day to play. Soon she'll take the steps we've taken."

Sara regards them with a sad smile. "Be children as long as you can. There are things I must do for the fiesta." María stands aside to let her aunt pass.

I think of following Sara, her head erect beneath the heavy jug. She never reaches up to steady it. But no. How often does a young male get to listen to two females, one just married and the other on the verge, who think they are alone?

"What's it like?" María asks, locking her fingers together and twisting her hands inside out.

"What's what like?" Ana sounds nervous, as if she knows what's coming.

"You know. When you and Byron are together."

"You mean… In the dark?"

"Yes. Grandmama explained it to me. I'd almost figured it out. It sounds nice, like giving each other the same gift. We don't rush like goats or dance about like dogs, do we? There isn't room in the hut. No matter how often I've imagined it, I'm sure I'll be surprised."

Ana looks quickly around, as if seeking a way to flee. "People never discuss these things," she hisses. "I've never talked about them with anyone, not even you. Byron and I don't even talk about what we do."

"I don't want to embarrass you," María persists, "but it's something you've done and I'm about to do and our parents have certainly done or we wouldn't be here. We're best friends, aren't we. So why can't we talk about it?"

"That's true," Ana says, slowly turning crimson. "I just can't imagine ever talking about it."

"But it leads to children," María continues. "They'll tell me twenty times during the fiestas how good it is to have them. So the things men and women do to start them must be good."

"Must be," Ana agrees, "but if it was good to talk about, why does nobody talk about it, except our grandmothers right before we do it?"

I too am startled by María's questions. In all my eavesdropping—or call it research—in this village and others, I have never heard a young woman plunge so frankly where others fear to tread. This trait will serve María well five years hence.

"Did one of Byron's grandfathers talk to him?"

"He said so."

"So Luis's grandfather must have talked to him. When he waved goodbye, he, too, must have known what will happen. Haven't you heard your parents doing it in the dark?"

"Usually I just go back to sleep."

"Not me, not after I knew what it was," María said warmly. "I lie there and wonder what it's like. I'm so glad I'm about to find out."

"Aren't you afraid of the pain? I was, after Little Granny told me about it."

"Not me. I want to get on with being a woman."

Ana catches her breath. "I'd be so ashamed if anybody heard us."

"You face the village. I'll face the trail. If anybody comes, we'll talk about Luis's tamales."

"Well…" They face each other across the rock. Ana looks anxiously past María's shoulder. Looking into Ana's eyes and paying no attention to the trail, María asks, "Did it hurt the first time?"

"For a moment, but it was worth it. It only hurt once, and a tiny bit the second time." Ana smiles. "Soon it felt good. Little Granny never mentioned that part."

"Grandmama didn't, either. She only said we do it for the man, and he does it to give us children."

Ana reflects. "When I used to hear Mama and Papa at night, I'd wonder why they took the trouble. They were always so tired. But you'll see. You'll take the trouble."

"Were you embarrassed the first time, with Byron's family lying so close?"

"They weren't. They put fresh flowers in their hut and spent the night with friends."

"I hope Luis's family does that for us." María shrugs. "It doesn't matter if they don't, but I hope they do."

"They've received you well so far, haven't they?"

"Oh, yes. You know they're nice people. I wish he'd get back."

"He hasn't been gone an hour."

María and Ana talk more warmly than they have talked together since before Ana's first fiesta, or so they reassure each other. Clouds passed over, leading new clouds after them. The sun swings slowly down the sky. María peers more often into the valley. Finally she stands at the edge, maybe hoping to reassure herself by indulging her concern.

The hour when Luis should have returned comes and lingers like a cloud frozen overhead and gradually passes on. The road remains empty. Ana, sitting on the rock, invents words after trivial words to divert María, then reason after plausible reason to reassure her why Luis is not back. María's words grow brief and jerk tight. Now and then her brow pinches between the iron tongs of panic.

At last Sara trundles back. "Still here? You're a lucky bride to have so little to do."

María turns to her aunt as if awakening from a troubled sleep. Her face relaxes in a smile. "I have much to do, but I can't leave until Luis returns."

"All those tamales are heavy." Sara says, "even for such a strong man."

"Maybe they weren't ready when he got there," Ana adds.

"You said that already. Of course you may be right."

"He probably stopped to rest and fell asleep." Sara's voice is too casual, her smile too tight.

"How could he fall asleep today?" Ana asks innocently.

"How indeed?" María sounds annoyed.

Ana absorbs the rebuff and tried a new tack. "You don't suppose some soldiers have delayed him, do you?"

Sara frowns and shakes her head at Ana. María, not seeing the silent reprimand, say, "Of course not. He always carries his identity card. He's not doing anything wrong, just carrying a load of tamales."

"That's all he's doing," Sara says with a resignation that escapes the younger women.

"Look, I know you're both trying to help me, but the only thing that will help me is seeing him on the road."

Sara nods but manages to change the subject until María suddenly pounds her fists on her knees. "It doesn't take this long! The sun's nearly to the mountains! I'm going after him!" She starts for the trail.

"He may need help with something," Sara said equably, "but you're not the one to go. I'll get your fathers." She turned towards the huts as María's older sister rushed out.

"Brenda!" cries María.

"There you are. I've been looking all over. The fiesta soon begins, but where's the bride, where's the groom?"

"Something's happening to him, something terrible." María's fingers tremble at her mouth, her eyes wide with fear. "I hear him scream inside my head!"

Brenda hugs María, her forehead against María's chin.

Quickly it is decided that María's father, Luis's father and both of his brothers, Old Pablo, and two other men will go search. María begs them to let her go too, but they say no. Brenda and their mother hold her at the top of the trail as the seven heads bob single file down into the gloom. Ana stands silent yet close. Tears streams off María's quivering chin. She buries her face against her mother's shoulder while Brenda reaches up and strokes her hair.

I, too, am fearful. I, too, go to the other village that other wedding eve, flying between the trees through the reddening dusk. The road below is dark and empty. So are the bushes along it. I see no trace of Luis or his burden.

I am still a young quetzal, but I remember much from having been a man. I know enough to fly to the local army post. As I perch in a tree by the barbed wire, long tremulous screams rise and fall inside a long low gray building with lighted windows. Is that the playful boy I had watched grow up, the man who is or was about to marry María? The army kidnaps many men, but in this little outpost today, who else can it be? I cannot sleep until very late, after the screaming stops.

The roosters crows and the sun slants warm across the treetops. I smell the soldiers' breakfast cooking. Soon, more screams pierced the morning. They can, of course, be coming from any man.

Chapter 9

Ana's fears and desires do much to shape her outlook. María, in contrast, needs to know the actual reality, be it good or bad. When things go awry, as they do, every village needs a María to save it from its Anas, who are often passive and in what you call denial. My people have learned much about their reality from their elders speaking at wedding fiestas. María and Sara will learn much more when they spend an evening with two Catholic nuns in Guatemala City after the GAM march. What the villagers have learned from their elders, and especially what María and Sara learn from those sisters, will stand everyone in good stead today, some of our friends more than others.

Two years ago, María and Sara made the journey to Guatemala City to march with the GAM and pass the night with the nuns who changed María's life. I can tell you what happened because I went with them, my first flight into broad, bright metropolis which stinks of the fumes that cars, trucks, and buses spew up and down the tree-lined avenues faster than I can fly. This city is dangerous for resplendent birds, as it is for these two women who mean so much to me. They arrive before I do, to sell weavings at a tourist hotel.

Flying through the gray first light on the day of the march, I notice brightly colored bundles lying between green bushes along the roadside miles before I reach the city—Mayan women sleeping, I suppose, on their way to the march. Orange tile roofs of homes that are as big as government buildings pass beneath me. Around them lie green parks still in shadows as the sun's first rays spark off shards of glass imbedded atop the high walls around them. The capital city is noisily awake as I alight in a lofty flame tree near the headquarters of the National Police and conceal myself within its green fronds and orange bursts of blossom.

It is worth the risk I am taking to gaze down upon the rainbow carpet of women, some barefoot, some with babies on their backs. Though many have tied triangles of colorful cloth across their lower faces like bandits, someone who knows the weavers' code can tell the places they come from by the patterns woven into their garb. How great must be the grief that brings so many so far!

Joining the women come young men, also wearing masks and shirts that say "San Carlos University" and men from the labor unions. All march not as soldiers but in a jostling flow of free people. They teem among the cars and buses and swarm about a big Coca-Cola truck where the driver is struggling to wheel cartons of bottles through them into a grocery store.

Women at the forefront of the parade hold a wide white banner emblazoned in black with their name, GRUPO DE APOYO MUTUO, which means Mutual Support Group and is the GAM that Ana said she did not know about. Big red letters across the banner say in Spanish "Respect for Human Dignity, Life and Liberty!" Though many of the Maya in the march cannot read it, all of them are demanding it.

Other women hold aloft swaying placards that bear long messages beautifully lettered though too small for me to read. Tacked to wooden T-crosses that sway in the vanguard are huge photographs of two GAM martyrs. One shows a young man wearing a dark jacket, white shirt, and neatly knotted tie—the GAM leader who later has cotton in his mouth to conceal what the people whom the marchers were now defying have done to him. The other photo, bobbing beside it, shows a beautiful young woman with black hair that billows past her keen oval face. There is no picture of her brother or her boy who was two years old and had his fingernails pulled out.

The marchers shake their fists and hold flowers in their other hand as they swarm about the police building, shouting in what sounds like all twenty-two languages of the Maya, some shouting in Spanish which the police can understand, a seething arc of life and color before the silent facade. Tears glisten on many cheeks and blot into bandanna masks as the women cry out for their husbands, their fathers and mothers, their brothers and sisters, their sweethearts, their sons and daughters. Their courage makes me quiver on my branch. Though they seem to cry out in vain, their cry will echo through the years and bring tears to many eyes and fire to many hearts.

My own heart jumps as I see Sara hurry past on the opposite sidewalk with her shawl across her shoulders. Soon the familiar figure hurries back, the shawl cowled so that only her broad brown nose shows beneath its shadow. Back she comes, her face tilted up, her cheeks sucked in, and the motley shawl folded upon her head in the manner of Mayan women. Do her disguises fool the men behind the hidden cameras into thinking she is three women instead of only one? Even as I fear for her safety, she strikes me as being like another quetzal watching over our people—she as helpless as I am if help is needed, yet undaunted. I do not see her again before the women finally disperse, a tide of many-colored grief and anger ebbing from the hollow rock that houses the police. Where is María?

She joins Sara on the pavement below me. Since I am sure they will return on the avenue they arrived on, I allow them to ramble away before I fly to wait in a tree beyond them. The marchers are scattered by now, a few bright garbs among the drab, hen-like people of the city.

Where are my dear ones? How fast they must be walking, I think as I flap through the fumes and glance from sidewalk to sidewalk. Below me now is only an occasional Maya too far from the march to have been part of it. Can my women have been passing beneath a tree as I flew above it? I skim back daringly low along one sidewalk, not caring how many people see me, gone before they can more than gasp, then back along the other sidewalk at the same reckless height. Where are they?

Don't panic, I tell myself as I rise comfortably above the rooftops. Form a plan. Since the police are not likely to identify the masked women later on, even from the photos they must have taken of the crowd besieging them, this very moment is their last chance to disappear any of the marchers. The familiar Jeep Cherokees with smoked windows are not careening through the streets, but sometimes the death squads work more subtly. I begin to fly in big circles. If people see me, they must think, What a crazy bird! So intently am I looking at each bright woman that my fear recedes, but not far.

At last I spot them, the short one and the tall, rocking along the same avenue but in the opposite direction from where I expected them. Are they lost? I alight in a thick tree and watched them pass, their toes thrusting out from beneath their skirts below me, María talking breathlessly and Sara nodding now and then. When they are nearly out of sight, I speed to another tree and await them again.

What? I glimpse the red, violet, orange, and indigo of their skirts disappearing into a side street. Racing up I catch the tag of their skirts swishing through a doorway three houses down. What to do? I perch in a tree across from that humble house and wait. Singly and in twos and threes, other brightly clad women come to that shadowed doorway until perhaps twenty have passed inside. Odd, I think, that the skin of a woman who sometimes opens the door for them is not even ladino tan but tourist pink.

Time creeps along as daylight fades into the reddish city dusk. Bright headlights and red taillights race endlessly on the avenue, and perhaps I doze. Is that Sara's gravelly laugh? It was faint and hard to distinguish amongst the traffic that roars past the corner. Is that it again? The dark honey of María's voice bubbles unmistakably from the patio within the house. I glide to it and alight in a thick bougainvillea that rises higher than the roof. Its green and purple hides my green and scarlet in the faint gray light.

Sara and María sit below me at a battered wooden table across from the pink-skinned woman and a tan one. A candle flickers in a green glass jar. From their conversation I learn that the other two women are nuns, Sister Justine, a Maryknoll missionary from your State of Indiana, and Sister Milagros, a Maya from the highlands who teaches in a school for Mayan children in this vast city.

"The candlelight is nice," María said. "Like home."

"It is, isn't it," Justine said warmly.

"The authorities watch our electric bills." Milagros's sour realism sounds like Sara's. "If someone suddenly uses a lot of electricity, they suspect she's hiding subversives."

"Even nuns?" María asks.

"Especially nuns." Milagros sounds disgusted.

"Not that we hide any," Justine adds, "but they suspect everyone who accompanies the poor."

"How well they understand the Church," Sara mutters.

Milagros and her sisters, I learn, have opened their home, quietly and at great risk to themselves, for some of the marchers to rest the night so they can leave the city with the random flow of Maya in the morning. All the women have eaten a supper of steamed vegetables, tortillas, and chicken broth that had rice and carrots in it. Most of the women are already asleep inside.

Milagros, sitting across from Sara, looks enough like her to be her somber sister. Justine, who is younger, is the only North American I have ever heard speak Mam. She and another nun learned it upon arriving in Guatemala two years ago, it seems, and have opened a school in a large village across the mountain from my friends' village. Like them, she made the long trip to the march with several women of that village who are now asleep inside, because being accompanied by a North American keeps my people safe usually but not always.

"You're so nice to let us stay here," María says. "You must come and visit us."

"I'd love to," Justine says, "but I'd never find my way."

"I'll cross the mountain and fetch you. It's only a day's walk."

"You don't know fear, do you," Milagros declares.

Sara nods. "It's her defect."

"What do you mean?" María draws herself up in mock umbrage. "I was scared in front of that fortress today. They were probably pointing machine guns at us through the windows."

"Cameras at least," says Milagros.

"But you stood there anyway," the younger nun adds.

"The worst that can happen, I thought, is that they'll shoot us and I'll be with Luis in Heaven."

"The worst that can happen," Milagros says "is they take you inside the Old Politécnica."

"I didn't think of that." María's shoulders shudder as she regards the flickering flame. The Old Politécnica is a military school that is also a well-known torture site. It's where the secret police will torture an American nun named Sister Dianna Ortiz several years hence.

Milagros smiles, and her smile fades as she speaks. "I thought of you today as I sat here in such peace, watching the sun play on the bougainvillea. Each of you was out there because a person you love was snatched away for some cruel purpose that they never explain. How futile, I thought. What can you accomplish? Yet how much nobler than doing nothing! Your courage will burn like a beacon. A little of your light may even reach Justine's homeland. I thanked God you were there as I prayed you were safe. The hope of the hopeless is the strongest hope there is."

Sara twists her hands as she does the rare times she is embarrassed. Justine looks down self-consciously at the dark surface of the table. "What she says is true," she assures them.

"You are too kind." It is María's turn to blush. "When we stood with our flowers and our fists, I too thought, what can come of this? But in the midst of my tears and fury, I felt how good it is for others to know that we stand here like this. Dear Luis filled my heart. My grief has never known such company!"

"I was afraid the police would shoot you and claim self-defense," Milagros says. "I kept thinking how they burned up the thirty-nine protesters inside the Spanish Embassy a few years ago."

"And snatched the one survivor from his hospital bed that night and tortured him to death," Justine finishes a litany that nuns like them know well.

"Is Luis a loved one you lost?" Milagros asks.

"On the first day of our wedding. So long ago, but today it seemed like yesterday."

Pain shapes Milagros's face. "That must have hurt like being burned alive."

"If only they'd left him in the road. Even if they'd cut off his head like they sometimes do." María winces. "But not to know. To feel hope come and go for months and years. To fight with my friends who said he was dead." Her voice snaps from anguish into anger. "And fight with a friend who insisted he must be living someplace else."

"Ana?" Sara asks.

"Ana."

"You mustn't be too hard on a person who cannot face what really happens," Milagros says soothingly.

María nods. "I told myself that. I said to myself, 'If it took me years to accept what happened to him, why am I so hard on Ana for not accepting it?' But she shut me out with her jolly wall of sunshine, and her smiley white teeth that made me so angry. 'So that is my friend,' I thought, and I talked with Sara and others but never with her about the questions that burned through my brain. 'Is he eating? Is he sleeping? What are they doing to him today? Is he alive?' Even while I asked, the feeling grew within me that they had already killed him."

"When they leave you the body," Sara murmured, "you can bury it. If they disappear him, they force you to kill him in your heart. Or your life, too, is over."

"I'm so sorry." Justine squeezes María's brown hands between her pink ones. "The Terror brings on many forms of denial. I saw an ugly one last September. I met with some other North Americans at a hotel not far from here. I was the first one down for breakfast. The headline in the paper said, 'FOUR BODIES FOUND AT SAN CARLOS UNIVERSITY.' The hostess must have thought I was one scared *gringa.* 'Don't worry,' she told me, 'they're just killing students.'" Justine's face darkened in the dim light. "She was smiling. I wanted to slap her face."

"What had they done?" María asks.

"Led a teachers' strike for higher pay. Eight more strike leaders were disappeared about the same time. Three of them turned up dead."

Milagros looks into the dark wells of María's eyes. "How long ago did they take Luis?"

"It's been more than three years. Once I accepted that they had killed him, I wanted to do something strong."

"Revenge?" Milagros arches an eyebrow the way Sara does, and shadows dance across the hollows of her face.

"Something useful. I even thought of becoming a nun."

Milagros and Justine exchange looks. Sara smiles and lowers her eyes.

"We're always here if you want to talk," Milagros says.

"I'm just across the mountain," Justine says.

"It can be a beautiful life," Milagros adds, "but if it's not for you, it can be a quiet form of hell."

"Poverty and chastity she's used to," Sara says with a faint smile. "But don't you also require obedience?"

"I obey my parents."

"You know what I mean."

"Life has changed for many nuns," Justine reflects.

"In some ways," Milagros says. "I love teaching children how to read. It arms them so much better than guns would."

"You're very attractive," Justine says. "Surely some man will give you another choice."

"Her father opened the door for two men after Luis," Sara explains, "but she wouldn't consider them."

"There must be others," Justine says. "If your village is too small, come stay with me in mine for a while. You could help me at the school."

María smiles, her cheeks flushing deep red in the yellow light. "Thank you."

Sara rises to meet Justine's challenge. "There's a fine young man in our village. He had a wife and two children, but a bomb from the sky sent them to Heaven."

"From an airplane?" Justine sounds surprised. "Why would they bomb you?"

"We've often wondered," María says.

"We think maybe the pilot was afraid that if he flew home with his toy, they'd say he hadn't completed his mission, so he got rid of it on us." Sara shrugs.

"Even when his grief ends," María says, as if dismissing the subject, "that man's too old to look at me."

The older women smiled. "His age wouldn't stop him in my country," Justine says.

"Nor in ours," says Milagros.

"The older you grow," Sara said, "the younger he becomes."

The candle flickers in the darkness of the patio beneath the red glow of the city. Cars, trucks, and an occasional bus or jeep roar faintly on the avenue beyond the rooftops. Justine pulls on a sweater, and the others clutch shawls about their shoulders. Justine mentions that Padre López comes often to her village.

"We keep him in our prayers," said Milagros, who is also his friend.

"You should pray for anyone who rides with him," says Justine. "I've never been so scared in my life."

"He looks safe to us," María says. "I've never ridden with him."

"He's an excellent driver," Justine says. "He has to be to keep control when he bounces through the potholes."

"If he's so good, why doesn't he slow down?" María asks.

"He says it's safer going fast."

Milagros sees disbelief on María's face. "He's been shot at twice from the bushes."

"Our Padre López? They shoot at a priest?"

The nuns nod.

"It means a lot that you come to our country and take chances for us," Sara says to Justine.

"Yes!" María clasps Justine's hands across the table. "So much evil comes from your country."

"Many missionaries have come to help," Milagros says, "and some have been killed."

"Father Stanley Rother, Brother James Miller, Frank Holdenreid, and over in El Salvador the three nuns and the young woman who worked with them," Justine recites.

María shudders and gaves a little cry. Wide-eyed, she stares up past the glow of the city, past the stars, as if at her future or perhaps only at the fate of those North American missionaries.

"They died for our people." Milagros's eyes are moist.

The women are silent. Finally María said to Justine, "So no one is safe. Not even you."

"Not even me." Justine smiles faintly.

"And the North American people? Surely they must feel as we do about such things."

"No one has told them. I wrote to my parents in Elkhart about it. They wrote back that I'd shocked them. That I must be mistaken, it couldn't be true."

Milagros turns to Justine. "Tell me if I presume too much. I suspect that your government is happy if the death of a few North Americans frightens off you women religious who threaten their sacred business as usual."

Justine nods.

"You're both teachers," Sara says. "Do you think the officials of both countries arranged these murders to teach troublemakers a lesson?"

The nuns look at each other. "Probably," Justine says.

"It would fit with many things," Milagros adds. "Our government and yours use terror to teach our people to be contented. It usually works, or they wouldn't bother doing it."

"My country, my country." Despair fills Justine's voice. "It does so much good in the world—sends help where an earthquake strikes, feeds hungry people…. I guess it doesn't feed hungry people in Guatemala." She tips the green glass between her fingertips so that the wax flows around the flickering flame. "I learned about death squads from a man who used to be a soldier. He told me the men in his outfit were often asked to volunteer for special assignments in civilian clothes. He said he never volunteered, but the men who were bullies often did. Later they'd laugh and brag about the fun they'd had, especially with the women they took."

Justine looks into their eyes, Sara's and Milagros's deep with knowing, María's wide with learning. "The official terror is no secret here. Why isn't it known to the White House, the *Casa Blanca*, where our President lives?" She struck her fists on the table. The flame flickers sharply as the jar bounces. "I'm so ashamed of my government for supporting your army. Poor Maya like you ask me how such terrible things can happen. How can I explain why the United States assists and maybe even directs these crimes against defenseless people?"

"It's not your fault." María sounds motherly as she speaks to the older woman. "You're doing all you can, perhaps what I should be doing."

Justine's voice smolders. "My people, even my parents, do not have a clue what it's like to be on the receiving end of U.S. power!"

"You needn't try to explain the evil in your government," Sara says. "We can't explain it in ours."

A dam bursts within gentle Milagros, and her anger flows. "Both governments help the rich while we try to help the poor. For this they call us Communists. They murder us if we complain about this war between the rich and poor even while they're winning it. So our children keep dying, dying, dying. Their bodies are the bloody red bricks of the temple called Capitalism."

"I pray for the officials, too," Justine says primly, "though sometimes it's hard."

"I pray that God will soon have them in His classroom." The anger in Milagros's voice reminds me of the anger that sends some people into the mountains to kill and die with the guerrillas. They may be less reflective than Milagros or maybe only younger.

"Are you sure you'd rather teach children to read than prepare them to carry guns?" María asks.

"Beyond any doubt," Milagros says quietly. "You may find it hard to agree.

Young people like action. But you may agree when you're my age. I pray you reach my age."

María smiles. "Do you want to frighten me?"

"No, no. But a free spirit like you faces great risks."

"That's true in my country, too," Justine says, "though the stakes are usually lower."

"It's probably true everywhere." Sara shrugs.

Milagros takes María's hands and looks into her eyes for a long moment. "I think that today you have buried Luis." She pauses as María looked puzzled until a smile opens across her face, radiant in the candlelight. Milagros continues. "Perhaps today opens new paths for you to choose. I hope and fear which one you'll take."

The candlelight flickers in María's eyes. "You're amazing, Sister. Today I felt that Luis was standing beside me in the crowd, giving me strength from wherever he is. Yet I feel that by facing the ones who killed him, I have buried him at last."

Half standing, she reaches past the candle, tears glistening along her nose, and presses Milagros's withered cheek against her own. "Dear Luis.... Dear, dear Luis... *Vaya con Dios*."

María sobs against Milagros as the older woman rubs the back of her neck.

"*Requiescat in pace*," Milagros murmurs to María and Luis. Her eyes, too, shine moist in the flickering light as María weeps, the other women watch, and the traffic speeds faintly on the avenue.

The talk turns to other things. When the candle finally gutters out, the women stand stiffly from their chairs and shuffle inside for a few hours' sleep before the first light chased the hellish red glow from the sky above the city. Often I have heard nuns involve themselves in politics, which they call acting on their faith, and I have heard some people ask, Why can't they simply stay in their cloisters and pray?

I roost high in the tree in front of the house, so as not to miss Sara and María when they emerge into the morning bustle. Once I see them safely around the police headquarters, I allow myself to spend an hour as a tourist, flying about the busy city and out to the airport which had helicopters and narrow planes that carry bombs parked beside the runway and painted like the soldiers in the blotchy greens of a feverish frog. It is on this tour of Guatemala City that I see the mighty eagle that is entombed in stone upon the wall of your embassy, a bird of freedom for you if not for us, for it is mated with Terror in this small land that some of you may not know where to find on a map.

Chapter 10

Sara asked María what is normal in a time when the Terror strikes at will. What indeed? My people fear to speak against the army to anyone they don't completely trust, and many like Ana refuse to even think against the army. They erect walls across their minds where nothing happens on the other side and no one risks his life to spray-paint graffiti that calls for resistance and liberty across the endless facade.

In many villages, though, doughty people walk casually into the forest as if to gather firewood, but actually to meet as if by chance and talk about their God, while the flock who are like Ana to sit in church and listen to safe parts of the holy Word. I have flown above the bodies of many of those catechists whom Sara mentioned and also above the body of that brave North American priest Father Stanley Rother, whom Sister Justine mentioned to María and Sara, as it was being carried out of his home at Santiago Atitlán. I understand that your government accepted his murder as calmly as it did the rapes and murders of the four North American church women in El Salvador. Thousands of Father Rother's parishioners, dozens of priests, two bishops, and a U.S. reporter attended his funeral, but no one from your Embassy.

One day a year ago, a walk into the forest begins the second romance of María's life. It is warm and bright this Sunday afternoon, though the trees still drip from a shower that passed over at noon. I perch beside a clearing up the mountain from the village. Other birds talk across the slope, and sunlight dances about the clearing as the breeze strokes the limbs of the trees.

Villagers trudge up the forest, no two the same way so as not to trample a path that soldiers can follow. Here comes Padre López, who is a *ladino* whom my people trust. Over there is Ernesto, who is broad and taller than most of my people and never smiles. As usual, more women arrive than men. They sit in a circle on woven mats that can hold firewood. It is most pleasant among the sun-dappled trees to be with these people who climbed the mountain and take this risk for their faith.

Old Pablo is not here today, but that is not unusual. Neither is Sara. A young woman named Teresa asks after her. Another named Inez says she is sleeping because she was up all night to pull a baby boy into the world for Alma and Roberto Perez. My plumes droop at the news that I will not be seeing Sara here today, but here is María, her frisky former self again after those nuns educated her the day of the GAM march. I hear that many of you North Americans have also been educated by nuns, but probably in a different way. Earlier María fashioned a bouquet of crosses out of broad blades of forest grass. Now she lays a green cross on the ground before each surprised person.

"Why don't we have a Scripture reading for new little Armando?" says Inez, who married three years ago but has yet to bear a child.

María's eyes kindle. "How about the one that says you must be like a child to get into Heaven?"

"It's in the Gospel of San Mateo and also in San Marcos, somewhere." Teresa is showing off. Her voice trails off.

"I like it best in San Lucas," says Ernesto, his first words to the group in several weeks.

A very thin man named José, whose dark skin is lined like old leather, hands Ernesto a plastic bag that has patches of damp earth clinging to it. Ernesto unfolds it, brushes the dirt from his fingers onto his knee, and pulls forth another plastic parcel, from which he draws yet another plastic parcel, and finally a thick Bible with a frayed black cover and a worn spine.

"I think you'll find it around Chapter 18," says Padre López.

Ernesto scans some pages that rustled like dry leaves between his fingers. As he reads from the Word, his voice resonates deeper than when he talks. "Now they were bringing even infants to him that he might touch them; and when the disciples saw it, they rebuked them." He pauses while a woman named Olivia, who is about Sara's age, translates from the Spanish into Mam. "But Jesus calls them to him, saying 'Let the children come to me, and do not hinder them; for to such belongs the kingdom of God.'" Olivia translates. Ernesto concludes, "'Truly, I say to you, whoever does not receive the kingdom of God like a child shall not enter it.'"

As Olivia finishes, the circle falls silent. Birds still talk through the trees as the breeze brushes the leaves. Finally José speaks. "Maybe that's about going to Heaven and maybe not. But surely it's about receiving the peace of our Lord right here and now."

"How can we receive peace when there is no peace?" Inez's voice is bitter, as though she does not expect an answer to her question.

"By being like a child, Child," María says with a laugh. Inez's face falls.

"I think you're basically right," Padre López says to María after an uncomfortable pause, "but I don't think it means showing the insensitivity that children sometimes show."

"I'm sorry," María murmurs to Inez.

"The question," Padre López says, "is what does it mean to receive the kingdom of God like a child after we've grown up and, as Inez says, there is no peace?"

The warm, comfortable silence returns. These women and men are used to silence and know that silence is as much a part of their reflections as talking is. From time to time a person speaks, and another answers or says something new. All heads turn as the underbrush crackles downhill. More and more of a woman's colorful clothes come into view, and Sara plods into the circle. After a flurry of questions about the new mother and baby, Olivia paraphrases the passage from San Lucas for Sara, and the peaceful rhythm of the reflection resumes.

"Jesus said to turn the other cheek and to walk the extra mile for the bully," Ernesto says slowly, after a particularly long silence. "Last week in the fields those two sayings came together for me in a new way. Today I see that they also go with becoming like a child."

"What do you mean?" María demands, her eyes flashing. Never before have I seen her speak so intensely to a man in this circle.

"All three of those teachings led me towards peace with the men who destroyed my family."

"Do you mean that only a child could turn the other cheek to such evil people?" Scorn fills María's voice.

Ernesto does not take offense. "I can neither hurt nor help the men who sent the bomb, but my own life is better during the times I don't hate them."

María's face darkens, and now she sounds perplexed. "How can you live at peace with people who took those lives and hurt you so?"

"Hating the killers does not bring back the people I loved. I thank God the bomb landed down the slope so they were the only ones killed."

"Red chunks of your loved ones landed on the roofs of other huts and all over the ground. And you are at peace?"

"Forgiving those unknown men brings me the only peace I've been able to find."

"Maybe you value your peace too much."

All eyes watch Ernesto and María, who do not notice them even during the silence before he replies. "I thought deeply about hunting down the killers, or anyone who flies those planes. Vengeance still tempts me, but if I yield to it, what is my faith? Where is my peace?"

"I can't criticize you." María smiles faintly. "When I finally accepted that the army took Luis, I thought of joining the guerrillas, but you see I didn't."

"They died, María, and most of my heart died with them. I'm thankful that at least they died too fast to feel any pain."

"That's a blessing. I'm sure death came as a blessing for Luis, after more agony than he could bear." Her brow furrows. "But how do we explain that you have peace after only two years while I'm still searching for it after four."

"You raise a deep question in me, too. I am at peace, yes, but barely alive. Will I ever again have anything like your spirit, your childlike joy, your drive to do things? Do you know a secret that I may never learn?"

"I wish I could make you smile." María's voice is a warm hand stroking his brow. "I'd give you my secret, but I don't know what it is."

"I no longer hate…"

"But you don't love either." Her lips form a wan smile. Her eyes leave his to glance at the twenty faces around them as if she is awakening to their presence. "I wish we could continue, but we're taking up everybody's time."

"This talk is important for both of you," Padre López says. "Perhaps you'll find a way to continue later."

A smile of benediction flashes across Sara's face while a man named Jorgé regards the ground with a face of stone. He is one of the men who knelt before María's door with Old Pablo in the middle of the night a year or two after Luis died, and he joined this religious community shortly after María did, though he usually remains as silent as Ernesto was until now.

As the reflections continue, other people speak about loved ones they lost and what it can possibly mean to receive the kingdom as a child in a time of Terror.

"God permits much agony and early death," says old José, "but that does not mean He has forsaken us."

"Knowing this means having faith," says Sara, and all are silent for a time while the birds talked on.

As the reflection ends and people stand to amble down the hill, María and Ernesto fuss about and chat with others until they are among the last to start towards the village. They walk side by side, with Sara following at what you may call a discreet distance. As they pass beneath me, María is talking, and Ernesto smiles.

When I visited this village during the months that followed, I caught glimpses, as if through windows along a wall of time, of María and Ernesto giving each other their gifts—hers of life and his of peace. She sometimes brought him lunch while he was working in the fields, and he would save for the next day the tortillas he'd made himself that morning. Sometimes they would stroll to the grassy plot beneath me now, to watch the sun go down. She joined the Spanish lessons that Old Pablo was giving to him and several others in the church building. Old Pablo had been many places and done many things and spoke Spanish well, though he did not write in any language. Germán sometimes helped with the lessons, since he had learned to speak passable Spanish from his mother, who came from Quetzaltenango and moved back there after his father died. Padre López encourages my people to learn Spanish so they can get along in the cities when they have to and *ladinos* will be less able to cheat them.

Sara learned some Spanish years ago when she went down with other families to pick coffee on the *fincas*, the huge farms, in the lowlands to the south. Then came the awful day that an airplane sprayed her and Paz, who was eight years old and was picking coffee beans beside her, with an insecticide that you North Americans ban in your country and sell in ours. Sara became sick, and Paz died that night jerking horribly under the same blanket. I understand that deaths like hers are part of the price of keeping your coffee cheap. Since then, Sara has not returned to the plantations, nor has she learned more Spanish though Padre López sometimes prods her to.

On other Sundays when I perched by the clearing in the forest, I saw María and Ernesto walk down the mountain, always the last except for Sara. I know that Sara has discussed their courtship with her sister, María's mother, because I had perched on the thatch of their hut on the evening that María's mother, after much hesitation, told her father. Silence followed—as her father reflected, no doubt—until I heard his deep laugh. "She is twenty years old," he said at last. "Her time is passing. We'll hope for the best."

These afternoons that María and Ernesto walked side by side down the mountain, they never touched with their hands, but he smiled often, and sometimes she grew careless and bumped her lithe body against his and he smiled. Is it true that the man always dances the first steps towards conceiving a child? But what does that matter so long as María and Ernesto are fulfilled? They climbed the mountain to look for God, and they found each other. Perhaps that is a way of finding God.

III The Jaguars Pounce

Chapter 11

Let us return to the present. The morning is gone. María has just exclaimed "Joyful day!" because her marriage to Ernesto is to begin in a few hours, and Old Pablo is about to grab some tortillas and head for the fields.

Sara looks towards the trail and says to Old Pablo with fear in her voice, "I think you'd better speak softly and wait."

The others follow her gaze towards the sound of grinding gravel. Old Pablo claps his hands across his mouth as terror bulges his eyes, but he shrugs himself into nonchalance as a small man wearing insignia of a lieutenant in the Guatemalan army rounds the hut. A large sergeant follows, leading a man by a rope tied around his waist.

Both soldiers wear black berets and blotchy greens. The lieutenant's are pressed, the sergeant's rumpled, their legs tucked into leather boots. The lieutenant holds a semi-automatic pistol in his right hand. The sergeant has an automatic rifle slung across his back. A small radio swings from his belt. Their uniforms make it hard to guess their ages, maybe twenty-three, maybe thirty-two.

The prisoner's face is bruised and bloody, his nose askew and discolored, his shirt torn and splotched with blood, his hair a matted tangle. He is perhaps twenty-five though that, too, is hard to tell. As he limps, a knee black with dried blood winks through a rip in his trousers.

The faces of my friends freeze as though a volcano has instantly encrusted them with lava. Only Ana's eyes betray fear before they, too, congeal. Thus for centuries my people have faced invaders behind Mayan masks of stone.

"*Buenos dias*, my friends," the lieutenant says through a tight smile.

"Welcome to our village, sir," Old Pablo says, also in Spanish.

The natty little man hooks his free thumb into his belt and slowly inspects the scene, the pleasure of control evident in his smile as he forces everyone to wait. Old Pablo glances at the plastic flag lying on the grass, but the officer does not seem to notice it. At last his gaze returns to Old Pablo. "We come upon a happy scene."

"A wedding fiesta tonight." Old Pablo's voice is also tight.

"Really?" The lieutenant turns. "Bring forward the prisoner."

The sergeant jerks the man, who has been standing with head bowed perhaps three meters behind him.

"Germán!" Ana gasps.

"You know this man?" the lieutenant snaps. Ana stares in terror at these words she cannot comprehend. The lieutenant turns to Old Pablo. "Translate!"

When he does, Ana answers, "He...He looks like someone I know." Old Pablo translates again.

The lieutenant does not seem to hear. "On your knees!" he orders, pointing grandly downwards. Germán complies, favoring the bloody knee. The sergeant slaps his head. "That's right! Head down! Sergeant, cover the prisoner."

The big man drops the rope, unslings his weapon, and levels it with his finger at the trigger. The muzzle wavers a few centimeters from Germán's matted hair. The lieutenant holsters his pistol. "He claims to come from here."

"We persuaded him to tell some truth." The sergeant sounds pleased.

"You may know him," the lieutenant says.

"His name is Germán Culán," Old Pablo says. "He lives here with his wife and two children. He went to Quetzaltenango to care for his mother, who is sick."

The soldiers exchange glances. "If you know him, you will know how to deal with him," the lieutenant says.

"What do you mean?" Old Pablo asks.

"Do any of you belong to the civil patrol?"

Old Pablo, blushing perhaps because the lieutenant has ignored his question, gestures to Ernesto. "Him and me."

"I thought so, or I could not understand the rifle." His arm stiffens towards it. "I need not speak of your duty to deal with Communists if they hide among you, even if they live among you...I see that your flag of Guatemala is on the ground," he adds without looking towards it.

"It's windy up here on the hillside." Old Pablo props the flag against the hut.

"I don't feel any wind," the lieutenant says.

From my perch I see the leaves fluttering gently around. Yet I notice something different. The birds and animals talk as before, but they continue alone. The shouts and laughter of the children are gone. Between the thatched roofs I see women shooing a few little figures into huts.

"By the way," the lieutenant asks Old Pablo casually, "how many bullets do you have?"

"Four," Ernesto says.

The lieutenant turns quickly, surprised perhaps at Ernesto's Spanish. "Show me."

Ernesto pulls the cartridges from his pocket and holds them up as he did for Ana.

"I have ten bullets in my hut," Old Pablo adds.

"And there's one in the rifle," the lieutenant says impatiently.

"It's not loaded," Ernesto says.

The lieutenant seizes it up, slams open the bolt, peers into the breach, and thrusts the rifle to the sergeant, who props it roughly against the wall. "You Indians amaze me. What good is an empty rifle?"

"We do not have your excellent training," Ernesto says, glancing at the muzzle poised at Germán's head like a fer-de-lance about to strike. "We are afraid of accidents."

"Is there a problem about Germán?" Old Pablo asks. The sergeant laughs.

"My men captured him twenty kilometers from here and interrogated him. He did not belong there. This morning we received new proof which we cannot tell you about. He is a Communist, a member of the guerrilla army."

"Why do you tell us this?"

"In the old days it was simple. We would have shot him. But democracy is arriving in Guatemala. You, the people, have elected a civilian President." The lieutenant sounds like a teacher to a circle of children. "It's not easy to have democracy after more than three decades of army rule. We are learning to exercise patience even though it costs us efficiency."

"Do you expect these Indians to understand this?" says the sergeant, who has stepped back and is sweeping his machine gun slowly back and forth across the villagers. The lieutenant frowns at him.

"Are you turning him over to us?" Old Pablo asks.

"In a democracy, the people decide." The lieutenant points to the rifle. "You can shoot him, or you can free him. It's up to you."

"It's up to us whether to let him go home to his wife and children or else kill him?" Old Pablo sounds unbelieving.

"Democracy gives responsibility to the people. It's what people like you say you want and the guerrillas say they are fighting for. Perhaps today you will feel the burden of responsibility that the army has borne so long."

"What's he done?" Ernesto asks.

"I just told you—he's a Communist," the lieutenant snaps. "I've told you all I can," he continues calmly. "We shall withdraw so no one will say we influenced your decision. We'll return when we hear a shot. If you send him home, shoot in the air."

The lieutenant wheels to go. The sergeant swings his weapon away from them to follow his *jefe*. The lieutenant turns back and says darkly, "Do not take too long. The army has other things to do."

"Hold still," Old Pablo says to Germán, once the soldiers are out of sight. He steadies him under an arm and cuts the ropes around his wrists and waist with the machete. Germán lurches free and stumbles into Ernesto's arms.

"It's so good to be back." Germán smiles as tears cross the dried blood on his cheeks and vanish into his mustache. María takes him from Ernesto and hugs him.

"I'll bring water," she says and disappears into the village as Ana, Sara, and Old Pablo embrace him in turn.

"Here, sit down," Ernesto says. Germán puts a hand on the rock, starts to sit, winces, and tries again. He settles with his arms resting stiff against his knees and looks up at them like a puzzled child.

"I can't believe I'm here." He laughs. "It's wonderful!" He sobs. "When I could not move or bear the pain, I didn't think I would see any of you again."

"How awful!" Ana looks as horrified as she sounds.

María returns with an earthen bowl. Germán drinks in loud gulps, the water spilling from his mouth into dark ovals down his shirt. At last he hands it back. María wets a cloth that was lying beside a ka and tenderly washes the blood and grime from his face. Ana watches for a moment, then joins in with another cloth. Old Pablo repeats in Mam the fatal choice that the lieutenant has left them. Germán looks aghast. The others mutter softly, something like "My God!"

"I'll get Lourdes," Ana says as Old Pablo finishes.

"No," María says.

"Why not?"

"What we have to discuss cannot wait," Old Pablo says.

"It's best if she doesn't have to hear it," Germán says to the grass between his feet. They watch him as he turns from one to another of them.

"When you're ready," Old Pablo says, "tell us what happened."

"I was going to my mother." Germán is suddenly anxious. "Has anyone heard how she is?"

"Mateo Mendez saw her," Old Pablo says. "She's not well, but he thinks it's not serious."

"I'll go to her as soon as I can."

"Of course," Old Pablo says.

Ernesto shakes his head. "It will be dangerous for all of us, Germán, if you leave before the soldiers are satisfied."

Germán throws up his hands and smiles. "Whatever you say. It's so good to be free!"

"The lieutenant said to hurry," says María.

"It's crazy." Germán laughs. "The more I told them I know nothing, the more they hurt me."

"Why don't you start from where the soldiers captured you?" Ernesto says. He sits on the ground before their shattered friend, as do the women. Old Pablo keeps standing, glancing from time to time down the trail. Germán slides awkwardly off the rock and sits on the grass with his back against it. As he speaks, his battered face keeps grimacing.

"I was walking on the road to Quetzaltenango two days ago. A truck stopped in front of me, another one behind me. The road filled with soldiers. They beat me. When I told them I come from here, they said, 'You're lucky. We're going there soon. Maybe we'll drive you.'"

"How friendly," Sara mutters.

"They beat me some more and locked me in a room. Yesterday they put electricity on me, my most sensitive parts. I…" For a moment the memory freezes his face. "I cannot describe…" He wags his head like a dog shaking off water. "This morning they tied me like a goat and threw me at their feet in the back of a truck." He jerks his thumb over his shoulder. "Down there, they beat me again because it's my fault this hill is so steep."

María, "We heard you scream."

Sara, "We saw the trucks."

Ernesto, "Did you tell the soldiers why you were going to Quetzaltenango?"

"Before they even beat me. They said no one from this village can have a mother in a city."

"Stupid *ladinos*!" Old Pablo shakes his fist at the trail.

"They think we're as simple as our huts." Sara turns aside and spits.

"I said, 'Take me to my mother, I will show you.' They said, 'A guerrilla will have a woman waiting who is sick or pretending to be.'"

"They probably had tricks played on them before," Ana says. Sara and María turn on her as fast as owls.

"I said, 'Ask me questions that only a mother and son will know. Then ask the woman. She will give you the same answers.'"

"Fast thinking." Old Pablo nods his approval.

"I was very frightened."

"Why didn't they do it?" Ana asks.

"The sergeant said, 'What if she is your mother? That doesn't prove you're not a guerrilla.'"

"The pig!" Sara turns as if to spit, but doesn't.

"The lieutenant said, 'Work on him. See if he changes his story.' But it's the only story I know."

"That's how it was when they tortured me," Old Pablo says. "The less you know, the more they think you're hiding. You stop feeling like a person."

Germán nods. "I always said I'm not a guerrilla. So the sergeant said, 'You're a tough guerrilla.' He put more electricity on me until I prayed he would make a mistake and kill me." He shudders. "The lieutenant came in and said, 'We can't waste time chasing your story to Quetzaltenango. Your village knows more about you than our torture can make you tell us. They will decide what to do.'"

"He mentioned new proof, Germán," Ernesto says. "What did he mean?"

"I don't know."

"See how the soldiers demand we trust them." María's eyes flash. "They make us decide whether to take his life on their word which is not truthful."

"The army has given choices like this to other villages," Old Pablo says. "I used to reflect on how we'd face it if they ever gave it to us."

"And?" Sara asks. Everyone looks at him expectantly.

"I decided we probably wouldn't have to face it." He shrugs. Their faces fall.

"This morning the lieutenant told me a North American newspaper reporter is nearby and maybe I will be his story. But what can a *gringo* write about me?"

"'An innocent *campesino* is tortured,'" Old Pablo says, more wisely than he knows. "That will not be news in North America."

"Maybe the reporter will tell the North Americans how the army uses their guns, their training, their electric toys," Sara says.

"The sergeant said, 'We defend the United States from International Communism. Finally they notice us.'"

"He carries a machine gun from there," Old Pablo says, "Their famous M-16."

Ernesto smiles. "Maybe I should have gone to El Norte and shot their President after all."

"You? The peacemaker?" Again Old Pablo sounds unbelieving.

"Peace can come if they stop sending weapons," Ernesto says.

"Weapons are their god," Sara says. Ernesto, María, and Old Pablo nod.

"I'm sorry," Ana says crossly. "We can't go off on politics."

"Right," María says. "Who knows how soon they'll be back?"

"We are in a terrible position," Ana continues.

"Where politics put us," Sara mutters.

"I never suspected that Germán may be a guerrilla," Ana says. "But the army wouldn't say it if they don't believe it."

"Do you believe a stranger in a green monkey suit before you believe what you know?" Sara demands.

"They left it up to us," Ernesto reminds Ana gently.

"A blessing of our democracy," Sara says.

"They cannot want us to kill an innocent man," Ana says.

"Ha!" Old Pablo's eyes dance. "That never stops them!"

"They told us he's guilty," María says.

"Maybe he's done bad things we don't know about," Ana says.

"Ana!" Sara's tone is so corrosive that the men look at Ana with pity.

"You trust them as if we had never talked just now," María says bitterly.

"No!" Ana shrinks as though she will disappear into the ground.

"Look," Old Pablo says briskly. "We must make the decision, or it will go hard with us and maybe with the village."

"We must not try their patience," Germán concurs.

"Agreed," Ernesto says. The women nod.

"We must analyze carefully," Old Pablo says, "as if Germán were a stranger."

"I cannot do that," Ana moans.

"Do your best," Old Pablo says pleasantly. "First we must decide who will make the decision, us or the village."

"You're the Elected Representative, Pablo," Ernesto says. "We all know Germán. Why not us?"

"Perhaps we can." Old Pablo sounds almost convinced.

"But if the decision will make the army angry with the village," Ernesto continues, "the village should decide."

"A good point. As the Elected Representative, I may have to call everybody together."

"Does anyone think the army will be angry if we shoot him?" Sara says.

"Sara!" Ana looks shocked.

"My little joke," Sara says.

"I cannot laugh," Germán says.

"I'm sorry."

"No. I agree," Germán says. "I know what they are."

Ana has begun to pace, working her hands together. "Pray God that this will not be the decision. If it is, I will feel better if the whole village makes it."

María, "It takes a long time to bring sixty men and boys in from the fields."

Old Pablo, "Also a good point."

"That *ladino* lieutenant talks to *us* about democracy! Democracy is a tradition of the Maya." Sara spits again. "Their *ladino* President is a marionette. The army pulls his strings and he dances across the mouth of hell, so the stupid gringos from *el Norte* won't see the fires inside."

"What do you mean?" Old Pablo says with mock seriousness. "*El Presidente* is like us, free to do anything the army lets him."

"They hold the power of life and death," Sara says. "They decided to pull a blanket of democracy over the Terror to hide it, so now they play at sharing the blanket with us."

Ernesto, "They use democracy as a new way to torture us."

Ana looks around in frustration. "You're going off on politics again."

Old Pablo shrugs in agreement. "It hurts less when we are angry at familiar things."

"You're *all* right," María says. "Now let's get going."

Ernesto, "We all believe he's innocent. If the village assembles, someone may denounce him to settle a grudge."

Old Pablo, "No one in *this* village has ever denounced anyone."

Sara, "But they've never faced a choice like this."

"Why don't *we* make the decision," María says. "If Germán agrees with us, that will be that. If he doesn't, Old Pablo will assemble the village."

"A good solution," Old Pablo says. Sara and Ernesto nod yes.

"Well…" Ana hesitates. "All right."

"What do you think?" María asks Germán.

He begins to tremble. "If you decide to shoot me, I can ask the village to let me live?"

"That's it," Old Pablo says.

"It sounds all right," Germán stutters. "But you know I am innocent! You should not want to kill me!"

María throws up her hands. "Mother of God, Germán! We don't!"

"But we must also think of the village," Old Pablo says.

"I know that."

"I wouldn't shoot you if you *were* a guerrilla." María puts an arm around his shoulders. Ernesto regards them.

"None of us would," Sara says, glancing sharply at Ana.

"I feel better." Germán's shoulders relax, and María removes her arm.

"One more thing," Ana says, surprising the others. "We five must all agree."

"What?" Old Pablo sounds puzzled.

"If we don't all agree, then *any* of us should be able to assemble the village."

María stands before her. "Ana, you're the only one who doesn't believe the army is evil. Your decision may be different from ours."

"I know."

"Right," Old Pablo says. "Ana has a good point. If we all agree about Germán, our answer is probably what the village would say. If we disagree, most of the village may not agree with most of us. So then it's best if we ask them. All right?"

The others nod yes, though María's mouth is set.

"At least we agree on that," Sara says.

"We'll probably agree about Germán, too." Ana sounds sure.

"Not if we don't get going," María fumes.

Ernesto looks at each of them. "Now, how do we decide?"

"Probably we must have a trial," Old Pablo says.

"What do you know about trials?" Sara demands. "Will you be the judge or the lawyer?"

"We will question Germán," Old Pablo replies, his dignity bruised. "We'll decide from his answers and our other information whether he's innocent. Forgive me, Germán, but you see how serious this is."

Germán nods. Sara says, "You surprise me, Old Pablo. You be the judge."

Old Pablo reflects. "Since we are all ignorant, we will all be judges." They look at each other. "Who will start?"

After a moment Ana draws up her chest and plants her feet before Germán. "Are you a guerrilla?"

"No."

"Were you ever a guerrilla?"

"No."

"Have you ever given food or encouragement to the guerrillas?" Ernesto asks.

"Only in my prayers."

"Then you are sympathetic to the guerrillas?" Ana asks.

"I am sympathetic with ending the way *ladinos* treat us. Aren't you?"

"Of course," Sara says.

"This is, ah, not useful. It's not what he prays for but what he's done." Old Pablo nods for Ana to continue.

"Are you a Communist?"

"I live in a community. Is it that?"

"We talked a little about Communism in our Christian base community," Ernesto says.

"It's dangerous to talk about it," Ana says, "unless you also denounce it."

"It's about who owns businesses, not about life in our village," María says impatiently. She walks over and looks into the valley.

"Communism is simple," Sara says. "It's whatever the army doesn't like."

Old Pablo nods his agreement. "If Germán doesn't know what it is, that's all we need to know."

"Do you know how to shoot a gun?" Ana points to it.

"You probably put in a bullet and push the trigger."

"Have you ever fired a gun?" Ernesto asks.

"No."

"It's easy," María says, suddenly girlish. "Ernesto showed me how." She continues to stare at the gun.

"Why are you not a member of the civil patrol?" Ana asks.

"I wasn't asked."

"Lucky you," says Ernesto.

"Only half the men in the village waste their time in the patrol," Old Pablo says. "It means nothing that he doesn't."

"If he were a guerrilla, he might have joined to avoid suspicion," Ernesto says.

Germán raises his hand to draw their attention. "I will tell you, I once thought about joining the guerrillas. My brother took part in a labor strike. He was not a leader, but a man pointed a camera at him while he was standing near the leaders. They didn't even get the higher pay they struck for, but the leaders and my brother were disappeared and later found with marks of torture. I was angry, but our mother said, 'I have lost one son for nothing. Don't do it.' I also asked myself, What do I know about fighting? I'm too clumsy. My duty is to my family." He sweeps them with his gaze. "Perhaps some of you have thought like this?"

Ernesto and Old Pablo nod yes. Ernesto says with certainty, "Our duty is to the living."

"So is the guerrillas' duty," María snaps. "I wish I could send for some to shoot these soldiers."

She starts to pace back and forth, working her hands together before her throat, her black brow notched in thought. She is near the trailhead, and though her feet swish the grass, the others do not notice that she has left them.

"Is it true," Ana continues, "what you told people about going to care for your mother?"

"Of course. I wish I were there right now."

"I know his mother has not been well," Old Pablo says.

"And Mateo Mendez told you she was asking for him," Sara reminds them.

"Who told you she's sick?" Ana says.

"Mario Tzul, when he came back from selling a load of weavings."

"I've heard enough," Old Pablo says. "He's innocent. No question about it."

María, still unnoticed, scuffs the grass savagely with the ball of her foot. Thunderclouds have gathered on her brow.

"I agree," Ana says, sounding happy to exchange the inquisitor's burden for the decision she sought. "The soldiers must be mistaken. I'm sure they'd be angry if we took the life of an innocent man."

"I…" Sara hesitates. Old Pablo and Ana turn to at her. "I will not say he is guilty."

"He *is* innocent," Ernesto says, "but what will happen worries me."

"Then we agree?" Old Pablo asks, but does not pause for anyone to answer. "I'll fire the shot in the air."

He stoops for the rifle, but stands up without it when Sara says, "We haven't heard from María."

All turn to her. She faces them with her feet apart, fists quivering by her hips. Her voice is so fierce that the women and children in the nearby huts must hear her. A chill goes through me as she speaks.

"Germán is guilty! He must die!"

Chapter 12

Ana and Germán gasp. All of them gaze at María in uncomprehending horror. Birds go on talking through the forest.

She steps into the group. Tears glisten along her nose, and she sniffles. She is trembling but no longer shouting. "We are not facing reality. Germán is guilty because the army says so. He is not being judged. We are."

Ana's eyes are bulging. "What do you mean?"

"He's dead either way." María is almost calm as she packs flesh onto the bone of her fatal insight. "Do you think he can live after the army tells us Maya that he's a guerrilla? If we spare him, then we support the guerrillas."

"They do think like that," Sara muses.

"So it doesn't matter if the soldiers are wrong and don't have secret proof?" Ernesto speaks slowly, as if María's words are so terrible yet plausible that he must make extra certain that he understands them.

"What are you, María?" Ana's eyes remain wide. "Who is inside my friend?"

"What of my family?" Germán sounds miserable.

"Truth is what the army says it is!" María, not diverted, tells Ana.

"This is a terrible truth," Sara says.

"So truth comes from the barrels of their guns," Ernesto says. "Padre López said that once."

Old Pablo pinches his chin between his thumb and the crook of his forefinger. "The army has wiped out many villages for less reason."

"If it has to be the village or me..." The turmoil within Germán clutches like the claws of a hawk inside his face. "I want to live!"

"We cannot shoot you if our own risk is small," Ernesto assures him.

"I know you're not a guerrilla—" María's first soft words since she stunned them.

"I... I believe you."

"I wouldn't blame you if you were."

"María!"

Her eyes flash at her beloved. "There is a time to stop turning the other cheek!"

"I hope you will reflect on that." Anger seeps out around Ernesto's words.

"I'm sorry." María puts her hand on his chest. "You're the last person I want to quarrel with."

Ernesto remains agitated, though no longer with her. "We are arguing whether to kill a friend!"

"We are analyzing whether the army will wipe out the village," Old Pablo says.

"You are my beloved." María looks into Ernesto's eyes, as heedless of the people around them as she was on that other sunny afternoon when they discovered each other. "But I cannot say that the risk to the village is small."

"I love you no less, and I respect you the more for what you are trying to do."

"But you don't agree."

"I don't know."

"I can't stand this!" Ana shrieks, her fists pressing her cheeks. "This must be horrible for Germán."

"A good point." Old Pablo turns to Germán. "Would you wait over there?" He gestures to the hut by the trail. "There is much force to what María says."

"You too?" Germán sounds betrayed.

"We didn't rush to say you're innocent," Old Pablo says. "We won't rush to say you're not."

"My brain is at war with my heart," María tells Germán.

"God gave us brains for times like this," Sara says.

"We'll talk with you again before we reach a decision," Old Pablo says.

Germán struggles to sound calm, but fails. "I can't believe this is happening. Aye! My village! My home!"

"Dear Germán," María says. "What else can we do?"

"Nothing. This is more horrible than the electricity." Germán turns his back to the others, subsides gingerly to his knees by the hut as though to pray, and sits on his heels beside the rifle and the plastic flag, which has fallen again to the ground.

"The poor man," Ana says.

"Show me I'm wrong." María sounds distressed at her own strength.

"You're right, María," Ernesto says, "we must discuss these things."

"Wait! Maybe there's a third possibility," Old Pablo says hopefully.

"What is it?" Sara asks.

"I don't know."

"There is Germán. There is the rifle." María points, suddenly cheerful. "The bullets are not in it. Perhaps he will escape into the trees."

Old Pablo strokes his chin. "The soldiers have such contempt for us, they might believe it."

"It will be the same to them if we call him innocent or let him escape," Sara says. "And they'll be right."

"Perhaps the whole village may escape," Ana says excitedly, "into the forest and up the mountain where the soldiers do not like to climb. They'll grow tired of waiting for us and go away."

"Then they'd *know* we're guilty," Sara says.

"They'd send soldiers up in helicopters," Ernesto says.

"Or come back after we return," Old Pablo says.

"But today they'd destroy our homes," María says, "burn our fields, and kill our animals."

"A few may escape through the trees," Old Pablo says, "but most of us would die."

"If we shoot Germán…" Ernesto shakes his head. "Which of us would aim the gun and pull the trigger?"

"Um!" Old Pablo nods and shudders.

Sara turns to María. "You force us to face what we do not wish to face."

"First she did it to me." A smile of satisfaction crosses Ana's face. "Now she does it to everybody."

"Someone has to," María retorts.

"We should thank her," Ernesto says, "not blame her."

Sara adds her wisdom: "The one who brings bad news is seldom thanked."

"She makes us face evil, but evil is not always correct." That's Ana's wisdom.

"A good point," Old Pablo says again. "We must analyze carefully, with as much courage as María."

Ernesto: "Sometimes one must take a great risk or even die for what's right. We may sacrifice Germán as the Hebrews sacrificed a lamb on the altar of Yahweh…"

"As our ancestors would sacrifice a virgin." Sara's eyes pierce María, who sets her shoulders beneath her aunt's gaze and says nothing.

"But it's *wrong*," Ernesto replies, "to sacrifice a friend to the false god of the army."

Old Pablo interrupts, "The army looks stronger than God in Guatemala."

"Perhaps we must assemble the village," Ernesto finishes what he was saying. "If they agree, we'll tell the lieutenant, that from all that we know, we cannot say that Germán is a guerrilla. He is too simple to be a Communist. He's just a *campesino* trying to feed his family and serve God…"

"Like the rest of us," Ana interrupts.

"'So we could not shoot him. Then we will have done what is right, and the lieutenant will do what he will do." Ernesto searches their faces.

Old Pablo, agreeable as usual, speaks first. "The moral force of a whole community can be very strong. The lieutenant may realize that it's time to forget about us and go on with more important business."

"You'd be right if these soldiers were reasonable," María says.

"But they find Communism in normal things," Sara adds.

"Wait!" Ana's face is alight. "Germán said a reporter from North America is nearby. Would they dare to massacre the village when he'd report it to their friends in his country?"

"He'll soon be gone," Old Pablo says. "Then the army will do whatever it likes."

"As always," Sara says.

"No matter what you tell me"—Ana sounds serene—"I know in my heart that we cannot shoot him."

"Yes, Ana"—Ernesto sounds relieved—"I feel that, too."

Ana, suddenly close to tears, wrings her hands. "How can everyone agree what to do when we keep disagreeing like this?"

"We're not getting anywhere," María says. "I think we should pray. I fear the delay, but it may speed things up."

"Yes," Old Pablo nods. "It's easy to forget to pray."

"This morning in the forest," Ernesto says, "my head was full of the prayer that María and I will say tonight."

"I've memorized it, too."

"Of course," Sara murmurs, smiling at María. Ana smiles to herself.

"Perhaps it's a good way to start," Ernesto says.

"Go ahead," Old Pablo says. All, including Germán, bow their heads. As the voices of Ernesto and María entwine, Sara raises her tear-filed eyes and regards them.

"Father and Mother, one God, Heart of the Sky. May you give us light, may you give us heat, may you give us hope and punish our enemies—all those who wish to destroy our ancestors and ourselves. We, poor and humble as we are, will never abandon you."

"It's well you say that prayer now." Sara snuffles, though her face remains impassive. "I may not be your grandmother tonight."

"It doesn't seem likely." Ernesto looks at María and shakes his head.

"Nothing must interfere with our fiesta," María almost shouts, then shrugs her graceful shoulders and subsides. "But I guess it already has."

Ana, "Perhaps God will show us a way to save everybody."

Sara, "God lets us see things that we do not see alone."

Old Pablo, "And accept what we must."

María, "Please, God, let me be wrong. And don't let the army attack while we're praying to You."

They lower their bodies to their knees, many-colored skirts and drab trousers on the thick green grass.

"Let us open our hearts and minds to the Lord," Old Pablo says.

"A Lord who lets such wonders come to Guatemala," Sara says, "and the Terror."

Chapter 13

With their heads bowed they will not see me leave. It feels good to stretch my wings through the breeze after clutching that limb so long and attentively. The sounds of birds and the animals of the village follow me aloft.

Aye, María! There are the lieutenant and sergeant sitting behind a bush not thirty meters down the trail. Can they hear my friends? There is another soldier. And another. I wheel higher. Down the hill, up, and on the sides, soldiers rest with their guns behind bushes and trees. They encircle the village!

Among the huts all is unnaturally serene. A few women go about their carrying and weaving, but most people have disappeared, probably watching the children inside their huts. They are a patient people and must know that Old Pablo will tell them when it's safe to return to their lives—if they have lives to return to. Off in the fields, the men work among their corn and beans. Perhaps no one has told them what's happening.

I glide into the valley and skim the trees along the road. Grass grows in the middle. Holes from the rains pock the tracks, and now and then a rock rears from the earth like a fish that never swims. One track is wider than the other, worn by the feet of my people.

I see the two trucks parked in the middle of the road. On the hood of one, two soldiers are sitting and smoking cigarettes with their backs against the windshield. Their assault rifles lie within easy reach on the roof of the cab. I alight on a limb behind them. They talk quietly, laughing now and then, and do not look worried about guerrillas.

I return silently to my friends. They are still on their knees, heads still bowed. Such dangers surround them, but what can I do? Squawk? We quetzals do not do that. Fly at them or flap in their faces? What good could it do if I break the silence of my kind? I resolve to find a way to communicate with the people who can change things if they care to, that is, with you North Americans. Meanwhile I, too, pray to the Creator of us all.

Clouds cling about the peaks of the high mountains in the distance. Big white clouds move across the sky far beneath the high ones and sometimes cast a shadow over the village, fields, and valley. Since my friends are still at prayer, I glide into the bush uphill from the lieutenant and the sergeant.

I can see bits of their uniforms through the leaves, but they will not notice my bright scarlet breast unless they turn around.

"How much longer will you give them?" the sergeant asks.

"The reporter is spending the night at the post. So he can experience counterinsurgency in the field." The lieutenant's is the higher voice. "It doesn't matter if he comes out here today or tomorrow."

"But we must get the men back for supper." The sergeant sounds concerned. "*Our* supper."

"Of course." The lieutenant's tone betrays his boredom with his inferior. "The Indians have not assembled the villagers, probably because I told them to hurry."

"If it's only those few who make the wrong decision, that won't stop us from attacking the whole village, will it?"

"Oh, no. We can't force the correct choice on them, but the village will pay the price if they fail to make it."

"What do they need to talk about?" The sergeant stabs his thumb over his shoulder. "Either they shoot him or they're with him."

"There is such a thing as being too logical, my friend, especially with Indians."

"You told them all they need to know." The sergeant pleads like an adolescent working on his father. "If they take too long, they insult us."

"Maybe so," the lieutenant says, "but it's our duty to give them a chance. Like sometimes you don't send a death squad for someone until he ignores several warnings."

"It's our duty to suppress Communism." The sergeant is pumping himself up with righteousness. The lieutenant makes a shushing sound, and the sergeant lowers his voice. "If we make a mistake now and then, that's a sacrifice these Indians must accept. Like sometimes you ask the *gringos* to bomb a whole village when guerrillas hide in it. I will tell that to the reporter—with your permission of course."

"That, ah, might not look right in print," the lieutenant says. "The international press puts a bad slant on much of what we find necessary. Sometimes I think that press is in league with the Communists."

"I remember when the army took me. I was just a simple kid with no idea about Communism." The sergeant's tone shifts from nostalgic to proud. "The army made me what I am."

"So you were recruited in the usual way?"

"I was hitchhiking home from a movie with some friends one night. Headlights came up to us. A truck stopped. Suddenly we were looking into the muzzles of six Galils." He laughs. "We thought they'd stopped to take us home."

"In a sense, they did."

"I saw that later. At first I hated the army. They were very harsh, but it was for my own good."

"That's the idea. Destroy the boy. Show him he's an animal, to make him a man. I understand you do that very well, Sergeant."

"I do my best, Sir." Modesty and pride mingle in his voice.

"I understand," the lieutenant continues, "that you're especially good at urinating on their food and making them eat it."

"Ah, me," the big man says, "A dog has enough for every tree, but no matter how much water I drink beforehand, I never have enough for every man's dinner."

"No system is perfect," the lieutenant says. "You do turn out fine soldiers."

"Thank you, Sir. I will say, it was good to leave that training company and see action again." The gruff man's tone becomes personal, almost apologetic. "Maybe that's why I'm so eager to play with these Indians until they lose everything."

"How do you like your new weapon compared to the Galil?"

"They made a big fuss when they issued the new ones, but either one will kill an Indian."

"I hear the guerrillas prefer the AK-47 because it hits harder."

"Communists make the AK-47." The sergeant sounds oddly like Ana when she thinks someone is not being correct.

"But the AK-47 doesn't know that. It's nice of these Indians to give us this time to discuss our trade."

"I'll sneak up and see what they're doing." The sergeant starts to rise.

So do I. When he comes around the bush, my perch will be beside his chin. With my long plumes trailing, I must be well beyond his grasp or we quetzals will be one bird closer to extinction. As I circle upwards I see the lieutenant put a hand on the sergeant's shoulder and the large man subside like an obedient cur. Oh well, it's time to return to my friends. They kneel as before, silent and oblivious.

"We'd better finish," Old Pablo says, his white thatch still bowed.

María rises onto her toes, stretches her arms, and goes to gaze into the valley. Germán stretches and sits with his arms around his drawn-up knees. His back is still to the others. Ana scrambles from her knees and sits on her mat. Sara steps behind Old Pablo and massages his shoulders as he draws up his knees like Germán. Soon he stands and paces while she tidies up, laying the grinding materials, water bowl, and Germán's ropes near the rifle. She leans the flag against the hut again and wedges the tip of its stick into a crack in the wall so it won't blow over any more. Ernesto is the last to arise.

A woman named Emma who is about Sara's age walks forward from among the huts as if she has been waiting for them to finish praying. In one hand and across the other forearm, she holds a large plate covered with a blue and pink striped cloth, and in the other hand, a small plate covered with a green and red cloth. She gives the small plate to Germán. "Your Juanita made them for you."

He lifts the cloth off three steaming tortillas. His voice chokes and he is unable to thank her. He smiles up at her through his tears before he begins to devour this food that his daughter has beaten flat between her little hands and cooked for him.

Emma offers the large plate to Sara, who lifts the napkin from a steaming stack. They thank her and go at the tortillas. Old Pablo says he didn't know how hungry he was. María and Ana notice how ravenously Germán finishes his, and give him the rest of theirs. María returns to her vigil over the valley, little knowing that she is gazing past the heads to the lieutenant and sergeant as they sit hidden behind the bushes below her.

"Everyone is very worried since the soldiers came," Emma says, "but we thought it best not to disturb you."

"I'm sorry you must worry, but you were right to wait," Old Pablo assures her.

"I hope it's all right…" she begins anxiously.

"And, as you see, right to bring the tortillas."

Relieved, she asks him, "Is there anything we can do?"

"I don't think so." He looks to Sara and Ernesto, who shake their heads. "The situation is serious, but it's best to keep on as we are." He hesitates. "No one should act alarmed, but it may be necessary for everyone to run into the forest and up the mountain. If that happens, don't stay together. Scatter. Don't take any more than you can run with, the babies, a little food, a blanket."

Emma's face grows increasingly grave as he speaks.

"Someone must tell the men," he says, "but the first thing to tell them is, not to show alarm. They should come in from the fields casually, as if leaving work early for the fiesta, which I told the lieutenant about."

Emma repeats Old Pablo's points until he assures her she has them right. She disappears between the huts, napkins and empty plates in hand.

María pirouettes away from the edge and walks lightly back among them, a broad smile lighting her face. "The men will come in early. They'll come for our fiesta," she says, and reaches out to muss the front of Ernesto's shirt. The others look perplexed, even Germán, whose back is to María. Yet the others, too, seem oddly carefree, as if they have passed their burden to Emma to carry away on her empty plates, and they no longer feel its weight.

"Emma makes the best tortillas," Ana says.

Ernesto nods. "It must be hard for the others, wondering what's happening."

"It was so nice of her to bring them," Ana says.

"And so dear of Juanita," María says, nodding towards Germán.

"A tortilla is a tortilla," Sara says, "but these were very good."

"Why don't we invite the lieutenant and the sergeant to stay for our fiesta?" María says, almost child-like.

"We'll collect all the *guaro* in big jugs," Ana says, "and send it down to their men."

"Save some for me," Old Pablo laughs.

"We and the soldiers will eat and laugh and be friends together," María says.

"And turn water into wine." Even Sara sheds her gloom. "This is more Christian than I can believe."

"Good point," Old Pablo says. "It may be harder for them to kill us after we invite them to our fiesta."

"They'd think we're trifling with them." Ernesto's curt words dash icy water on their glow.

"Of course. I don't know what got into me just now." María presses her hands across her skirt. I guess she tried to escape the horror of their plight by fleeing into what North Americans call denial. Fortunately for everyone, she will soon return to reality.

Sara puts her arms around her and Ernesto. "My poor children!" As she looks up at María's face, I sense that she is also thinking of Paz, who was eight years old.

Now they are as before, tormenting their brains to decide what kind of fiestas awaits Germán, the village, and themselves. They look like a peaceful little group if one does not notice their faces, their stances, their voices. The gentle afternoon bears them like a canoe swiftly down a rocky river. They dig their paddles into the foam and drive towards the shore as the current sweeps them towards the falls. Its thunder whispers through the sunshine.

Chapter 14

María releases herself from Sara's hug. "How soon will the soldiers grow angry because they don't hear the shot?"

"Soon," Old Pablo says. "Very soon!"

Ana pouts like a child awakened from a pleasant dream. "They have tossed nine vipers in our laps!"

"They're probably enjoying a siesta or a cigarette while we struggle with their gift," says Sara.

"Then they'll yell at us for wasting their time," Old Pablo says.

"We must hurry." Sara shrugs. "But what we must decide is too important to hurry."

"The lieutenant may wave his pistol," Ernesto says, "but we'll tell him we almost have a decision. I think he'll wait an hour before he orders a massacre."

Old Pablo nods yes. "Unless he goes ahead with it."

Ana looks around wild-eyed, as though things unseen are pressing her in. "I don't want to be here!"

"You are very important," Old Pablo says.

"Even if I can't agree with you?" Ana covers her desperation with her winning smile.

"Especially if you can't," María assures her.

"Some thoughts came to me while we prayed," Old Pablo says. "Why don't we each speak in turn?" The others nod yes, even Germán whom they do not see. "Ana?"

She sweeps a little arc of green blades back and forth with her foot, watching the foot and not the others as she speaks. "I have known Germán since I was a little girl and he was a big boy. Lourdes and I have always been close. Their children play with my Gloria. When the small man said Germán is a guerrilla, my first idea was, he never had time for that. Just now I asked him the most questions…"

"You questioned him very well," Old Pablo interrupts.

"I surprised myself. I think the army has made a terrible mistake. They didn't mean to. I thanked God just now for what you said, Ernesto. They will have to believe he's innocent after we tell them what we know about him and they see how honest we are. Everyone may live."

"Oh, child," Sara says like a mother in pain. Red covers Ana's face, but her mouth hardens.

"You know that the army has destroyed other villages," María says.

"Ones that helped the guerrillas." Ana says.

"They say Germán is a guerrilla. If we help him…" María's pause is pregnant.

"You're so clever," Ana spits out, "but that's not what I think."

"You'd rather not think at all!"

Ana's hands are on her hips, her face thrust towards María. "Better that than think subversive!"

"If we argue, everyone will lose," Ernesto says calmly.

"We must walk together, not push each other apart," Old Pablo says.

"You're right." María sounds contrite. "Ana's not the enemy."

Ana relaxes and nods yes.

Sara sighs. "They divide us against ourselves."

"I must tell you, Ana, I'm not sure of what I said before," Ernesto says. Ana's face falls. "Sometimes I feel as if I am standing on firm ground and don't realize that I may fall out of a dream onto sharp rocks."

"Most people live like that," Old Pablo says.

"María says I do," Ana blurts.

"Your dreams are for tomorrow," Sara tells Ernesto.

"Long ago, nations were like infants, too clumsy to destroy each other even when they wanted to," Ernesto says. María turns on him as if to say, What now? "The Maya were like that. But today every soldier carries a machine gun. A bomb can land on any hut. Everyone must denounce violence or everyone will die."

"You're like our ancestors," Sara tells him. "They knew much about the stars and much less about war. So barbarians came from Europe with greed and guns and Christianity and made them slaves. Which we still are."

"One must sometimes do a wrong to prevent a greater wrong." Ernesto gestures to Germán. "Must we send in a bullet that makes his life depart? Turn the miracle of this man into a sack of meat that will soon go bad?" He looks at the others, who look back expectantly. "I have one last idea."

"May our prayers not blind us," Sara says.

"Suppose we tell the lieutenant, 'From all that we can discover, Germán looks innocent, but you are a just man and you alone know if your secret proof is strong enough so that he must die. We will shoot him if you tell us to—which shows our obedience and probably wouldn't matter to Germán…"

"It would matter a lot." Germán's voice startles them. They turn to him, but he is still facing away. "I would feel betrayed if I were not hearing how hard you struggle."

"He's right beside us," Sara says. "Of course he hears us."

"I am thinking that I must die after all." Still he does not turn.

María kneels behind him, grips his shoulders. "God help us all, Germán!"

"God may save us by showing us how to save ourselves," Old Pablo says.

"Don't count on it," Sara says.

"This grows harder," Ana says haltingly.

"I will try not to speak." Germán says. Almost without moving, he slumps. "This is so hard to believe."

Ernesto sounds confident as he concludes his plan. "If we show the army how ready we are to obey them and to kill their guerrilla if they tell us to, we may pass their test and even Germán may live."

"The lieutenant is evil, but he seems intelligent," Old Pablo says.

"Except for thinking we're stupid," Sara says. "The racist pig!"

Ana looks at Ernesto as she has often looked at María today, as if his words are unspeakably cold. "If we spare Germán, God will spare us."

"We know of many villages that God did not spare," Sara says.

"But not which ones He did," she retorts. "They just live on like ours."

Again María confronts them, her voice strong. "Do you think the lieutenant will tell his colonel, 'The Indians convinced me that their comrade is innocent?'"

"Would the colonel accept it if he did?" Old Pablo asks. Ana is regarding María intently again.

"Unless those officers say, 'You stupid Indians are right and all of us superior soldiers are wrong,'" María continues, "then Germán is dead."

"This means he is dead," says Sara.

"Certainly." Old Pablo is so agreeable that I wonder if he grasps their peril. His next words show everyone including me how seriously he takes it.

"There is something I should tell you about colonel who commands this lieutenant," he continues. "Shortly after I became the Elected Representative, he called all the Elected Representatives in the district into his office. Some of us had to walk days to get there even though he could have sent his soldiers to bring us in their jeeps. When we were all sitting in a room at the army base, he walked in and said in Spanish, "I have the power of life and death in this district. You will return to your villages and conduct yourselves accordingly." A soldier who was a Maya translated. The colonel left the room and left us to walk back to our villages. All that way to hear only those words! But the fear they struck in me fixed them in my mind. Shortly after this, his soldiers killed Luis. Since then, they have wiped out at least eleven villages in this district."

Again, Ana looks shocked. Ernesto puts an arm around her shoulders and gives her a little hug. I am surprised that Old Pablo does not know that soldiers under the colonel's command have wiped out at least fifteen villages, sixteen counting the village this morning.

"That's just what the colonel told Padre López and the other priests," Sara says.

"So there's nothing to gain—not Germán's life—by risking the village at all." María lets out a breath and relaxes a bit.

"María!" Anguish twists Ana's face and drives her words. "Those tortillas that Juanita sent to her Papa! How can we take him from her?"

"Isn't it better for her tears to moisten the corn she grinds tomorrow than for her body to rot beside his?"

Ana, too horrified by María's words to hear her pain, confronts her, eyes flashing, much as María just stood. "Only a monster talks like that!"

"Is this easy for me, Ana! Am I not torn?" María is as fierce yet vulnerable as a feral cat. Tears flow from her eyes. "Would I say all this if I did not fear for Ernesto—for Mama and Papa, for your Byron, Gloria, and Miguelito, for everybody!"

"Forgive me!" Ana embraces her. María puts her arms around her and strokes her hair.

They separate as Sara begins to speak, also looking at the ground. "Only yesterday I watch Germán and Ernesto at play. Only last night Lourdes squats above the birthing mat pushing and moaning as I pull out her children and Germán's by their heads. He kneels with a candle, worry on his brow." She raises her eyes. "Theirs all came at night. Now shall I..." Her voice trails off for a moment. "I have birthed the babies of many families and I love them all. I cannot hold a basket in each hand to weigh the lives of people I love."

Old Pablo puts an arm around her shoulders, squeezing her until one of her feet leaves the ground. "You have lived nearly as long as I...."

"Only because you're younger than you look."

He releases her, but I see that she is touched.

"What is your wisdom?" he asks her.

"What I feel is not enough?"

"We need your wisdom."

She collects herself. Acid fills her voice. "I have seen the army kill and kill, bodies by the roadside, some with stuff running from their necks, severed heads they kicked into the weeds like soccer balls, and I try not to breathe. Vultures root and rip, flesh in their beaks, slime on their claws. The army doesn't make war on a few guerrillas. It makes war on *us*, their own people. What will it matter if we save the village today? They may destroy it next month… a year from now… when someone cares enough to climb the hill and steal our fields that are not level. The soldiers root in evil, flesh in their beaks, slime on their claws. They do not think like children of God. They kill for reasons that we common folk would laugh at if our hearts were not strewn in pieces across these blood-soaked hills."

"Their thoughts slither like snakes." Old Pablo picks up on Sara's vision of their plight. "Not long ago a company of soldiers made camp in guerrilla country. Other soldiers came and found that they had not posted guards. 'Why not?' those soldiers asked themselves. 'It must be that they don't fear the guerrillas. Why not? It must be that they are with them.' So the other soldiers shot them all and stacked their bodies like firewood in the forest."

"Their sick minds are what killed Luis," María says. "They think that any *campesino* who carries that many tamales must be feeding the guerrillas."

"I can't believe that!" At the shock in Ana's voice, Sara and María exchange anxious glances. Ana continues, brightening as she goes on. "He must have told them that the family of the groom brings the tamales to the fiesta. When he said that, they would have let him go. So maybe it wasn't the army after all!"

"They pay no attention to our traditions. Even though many of them are Mayas too." Sara turns and hawks. Her spittle hangs from a blade of grass.

"You don't believe they tortured Germán"—María is suddenly angry—"or gave us nine vipers?"

"I don't say you don't love Ernesto"—Ana matches her anger as though they had never reconciled—"but I want to tell you something. You carry a big hatred from what you think the army did to Luis. It's like a big jug of water on your head for five years. Tell me, María. Tell everyone. Is it your hatred for the army that drives you towards killing Germán?"

The others, except Ernesto, look to María. She stares across the valley, the light gone from her eyes once again. "You know me so well, Ana, in spite of the wall between us. Hatred is a burden I've often tried to shed. Sometimes I feel free like Ernesto, but then I wake up in the dark and find it, as you say, heavy on my head. I hear Mama and Papa sleeping, and I envy their peace.

Soon, I pray, I'll awake beside Ernesto and feel the hatred gone for good."

The light rekindles in María's eyes, and Ana shrinks before its fire. "Yet sometimes my fury is not a burden but a joy. I'm part of an avenging flame that will purge the highlands of these evil men and cleanse our mountain air!" She returns to the moment. "My burden never leaves for long. It comes back like a cat that you take off in the forest to lose. But I do not think it has bent my analysis of our reality." She turns to the others. "If you think I'm wrong, say so."

The others meet her challenge with silence. She and Ernesto look into each other. He smiles. She relaxes and smiles.

"Ana, the soldiers saw that Luis had more food than one family can eat." Ernesto's voice is kind. "They have killed many people for that. We learned after he died that they do that."

"For example, if you carry a hundred aspirins in a bottle," Old Pablo says, "they think all that medicine must be for guerrillas, so they have killed people for that, too."

"But a big bottle *has* a hundred aspirin," Ana says. "Friends pool their money, and one walks to a store and buys it."

"You'd think the army would know that, wouldn't you," Old Pablo declares.

"The way they think," Sara says, "every bird that shits on them must be a Communist."

What a good idea, Sara! Speechless I may be, but soon my message will reach the sergeant's ear and put it into his head that even a bird can be a Communist.

Chapter 15

Below me in the soothing sun of late afternoon, three women and two men who have done nothing wrong discuss the nine vipers that slither through the grass around them while Germán gazes away but cannot miss a word. I look into the foliage down the trail and do not see the soldiers. Are they the same ones that ravaged the other village this morning where each body on the blackened earth was as beloved as Germán, or as Sara would say, some more, some less? Do soldiers brag to each other about these victories over Communism?

Between the thatched roofs, I see Lourdes with her children by their hut, the only children in sight. She is kneeling with her arms about them like the wings of a hen with her chicks. They are looking this way, as though the huts do not block from their sight the hunched form of her *compañero*, their Papa. Lourdes hugs their little bodies tight against her.

I worry that Germán will run to them, a human thing to do that would cost even more time. Or that he will run the other way, into the forest and up the mountain, not knowing that soldiers are there to greet him, and maybe spark a massacre. But these possibilities do not seem to worry my friends, and they are right. Brave, responsible, miserable Germán awaits his fate.

I vow that I will report this fatal day to every North American who cares to heed it.

Chapter 16

"I can't believe these soldiers are as evil as all of you think they are," says Ana like a person who says she is sorry when she isn't. "But it's four to one against me. You can do what you want."

"You see so much, Ana," says Sara, "but you won't see this."

Ana recoils. María tells her gently, "Dear Ana, we need you to test us, especially me. I've borne such hatred on my back while you've been raising your children."

Ana starts to weep. "Time after time you beat me down. Just now…"

"We try to convince you in order to convince ourselves," Ernesto tells her.

Ana sniffs back her tears. "I know you want to do what's best."

María puts an arm around her. "We're all scared."

Old Pablo, "You see how I have wavered."

Ernesto, "None of us is as certain as we want to be."

Sara, "Responsibility is hard when you take it seriously."

Old Pablo, "But soldiers shoot children without a thought."

Sara turns to María. "You started this analysis. Are you still certain?"

María begins to pace back and forth, her lower lip quivering. "The army and police have murdered village after village and many thousands more in the cities. One hundred and forty thousand bodies found so far, very many with marks of torture. Can you imagine how many villages those dead people would fill? Or what agony each tortured person must have felt? Over forty thousand more people disappeared, so people like me can say, 'Maybe they're still alive,' and never give them the burial their tortured souls long for. Hundreds at least dropped from helicopters into the volcano Pacaya and over the ocean."

"That's not true." Ana's force matches María's. "You can't know these things! No one is so evil!"

"The Archbishop's office in Guatemala City records the numbers," Ernesto says. "Padre López showed them to some of us."

"The army admits it has destroyed four hundred and forty villages," María says.

Ana looks dazed. "I didn't know there were so many villages in Guatemala."

"Gentle Ana," María says. "These stupid numbers show what the army may do to us."

"Miguelito probably needs me," Ana blurts. She starts towards the silent mass of huts.

"No one blames you for wanting to go," Ernesto says, "but…"

"Your mother can care for his diarrhea," María says. "You must stay and decide about his life."

"Germán's."

"And Miguelito's."

Ana returns.

"It isn't you we're fighting," Sara tells her. "It's our own humanity."

"I'm your humanity?"

"Of course," Sara says. "This army that you trust puts us at war with our best part."

"I feel better." She looks relieved. "Really, I must check on Miguelito." She notices Old Pablo looking askance and adds brightly, "The minutes I'm gone will not be lost. You can decide how to fight me, your best part."

"Well…" Old Pablo hesitates. "You know how important it is to come right back."

Ana nods and hurries off between the huts. Germán is standing now. His eyes follow her into the village.

"It's lucky that María and I were working on her before you returned," Sara tells the men once Ana is out of earshot. "Otherwise you'd never move her in time."

"Do you think we'll do it?" Old Pablo asks.

María arches a rich black eyebrow. "Must the life of the village depend on it?"

"No," Old Pablo says slowly. "But we must represent the village. A lot of them think like her."

Sara nods. "Which is hard to believe when you think of all they know."

"I may be more of a problem than Ana," Ernesto says. They turn to him. "Perhaps it's better to risk dying as decent people than live as murderers."

María confronts him. "Is it decent to risk a hundred and sixty of our family and friends for your idea of decency?"

"Not without asking them," Ernesto says. "I *think* you're right. But it's hard to abandon what I believe about violence."

"I hope you'll…," María says harshly to her lover, but a shout from Germán cuts her off.

"Lourdes!"

The distraught woman rushes past them, her gaily-colored skirt tossing, her black hair streaming behind. His brown arms cross the back of her white blouse as they cling together. She searches his face for a long moment as his eyes caress her, then presses her cheek to his shoulder and softly strokes the back of his bruised head. The others regard them with pity and distress.

Ana runs up, her bright skirt brushing the grass. "It's all right." She pauses to pant. "I told her she can't stay."

"Forgive me," Lourdes says to her husband. She disengages herself and faces the others. "I had to see him. Everyone is frightened." She catches a sob and her eyes are big. "The woman who saw the soldiers drag him up here didn't even recognize him." She is weeping but continues. "The men are coming in from the fields, Old Pablo, as you told Emma."

"Good," Old Pablo says, adding in singsong, "The danger may not be great."

"Maybe greater than you know." Lourdes rubs her wrist across her nose. "Soldiers were seen moving through the bushes on the other side."

"They may be spying," Old Pablo says. "Possibly we're surrounded. All the more reason to keep calm."

"If we're free to decide," says Ana with a note of discovery, "why would soldiers spy on us?"

"Exactly," María snaps. "Why wouldn't they have left at once?"

Ana stands with her arms arched from her body like a bird that cannot fly. Old Pablo puts his hand gently on Lourdes's shoulder.

"Yes, I must go." But instead she clutches Germán. "What's happening? Why can't you come with me?"

"Because of the soldiers," he says softly, pressing her to him again. "It will be explained to you soon."

She draws back, still holding him. Horror twists her face. "Explained?" The horror deepens about her mouth and bloodshot eyes. "Who will explain it?"

He speaks without hope. "I don't know."

"Oh, God!" She releases him and screams at the others, "No!"

As they stand helpless, she doubles over, pounding her fists on her knees. "No! No! … *No! No! Nooooo!*"

Ernesto takes her arm as if to soothe her, but she jerks free and runs off sobbing pitiably. They look after her, then at each other. Germán sits with his back to them, his knees drawn up, his head buried in his arms, his shoulders quaking with his muffled sobs.

"I couldn't stop her," Ana says. Tears glisten on her cheeks. "Thank God she's seen him."

"It's not your fault," Old Pablo says. "She did well to wait as long as she did."

Ana kneels beside Germán, a hand on his shoulder, a palm on his back. She quakes as he quakes, her little cries bleating through the sunshine.

"It is so much harder now," Ernesto says vacantly, "to think of making her a widow."

"Or making her dead," says his bride.

Ernesto turns on her. "She tears at our hearts, María! Are you not moved?"

"As moved as you! But I remember our position." Then in desperation, "What do you want from me!"

Ernesto, downcast, turns away.

"Lourdes!" Germán lifts his head and cries out to the mountains. "Julio! Juanita!"

"Like the soldiers, they await the shot," Sara says with infinite sorrow. Suddenly she snarls, "I would shoot every goddamn soldier!"

"It was all I could do not to follow her," Germán says without turning. "But what she says doesn't change things." He suppresses a sob. "I pray it doesn't make me weaken."

María comes over and puts a hand on his shoulder. "What you do, you will do for her and your children." He rubs her hand.

"Dear Lourdes. Dear María." Tears flow down Ana's cheeks. Suddenly she turns on María. "You talk as if it's all decided."

"I don't mean to. I only..."

The roar of truck engines cranking in the valley cuts her off. They look at each other in terror. All except Ana and Germán go and peer down.

"What's happening?" Ana says.

"Come see," Sara says.

"I can't."

"The trucks are heading down the valley," Ernesto says. "Now they've stopped."

"Are the soldiers leaving?" Ana says. She turns to them and notices that Germán is watching them anxiously. She steps close behind him and returns her hands softly to his shoulders.

"There are no soldiers," Sara says.

"Maybe they're still resting in the trees," Ana says hopefully.

"They're telling us to hurry," María says.

"Right," Old Pablo says as they return to Ana. "A little message from the lieutenant. If we don't decide quickly, the blood of the village..."

"Only we won't know it," Sara says.

"Really, Sara," Ana says.

"Death is looking into your face, Ana." María's voice is as harsh as their plight. "Best you look back."

"Attacking her won't win her over," Ernesto says.

"It's all right." Ana's voice is calm and firm. "She's upset with me."

"I'm sorry," María says.

"Good," Ernesto says. "If we take the time to assemble the village, I'm afraid we're done for."

"We can change our rule that all must agree," Old Pablo says.

"Which will also take time," Sara says, "if we don't all agree to it."

"Aye, María!" María says in exasperation. "Let's get going!" She turns to Ana, as do the others.

Chapter 17

My friends know that at any moment their time, even their lives, may end, yet they argue on. I must find out when the moment will arrive. As they regard Ana and she regards them, I lift silently from my branch and glide down to the bush by the trail. The two men who hold so many lives in their hands still sit on the other side. I breathe easier though not for long.

"After all the weeks you and I have gone into the field, sometimes into danger," the lieutenant says, "we finally have time to learn a little about each other."

"I already knew you are a brave leader and a smart man." The sergeant snaps from fawning to anger. "We can't give them all day. If we don't attack soon, it'll be dark. Someone may escape."

"Since we've been talking about our personal lives," the lieutenant says soothingly, "I will tell you something that not many people know."

He hesitates, the sergeant looks expectant, and he continues. I sense that he is taking a personal risk so the sergeant will stop pushing him to attack.

"If I give them longer than some others would, it may be because I once had to make a choice like theirs. I know it can be hard to see what's obvious and do what's necessary."

"Oh?" The sergeant catches his breath as if a quarry were stepping into his sights.

"A man I grew up with became a labor leader," the lieutenant reminisces, oblivious of the sergeant's eagerness to hear what he may admit. "I was sad that he'd chosen the wrong side. I ran into him on the street one day in Guatemala City, and he asked me to his home for a beer. Perhaps I was foolish to go, but I feared I'd never see him again because he'd soon be dead. He had a nice little house with a pretty wife and three children who laughed and played with their papa's friend in the funny green uniform. I began to think maybe it was time I got married.

"Over our third beer he started saying things that I should have expected but couldn't believe—teachers need higher pay, Indians deserve human dignity, the rich exploit the poor—it was straight Communism. If my face fell, he didn't seem to notice. He said how angry he was not to win a teachers' strike that he'd just led. He even asked me to use my huge influence as a lieutenant to end the army's tactics that he called human rights violations. I left quickly and did not sleep a minute that night. Had he misspoken? Had I misheard? But he was clear, and so was my duty. We had once been like brothers, but to protect the nation from his Communism, I denounced him to the National Police the next morning. The next day they disappeared him."

"Did they torture him well?"

"I never saw the body. They knew where to reach me, but I never heard a word. My sister told me that neither did his family." The lieutenant muses. "It's interesting to see these things from the other side."

"Did the colonel give you today's assignment because you, ah, once had the same problem we've given these Indians?"

"I don't know if the colonel knows about it, unless the last colonel told him." A tremor passes through the lieutenant's voice, as if he has stepped into a trap and sees that his best course is to plunge forward. "Today's assignment has been given to others before me and will be given to others later. I don't think the incident with my former friend is why we got this job."

"Tell me, Sir." The sergeant speaks with a twist of contempt, as a subordinate no longer. "Suppose they do shoot the prisoner. Won't you order us to attack the village anyway?"

The question floats like a vulture on the wind. When the lieutenant answers, his tone is shrewdly man-to-man. "I think I read your mind, Sergeant. You have your eye on the little one with the big tits."

"Ha! She is a *cat*," the big man responds, happy at being flattered. He adds with a shrewdness of his own, "I think you want her, too. Of course, there's enough for both of us."

"If I take anyone," the lieutenant says, "it will be the tall one. She has less tits but more fire."

"Well?" the sergeant demands. "Are you going to do it?"

"Too much terror works against us," the lieutenant answers smoothly. "It sends more Indians into the mountains to fight us, and they fight more fiercely after we kill part of their family. It's what our advisors call a trade-off."

"Those *gringos* think they know everything," the sergeant says. He continues darkly, "What will the colonel say if you spare this village after they take so long to shoot the Communist? Which side will he say you're on?"

"A little terror can save many lives. The more these Indians realize we mean business, the better for everyone." The lieutenant is leading the sergeant now as a matador leads a bull.

"They're so thick! The ones we spare need many examples to see the point."

"So do sergeants who threaten their lieutenants," the lieutenant snaps like a pouncing jaguar.

The fury in his thrust takes the sergeant aback. "I… I agree, Sir. I was only trying to warn you how your wise decision can be misunderstood."

The lieutenant turns to the shaken man, smiling ironically, and goes on as if nothing has happened. "If they make the right choice, destroying them anyway would have to be on my own authority. I can't ask the colonel over the radio."

"Unless we report that they refused to shoot him." The sergeant sounds relieved to be talking business again. "If they're all dead, no one will be the wiser."

"A good point, Sergeant. I'll think it over." The lieutenant settles down against a rock by the bush and slides his beret over his eyes. Suddenly he digs his hand into his side. "If these bugs will let me."

"Excuse me, Sir. I must prepare for the attack." The sergeant ambles a few yards down the trail, lurches behind another bush, and unzips his pants. He may see me when he looks up, and I have heard enough. As his urine gushes into the bush, I return to my friends. Ana is still facing the others as if they have endless time.

After a jaguar pounces, he sometimes toys with his prey like a cat with a mouse. Now and then the mouse escapes, but usually not. Though the sergeant is big and cruel, he is the mouse and the lieutenant is the cat he was stupid enough to threaten. I do not envy his weeks ahead. And I fear the more for my friends today.

Chapter 18

Ana's face is calm as a statue. Her arms rest by her sides. "My mind tells me to agree with you…"

"But you don't," Old Pablo offers.

She nods and lowers her head. Her words jerk out in little freshets. "I am so torn. All my life I've looked up to those above me—my parents, you Old Pablo, the army. Where would our village be if people did not look up to those above them? Now I feel as if the lieutenant has ordered us to shoot Germán. I want to please him, but what he says is wrong. Shall we take away Germán's life to please this powerful man? Shall I listen to Lourdes weeping in the night and know that I am to blame? But everyone may die if the lieutenant is more evil than I can believe…" She shakes her head, more tears flowing from her eyes.

Ernesto puts a hand on her shoulder. "Whatever evil comes, you are not to blame."

"Ana," Sara says gently, "do you know why we call Pablo Old?"

"Because his hair is white."

"Why did his hair turn white so soon?"

"He was tortured. Everybody knows that."

"Do you know what they did to him?"

"Nobody knows, except probably his family."

Old Pablo murmurs, "I no longer have a family."

"She may understand," Sara says, "if you tell her."

Moments pass before he responds. "I felt the pain all over again when I told my wife about it. I have not talked about it since, though it often haunts my dreams and I wake up trembling and sweating."

"If you think it will help…" Ana sounds dubious.

"I wouldn't ask you to do it if our lives were not at stake," Sara says.

"Well…" Old Pablo seems embarrassed.

"It may help us all," Ernesto says. Sara gives him a piercing look, and he looks away.

Old Pablo clears his throat. "After they captured me, they did three things—after they beat me of course."

"What had you done?" Ana asks.

"The usual. Nothing. This was before I became the Elected Representative for the village and the colonel made me the head of the civil patrol." His face shows deepening pain, but he plugs on. "First they put my head in a plastic bag with powder in it that kills ants. I shut my eyes and mouth, but the powder got into my ears and nose. I gasped for air, which took it into my mouth which set it on fire…"

"Their famous *capucha*," Sara says. "They should take the bird of freedom off our nation's flag and put that bag on it instead."

"I nearly died, jerking and vomiting on the floor when they put me back in the cell. No toilet. Several days later, they used a torture that their North American advisors taught them…"

"This comes from a civilized people," Sara tells Ana, who looks as though she smells a dead rat, "so it can't be so bad."

"They put a towel over my head and tied it around my neck. They tied me to a board, my head lower than my feet. I didn't know what was happening. The towel grew wetter and wetter until I felt I was drowning. I can't breathe! I can't breathe! I struggle against the ropes and can't move! I scream that I will tell them anything, but, like Germán, I have nothing to tell. Each time I pass out, they press the water out of me and bring me back. The towel fills with water again. All night I dream I cannot breathe but they order me not to die. They told me afterwards I was lucky, that a few days earlier they accidentally drowned a prisoner and couldn't revive him."

"You poor man!" Ana's face reflects his anguish as he relives it. The brown of her eyes looks small in the whites. "Did the other man die?"

"He died. The next day an officer and three soldiers drove me into the country." Old Pablo is speaking softly and his eyes are vacant. He has left his friends, who are stark still, and he is back in the grip of the soldiers. "They make me take off my clothes. They handcuff my wrists behind my back. A soldier kneels by each leg and holds it so I cannot move. Again I don't know what will happen, but I don't like standing naked by a road with two men holding my legs. The officer pulls a ball of twine from his pocket and passes it to the other man. He makes a noose and slips it around my testicles and tosses the ball over a limb of the tree we are under…"

"My God!" Ernesto gasps. Ana's mouth forms a terrified O.

"He wraps the twine around a heavy stick and stands off to the side. The others let go of my legs, but I know what I will feel if I move. 'This is your last chance,' the officer says. 'Talk!' I tell him that I wish to Jesus and María I could tell him anything he wants to know. The soldiers pull on the stick. The twine goes tight, but they do not stop. I scream and scream! I go up on my toes and the pain is huge. They keep on backing away until I am lifted from the ground. I spin around so my legs go up. You cannot imagine... Agony floods from my crotch through my body like the explosion of love.

"My head must bump the ground, but I don't feel it... Praise God, the agony starts to drift away, like chicken feathers on a breeze. The next thing I know, I am lying on the ground. The soldiers are gone. The handcuffs are gone. My testicles are on fire and fire throbs through my body, but it is not as sharp as before. I'm cold. An old man heard my screams and hid behind the underbrush until the soldiers left. He untied the noose, which he said was hard because my blood made the knot slippery. They cared for me in his village until I could walk again, and I walked home."

Tears fill Sara's eyes. Germán and Ernesto shake their heads. María's mouth is set. Ana's hands cover her mouth.

"I cannot imagine..." Ernesto echoes Old Pablo.

"This is how the army saves us from Communism." A hatred that time will not dim fills Sara's voice.

"Dear Old Pablo," Ana hugs him around the waist.

"This is the army that gives us Germán," María says.

"I was still a girl," Ana says. "I think you look younger now than you did then. Except your hair."

"Well, Ana?" María says.

"It is hard to believe that human beings can do these things." Ana still sounds torn. "But it must be true. I trusted them too much."

"Then you agree that we must shoot Germán?" Sara asks.

"God forgive me..." She covers her face with her hands and her shoulders heave. "I agree."

Ernesto and María put their arms around her. Their look is not triumph but sorrow. Her hands press her cheeks so hard that trails of white follow her fingers. "They make us as heartless as they are."

"Is it settled?" Sara asks.

"I must tell you what came to me as I prayed," Old Pablo says. They turn to him, even Germán, who quickly turns back.

"The army demands blood." All except Germán nod yes. "So be it. Let's tell them we found the true guerrilla. He's not Germán. He is *me*."

He looks from one to the next. Wonder turns to admiration on their faces.

Sara grabs his arm. "No!"

"You can't." María sounds equally firm.

"Will they accept it?" Ana asks.

"They suspected I was a guerrilla back when they tortured me. The lieutenant can check this on his radio."

"They will torture you again," Ernesto says. "I don't question your courage, but suppose they force you to tell them about our trick."

"Not..." Sara trembles. "Not if we shoot him."

"Exactly," Old Pablo says. "My blood will be their proof. You would not shed it lightly. They will shrug at life's surprises and go their way."

Sara puts her arms around Old Pablo, clutching bunches of his shirt as she sobs. He pats her back. She goes to the rock and sits with her head bowed, her hands to her forehead.

"Why is your life worth less than Germán's?" Ernesto asks.

"My wife and children are dead. I am probably no longer a man. It will not be a great loss to you or to me." His eyes flash beneath his black brows. "It is my place to do this for the village."

Ernesto and María put hands on his shoulders. "You are brave," María says, "but it's no use. They would see what we've done."

"And they'd think that only Communists can do such a thing," Sara growls.

"Then I fail at this too." His voice is empty.

"You have spoken like a man," Ernesto says. "But your sacrifice would be useless."

"You have agreed with us," Ernesto says to Ana.

"You have won."

"It's not winning if we help you to see reality and save the village," Sara says gently and rises from the rock. "We must talk with Germán."

"Not yet." Ernesto shakes his head and begins in a reflective tone that pulls Sara's mouth tight with anger. "My brain says we must shoot him but I, Ernesto, still can't agree."

"What if someone were trying to kill me and our children?" María asks savagely.

"I would kill him. That's different."

"And if that man had already killed us?"

"I would want to kill him, but what good would it do?"

"We're so different! I would not rest until his brains lay on the grass before me like that mash!" She points to the remnants of the ground corn.

"If you would have killed a man to save your family," Old Pablo asks Ernesto as if the answer were obvious, "then why not kill a man to save your village?"

"We cannot kill the right ones," Sara mutters.

Ernesto struggles. "They have made it self-defense to shoot a good and innocent man. I won't stand in the way."

"It will be better if you join us," Old Pablo says. His raised eyebrow invites Ernesto to agree.

"We don't have time for *better*," María says harshly.

Ernesto regards María and Sara and Old Pablo. His isolation does not seem to bother him.

"I've wavered like a young tree in the wind," Old Pablo says, "saying 'good point' so often…"

"Only a fool does not waver," Sara says.

He blossoms at her words. "It's time to talk with Germán."

"He may ask us to assemble the village," Ernesto says.

Germán turns as he sits, putting his hand on the ground so he won't topple. "I…"

"If you want them, tell us," María says.

"Please come back to us," Old Pablo says.

"I never left you." He rises from his knees and turns to them, completing their circle. "I am more afraid than you are what will happen if we take too long."

Old Pablo's voice has calm authority. "There is time to tell us what you think."

Germán starts to tremble and looks around, embarrassed that he cannot control his frame. "It is best if I am the only one."

"You agree to die?" Ernesto says.

Germán nods yes. "Just now Old Pablo was ready to die for me."

"And you will be as brave," Sara says with a sadness that has no end.

"As you told Ana of your torture, Old Pablo, you convinced me too. If I must die, best I go quickly and save my family and many others." He continues with feeling, yet he has stopped trembling and seems more at peace. "I love this life. It's been hard but beautiful—the sun rising over the mountains dark and green, corn rising under the sun, green stalks that hold the black and gold and white kernels. I ache for Lourdes and the children and the years I won't live in our hut with them."

"Aren't you afraid?" Ana asks.

"I tell myself to trust God. That helps some. I feel I am on the edge of a cliff and will soon plunge off."

"So brave," Ana says.

"Can you forgive us?" Ernesto asks.

"Of course. In your place, I would do the same."

"Can he say goodbye to Lourdes and his children?" Ana asks.

"I long to hold them, but taking the time may bring death... Tell them I love them. I do this for them." His voice falters, and he wipes his eyes. "Tell Julio and Juanita to be good, keep on being good and obey their mother... I wanted to walk with my grandchildren as the sun sets between the mountains and tell them the stories I heard long ago..."

"Your children and grandchildren will be proud of you," Old Pablo says. Tears stream unheeded down his cheeks. "The village will honor you."

"I'll provide for your family and tend the corn on your land," Ernesto says.

"When Lourdes is a widow, they will also get corn from the common ground," Old Pablo says.

"The children's godparents will help," Germán says.

"I'm Juanita's godmother," Ana says brightly.

"I'll go to Quetzaltenango and care for your mother till she's better," María says.

"Lourdes will tell you how to find her," Germán says. "I'm very grateful for all that you will do. It makes it easier."

"Let's pray together," says María. They all form a circle, arms around each other, their heads bowed, like one of your football huddles. Old Pablo speaks.

"Father and Mother, One God. We pray we have chosen the smaller evil and you will forgive us for taking this life. We ask you to hold Germán in your heart. He is a martyr an accepts death to save many people. Your Son did that. Please protect his family and our village. Your will be done. In the name of Jesus and María, our Lady of Guadalupe. Amen."

"Amen."

IV   The Eagle Soars

Chapter 19

One by one they embrace Germán. Their eyes are wet. Each has a few quiet words with him. Ana starts to release him, starts again, and finally does. Ernesto is the last. Germán kneels by one of the huts, his back to the others, his head erect.

"Excuse me, Germán," Old Pablo says. Germán looks back over his shoulder. "Would you place yourself over there."

Ana looks on astonished as Old Pablo points to a hut by the trail. "Why can't he die where he wants to?" she shrieks.

"It's all right," Germán tells her as he goes to the other place. "We don't want the bullet to pass into the village." He kneels again, his back to all. No one speaks.

"Well?" Sara says at last. "Who will do it?"

"It's my place," Old Pablo says slowly, "but I took a vow after my torture not to hurt a living soul. If someone else would like to… "

"I hate this," Ernesto says. "I will do it if… "

Germán's voice, almost disembodied in the silence, startles them. "I hope you will decide quickly."

"Here!" María snatches up the rifle and thrusts out her hand. Ernesto pulls a cartridge from his pocket and puts it in her palm. She slips it into the chamber, closes the bolt, and goes down on one knee. She aims at the back of Germán's lank black hair, which is maybe a meter from the muzzle, as they both face the distant mountains.

"Noooo," Ana wails. She buries her head against Sara's shoulder. Sara puts her arms about her. Old Pablo, Sara and Ernesto watch, not seeming to breathe, horror on their faces.

"You will be with God, Germán." María's voice turns from reassuring to hard. "You will be avenged!"

There is a long instant of silence, not a bird nor rustle of leaves, nothing. Flame flashes from the muzzle. A crash shatters the silence. María jolts backwards as Germán's head jerks forward. Those stories he wanted to tell his grandchildren spurt from his brow and splatter the grass. His body crumples.

As the shot echoes away, María stands and pulls back the bolt, flipping out the little brass tube, which strikes the bare path with a ping. Ana turns, screams, and reburies her head against Sara. The others, stunned, drained, relieved perhaps, stand motionless.

"He did not feel it," Old Pablo tells Ana as she quakes against Sara.

María drops the rifle, which clatters on the path, and kneels beside Germán. She places a hand gently on his back and the other on his forehead, like a mother checking her child for a fever. When she stands, she is shaking. Bloody white substance drips from her fingers. Ernesto comes to her, hesitates, and they embrace, smearing his shirt with red, as they look down at Germán.

Boots crunch on gravel on the trail as scarlet spreads through the grass around Germán's matted hair.

"So soon," Old Pablo says softly.

The lieutenant and the sergeant walk briskly up. The lieutenant holds his pistol in his hand. The sergeant swings the muzzle of his M-16 across the group. As the lieutenant speaks, the sergeant notices the rifle on the ground. He picks it up, looks into the breach, and sets it against the hut.

"Congratulations!" the lieutenant says smiling. "You have made the correct decision." He notices Ana, who is still sobbing against Sara, and speaks as if to comfort her. "This is too much for our little friend. Our enemies are cruel. If you knew what we know, you would understand."

Ana does not respond. "Translation," he says sharply to Old Pablo, who complies. Ana peeks out and returns to Sara's shoulder, shivering as though she feels for the first time the chill that has crept into the air of the waning afternoon.

The lieutenant gives up on Ana and turns to the corpse. He places a foot on its shoulder and rolls it enough to see Germán's face. I see it too. It looks at peace beneath a dark red, ragged hole in his forehead. The sergeant inspects the body but does not touch it. At last Sara and Ana separate.

"Justice has been done," the lieutenant says.

Sara spits. Both soldiers whirl in her direction.

"What was that?" the lieutenant demands.

"A bug flew in my mouth." Sara, not understanding his words, speaks to the irritation in his voice.

Old Pablo translates. "I saw it," he adds though he had not been looking at her.

"No matter." The lieutenant smiles and holsters his pistol.

"You got here very quickly," Old Pablo says.

"We had not gone far."

"We forgot to tell you," the sergeant says with a sneer, "that soldiers are surrounding the village. In case somebody tried to escape."

"To protect you in case other guerrillas tried to rescue him. Sergeant, the radio."

The big man unhooks it from his belt, hands it over, and relaxes apart from the group with his assault rifle crooked in his arm, as the lieutenant holds the radio like a bulky telephone.

"Omega Bravo Leader calling Omega Base. I wish to report."

A voice I cannot understand crackles from the radio.

The lieutenant smiles. "Yes, my Colonel. One shot, in and out. Quite professional."

More crackles.

"You may tell the reporter that the people have decided as the army would have decided. We protect the people from Communists, but they are the ones who knew this man was a Communist, certain enough to kill him. We soldiers only suspected. Today they protected all of us."

Crackles.

"He can see for himself. His Spanish is good. He will understand what we tell him."

Crackles.

"Soon, before it grows dark. We shall wait on the road."

Crackles.

The lieutenant hands the radio to the sergeant and motions to Ernesto and Old Pablo, "You! You! Drag it into the hut!"

Sara comprehends. "People live in there!"

The lieutenant turns to Old Pablo, who tells him she is worried about putting blood on the floor of the people who live there.

The dapper man confronts Sara menacingly. "Do not worry, Mother. Your mountain air will cleanse their home. You have rich earth to replace the floor beneath his head. Translation!" Old Pablo complies. "We must prepare the reporter to see the corpse. After he goes, do what you like with it. Translation!"

Sara glares at him with sullen defiance as Old Pablo tells her his words in Mam, and he adds that she must control herself.

"The sun is nearly down," she mutters.

"She says she didn't think of that," Old Pablo says in Spanish.

The lieutenant and points to the body. "Now!"

Ernesto and Old Pablo grab the body under the armpits and drag it, blood dripping from its drooping head, into the hut until I see only the trousers, ankles, and shabby, dusty shoes.

The lieutenant faces Sara and Ana and motions Old Pablo to come close for translation. He stands about three meters before the women. Old Pablo is between them but to one side.

"You are angry, and you are sad. It will pass. Death in war is hard when it comes to a friend." He looks pained—maybe he is recalling the friend he denounced. "You did what you had to."

Without warning Ana springs at him. "Viper! Viper!" She hammers at his shoulders with her fists. He throws his arms around her, binding her arms against him. Ernesto starts towards them to pull her away. Sara and María gasp as the M-16 rises to the sergeant's shoulder.

"Halt!" the lieutenant shouts, as much to the sergeant as to Ernesto, who freezes and nearly topples over. The sergeant looks to the lieutenant, who says, "It's all right."

Disappointment on his face, the sergeant slowly lowers the weapon. Ernesto relaxes and straightens up. The lieutenant releases Ana, who has ceased to struggle. She walks proudly to Sara and stands with her back to the lieutenant, who ignores the provocation.

"We should take her down to the men," the sergeant says. "They will teach her how to love the army."

Old Pablo does not translate.

"No… " The officer makes up his mind. "A Communist has no value and must be disposed of for our people. But in a democracy we make allowances for those who find this hard the first time."

"I apologize for our young friend," Old Pablo says, in the tone of one senior to another. "She's a close friend of his wife."

"His widow," Sara growls in Mam.

The lieutenant nods towards Ana and tells Old Pablo, "It's over. See that she doesn't get near the reporter." He turns to the trail.

"Lieutenant," the sergeant says.

He turns back. "Yes?"

"Have you considered the plan I proposed for the village?"

"Fully."

Terror fills Old Pablo's face. The others look perplexed.

"The men are ready." Menace fills the sergeant's voice. "Have no fear that anyone will escape."

Sara's mouth sets. Anger flashes across María. Ernesto's eyes dart from the sergeant to the stone arms lying on the kas. Ana remains perplexed.

"I have no fear, Sergeant." The lieutenant's words flow like oil. "You must agree that a propaganda victory in the North American press is worth more than half an hours' sport with an Indian village."

The sergeant is taken aback. "I agree, Sir. Very good, Sir." He bellows down the trail, authority in his voice, "Squad leaders! Assemble on the road!"

"Perhaps we shall meet again on a happier day," the lieutenant says. He and Old Pablo exchange faint smiles before the younger man walks down the gravel and out of sight.

"My God," Ana gasps. "If that reporter wasn't coming, they would have killed us all."

"That was the sergeant," Old Pablo says. "The lieutenant would have kept his bargain with us."

Ana turns to the others, her feet apart, fists clenched on her hips and face livid, much as María stood so long ago when she first said that Germán must die.

"Vipers!" Ana shouts. "Barbarians!" The others look nervously down the trail. She relaxes a bit, and sobs catch in her throat. "God forgive me, María. I see how you feel. They made us kill Germán!"

"I do what I have to," María says vacantly. The depth of Ana's turnabout passes her by.

"You did not kill him," Ana assures her. "They did."

Sara puts an arm around María's waist but speaks to Ana. "You did what most people won't, Ana. You opened your eyes."

Ana's voice falters as she looks from one woman to the other. "I was afraid you didn't like me anymore." Sara hugs her. María, still in the grip of her emotions, not comprehending Ana's, gives Ana a wan smile.

"It's a hard way to learn," Old Pablo tells Ana gently.

She puts a hand on his breast, the other on his shoulder. She, too, is gentle now. "Not as hard as yours."

Old Pablo shakes his head and chuckles. "I thought the lieutenant was done for when you attacked him."

Ana looks flustered. Sara smiles and says, "Remember? You worried what María might do to the soldiers."

A smile lights Ana's face. "I did, didn't I."

María walks trance-like to Ernesto. She puts her head against his shoulder and clutches him. With his arms around her, she weeps more pitiably than I have seen her weep since Luis was taken.

Ana looks to Sara, who says, "She tried to tell us all afternoon that she's only human."

"It's all right, María," Old Pablo says. "You heard the lieutenant. Germán saved the village. Thanks to you."

María releases herself from Ernesto. She snuffles and rubs her nose, which is shiny red. "I do not weep for what I have done," she says, "but for what I must do."

Old Pablo looks questioningly from her to Ernesto. They are locked on each other's eyes, Ernesto unsure, María with lips tight and quivering. Tears tremble off her nose. At last Old Pablo shrugs and turns to Sara and Ana. "Why don't you go to Lourdes. I'll assemble the village and tell them what's happened."

"Old Pablo?" Sara suddenly hugs him tight. His hands hesitate and he presses her to him. Now she stands back and looks into his face, her hands on his shoulders, sorrow and hope in her voice. "You are a man!"

She disappears between the huts, Ana close behind. Old Pablo shakes his head smiling and walks slowly after them.

Ah, well. Perhaps Sara will not live alone much longer. I shall not fret if Old Pablo feels the warmth that once was mine.

Chapter 20

María and Ernesto face each other as Old Pablo ambles from my sight among the huts. I grip the limb tighter and tremble as I see below me the little girl playing with Ana at the rock, the young woman waiting there for Luis, waiting for Ernesto, and now the woman who has taken the life of a friend—doing what must be done that the others would not do.

"There was so much I wanted to say to you." The words burst from Ernesto.

"I wanted to ask you your thoughts and tell you mine," María responds.

Ernesto pauses. "What is it that you must do?"

"It will be harder than what I just did."

"What is it?"

"Avenge him."

"I feared you would want to." His face falls yet shows a strange relief.

"The joke is on the army." She gives a bitter laugh. "They said a guerrilla was here. There wasn't, but now there is.... The truth is what the army says it is."

"Germán gave his life to save the village. But what good can come if you give yours?"

"I will probably die, soon or not so soon." She looks at the ground, then faces him fiercely. "For the children we would have buried!"

"I thought we agreed about violence."

"That was my dream, but violence just saved the village." She looks to the sky, as though her dream still floats there, and back to Ernesto. "I was hard on Ana because she didn't see what must be done. But neither did I."

"I hope you'll reflect before you do this."

"I shall, and, like Germán, pray that I don't weaken."

He shakes his head as though he knows he cannot change her. "We must finish our marriage quickly, before you leave."

"Ernesto? What's really hard... " She bites her lip. "Something I cannot say." Tears flow off her nose as her mouth twists in a cruel parody of a laugh.

"You will not marry me," he says softly, with the quick despair of one whose heart has broken before.

"Ernesto!" She clutches him, her shoulders quivering. "Already I feel what Germán gave up."

He looks into her face without comprehending.

"To hold Lourdes in the night." Her fists clench at her sides. "As I must hold you… I must feel our babies inside me, our babies at my breasts!"

Her arms scythe about his neck, and they embrace as though to crush each other.

"Don't go," he says, stroking her hair.

"I must!" She begins to push free.

He locks his arms behind her back, holding her to him. "Don't!"

"What's this?" She struggles. "Let me go!"

"No!" He pulls her tighter.

"Ernesto!" She collapses against him. "You!"

"María!" He comes to himself and drops his arms to his sides. "Forgive me!"

They part, the width of a hand separating their heaving chests. She looks into his face. Slowly, slowly, her arms circle his neck tighter and tighter until the shallow cones of her breasts flatten against him and her heels leave the grass. His hands go hesitantly to her waist, and they embrace for a long gentle moment as if to become one flesh.

She stands back. His arms hang again at his sides like withered corn-stalks. A smile of triumph breaks across her face, her eyes dancing. "At last, Ernesto! You fight for what you want! Even if it's me you fight against!"

"I feel ashamed."

"No," she beams. "It was only for a moment. What matters is, your fire burns! We *are* alike!"

"At last." He smiles faintly. "And too late."

"My poor Ernesto." They gaze into each other's eyes as tears roll down their cheeks. "Today I have killed a friend and wounded my beloved." Her voice hardens. "My wedding days bring bad luck. Best I stop having them."

"I'll wait for you."

"I waited too long for Luis."

"You never said it was too long."

"Today I face many things."

Ernesto paces in a tight little track and turns to her, his face brightening. "You speak of God. You once talked of becoming a nun. The church of the poor does great good, or why would they kill so many of its people?"

She shakes her head. "God's ways are too slow."

Ernesto draws back. "María! That's sacrilege."

"But God knows it's true."

They are standing close again. "You should be a husband and a father again. Perhaps one day Lourdes… "

Ernesto looks at her with great sadness but does not speak.

"Lourdes is a fine woman," María says half-heartedly. "Her children need a father."

"I want *you!*"

"Ernesto!" She says with a flicker of hope, "Come with me."

"I have no children," he muses. "You're the only wife I'll ever want." He smiles ruefully and shakes his head.

She returns his smile, lovers joined in parting. "No, you wouldn't be my dear Ernesto if you became a killer."

"What about you? You'll be sharing danger with many men. Perhaps you'll be drawn to one and become his *compañera.*"

"I cannot think like that." In a flash her warrior's armor falls at their feet, and she stands as if naked, her body soft and open for her lover. "I want you so much!"

Their eyes meet as each steps forward. But the armor rises to sheathe her again like a supple green husk over a golden ear of corn. She shakes her head. The hope on his face goes out like a candle in the wind.

"It will be dangerous if you leave too soon."

"I'll go to Germán's mother. If soldiers capture me, I'll say, 'Don't worry. I'm the one who shot Germán.'" Her voice trails off. She does not move.

His mouth turns bitter. "The violence has cost me two wives."

"And twice, your children." Her breath catches as she tries to smile. "This is as hard for me as for you. I love you…even more than I did this morning… Oh, Ernesto!" She snuffles. "I'll leave with the next load of weavings."

"I will pray for you always." He shrugs the way Sara shrugs when nothing can be done. "What else can I do?"

"Unless you hear I'm dead."

"Always!" They embrace fiercely, with an energy that shimmers in the air as she turns to leave. "*Vaya con Dios*, María. Go with God."

She strides quickly into the village, not looking back. He gazes after her for a moment, then snatches up the rifle, pulls the cartridges from his pocket, and holds them aloft with outstretched arms, offering them to the reddening sky. The low sun sculpts black shadows across the eternal planes of his face. In his utter defeat he becomes a Mayan statue, at one with the civilization that the barbarians from Europe subdued centuries ago but have yet to destroy or even discover.

Lourdes rushes up, her skirt and black hair flying. She grasps Ernesto's shoulders, a fearful question on her face. He points without looking. Her hand comes to her mouth as she turns.

"No! No! Nooooo…"

Scream upon scream pierces the twilight. No one answers. Tenderly she goes to her hands and knees at the doorway to the hut where Germán lies and covers his body with hers. All I see are her brightly colored skirt and little bare feet between his dusty shoes. Her moans rise from the earth as Ernesto gazes down at them, man and wife together for the last time, as he and María were moments ago.

He turns away, grief and anger crossing his face. Suddenly he flings the cartridges over the edge, and they whisper briefly through the bushes below. He picks up the rifle, swings around, and looses it with force. It spins through the air and strikes my tree with a crack like a gunshot. I feel a tremor where my claws grip the limb as it clatters to the ground, the wooden stock split from the metal.

"The horror!" he cries. "The horror!"

Chapter 21

I look on, as helpless as Ernesto, until I can stand no more. Tipping from my perch, I fly upward and swoop back through the gloom. For an instant, I see twisted corpses among blackened circles on the ground below. But no. In this village, life goes on for all but one, though it will not be the same for those who love him. Beyond these remote villagers, no one knew him and very few know them, except his mother who still waits for his knock on her door in Quetzaltenango. The tamales that the women prepared for María and Ernesto's fiesta will be eaten, though tears may thin the salsa.

Old Pablo's voice rises from a cluster of men and women who stand around him. A knot of women surround Ana, who is kneeling between two children and pressing their slender forms against her, while her own little Gloria regards them with tears in her eyes. Only Sara looks up. As I pass above, our eyes meet, and she calls softly, "Tomás!"

María is talking quietly with her Mama and Papa near the door where Old Pablo knelt beside her suitors on ten nights of her young life. I love her as Sara loves her, and my heart scalds as I think of her life. If she dies, I think, a fierce new eagle may soon be flying through the highlands.

But this is her day. Today she sprang free. Thanks to her, the village lives. Perhaps after all, she will one day be a matriarch, though I do not think so.

I fly onward towards the flaming sky. A new scarlet flows across my breast. It is the blood of my people, which is shed for you.

Book Two: Brenda's Luck

Chapter 22

"Don't go!" María sobbed as she hugged me at the top of the trail to the road. "I can't believe you're going."

"It's best for all of us," I said through my tears. "I'll be back as soon as I can."

"First I lose Luis, now my precious sister!"

"It's only for a time. I'll be safe," I said loosening my arms from her back. I hated to leave but didn't want to keep Padre López waiting.

One thin tortilla apiece with nothing on it was the only breakfast that Mama, Papa, María, and I ate this morning of my departure, the same as the meal we ate last night. We went quietly about our chores this morning until the padre's horn honked from the road. Aunt Sara and my dear friend Frida stood at the top of the trail to say goodbye.

My leaving was especially hard on María, and her words pierced me. "Two years ago I lost the man I loved," she said between sobs as I wept more quietly. "Today I'm losing my sister. I stood here then and waved as he walked away. Today I'll watch you disappear in a car."

"It's hard for me too, but it isn't forever. We have to believe this."

"Oh, Brenda! I don't know if I'll ever see you again!" She released me and turned away. Still weeping, she buried her face on Mother's shoulder. She and our parents would have more food without me, and so, I hoped, would I when I reached my unknown employers in San Salvador. Was it worth it to rip me out of my family for God alone knows how long? Who knew how long the famine would last and the toll it would take? When Padre López offered me this chance, we talked it over and agreed I'd best take it. Now I couldn't very well say, Padre I've changed my mind. Leaving home was like going through with a marriage to a man I wasn't sure was right. Funny that this crossed my mind last night, since a chance to marry had yet to come my way. It didn't occur to us that after the famine ended, the civil war might still delay my return.

I tore myself away and scrambled the family's battered suitcase down the trail while the others stayed at the top. We had agreed they would not come down, so as not to burn the energy it would take to climb back up. It was bad enough that someone had to go down every day for water.

At the car I turned and waved to the silhouettes of the people I loved the most. Their arms brushed the sky as they waved back. A final wave across the roof of the car and I climbed in and couldn't see them anymore.

The padre drove off with terrible jolts from the ruts and stones and at a terrifying speed. Half a dozen tortillas wrapped in a blue and white napkin were wedged between the dashboard and the windshield.

"They're for you because you must be famished. Eat them slowly so as not to upset your stomach."

He said he was driving fast to avoid being shot at, and I thought that being shot at might not be as bad as smashing into a tree. At the bus stop he gave me a leg of chicken, some biscuits for later, my tickets, and a letter for his friend Padre Quinones, who was to meet me in San Salvador. At the steps into the bus, he put his hand on my head and gave me God's blessing. I wept again and squeezed his hand and scrambled up and inside.

All I remember of the ride to Quetzaltenango was more bumps, the diesel smell from the open windows, and the squawks of chickens on the roof. I was nervous about changing buses there and again in Guatemala City, but the padre had left plenty of time between trips, and I was pleased to find I had enough Spanish to ask strangers for directions and buy more food at little shops in the terminals with some money he also gave me. The bus to Guatemala City was smoother and didn't have animals on the roof. I gazed out the window, beyond the bustle and sadness of leaving home, and took stock of where I was. The countryside was green and pretty. Except for jeeps that passed now and then holding soldiers with guns pointing upwards, you wouldn't know there was a war.

This morning was the first time I'd ever ridden in a car, and right now was my second bus ride, all in the same day. The reason I was here and not at home was that I loved Spanish and Padre López thought I knew enough of it for this adventure. Spanish is so different from Mam. It flows easily from your mouth, whereas Mam chugs almost like the beginnings of a cough. I grew up with those sounds and never gave them a thought until I began to learn a language that didn't have them. My love of languages would continue to shape my life. As you see, I am writing this in English.

Frida and I were learning Spanish together, practicing the phrases we got from Old Pablo, who could speak it, and sometimes from the padre when he had time to spare during his visits, but we had no grasp of the grammar, and the only writing I had seen on paper might has well have been from chickens scratching in the dirt. Frida caught on faster, but I practiced more, so we were about even when the padre made his offer.

I think our motives were why he chose me instead of her—her family was hungry too. She wanted to learn enough Spanish so she could leave the village, which she felt confined her, and make a life for herself in a city. That's why she turned down two young men who wanted to marry her. Though no man had wanted to marry me, at least not yet, several had knelt at our door for María. Like some other firstborn girls I knew, I was the more stable, but I had to admit that several young men had found my little sister more attractive. I say "little," but she was the taller.

My motive was, I wanted Spanish so I could protect the villagers from the *ladinos* who would cheat us Maya out of our property by conning us into signing documents in Spanish that we couldn't read. I even planned to spend a few weeks in Quetzaltenango and stay with Frida if she was there by then or with Germán's mother, who worked in a hospital, and take a course on Mayan rights. I was pretty sure that Padre López chose me for the job in El Salvador because he expected me to return and help my people, as I had every intention of doing. Not that he criticized Frida's choice. He never criticized anyone, at least not that I'd heard of. I've wondered whether this was simply his good nature, or whether as a *ladino* who actually cared about us Maya, he wanted to be extra careful not to condescend.

It was another chicken bus that took me to San Salvador. The trip lasted from late evening until after first light the next day. It seemed endless. I tossed and turned in my seat, half squashed by a fat, grizzled *ladino* beside me who smelled of stale sweat and garlic, which I like but not on him. I slept little, too uncomfortable most of the night even to feel homesick.

Padre Quiñones found me easily at the bus station because I was the only passenger wearing Mayan *traje* and carrying a many-colored Mayan satchel. He was tall and thin with a deep voice and not a word of Mam, but my Spanish was enough. He drove at a sane speed through the city to the home of the Rodríguez family, where I was to serve. He said they were nice people and belonged to his parish. The rest of the drive, he asked me about my family and life in my village and Padre López and the famine.

The Rodríguezes lived in a big house with white stucco walls, which I had never seen before, and an orange tile roof. It sat in a big lot that was like a little green park with purple bougainvillea bushes and bright flowers against the high walls, which had broken glass imbedded on their tops. Gracefully curved iron bars protected the house's windows.

Señora Rodriguez, who had a wiry body inside a simple dress, showed me swiftly around the big rooms and introduced me to her husband and children, two boys and a girl, who were finishing their breakfast. Señor, who was wearing what I would learn was a business suit, stood up and said, "Welcome to our home." He kissed Señora quickly on the cheek and left through a large, gracefully carved, wooden door, which I could see through an opening from the dining room.

The children were still at the table. "Why is she wearing those funny clothes?" said the smaller boy, whose name was Miguel.

"Those are the traditional *traje* that Guatemalan Indians wear. You'd better take a good look because she won't be wearing them long."

I felt warmly surprised that Señora knew the word, but hearing I'd not continue to wear them felt like a slap in the face. Plunged into one new world after another since yesterday morning, I was aching for my family and village, but at least I felt snugly at home in the garments my mother helped me to weave beside our family hut. Hearing that I could no longer wear them made me realize that they were part of who I am. I tried not to show that I was devastated.

"I hope Miguel didn't offend you about your clothing," Señora said.

"Oh, no," I lied, sensing that *no* was the correct answer.

She gave me a quick tour of the house except for her and Señor's suite. Each child had a separate room and a bed that was big enough for a grown man and woman to lie in together. These were the first beds I had ever seen. Last, she showed me to the little room over the garage that would be my home inside theirs.

"Your *traje* is very beautiful, but it would soon wear out with the work you'll be doing. I hope you'll save it for special occasions."

Saying "I hope" was often how she gave me an order. Several sets of plain, different-sized clothes lay across my bed, which was no bigger than it needed to be. She had me try them on in front of her and said she'd order three sets of the ones that fit best.

"Indians in this country used to wear traditional clothing too, until a great tragedy befell them many years ago. Since then, they've dressed like everybody else."

I would learn later, during my political education after I left the Rodríguezes, that the tragedy she referred to was so much greater than most of the tragedies that befell us Native Americans that it had its own special name, *La Matanza,* which means The Massacre. In putting down a small rebellion in 1932, the army killed, they say, thirty thousand of us, mostly civilians, a lot like what the army was doing now in Guatemala. In the violence after the main extermination, like the aftershocks of an earthquake, the Native Americans of El Salvador found they were most likely to survive if they dressed like *ladinos*.

Señora said that since I was probably tired from my overnight ride, she would take care of the breakfast dishes and I could start work in the afternoon. I thanked her and mean it. As soon as she closed the door, I threw myself on the bed and slept.

The room contained a chest of drawers with a mirror on the wall above it. In front of the window were a wooden chair painted pale blue and a wooden table with a Bible on it. The window faced the front gate, which the handyman opened for Señor's car and closed after he drove through. On Sundays, Señor worked the gate himself. This was one of the ways they did not live as luxuriously as they could afford to. When I sat at my table, I could see past the iron bars of the gate to slivers of the world outside, and I felt less enclosed. I had hated to leave my village and often repeated my vow to return as soon as the famine ended. From my window I could see the morning sun glinting off the glass shards on the wall. It was quite beautiful, though it shut in the family and me.

As the days passed, I got used to wearing the clothes that Señora had bought me, but sometimes in my room at night, I put on my real clothes and looked at myself reflected in the black window. Alone in the evening, I missed my loved ones the most, especially María and Frida. Frida was a year younger than me and a year older than María, and the three of us were very close. Ana had been one of us, but after she drew away from María, it was just us three.

My hours of work ran from starting the breakfasts till finishing the dinner dishes, usually with a break in the afternoon, and I had an hour or two to myself in the evening before I needed to sleep. Señor and Señora were nice people even though they spoiled their children. "You have to do what Brenda tells you to," Señora instructed them on the first afternoon. I told them to do stuff as little as possible, and they were usually good about doing it.

One afternoon when they were home from school and Señora was out, they asked me to take them to the country club for a swim. "As soon as you clean up your mess in the living room," I said. Papers and crayons and other things covered the floor. They promised to clean it up as soon as we got back. I was sitting in a stuffed chair with my arms folded, and I shook my head no. About twenty minutes later they returned. "Can't we go now?" I shook my head. Ten minutes later, the same thing. They cleaned up the mess, and I took them swimming. Later they told their mother. She said,

"I'm glad you and Brenda understand each other." After that, they seldom disobeyed me.

Soon, I felt the children were beginning to like me. Once they found out that I wanted to learn more Spanish, they turned me into a game. One or another would point to phrases in my Bible and tell me what they meant, and a few minutes later ask me what they meant. Sierra, the girl, gave me a grade school grammar book she was done with, and as I was beginning to read, I devoured it as best I could. The more I learned, the more delighted the children were to play their game of Spanish with me. The maid before me, they said, knew Spanish and didn't want to learn about anything, and that was no fun.

The country club was close enough to walk to it, though the family sometimes drove—Señora had a car too, a big white van. There they played tennis and splashed in the pool while Señora sat with other mothers and more or less kept an eye on them. I did the laundry and kept the house immaculate so that Señora was free to chatter with her friends on the phone, read her books, and go watch her kids at the club when they weren't in school. Sometimes the family ate lunch at the club and took me along. I had to sit with the other servants away from the pool. None of us had swimsuits, and I didn't know how to swim, though on hot days I wished I could splash in the water.

Señor drove into the City to do work that he never talked about. I thought at first it must pay him well. Later I realized that maybe it didn't because he came from a wealthy family. People said that fourteen families ruled El Salvador. Actually it was more, and the Rodríguezes were one of them.

Then there were the horses. The family owned several and belonged to a riding club a few miles farther outside the city. The children were great horsemen, always tacking up in their rooms the ribbons they'd won at horse shows—blue, red, white, yellow—crinkly cloth badges with tails hanging down. There were not many places they could ride beyond the club's meadows because a civil war was going on in that nation too. Leading the life that Señora and the children led, they seemed hardly aware that death squads were working in the City, disappearing suspects and leaving bodies in the streets, or that the army was fighting guerrillas and killing civilians in the countryside.

It felt luxurious not to be always hungry, and after a few months, Señora had to buy me a few new clothes because I'd outgrown the ones that fit me at first.

I knew something about the war from going to church. Nearly every

Sunday the Rodríguezes would drive in Señora's big white van to Padre Quinones's church in the City. Señor always took the driver's seat, while I scrunched in the very back. They let me spend the afternoons at the church—as long as I took a bus back in time to fix their dinners. Señora made their Sunday lunch and left the dishes in one of the sinks for me. On those afternoons, I would attend the church's adult education programs or simply hang out with the nuns who came for tea. Sometimes I would go to the sisters' convent or the house where the Maryknoll missionaries from North America stayed, and I would practice my Spanish and try to learn what was really going on in El Salvador.

As my love of language had changed my life, so would my curiosity about the real world, for better and worse. One of the sisters told me that Padre Quiñones had known Monsignor Oscar Romero, who was assassinated by a death squad a few years earlier, and maybe I would want to ask him about him. I did.

"He was the bravest person I ever knew," the padre said with a tremor in his voice. "He did God's work, and they killed him for it. He was a saint if ever there was one." He paused. "Señor Rodríguez probably knows I think like this, but it would be best if you don't tell him what I just said."

I assured him I wouldn't and began to wonder what the relationship between these two men might be. Years would pass before I found out.

I had understood that I could go home to my village when Padre López sent word to Padre Quiñones that they'd had a decent harvest. I was saving nearly all my salary to buy the bus tickets and food I'd need along the way, and I wanted to repay Padre López for the money he'd spent to get me here. Leaving the Rodríguezes after a short time would probably be all right with them. They considered it a part of their Christian duty to help young women in difficulty. When one of us wanted to move on, they agreed, sometimes sadly, to see her leave them and make room for the next one.

After a few months on the job, I began to worry about whether I had understood correctly about going home. One Sunday I asked the padre.

"I think you're right," he said. "I'll ask Padre López. In the meantime, it might be best not to get your hopes up. There's a lot going on that we don't know about."

Though he said this in his kindly way, it devastated me. If there was enough food in the village again, what could be going on that could keep me away? A few weeks later, I found out. He told me after Sunday mass that Padre López had explained to him that most villages in Guatemala, probably even mine, have *orejas*, which literally means ears and actually means spies for the army. An *oreja* would almost certainly tell the army that Brenda, who had been away for several months, had suddenly returned, that she said she'd been working as a maid in El Salvador and came back because the famine was over, but there was no proof that her story was true. The army, in spite of being very strong, was very paranoid—the padre explained *paranoid*—and would probably conclude that Brenda had really been fighting with the guerrillas, so they would kill her and probably her family.

"That means I can't go home until there's peace?" I asked in dismay, knowing that the civil war had already lasted many years.

"I'm afraid that's the safest way for you and your family." He must have seen that I was about to cry. "Wars do end, you know."

I could hold back no longer and burst into tears. He held me in a little hug and patted my back with one of his big boney hands. I let him try to comfort me for a few minutes, then broke away—rudely, I'm afraid—and shut myself in a stall in the women's toilet until I could stop sobbing. I'm lucky to be where I am, I told myself several times, and my loved ones are safest if I stay here. I believed this was true, but it didn't help.

More months passed. I liked the Rodríguezes well enough. My Spanish was coming along nicely, especially the reading and writing, and my work was not too demanding. But it was a dead-end job. If I could not return home, the best I could do in El Salvador would be the same old same old until the kids grew up, then try to find the same job with a family that would surely be less agreeable. The bad news about going home made me feel more isolated than ever. Apart from those Sunday afternoons, I had no one to talk to about the reality of El Salvador. I only talked with the family about necessities and stuff that didn't matter and the game of Spanish. If I got a different job, I'd create a place for them to help some woman who was in more trouble than I was.

I screwed up my nerve and told Señora Rodríguez how much I liked the family and appreciated the work, but I was used to being surrounded by people in my village and felt a little isolated now. I knew I was taking a chance by telling her this, but I was pretty sure she was a good person. She and I both knew that she'd have no trouble finding another girl. She wasn't angry and didn't fire me but said they knew that, much fun as I had with the children, I felt lonely. They'd hoped that by letting me stay in town on Sunday afternoons, I'd feel less so. She said she'd see what she and her husband could do. He asked a friend who owned an accounting firm whether they could use what North Americans call a *girl Friday*, he said yes, and after a sad farewell with the children, I moved in with three single women from the church who shared a room in the city.

I spoke Spanish well enough by then, but my reading and writing were poor, and beyond the simplest arithmetic, my math did not exist. So I sorted the mail and passed it around the office. I made Xerox copies and coffee on demand and fetched and delivered papers in brown envelopes around the city—getting to know parts of San Salvador very well—but I still wanted to learn more about the civil wars that El Salvador and Guatemala were both having. Their outlines were simple, but the particulars were not.

Padre Quiñones told me I could probably learn more if I joined a Christian base community, but I didn't want to talk about God or Jesus. He knew that the chance to worship was not what drew me to his church. I'd grown up in the Mayan and Catholic faiths, but I didn't see how a good God could allow such bad things to be happening in this country and back home. God's spokesman, Monsignor Romero, tells the soldiers to stop killing their own people, so an army assassin shoots him dead while he's saying Mass. Four missionary women come from the U.S. to help needy Salvadorans, so soldiers rape them and shoot them. What kind of a God permits this, especially to people who are trying to serve Him?"

The padre said my question was very old and very natural, and he hadn't found an answer that satisfied him. Then I said I knew I was supposed to love God, but God is a mystery and how do you love a mystery? He said he knew it's hard and must be one of the reasons that God sent Jesus—because it's easier to love a man than a mystery. So I said I'd have to learn more about Jesus. But I didn't. The padre was patient with my questions and offered to discuss my faith, but I said maybe later.

He made the fateful suggestion that if I really want to know what was going on in El Salvador, there were people I should listen to at the *Universidad Centroamericana*, which was run by several Jesuit priests. Then he seemed to think better of what he'd just said and told me that if I tried to learn more at the *Universidad* or anywhere else, to be very careful because people who ask too many questions make the secret police suspicious. I said I'd try not to ask too many, which I realized later was a stupid remark.

I started spending evenings sitting beside people I didn't know in the cafeteria and joining in whatever conversations didn't seem frivolous. I quickly learned that many students held radical views and were sometimes targets of the security forces. We avoided learning each other's names so they couldn't torture them out of us if, God forbid, they detained any of us. I was careful mainly to ask questions and not express my opinions. As you may suppose, I was becoming increasingly radical, as who wouldn't on learning about the oppression that most Salvadorans endured and the brutality with which the security forces terrorized most people into line? You see a decapitated body in the street, and you know to keep your mouth shut. Only I kept asking questions, and I guess somebody—either someone being tortured or a snitch, an *oreja*—told the secret police that I asked a lot of questions. I guess I thought I was too harmless to attract attention.

Maryknoll Sisters were present in both El Salvador and Guatemala, and of course they exchanged news and views, and sometimes they invited some of us to tea at their house. One of them told me that in Guatemala there were no political prisoners; people who were disappeared were often tortured and always killed. But while torture may have been equally common in El Salvador, some of the victims were allowed to survive. The sisters asked each other which practice instilled more terror in people: only seeing mutilated bodies in the gutter or seeing those bodies plus hearing about the agonies of survivors. Be that as it may, I had rays of hope after three of the people in my discussion group were disappeared. Sure enough, one of them reappeared in the Mariona Prison and another in a hospital. I had not heard how the third one fared before my own turn came.

Walking to work one morning, I found myself arm in arm with two burly men in jeans who guided me to a car while the other people on the sidewalk paid no attention except to shuffle quickly out of our way. They thrust me onto the floor in the back seat, and one of them sat with his shoes pressing on my body while the other one drove for maybe half an hour and stopped inside what seemed like an underground garage. The driver called the other one Max. Max called the driver Jorgé. Of the two, Max seemed to be in charge. He pulled me roughly out of the car and hustled me through a doorway.

They sat me down at a table in a fetid room. Max sat across from me and asked me questions. Jorgé stood behind me and slapped the back of my head, no matter what I answered. It seemed like the less I really knew, the more they thought I was hiding. At one point a tall blond man entered the room and wrote out questions for them to ask me. His questions were in bad Spanish which they did not correct. Out of respect for him, I guessed. After he left, the torture got worse. The men tore off my blouse and bra, which I found very humiliating, and instead of hitting me, Max would burn me with a cigarette. He did that often and it hurt terribly.

It occurred to me to make up the names of people I'd talked to. I hoped that real people didn't have these names and the men didn't find out right away that I was lying. I told them that some of the people, I didn't know which ones, were not enrolled at the university but walked in off the street like I did—so Max and Jorgé couldn't find out I was lying by checking the university's records. This was true. There really were other walk-ins like me. I was surprised that this trick occurred to me, but Max was writing down the fake names and Jorge shot the terrible pain into my body less often.

Finally they threw me onto a filthy mattress that was on the floor and raped me. O, the pain! It didn't stop. O, how heavy they are! I was a virgin, and it hurt terribly. After a while they seemed to be getting ready to rape me again when I heard someone enter the room.

"It's all right, men. She's had enough." Destroyed as I was, I could hardly believe what I was hearing. The voice belonged to Señor Rodriguez!

"I checked with our friend from the north," the voice continued. "She's not a subversive, and she doesn't know anything worth interrogating her about. You can check the names she gave you, but I doubt that they're real."

Why didn't you tell them hours ago that I'm not a subversive, I almost shouted, but I didn't.

"Our friend has been watching through the mirror. He asked me to tell you you've done good work." Señor paused. "It's all right. You may leave."

The door opened and closed and we were alone. Why did they obey this person I knew only as a nice man? How did he get into the torture chamber? In spite of the pain that wracked my body, I felt terribly embarrassed that this man I thought I knew was seeing me naked as he helped me to my feet. He collected my clothes from where Max and Jorgé had thrown them, and turned away while I put them on. I had to hold the blouse closed across my chest because the buttons flew off when Max ripped it from me.

Señor led me outside into the cool evening air. We were on an army base, and the guards pushed the gate aside when Señora's big white van came towards them. It had been morning when Max and Jorgé seized me. Now it was nearly dark.

"'I'm very grateful,' I told him as we drove on, "but I don't understand. You're a religious man, a good family man, yet you come into to a torture chamber and those horrible men obey you."

Señor did not reply. We drove towards the city in silence until he said, "I have no idea how much you actually know and refused to tell them. If they put your name on a death list, there will be nothing I can do for you. You must leave the country at once."

He drove me to my room and told me to put on clothes I could travel in— jeans would be better than my shorts—grab any small valuables and return immediately. I snatched up the satchel that held my *traje* and threw in some clean underwear and the toothbrush I'd learned to use. He drove me to Padre Quinones' church—which, he said, might be watched—and told me to cover my head with the shawl I had also grabbed, and tell the padre I'd been interrogated and had to leave the country tonight. As I was stepping down from the van, he gave me some money and said, "*Vaya con Dios.*" Starting to weep, I thank him.

I walked quickly through the dimly lit church and into the living quarters in the back. Luckily the padre was sitting at his table eating supper. I told him I'd been tortured and Señor said I had to leave the country immediately. My news that it was Señor who rescued me didn't seem to surprise him.

He telephoned someone and asked him to come over right away because the hot water heater had sprung a leak and the place was flooding. The man understood and drove me towards the border and across into Guatemala early the next morning. I may have slept a little in the car, but my body ached all over, and I hoped to God the men hadn't made me pregnant. Before we left, the padre had handed me a tube of burn ointment, and I hate to think what I would have felt through the night if he hadn't. I had to ask the man to smear some on the part of my back I couldn't reach. Of course, I wanted to visit my village, but he said that Salvadoran and Guatemalan intelligence worked together and it would be too dangerous. He also said that Señor Rodríguez may have taken a risk in rescuing me, but probably not much, considering who he is.

"Who is he?" I asked, but the man said I'd better not know in case I was tortured again. That's also why he wouldn't tell me his name. It would be years before I heard which side Señor was really on, or if he was on both sides at once if that was possible.

On we drove through the darkness and gradual dawn, to the Maryknoll House in Guatemala City in time for a late breakfast for both of us. The man told several of the fathers and sisters why he'd brought me. Though we had not been expected, they fed us well, then loaded the man's car with stuff for the Maryknollers back in San Salvador that they suddenly decided those folks needed—in case he was stopped and had to explain his trip. I wondered what he would have said if soldiers had stopped him while I was in his car. I thanked him earnestly for the terrible risk he had taken for me, and off he drove, out of my life as quickly as he had entered it. In spite of my doubts about God, I prayed he would be safe.

Here I was in the midst of strangers who meant me well and felt they had to get me out of Guatemala. I agreed, though I hated to go even farther from my village. They sent for a woman doctor who gently applied more burn ointment and told me I was in good shape considering what I'd been through. I said I feared the rapes had made me pregnant. She replied that her religion prevented her from doing anything about that, but then she locked us in a bathroom and had me squat in the tub while she took big syringe and flushed me out several times with something that wasn't pleasant. It was still less than twenty-four hours since the rapes and, she said, "I have to protect you against infection." Before unlocking the door, she added, "That's all I did just now."

It was the sisters who took charge of me. That night they put me in a room that was as big at my family's hut. Badly as I needed sound sleep, one nightmare after another stiffened me with terror— the first of many nights of terror through the years ahead. By the time the sky outside the window grew pale, I was still tired. Mercifully, after I downed a good breakfast, the sisters let me lie in bed all morning.

During lunch, a nun named Sister Darlene said she was driving to Mexico City on Maryknoll business the next day and would take me with her. I guess I'd been anxious because on hearing this, relief swept through me. When officials at the border or along the way asked about me, she said she'd explain that I was on my way to their Mother House in New York State to discern whether I was truly called to join their Order. Me a nun? I'd never thought about it. I still wanted a husband and children.

"For the next week or two, I hope you will consider joining us, so I can be truthful," she said with a smile. "As we drive, I'll introduce you to some English in case you ever need it." She paused. "Actually, I can't drive you into the United States. We'll have to make other arrangements for you in Mexico City. If you'd survived torture in, say, Poland, the U.S. *migra* would let you in in a heartbeat. Since it happened in El Salvador, your chances are almost zero."

This scared me. I didn't know anything about Mexico City except that it was huge and Guatemalan death squads sometimes came and killed people there. I didn't know what she meant by *other arrangements*, but I knew what *almost zero* meant.

First, I left Guatemala to help my family and me. Then I left El Salvador to save my life. Now I had to leave Guatemala quickly, or at least try to leave, for Mexico and possibly *El Norte*. What was happening to me?

Chapter 23

No one stopped Sister Darlene, who was a *gringa* and looked it, and me while we drove through Guatemala. She turned out to be a very interesting person, and I enjoyed talking with her all the way to the border, which we crossed into Tapachula, Mexico, and on to Mexico City. I may have been more curious than polite about her life as a nun, but she answered pleasantly. She chose to live it, she said, mainly on the strength of her faith, a faith I didn't share. I didn't tell her that, but I think she figured it out.

I admired the way she and her sisters and the nuns I had known in San Salvador devoted their lives to people in need. I didn't take seriously their beliefs about Mary being a virgin and Jesus being God's boy, but it struck me that believing in the ways that Jesus asked us to treat each other seemed to turn these women into especially fine people. But there are other reasons to be good. I didn't seriously consider becoming a nun, not because of what they'd ask me to believe, but because I was still bent on returning to my village, finding a husband if I could, raising several children, and protecting fellow villagers from *ladino* sharpies. I was getting old by the standards of my people. If a man I was willing to marry did not choose me, I'd help the widows to raise their kids.

I wondered whether losing my virginity the way I did would ruin my feelings about having sex with a man I loved, when that part came along. And would the rapes make me undesirable to a man who cared about me? They shouldn't. They weren't my fault, though I couldn't help feeling guilty about them. Should I have fought harder? Would it have mattered if I had? Max's words lingered in my brain: "Lie still. Make it easy for both of us." How practical. How many other women had he said this to? His words almost made the deed sound trivial, but it wasn't trivial, oh no. I'd hated what he was doing to me, and it hurt like fury. Having endured it four times, I feared it had changed me forever in ways I couldn't guess. I'd like to talk about all this with the woman sitting beside me, but I didn't think a nun would know much about it. It didn't occur to me that many nuns experienced sex, sometimes against their will, before they joined up, and maybe she was one of them.

The closer we came to Mexico City, the more curious and concerned I grew about what would become of me. During the second morning on the road, I asked Sister Darlene what to expect.

"I don't think you should stay in Mexico—an attractive young woman by herself—unless we can find you a place quickly. We Maryknollers are friendly with some Benedictine sisters there and maybe they'll have an idea for what you can do until it's safe to go home. It's not certain they can help beyond a few night's lodging. Refugees show up all the time, and they help as best they can, which sometimes isn't much. I hope you're okay with moving beyond Mexico because I have a feeling you'll be better off in the United States."

Me a refugee? In *El Norte*? It hadn't occurred to me that I could or would want to go to the U.S. My evenings at the university taught me why it's called "the colossus of the north." Right now it supported the Terror in both my countries. Why should I go even farther from home to such an evil land?

We drove in silence until she said, "Violent as my country is, most of it is safer than Guatemala, El Salvador, or Mexico right now. You have been through a terrible ordeal that may have affected your mind in ways you don't know about yet...."

That's not true, I thought. Apart from two nights of nightmares and some terrible memories that I did not dwell on, my mind felt the same as it always had. But she was trying to help me, so I didn't tell her these thoughts. Besides, maybe she was right that something had happened in my mind that I didn't know about. But I didn't think so.

"Torture marks many people for life, and most of them are never treated for it, but in the U.S. you could be treated." She may have guessed my denial, for she added, "If you need treatment, of course."

"I may be way off base," she continued. What base, I wondered, her Mother House? "But you told me you were learning Spanish—you're doing very well with it, by the way—so you can protect your fellow villagers from *ladino* swindlers. It's good of you to want to do that. In the United States, there's a way you could help not just your village but all the Maya of Guatemala."

"Me? That sounds impossible," I said before I could stop myself. Darlene—she'd said to drop "sister"—was smart and had seen a lot. I should at least consider her words.

"It probably does." She didn't take offence. "It would be through the Sanctuary Movement. Have you heard about it?"

"People at the *Universidad* mentioned it. I don't know what they said."

"It's a precious few churches, synagogues, and Quaker meetings—several hundred but a precious few—whose people want the U.S. to stop supporting the terror in your countries and stop sending nearly all their refugees back to the violence. These are gross violations of Christian and American principles, but that doesn't seem to bother most Americans—mainly, I hope, because they don't know about them. The purpose of Sanctuary is to shelter refugees—only a handful compared to what's needed—and tell the public the facts that the media won't tell them. If enough people know the facts, maybe they'll push our government to stop supporting the terror."

This sounded noble, but I wondered whether it could succeed. Still, I wanted to know more. "I'm just a young *indio* who doesn't speak English. What could I do?"

"Tell the truth about what's going on. American media either ignore it or lie about it. As a survivor of torture, you have a lot of credibility. You could tell them what the secret police did to you." She must have sensed that I shrank from the thought. "You wouldn't have to go into detail. Most survivors don't."

"How could I find people to talk to?"

"You wouldn't have to. The church where you'd be in Sanctuary would line up other churches and maybe colleges for you to speak at."

"Me? Talk in a church full of *gringos*? I'd be scared to."

"You'd be telling it quietly to a person who would be sitting beside you and translating your Spanish. That person would speak to the audience."

"This is a lot to consider."

"You need to know about the dangers. You'd be out in public as an undocumented refugee, which the Immigration and Naturalization Service, the INS, the *migra,* considers an illegal alien. You'd be denouncing the people who tortured you; and because our intelligence people spy on churches and talk to their intelligence people, they'd know it. If you aren't on a death list now, you soon would be. Being inside a church wouldn't protect you because our laws allow the *migra* to enter churches to arrest criminals. So far they haven't done it—we think to avoid bad publicity—but there's no guarantee they won't. If they came after you, our people would try to hide you or whisk you into Canada; but again, there's no guarantee. Have I talked you out of it?"

Maybe she had. "You've given me more to think about," I said rather stupidly. As we rolled across Mexico, I rolled Darlene's words over in my mind. Speaking out in public certainly sounded risky, but maybe I would not be the first refugee the *migra* would go after; if they started taking others, maybe I could flee to Canada before they got around to me. It reassured me that when I told my story, a translator would do the actual speaking. What did I just hear myself think? *When I told my story.* The *gringos* needed to know what their government was helping to inflict.

"For instance," she said, "a newspaper might say, quote, thousands of people have died in the political violence in El Salvador. But the truth is, the U.S.-backed government has murdered more than fifty thousand unarmed civilians. That's a bit different, isn't it."

"I'm disappointed," I said. "I thought U.S. newspapers could tell the truth."

"They usually they do, but they don't like to contradict government' policy."

So it's your government's policy to help murder my people, I thought. Her words were almost making me angry enough to yes to Sanctuary. Even if telling the *gringos* the truth didn't end their government's complicity, at least some of us refugees were doing the best we could for our people, not by hurting anyone but just by being honest. I listened to myself again. *Some of us refugees* were denouncing the terror. I guess I was including myself among them again. As I pictured sitting in front of a bunch of *gringos* in a church, it occurred to me that listening to a translator turn my Spanish into English would help me learn the new language.

After a long silence, I said three words that changed my life, "I'll try Sanctuary."

"I'm so glad. When we get to Mexico City, I'll make a few phone calls. Don't worry," she added before I had a chance to worry. "We'll be talking in code. By the way, you'll need a new name, not to protect yourself but your family. And your Sanctuary church will probably ask you to wear a bandana across yours face where anyone might take your picture."

"So I'll look like a bandit?"

"Yes. For the same reason. So no one can see who you are. Also because pictures of refugees wearing bandanas look dramatic in the local newspapers. They help publicize our cause."

"It almost sounds like fun. What name shall I take?"

"Up to you. A choice your parents could not give you. Enjoy it."

More miles passed. I didn't want it to be as long as Rodríguez because I might need to write it a lot. "How about Emma Diaz?"

"Emma Diaz it is. I'll call you Emma from now on, so you'll get used to it. Brenda's a lovely name, but you'd best forget it for now."

A long slow drive through the Mexico City traffic brought us to the Benedictine Mother House. Darlene introduced me to the sisters as Emma

Diaz and made two phone calls in the head sister's office. "I can't thank you enough," I said as I walked her to her car outside the nuns' huge building. "I truly hope we'll see each other again."

"Me too. I hope you'll write and tell me how you're doing in the States."

"I promise."

She scribbled her address on a pad she carried and handed me the slip she tore off. "If this note goes astray, you can always reach me through the Maryknoll Sisters in Ossining, New York."

We gave each other a big hug on the sunny sidewalk. With a lump in my throat, I watched her drive down the street until her little blue car disappeared in the traffic. She was the first North American I had gotten to know, and she was so kind. I was very glad she asked me to write to her because I'd hoped we'd stay in touch but didn't know how.

The Benedictine Sisters, *Las Misioneras Guadalupanas de Cristo Rey*, fed me well that night and put more salve on my burns. I counted nearly a hundred gentle daubs of the sister's finger. The agonizing jabs of the cigarettes had seemed to go on forever, but I had no idea it had been that many. The next morning another sister accompanied me on the thousand-mile bus ride to Hermosillo, where I would spend the night in another bed before trying to cross the border from Mexico to Arizona. I told the sister I didn't know how long it would take me to repay them for our bus tickets.

"Don't think about it," she said. "We already have all repayment we need. It's your willingness to speak out against the Terror. You'll be doing God's work, which is what we try to do."

"But what if I find I can't do it."

"Then you weren't meant to. But I think you are. What counts is that you're willing to try."

Weren't meant to. That was her faith, not mine, but I didn't want to question it aloud. She was a nice woman and we didn't talk much. The next afternoon a North American named Stacy, who had black hair down across her shoulders and a beautiful oval face, picked me up for the four-hour drive north towards Nogales. Shortly before we reached it, she turned off onto roads that got worse and worse but didn't slow her down much. It reminded me of riding with Padre López only we weren't likely to hit a tree because there weren't any, just huge scraggly bushes in the desert. After a while she pulled off the road close to a bush that leaned over the car.

"We have to wait until it's totally dark," she explained in Spanish that, like Sister Darlene's, went slowly enough for me to follow all of it. "The border's only a few hundred yards to our left. If we weren't under this bush and a *migra* plane spots the parked car, they'll probably suspect the crossing."

She handed me a sandwich that tasted strange but delicious. "Peanut butter and jelly," she said. It was so handy I wondered why I hadn't seen it at the Rodríguezes'. Nobody drove past us during the long hour or two we waited. Just think, I thought, only last week Señor rescued me from those men.

When we could see almost nothing, Stacy said to get out. She had to slide across my seat because she'd parked so close to the bush that her door wouldn't open. She took my hand and led me through the darkness for what seemed like a great distance. We turned off the road onto a trail that was so narrow I had to walk behind her. I stumbled several times and would have fallen if I weren't clutching her hand. Soon we came to a barbwire fence. The top strand was as high as Stacy's chest.

"The border," she said. It amazed me that this was all it was.

"Jack?" she shouted.

A very large man emerged from the darkness across the wire. They had me lie down and wriggle under it while they were on their knees holding up the bottom strand with one hand and pressing down with the other on my back, butt, and legs so the barbs would miss me. Jack took my hand in his huge paw and led me to a car while Stacy vanished in the darkness. She'd told me that to make sure Jack and I got safely away, she would wait in her car for an hour before she turned on the headlights and drove home through Nogales, just another *gringa* who'd spent a few hours south of the border.

Jack drove at a sane speed for an hour or so to a church in Tucson that he called Southside Presbyterian. Inside, a lanky, kindly man with glasses, a mustache, and barely a beard greeted us. Jack introduced him as Reverend John Fife; I would learn later that he was one of the founders of the Sanctuary Movement, that more than thirteen thousand illegal refugees like me would pass through his church, and he would soon be convicted of committing federal crimes for helping us but not be sent to prison. He led me into the church's sanctuary which had a huge, roughly cut, wooden cross at the front. Dozens of *latino*-looking people were at different stages of bedding down on mats on the floor.

"You must be hungry," he said in Spanish. "We all ate about two hours ago, but I'll ask my wife to bring you some supper."

I sat on a chair near the door watching these people on the floor, catching snatches of Spanish through the murmur but no Mam, and wondering what had driven them to leave their homes and which ones had been tortured. I felt safe here and must have dozed when I realized with a start that a *gringa* was standing over me.

"Hola!" she said and offered me a tray with a glass of milk and two warm tortillas wrapped around shredded chicken and salsa. She said she was Maríanne Fife and asked if I needed any medical attention. I told her, with my mouth full, about my burns. She left to fetch some antiseptic, and when I finished eating, she led me to the bathroom and asked if it was all right to lock the door. She said I was healing nicely and didn't need the antiseptic but would probably always be scarred on my breasts and everywhere else they'd burned me. She saw to it I was set for the night on a mat near the edge of the other forms, the first mat and floor I'd slept on since leaving home. The light was dim, and the room almost quiet. I shut my eyes and imagined I was lying beside my family in our hut.

The next morning Maríanne asked me about myself and why I'd fled north and would I like some counseling. I told her I'd been tortured only half a day, so I didn't need it. Later I learned she was not merely curious; she was also judging whether I qualified for going into Sanctuary. She said it usually takes time to place a refugee like me, but Darlene had telephoned her about me from Mexico City, and it happened that a small church in Texas wanted me right away. Would that be all right?

How quick! How wonderful! My face must have lit up. I said yes. Two nuns, a Sister Beatriz and a Sister Judy, who were leaving Tucson the next morning for their Mother House in Concordia, Kansas, said it wouldn't be much out of their way to drop me off. Actually, Fort Worth was about two hundred miles out of their way. So another two days in a car. They helped me with my English as we sped across endless *El Norte*.

The Second Congregational Church of Fort Worth was made of stone and had plenty of trees nearby on land that was as flat as a skillet. A man named Jonathan Barlow met us in the church office, and introduced himself as the chair of their Sanctuary committee. He did not look like a chair, and the sisters explained, in the ladies' room that we dashed to, what *chair* meant. The committee had prepared supper in the parish hall, and one of them offered to put the nuns up for the night. Through the meal and afterwards, we all talked about ourselves and the church. Jonathan translated for me.

I was getting the impression that Catholic nuns ran the Sanctuary Movement. They didn't—for the most part nobody did except maybe the Religious Task Force in Chicago—but I believe to this day that these women religious formed the backbone of the movement. Their Church gave them the freedom they needed to help people in need.

My room was an old Sunday school room next to the kitchen. The committee bought me the food I was used to for myself, and I prepared it for them before our weekly meetings. Much as I still missed home, I would come to love my life and the people I did Sanctuary with at the Second Congo—their nickname. I could write a lot about them, but not here except about my sanctuary work with Jonathan. He was thirty-one years old, divorced, and had two children. His former wife, Vickie, was part of the congregation, and they remained friendly. He was a librarian when he wasn't involved with his kids or Sanctuary. I saw nothing not to like about him, but he was a man, a *gringo*, and about the same age and size as my torturers. There's no reason you shouldn't trust him, I told myself, yet for a long time I didn't and maybe never did completely. Would he try to protect me if the *migra* burst in? I smiled and was pleasant to him but kept my guard up.

My talks at churches and a few schools and other venues around Fort Worth were not as hard as I had feared. Jonathan was most often the one who drove me to them and translated my Spanish to the audience and their questions to me.

At these talks, I would speak first, describe what I knew about the violence in both my countries, and relate my torture and escape. Then my translator would speak briefly about the U.S. role in the violence and the things that citizens might do about it, like discuss it with their family, write letters to their newspapers and Congresspeople, and be sure to vote.

"Criticizing America probably comes best from Americans," Jonathan explained.

"Sounds right to me," I said. "I wouldn't be happy if a *gringo* told me what's wrong with the Maya."

When I reached the torture, I would talk about the questioning and blows and cigarette burns without mentioning my breasts. About the rapes, I'd give no details at all except that I had been a virgin and they hurt. Such horrors as I related seemed to satisfy the audiences. Only much later would I learn that omitting the particulars of the torture went deeper than not wanting to gross out the white faces in the pews below me.

I remember my first Sanctuary talk the most vividly. I was sitting on a raised platform at the front of Saint Mark's Episcopal Church on a hot Saturday afternoon. Maybe fifty men and women were scattered through the pews below me. Jonathan had told me that wearing long shorts would be fine, but I felt exposed, so I kept my knees together and moved them to one side. He was sitting to my right, and to his right was a priest he called

Jim—not a real priest but an Episcopal priest—wearing the white backwards collar and black dickey under a black jacket. As Jonathan and I walked down the aisle, two husky men were lifting the pulpit from the platform to the floor. Now the top part of it hid Jonathan's shins from view, but nothing hid any of me except a red bandana across my lower face. As the moment for the talk approached, I tried not to show my galloping nerves.

The air conditioner hummed faintly. The hum of talk below me ended when Jim stood up. He greeted the upturned faces that I felt looking at my big shiny knees and said, "It's our privilege today to hear from the young lady in the bandana. She wants you to know she is wearing it, not to protect herself, but to protect her family in Guatemala who might be harmed if certain people learn she is here to talk to you. What a world we live in that this can be true! For the same reason, she asked us to call her Emma, which is not her real name. Here to introduce her and say a few words afterwards is our friend Jonathan Barlow, who is the chair of the Sanctuary project at Second Congregational across town."

Jim sat, Jonathan stood, and what he said about me passed in a blur. I know it was short because he told me in car that the audience would be there to hear me, not him. I felt very close to him because he was my only anchor in this sea of *gringo* faces. He had been nothing but kind and supportive from the moment I arrived, but I still didn't trust him and didn't know why. He stopped talking and held out his hand. I took it for a moment—the first time I had let a man hold my hand since before the rapes—and stood up. In his other hand, he held a microphone attached to a cord that Jim had warned us not to trip over.

"Buenas tardes," I said, facing the white faces but only loudly enough for Jonathan to hear. He already knew from our rehearsal what my first words would be. "Thank you for inviting me to your church and coming out on this hot afternoon to hear my story."

Jonathan translated my exact words, "inviting *me, my* story." He told me in the car that he has no patience with interpreters who say, "She thanks you for inviting her," because that shifts the focus to the interpreter. Facing the *gringos* with my hands clasped in front of my shorts, I spoke a few sentences at a time so he could remember to translate them about life in my village, the famine, the bus rides to El Salvador without mentioning that two real priests had helped me, the family I worked for—Jonathan had said I should mention that they were rich but nice—my job with the accountants, my curiosity to learn about the civil war, and my evenings at the university.

I knew the people were waiting to hear about my abduction and torture—they hadn't come to hear a Maya's travelogue—but the worse my ordeal became, the fewer the details I gave them. When I reached the rapes, I simply said, "Both men raped me." There was a slight gasp, from the people who understood Spanish I guess, and a greater gasp when Jonathan translated.

I did not tell them that Señor Rodríguez was the man who rescued me and simply said it was "friends" who got me out of El Salvador and across Guatemala, Mexico, and the Border—no mention of Padre Quiñones or the nuns or the guy who risked his life to drive me from the padre's church. Sometimes I got involved in my story and rambled on too long and Jonathan missed some what I said and I told him what he missed and he translated it like it was the next part of my story.

When I finished, the people clapped. Jonathan spoke briefly about the U.S. support for tortures like mine and the wiping out of Mayan villages like mine and what they, as good citizens, might do about it. There were a few questions, mostly about life in my village—it disappointed me that that's all they seemed to care about—and it was over. The priest handed Jonathan a freewill offering that people had donated on their way out for our Sanctuary work, $86 and some coins. We got in the car. I took off my bandana and breathed freely.

"That wasn't so bad, was it?" Jonathan said.

"Actually it wasn't." I paused. "Next time I'll wear jeans."

"I don't want to scare you," he said, "but there may have been a government spy in the audience. Jim told me there was a face he didn't recognize. Maybe only a passer-by who saw a chance to cool off."

My hand went to my brow. Cold sweat! The *migra* wouldn't have to break in; one of them was inside already! "I'm glad you didn't tell me before. Was I in danger?"

"I don't think so. He was alone. If he approached you, Jim would have stepped in front of him while I hustled you out the back. More likely though, if he was a spy, he wouldn't want to give himself away by trying to arrest you. That's why it's so important not to mention the priests and nuns who helped you. Those governments grab any straws they can to build a case against the Church. And if they knew two priests helped you, they could probably figure out who they were and maybe kill them. They kill priests now and then."

I didn't say anything. I knew from the university that their murder of Padre Rutilio Grande had done much to radicalize Monseñor Romero and their murder of Father Stanley Rother had not bothered the U.S. Embassy in the slightest. I believed that as long as I didn't mention anybody's name or the location of my village, I was the only person my Sanctuary talks could endanger. But, it occurred to me, if I didn't trust Jonathan, why did I tell him about Padres López and Quinones?

I decided, as Fort Worth rolled peacefully past, to keep on giving Sanctuary talks but more carefully than ever. As for Jonathan, it was too late to take back what I'd trusted him with. I hoped all the more that he was what he seemed. A faint shudder shook me.

"Is the air conditioning on too high?" he said.

Naturally, going to all these speaking engagements with Jonathan, we got to know each other well. He became attentive the ways a man does who finds a woman attractive, and I remained polite but distant. He took me places with his children like out for pizza—a wonderful U.S. invention, especially with anchovies—or to a nearby lake, and I even learned to swim though I preferred to sit in a chair and study his daughter's grammar book. He obviously wanted to remarry, but it wouldn't be to me, and I felt a little guilty taking up so much of his time—though it was his choice—when he might be spending it with a more likely prospect. I heard a woman call him "a good catch," but I wasn't fishing. Every man doesn't appeal to every woman, and vice versa, yet I wondered whether I'd find him attractive if those thugs hadn't raped me. A month after I arrived at the church, one of the committee women asked me whether I'd be willing to talk with a psychologist about the hidden ways my awful experience may have marked me.

"People who've been through what you have," she said, "often find therapy helpful. We'd be sure the doctor would be a woman."

"Thank you very much," I said, still speaking in Spanish, "but I feel fine. I'm costing you enough money as it is."

I did not mention the nightmares, which were becoming less frequent. Nor that at barbecues, I would try to stay upwind of the sizzling meat and anyone smoking a cigarette lest the smells throw me back me to Max's cigarettes. Nor that I'd started looking at the men in the congregation and even in my audiences to see whether I could possibly warm up to any of them. Nice as some of them looked, I didn't have the slightest man–woman feeling. I thought back to the men in my village. There was one named Ernesto that I had felt attracted to, but he married someone else. Then I learned in El Salvador that a bomb had killed his wife and children. If I went home and saw him today, would he still attract me? I had no idea.

I would learn later that it was during my time in Texas that María and Germán saved my village and everyone in it except themselves.

During my second year in Fort Worth, the committee was finding it harder to find places for me to speak. From more than a talk a week, it was now less than one a month. And I was growing tired of telling the same story over and over, even though I varied it each time to make it less boring and painful for me. Besides I didn't feel right being this dependent. I had wanted to get a job, as many illegals do, but they said it would be too risky here in Texas. Too many rednecks who'd turn me in, they said. They and I agreed it was time for me to move on.

Jonathan phoned the Chicago Religious Task Force "on behalf of an experienced office worker who wants to live independently and maybe give an educational talk now and then," I heard him say on the phone. The word around the movement was that the feds sometimes tapped our lines, but, I thought, they couldn't arrest him for saying that. Ten days later a man named Michael McConnell called back to say they might have such a job. Sister Beatriz would swing by with the details. Just like that. Drive hundreds of miles. I felt unworthy that these people would do all this for me. Some people said I was brave to risk being deported and killed. That sounded dramatic though I knew it was true. I didn't feel brave, just sad and angry. The U.S.A. was like a huge steamroller with the driver sitting so high up that he couldn't see the people he was crushing.

It was wonderful to see Beatriz again. I greeted her in English. I'd learned enough so that all the committee meetings were now in English, and I'd begun giving my talks in English. The Riverside Church on the Hudson River in Manhattan, she told us, has a refugee family—man, woman, toddler, and baby—living in a small apartment in the tower that serves as the church's steeple. The pastor was an activist named Reverend William Sloane Coffin, who had been one of the movement's famous spokespeople. Everyone knew that the government could have prosecuted him and several parishioners for helping illegals, but it never did. By now he had quieted down, but the church's Sanctuary committee was still active and, Beatriz added, well-connected. I didn't know what *well-connected* meant and visualized the electric hoses that plugged into wall sockets. It turned out to mean that they knew many activists in the U.S. and Central America. Right now they wanted a refugee who could live independently, hold a day job, and sometimes give a talk.

"That sounds lucky for me," I said. "How do I find a job and a place to live?" The idea of Manhattan scared me almost as much as Mexico City had.

"More luck," Beatriz said. "A husband and wife in the congregation run a small law firm. Michael told them your background, and they said they'd take you on as a receptionist. The old one just married a sailor and moved away. It's a dull job, but it pays. As long as no one gives you away, you should be safe. The *migra* don't usually look for illegals in expensive Manhattan law firms."

"Did Michael tell them about me on his Task Force telephone?" I asked. I had become a suspicious person. But working illegally in a scary foreign country, I thought, was enough to make any sensible person suspicious.

"Don't worry, Emma. Michael goes out to a pay phone whenever he makes a sensitive call, and we're quite sure the feds aren't tapping these lawyers' phones.

"Isn't it risky for a law firm to hire an illegal?" Jonathan asked.

"I thought so too, and so did Michael, so he asked Bill Coffin. The lawyers told him, he said, that if he and the Sanctuary committee could risk going to prison for doing the right thing, the least they could do was risk having an illegal on their payroll."

Beatriz didn't rush but didn't waste time. "Tomorrow morning," she said, "why don't I drive you up to Concordia, Kansas? It's where I'm headed, and we'll work out the rest of your trip from there?"

"Where will I live in Manhattan?"

"Their congregation is big and active. You can stay with the family in the tower till they find you a place."

"This is pretty sudden," I said. "I'll be ready by morning." I had dreaded having to say goodbye to these wonderful people, and now I'd be leaving so abruptly that I mostly wouldn't need to.

"This is sudden," Jonathan told me when we were alone. "I'll miss you. So will the kids."

"I'll miss them too. And you," I said, trying to hide my excitement about moving on.

Chapter 24

I sat behind a highly polished wooden desk with a leather top in a windowless room with a blue carpet at 8:30 on the first morning of my job at Sigourney & Sisson. On the wood-paneled walls that surrounded me hung portraits of elderly *gringos,* who I felt watching my every move. My desk faced a pair of glass doors bearing the firm's name in gold letters and a line of elevators outside. If a visitor had a coat or hat, I was to press one of the wooden panels on the wall to release the door of the coat closet. Since it was May, I'd be hanging few coats.

Arranged on the desk were two telephones, a yellow legal pad, a small white note pad, a brown leather cup of sharpened yellow pencils, and on a piece of wood shaped like a Toffler Chocolate box, a brass nameplate that said "Ms. Emma Diaz." Also a sheet with the lawyers' names on the left and little boxes across the page to check them in and out of the office. They'd have to repeat their names till I got to recognize them. The support staff wouldn't start arriving until 9:00 and the lawyers until 9:30, but Ms. Sisson explained while she was showing me around the nearly deserted office the previous afternoon, that somebody had to man the desk by 8:30 to deal with deliveries, the mail, and visitors who came in early because they didn't know any better.

She said I speak English like a native-born American. I think she meant that as a compliment, not realizing that we Maya don't acquire Hispanic accents and I am more of a native-born American than she is.

Sure enough, from a little before nine until a little after, the staff, mostly women, pushed through the glass doors, said "Hi" or "Good morning," and disappeared down the hall to the right or the left behind me. I said "Good morning" with whatever smile I could manage. It's hard to talk and smile at the same time, though women in TV commercials have the knack. I watched a lot of TV in Texas to improve my English. My roommates, women from the Riverside congregation, watched for pleasure.

The firm had thirty lawyers, which seemed like a lot though Ms. Sisson told me it was small for Manhattan. Ten of the lawyers, seven men and three women, were partners, which meant they shared the profits and couldn't be fired unless they messed up badly. Then there were the associates, ten women and ten men on salary. Ms. Sisson told me it was okay if lawyers arrived after 9:30 because what mattered was the jobs they finished. Arriving late usually meant they'd spent the previous evening in the office. Most of the lawyers, I soon learned, were usually still working when I left at 5:30.

By 10:00 I'd checked every lawyer in except a partner named Mr. Marlow. When Ms. Sisson stopped by at 11:00, she told me he was their main litigator—the lawyer who actually went to court—and was arguing a motion before a judge downtown. I would soon learn what this and a lot of other lawyer language meant.

About half an hour later an athletic-looking man with a full head of short black hair and a slender briefcase pushed through the doors. "Good morning," I said with the smile I was already getting better at.

"Hi. I'm Charlie Marlow. You may check me in." He started to turn away, then didn't. "You're Ms. Diaz?" Feeling suddenly shy, I smiled again and nodded yes. "Welcome to Sigourney & Sisson. I hope you'll like it here."

"I'm sure I shall," I started to say, but he was gone. During those few seconds, he struck me as a nice man with more energy than the other lawyers had. Maybe that's what it takes to work in court, I thought. Soon I started checking lawyers out for lunch. My own lunch hour was from 1:00 to 2:00, supposedly the least hectic part of the day, while a stenographers sat at my desk and another one walked me to a lunch counter a block south on 40th Street. "You can usually eat here pretty fast," she said. "That'll give you time to walk around the neighborhood. It's interesting but pricey."

It took me only a few days to stop worrying that the *migra* would push through the glass doors. Some of the people besides Mr. Sigourney and Ms. Sisson probably knew I was illegal, but everybody wrapped me in a cocoon of silence—how much out of kindness or indifference or not to piss off the senior partners, I couldn't guess. I did my best not to piss off any of them lest I provoke an anonymous phone call to the *migra*. I had wondered about the phrase *piss* someone *off* the first time I heard it. What did anger have to do with urination? I stayed in close touch with the Sanctuary folks at Riverside because I liked them and as a precaution I had no idea how to use.

My roommates were friendly enough, though not involved with the church's Sanctuary project except for taking me in after their third roommate left to marry a man in Indiana. One of them sometimes brought a friend home for the night, which was okay with me as long as he rinsed his dishes and put them in the washer in the morning. My share of the rent took more than half my salary.

I came to enjoy my job once I got used to the stretches of boredom. Most of the people seemed nice enough; a few always hurried past and never smiled. Some of them would pause, never for more than a few moments, for small talk. What's *small* about *talk*, I'd wondered? There were many questions I yearned to ask them about themselves and the City and the U.S.A., but I didn't want to pry or take up their time, and small talk is safe talk. Several of them guessed I was from Central America, but none of them seemed to have a clue about what their government was doing to my people. Maybe because of my broad Mayan nose, one of the lawyers asked me whether I'd found a favorite Chinese restaurant yet.

Late one afternoon Charlie Marlow walked in from taking a deposition at another firm. He looked tired but relaxed. There was no one else in the reception room.

"I hope you don't mind my asking," he said. "Do you speak Spanish?"

"*Si, Señor*," I replied, much surprised, and surprised to hear myself ask him in Spanish, "Why do you ask?"

"I was fluent eight years ago, but I'm growing rusty. You look *latina* to me, if you don't mind my saying so"—What if I do mind, I wondered—"and I was hoping if you know Spanish, I could brush up by exchanging our pleasantries *en español*."

"Actually I'm a Maya from Guatemala. Spanish is my second language." I was warming to the idea of speaking it with him, the first I'd spoken since leaving Texas. I wondered whether he was presumptuous to say I look *latina* but glad he didn't take me for Chinese.

"That explains why your English doesn't have a Spanish accent."

So he knows that much about us, I thought happily, but then felt myself blushing over the mistake I realized I'd made. How likely is a Maya from Guatemala *not* to be illegal? "Please don't tell anyone I'm a Maya."

"Your secret is safe with me," he said cheerfully.

I hoped I could believe him. "How did you become fluent?"

"Between college and law school, I served two years in the Peace Corps in Costa Rica. About the best experience I've ever had."

"'Night, Charlie. 'Night, Emma," one of the secretaries said as she breezed towards the doors.

"*Hasta la vista*." He smiled at me and left for his office.

I was aglow. This was the only man in the office I felt any man–woman interest in. We'd had our first conversation, and I was sure there'd be more.

"Goodnight, Mr. Marlow," I said half an hour later.

"Please. Charlie." Another smile, I returned it, and he pushed through the doors.

One afternoon after maybe two weeks of the pleasantries *en español*, he stopped at my desk. "It's very nice sharing these words on the fly. It's bringing back my Spanish, but I'm wondering whether we could have a real conversation over lunch."

"I'd like that," I said. *Wow* is how I felt, but also apprehensive. Was I breaking some unwritten rule?

"How about tomorrow?"

"Fine. I'm off from one to two."

"I know. I'll pick you up at one."

I knew by now that he wasn't actually going to lift me off the floor. It pleased me that though it must take confidence to speak in court, he seemed a bit shy with me.

We sat in a booth in a narrow restaurant after making our way through three blocks of speedy people on Fifth Avenue. Wanting him to talk first, I asked him to tell me about himself. He grew up in Ithaca, which he called an all-American city, in southwestern New York State, went to college at Cornell, which is a big university there, and joined the Peace Corp because he wanted to broaden his outlook, take a break from studying, and do something useful before becoming a lawyer.

"Why did you like the Peace Corps?"

"The comradeship. Being immersed in a new and vibrant culture. Doing work that helped people. Our first big job was assembling flushless toilets in a poor neighborhood, not very romantic, but there was a real need."

Then it was law school, also at Cornell, and a marriage that failed here in the City. I wondered whether he would tell me his version of why it failed, if we got to know each other better. Then it was my turn. Telling him about my family and our village and how we lived, I grew enthusiastic and also homesick. I left out the violence all around us.

"So how did you get from there to here?"

We were walking back on Fifth Avenue. I had expected this question, dreaded it, and was not going to answer it, at least not today, even if my reticence annoyed him.

"It's a long story, and we're almost back." Actually we weren't.

"No problem." He paused. "If you want to tell me later on, that's fine. If you don't, that's fine, too. I'd like to know you better, but I needn't know everything."

"It's a deal." I felt relieved, and also that he knew or suspected I was illegal, but I was fairly certain that he wouldn't turn me in. Was I already beginning to trust him?

We had lunch the next week at the same restaurant, and with our personal stories out of the way, I felt free to deluge him with the questions I'd bottled up about New York and the civilized gadgets that were new to me, and books, movies, TV, life in the United States and its different parts, and whatever he felt free to tell me—which proved to be more than I expected—about the people in the office. My mind was like a dry sponge hungry to soak up information. He seemed pleased to provide it.

When my questioning subsided, we kept on having lunches. I looked forward to them, and he must have too or he wouldn't have kept inviting me. After a short meal one day, we walked up the steps between a pair of gray marble lions and looked in on the New York Public Library, which was a block from the office. On several Saturdays he took me to the Metropolitan Museum of Natural History, the Brooklyn Bridge, which we walked across and back again—during that trip he pointed out the courthouses that he worked in in Foley Square—and a wonderful round trip across New York harbor on the Staten Island ferry. He pointed with pride to the Statue of Liberty. I did not tell him the mixed feelings I had about it.

"There are three worst things about Manhattan," I said one day, "being cut off from Mother Nature, the subway, and the hurry so many people are in."

"There can be only one *worst*," he said. I had asked him to correct my errors.

"Then don't tell anyone I have three worsts."

"Your second secret is safe with me," he said smiling. Would I finish telling him my first secret, I wondered, how I got from a Mayan hut to the canyons of this city? It was looking likely. But not yet.

Around then I gave a Sanctuary talk at Riverside Church for the parishioners who hadn't heard enough from the Salvadoran family in the tower. To my surprise, I spotted Calvin Sigourney and Loretta Sisson sitting near the back. Afterward, they came forward.

"My dear Emma," Mr. Sigourney exclaimed. "We had no idea what you've been through!"

"When Bill Coffin told us you needed a job, that was good enough for us," said Ms. Sisson. "We didn't want to pry."

"We're all in favor of the Sanctuary Movement," said Mr. Sigourney, "and we know that sometimes the less we know the better."

"So when the church bulletin announced your talk, we couldn't miss it." Ms. Sisson paused. "Does Charlie Marlow know what you've told us tonight?"

"Not yet. You're the first people in the office I've told, and Charlie's the only one I'm thinking about telling." So they knew about Charlie and me. I guess every culture enjoys gossip.

"That's right," Mr. Sigourney said with pleasant-sounding authority. "The fewer people down there who know you're undocumented, the better. Everybody here tonight knows it, but they don't know how to find you."

"Charlie's one of our favorites," Ms. Sisson said. "I'm sure you can trust him. It will be nice if he learns someday how brave you are."

I wasn't going to trust him on her say-so, though I was starting to trust him on my own. Twice he asked me to have dinner with him. The first time I told him I was busy. I happened to be giving a Sanctuary talk at the Friends Meetinghouse in Brooklyn. I hadn't told him about these talks and didn't then. The second time he asked I said, "Not yet."

I had been learning what I could about the sexual customs of Americans (I'd stopped calling them *North Americans*) or at least of New Yorkers, and understood that it was common for a young man and woman to take off their clothes and screw when they didn't have any notion of marrying or even know each other very well. I was not ready to do that with Charlie or any other man even though he and I were getting to know each other quite well and I was becoming surprisingly comfortable with him. I even missed him a little when we were apart. The truth was, I feared that if we had dinner and I refused to do it with him, he would stop seeing me.

What a wonderful phrase, *do it* is! Everyone knows that *do it* and *fuck* mean copulate, but there are times it's better to say one and not the other, or maybe use one of the many other words for the deed. Like *doing the deed*, and we all know which deed we're talking about, which has nothing to do with the title to property, for which you say *signing the deed* or *executing the deed*, which does not mean taking the deed's life. Why a word for an essential human function is considered dirty is beyond me. It adds to the mystery that *copulate* is okay and *screw* is in between. Similar usages fit the body parts we do it with. I was noticing, too, that the most common words in English are often the shortest. *God, cat, and, dog,* are four words with three letters *each*, which has four, as do *fuck, do it,* and *four. We* in Spanish is *nosotros*, three syllables, eight letters. I don't know whether these word games were helping my English, but they were *mine* (four letters) and they were *fun* (three). I asked Charlie about many phrases, but saved the ones about sex for my roommates, maybe with a glass of wine, which I liked better than *guaro*. Why, I wondered, I was playing word games about doing it?

Would Charlie take my saying no to dinner as meaning I was refusing to sleep with him. (How different are *sleep* and *sleep with*, the one so passive, the other so active.) That's why I said *not yet* instead of *no*. I supposed after I'd said it that Charlie probably took *not yet* as meaning *yes but later*. Was it possible I'd come to want sex with him? Back in Texas, Jonathan and I had been close, but I never considered doing it with him, though I'm sure he considered it with me. Men are so transparent sometimes. One thing I felt for certain: I'd have to really trust Charlie before we'd do it. Fond as I was of him—and growing fonder all the time—distrust still lingered in my heart. Maybe I was born to distrust men, or maybe the torturers put it into me along with their semen. I don't know which, but I couldn't be fair to Charlie or myself until I overcame it—unless I just crashed ahead, which I wasn't going to do. I wished I could talk about it openly with him, but I could not do that before I had a better idea of what I felt. I was not used to being confused about my feelings.

Then there were my nipples. The first time I looked at them in a mirror in Texas, the ragged red scars from the cigarette burns disgusted me. What the men accomplished by burning me *there*, of all places, defied my understanding. But the nipples were only two spots on my okay breasts, and the bruises were gone from the rest of my female terrain. The male sex drive overcomes many things. These ugly welts? Boobs are a big deal in the U.S.A. and mine wouldn't pass inspection. I'd try to figure out a way for Charlie to get used to my whole body before he had to see them. Damn the electric lights in his apartment! A Mayan hut after dark would be ideal.

Luck delivered an opportunity to maybe end my distrust of Charlie quite soon. My Sanctuary friends at Riverside had news from my village. The army had given them a terrible choice, and María saved all the others by shooting our friend Germán! *My God!* I thought. Then she joined the guerrillas to avenge what the army made her do. María! Germán! The news stunned me. My precious little sister. Though I hadn't seen her in four years, I thought of her often. Now I lay awake far into the night going over and over what I'd learned and what may have happened since. I had to know more. But how?

The answer came at lunch a few days later when Charlie said, "You know how much the Peace Corps meant to me." I nodded. "Before I met you, this was the year I'd planned to take my vacation in Costa Rica and see my old friends."

"That sounds wonderful. If you're going to do it, you'd better arrange it soon." This was July, and his vacation was coming next month.

"I guess I've hesitated because I'd miss you."

His word lit a warm glow I me. "I'd miss you too," I didn't mind admitting, "but it wouldn't be for long. Who knows when you'll have another chance?"

"Right! I'll phone some people down there and ask my secretary to make the reservations this afternoon."

"It's good we brushed up your Spanish."

"I tried to get Annie to go with me, or not make a fuss if I went alone, but she wouldn't do either. We had quite a scene." I couldn't imagine Charlie having a scene. "One of the many reasons the marriage failed."

I would have found this glimpse into his divorce more interesting, and maybe try to prompt him to tell me more about it, if the light bulb, as you say, had not gone on inside my head. "Since you're going to be in the neighborhood, do you suppose you'd like to stop off for a day or two in beautiful Guatemala?"

"How interesting. Tell me more."

Wanting to be honest but not confide my history yet, I spoke more carefully than usual. "I received some terrible news from home. It's a year old, but I just heard it last Sunday. My friends at Riverside told me my little sister shot a friend named Germán to keep the army from wiping out our village. Then she joined the guerrillas, which few people survive. It's hard to believe this could have happened, but I'm very afraid it did. If you're going to Costa Rica, maybe you'd enjoy seeing Guatemala and finding out."

"I don't think I could go to your village."

Wonderful!

"You wouldn't have to. Before I left home, my Aunt Sara was taking several women's weavings to Guatemala City and selling them on the patio outside the Camino Real Hotel. Many Americans stay there. If I could get word to her when you'd be there, maybe she could meet you." I paused. "I'm not sure about her Spanish, but a friend we call Old Pablo usually accompanies her. He could translate."

"So you can maybe arrange for me to meet your Aunt Sara. I don't want to sound wimpy, but an American woman who lives in Costa Rica told me Guatemala is too dangerous to visit. I know the information means a lot to you. I need to think about it."

"Of course you do. I don't want you risking yourself to satisfy my curiosity. It was dangerous in the Western Highlands when I left four years ago, and if the news about María is true, then it was last year. How it is in Guatemala City, I don't know. We can ask the U.S. Embassy. My friends at church may know."

Now he's going to really wonder, I thought, why it took me four years to get from there to here. I think I trust him enough to tell him. If he may be stopping in Guatemala for me and I'm thinking of sleeping with him, telling him my story is the least I can do. But not here, where our waitress and several customers are getting to know us.

"I'm inclined to say yes," Charlie said. "If other Americans are safe at that hotel, why not me? You're right, who knows when there'll be as good a chance to see those friends. But I want to sleep on it and check with the embassy."

"I'm so glad you're considering it. I'll check with my friends tonight." Did those friends in Costa Rica include the woman who warned him against visiting Guatemala?

We were walking towards the zippy throng on Fifth Avenue when I took the plunge. "I'd like to tell you the rest of my story, only please don't tell anyone else."

"I promise. I've been hoping you would."

"A famine hit the district my village is in in 1984, and because I'd started to learn Spanish, our priest was able to give my family one less mouth to feed by getting me a job as a maid near San Salvador. A year and a half of that was more than enough, so I became a girl Friday for some accountants in the city. No problem yet, but I wanted to learn about the political situation and the civil war—which is still going on—so I started attending discussions in the Jesuit university."

"Are you a Catholic?"

"Not really, and I didn't talk with any of the priests. If you seek the truth about El Salvador, the security forces think you're a Communist. One morning two secret policemen kidnapped me off the sidewalk and questioned me about the people I'd been talking with at the university. They beat me. They burned me with cigarettes. Many times." I hesitated. I was quite sure Charles would not consider me damaged goods for being raped, but if I was wrong, my next words might drive him off. "They raped me."

"Oh, my poor Emma!" He stopped walking and faced me. "Let me give you a gentle hug."

He embraced me as strangers hurried past. I felt such relief that he was not put off but drawn to me. His hug was so gentle, and I found my arms going around him, my hands on his back. What a relief that I liked his body against mine! As we continued walking, he was holding my hand.

"How did you survive?"

"I can't explain it. Suddenly the man of the family I'd worked for was in the room. He ordered the torturers out and took me to a priest who helped me flee the country." We dropped hands as we turned into the street where our office was. I reached the point where I crossed into Arizona as we entered the building's lobby.

"To be continued," Charles said. "May we have lunch tomorrow?"

That evening my friends at Riverside told me that Charlie should be safe for a couple of days' visit if he stuck to the Camino Real and the tourist sites. Could they get word to Sara and Old Pablo in time to meet him? It would be tight. Even if they still sold weavings at the hotel, they'd probably have to make a special trip in order to meet him. I thought they'd do it. My friends needed Charlie's dates by tomorrow if he was onboard. And they had a few more safety tips for him.

Much as I wanted to know what had happened at home, especially about María and Germán, I didn't want to put Charlie in danger. Yet I couldn't help thinking that if he would do this for me, how could I not trust him.

Chapter 25

Back in my apartment on Riverside Drive, I sat at the window and watched the sky redden as the sun set beyond the Hudson River and flat New Jersey. Daylight and the dark of night hold us in the present, I reflected, but the red flame of sunrise and sunset burns away the scrim that separates us from the ages. Hendrick Hudson and his crew of the *Half Moon* plied the gray waters below me three and a half centuries ago, or were they there right now in the shadow of the Palisades that rose from the far bank? Gazing past the river dark beneath the crimson sky, I saw the land roll on across the eastern states and vast Southland to the farms and wastes and teeming cities of Mexico where, during the century before the *Half Moon* bobbed across the Atlantic, the Spanish conquistador Hernán Cortés vanquished the Aztecs and dispatched Pedro Alvarado with his guns and war dogs, his horses and diseases, to subdue the Maya in a quest for gold and slaves and converts to the One True Faith. In that land, great green volcanoes climbed into the sky above the surrounding mountains, and in the jungles the steep-stepped stone pyramids of the Maya rose to once-bloody altars. Descendants of that wise and mysterious people were still the Maya, but stripped of much of their culture and all their power by haughty worshipers of the humble Christ. From this impoverished and demeaned majority of that nation came this brave and fascinating woman who attracted and challenged me.

Another war was raging in her land. It was more a slaughter than a war, I knew though not from most media. God forbid that they should report the U.S. support for mass murder in a tiny neighbor. My main source was the *National Catholic Reporter.* Someone had shown me several copies of it while I was in Costa Rica. Later I subscribed to it, not for Church news, but to learn what was really happening in the embattled countries north of Costa Rica. I was interested, too, to read about the Pledge of Resistance, the Sanctuary Movement, and others who were resisting the U.S. support.

One Saturday before I met her, I was browsing in the photography section in the gorgeous old Scribner's Bookstore on Fifth Avenue and came across a book called *Guatemala: Eternal Spring, Eternal Terror* by a young photo-journalist named Jean-Marie Simon,. Her photos showed a spectacular land and grim war. I felt attracted and repelled. I've long been drawn to the places of dream-like beauty that I'd see in travel books and the *National Geographics,* a pile of which grew in a corner of my bedroom, a monument to opportunities not taken. But I'd never seen a dead person or even a good picture of one, and here was a photo of a naked woman with her hands lying on her chest where someone laid them after cutting them off her arms. I bought the book, and after studying the beauty of the land and Simon's account of the state terrorism, I resolved that if I finally returned to Costa Rica, I'd try to stop in Guatemala and see what I could while staying away from the danger zones. How little I knew!

Emma may have been asking me —and her Aunt Sara and her companion as well—to take a slight risk to satisfy her curiosity about an event that was over and no one could alter. (I'd soon see it wasn't over.) But was her dear María the hero she'd heard she was? Had María done the right thing under the circumstances? Did their parents and Germán's widow and the rest of the villagers agree? The more I reflected, the easier it was to see how much it meant to Emma to learn what happened. I could be her link to all she'd lost and yearned to return to. How risky could it be for a *gringo* to buy a few native artifacts and chat with the *indios* who sold them at a U.S.-owned hotel, simply one of many tourists wondering about their culture and how they made their stuff?

Yet if Emma were not beginning to mean a lot to me, I might not be considering it now that I knew it would not be risk-free. I probably wouldn't do it for the firm's previous receptionist. Like most people, I play it safe most of the time. When should I punch through my caution and take a chance? I'd be doing a good friend a favor that meant a lot to her, and the idea of a nearly riskless adventure caught my imagination.

As the sky darkened beyond the river, I wondered where my relationship with Emma was going. Where did I want it to go? Like most men I believe, my default position is mild interest in many women, and when infatuation or love comes along, it narrows to an intense interest in one woman. I seemed to be narrowing on Emma. All I'd intended was to sharpen my Spanish, but I found her so alive and unaffected, so curious about so many things and how they worked. I enjoyed her company so much. We got along so well. She asked about everything, and I enjoyed explaining what I could. Though I had come to desire her, I thought too much of her and the values I sensed were hers to simply seek an affair that, at best, would cool down to a friendship if she stayed at the office afterwards. She often spoke of wanting to return to her village—where I could never follow her beyond a short visit, addicted as I am to books and indoor plumbing—but with a mind as inquiring as hers, could she ever go home after these years in an increasingly wider world? Return to no books, TV, supermarkets?

How do you tell the difference between love and infatuation before it's over? That I was even thinking like this brought home the possibility that I might want to spend the rest of my life with her. Really? Too early to tell, but I didn't rule it out.

Why don't you cut the bullshit, Charlie, and trust your feelings? But that's what I'd done with Annie. Those who don't learn the lessons of history, a great philosopher once said, are condemned to fuck up again.

Chapter 26

During lunch the next day, Charlie told me he would do it. I was delighted and said so. He was quite excited about it and so, he said, were his friends in Costa Rica. He realized his stop in Guatemala should be on his way home, so as to give Sara and Old Pablo as much lead time as possible. So, two days to talk with them after eleven days in Costa Rica. Unless what my friends had told me last night dissuaded him, he said, he'd ask his secretary this afternoon to book his flights.

"I talked to a woman in the embassy's consular office this morning," he said. "The U.S. has a travel advisory for Guatemala, meaning a warning, but she said if I stick to the touristy places, I should be perfectly safe. I am to tell her when I'll be there and where I'm staying."

"My friends think you'll be safe too," I said, "but they told me some precautions you should take that make me wonder."

"Like what?"

"Call the embassy, which you've already done. Try to get a letter from a senator or congressman that you'll carry in your pocket. All it needs to say is, 'Have a nice trip, and tell me if I can help,' but it will be on their official gold letterhead, and what it really says is, 'If you mess with this guy, we'll make trouble.' The people who might mess with you work for government, which generally yields to U.S. pressure."

"This takes me somewhat aback. Anything else?"

"You should carry the number of the local Peace Brigades office to phone if you need help, but be careful what you say because their line is tapped and probably yours will be at the hotel. The secret police do that routinely with American guests."

"So if I need help, maybe I can't use a phone. This is beginning to sound like a movie I can't walk out of. What's Peace Brigades?"

"A group of Americans, Canadians, and other internationals who accompany local activists —meaning stick to them—who are at high risk of being killed by the security forces in Guatemala, El Salvador, and several other countries. These people are only armed with a notebook and a camera, but their presence has apparently kept a number of activists alive. They say they aren't political, but protecting people whom officials want to kill makes that a hard sell."

We could not know that a year from now, the Peace Brigades office in Guatemala City would be bombed and two of its members would be stabbed on a sidewalk.

"So these people take these chances and they're still alive." Charlie said. "If they can do that day in, day out, the least I can do is be a tourist for two days and maybe buy some weavings. I'd like to see this 'land of eternal spring' whether Sara and Old Pablo show up or not."

"That's so nice of you, and brave too. But there's one more factor I should mention—while we're walking back."

"Only one more? What a relief."

It was my turn to pick up the check. The July sun shone down on Fifth Avenue, a hot, humid day.

"I haven't told you the rest of my story. There may be danger for you if the secret police know we're friends."

"The only people who know it are the people in the restaurant," he said, "and everybody in the office. But I'd like to hear the rest of your story."

I filled him in on the Sanctuary Movement and what I did in Texas and was doing here, denouncing the Guatemalan and Salvadoran's campaigns of terror while my sponsors denounced the U.S. support. While I'd feared his response to the rapes, I was quite sure that, unlike some of his law partners, he'd be okay with my Sanctuary talks.

"So if the Immigration and Naturalization Service busts you, they'll probably send you back to where you'll pay the price for denouncing the terror. You brave, brave woman! Let me hug you again."

This time we embraced longer and harder, and I liked it even better. It didn't matter that he's much taller than I. A passerby shouted, "Right on!"

"I'm beginning to like this," I said as we separated. "But now that you know what the secret police may know—that you're keeping company with a woman who's probably on a death list—do you think visiting Guatemala is too risky?"

"A risk that exists whether or not I see your Aunt Sara. I'm glad you told me. I've read about Sanctuary and admired the refugees who risk so much to denounce the Terror. I'm so, so proud of you for doing it! Which I hadn't suspected"—he lowered his voice—"though I was fairly certain you were undocumented."

I was glad he said *undocumented* and not *illegal*. Unfortunately, we had reached our building and had to drop the subject.

So my being violated by other men didn't alienate him, and neither did my Sanctuary talks—in fact they drew him to me—but as we rode up in the elevator, I still didn't know whether he'd do me the favor I'd asked for, and whether I'd be less drawn to him if he wouldn't. No worries, Brenda Emma! As he was leaving my desk, he said, "I'll have my secretary reserve the flights and a room at the Camino Real."

On a Saturday morning three weeks later, he drove us to the Newark Airport and left his car in the long-term parking lot. In his jacket were letters from his congressman and one senator. We still hadn't heard whether Sara and Old Pablo would meet him. At the gate, another embrace and this time a lasting kiss!

"*Vaya con Dios!*" I shouted after him. I was twenty-four, and this was my first real kiss. Many girls I grew up with must have finished nursing their children by now, if my village still existed.

Knowing I wouldn't see Charlie next week and the next, I missed him keenly. I asked one of my roommates how the pill works, just in case. She giggled and said she was happy for me. I visited her doctor, and he assured me that seven days after I started taking them I'd be protected—another strange term, *protected* from having a precious baby sucking at my nipples if they still functioned. I had thought of a plan to keep them from grossing Charlie out, but I wasn't ready to mention it until I'd done some research. I got the doctor's prescription filled right away, but nothing would happen unless I felt safe with Charlie. Did I? As his return date approached, the package from the drugstore stood unopened on my dresser.

Chapter 27

Visiting my friends in Costa Rica was all I had hoped for. The August weather in San José, which sits at four thousand feet between two oceans, was warm and fair except for the brief afternoon showers. A family of old friends—their children now well into their teens—and I drove to the coast for a weekend by the warm Pacific where we frolicked in the surf all afternoon wearing T-shirts against the fierce sun, then settled into rocking chairs on a terracotta tile veranda to enjoy *cervezas* as the sun sank into the ocean.

I had lunch with the friend who had warned me against going to Guatemala. We'd had a torrid affair about half way through my time in the Peace Corps and occasional encores thereafter. I found her still single and taking her pleasure as it came along, but I told her I was in a relationship at home and would have to pass. She took the rebuff as calmly as I'd expected and asked me to please be very careful in Guatemala.

On landing at the Aurora Airport, I saw, as she had told me, that before reaching customs, the Guatemalan passengers had to pass through one corridor and everyone else through another, making it easy for the secret police to disappear arriving Guatemalans without attracting foreigners' attention. In the lobby of the hotel, I noticed several men in brown uniforms who could pass for bellhops but were security men who worked with the secret police. If I act like other tourists, I almost convinced myself, they probably won't pay me much heed. Relax, Charlie, enjoy your *cerveza,* the chatter in English of the foursome at the next table, and the local food sampler the waiter deftly set before me.

The next day was bright and sunny. I hadn't put in a wakeup call and didn't finish breakfast until around 9:30. Sure enough, on the concrete patio outside the main entrance, a small woman in Mayan garb sat before an array of gorgeously colored weavings—skirts, shawls, wallets, purses, belts, blouses, and table runners. I asked her in Spanish if she was Sara. We had neglected to arrange a more subtle way to identify each other, though Emma had told me that Sara knew her as Brenda.

"Si, Señor," she said and nodded to an old guy in a white shirt and cowboy hat who was lounging nearby. He ambled over.

"Old Pablo?"

"Si."

I inquired about the weavings, examined some, set aside a few, and asked Sara to hold a few others that I'd decide on tomorrow. All the while, Old Pablo, facing away from a nearby man in the brown uniform, was telling me what had happened in their village since Emma left, while a small recorder spun in my breast pocket.

In short order, Old Pablo confirmed what we'd heard about María, Germán and the terrible choice the army had forced on the village: "It was on the first day of María's wedding to Ernesto. She was very strong and saw the reality that none of us wanted to see. She persuaded us all, even Germán, what had to be done."

"Did she persuade the whole village?"

"There wasn't time to assemble them. The six of us had to decide, and Germán of course. It was a terrible responsibility."

"Who were the six? Brenda will want to know."

Old Pablo lifted his hat and rubbed a kerchief across his brow while, I suppose, he searched his memory. "María, Ernesto, Sara and me, Frida, and Ana. María was the one who shot the rifle when the rest of us didn't have the courage. She was full of fury—I never saw her fury before—and left us to join the guerrillas and avenge Germán. Maybe Frida joined them too. She left the village when María did, and we haven't heard anything about her."

I bought several exquisite gifts, including a mostly purple vest for Emma and a red, indigo, green, and violet weaving to hang on a wall in my mostly undecorated apartment. As I headed inside with my loot, I nodded and smiled at the man in brown who'd been watching us, and he returned my smile. Up in my room, I turned off the cassette recorder after checking to make sure that Old Pablo's words had come through, and thrust it into a trouser pocket lest anyone search the room while I was out.

When I left for downtown, Sara was talking with another *gringo* and Old Pablo was lounging nearby. The brown uniform seemed to know he was only there to help her and maybe translate for inquisitive tourists like me, and he didn't bother him. My bus to the Central Square swayed down the broad Avenida Reforma past the large U.S. Embassy and the Old Politécnica military academy, which looked like a quaint little fort but which, I would learn, was a notorious torture site where a year from now an American missionary named Sister Dianna Ortiz would be interrogated, burned with cigarettes, and gang-raped. It rained that afternoon longer than the afternoon rains in Costa Rica.

The next morning was again bright and sunny. As I emerged onto the patio, I notice several limousines parked along the curb for some sort of meeting that was going on in the hotel. The drivers and men I took to be bodyguards sat in them or lounged against them. They all seemed relaxed. I examined each weaving I'd asked Sara to put aside while Old Pablo told me that about a year after María joined the guerrillas, they heard she had been killed in a firefight with the army high on the side of the *Volcán Tajumulco*, in the west near the Mexican border. They heard she had fought fearlessly, and old Pablo knew that the brave ones often die soon. But he was never able to verify the report of her death. Her parents hoped she was still alive, but they often grieved.

Nearly all the villagers, he said, had come to understand that María had saved them. It meant a great deal to them, above all to Lourdes, that Germán had agreed with what had to be done. A few people criticized María at first, but she was quickly gone. Everyone feared, of course, that the army would come back and kill them all. It happened often and was a common fear among the Maya in that region. I knew that the army had admitted destroying more than four hundred villages. It would turn out to be many more.

"Ernesto helps to care for Germán's widow and their children," Old Pablo continued, "to be the man of her hut, though he always returned to his own hut to sleep. Her youngsters called him '*tio*'—'uncle'—and for him they were almost becoming the children that he and María would never have. No one, though, could replace the children he lost to the bomb. He and Lourdes sometimes sat together in front of her hut and talked into the evening, but both were too immersed in their grief for more to happen."

Sara and Old Pablo were now happily married. When I looked at them closely, they were not as old as I had thought.

I paid for my second day's purchases, and Sara was putting them into a large paper bag when we witnessed a horrifying attack. An army officer in a camouflage uniform emerged from the hotel with several men in business suits. Old Pablo whispered that this was the colonel of their district, the one who had directed the lieutenant to give the villagers their awful choice.

The officer was about to pass beside me when I heard a rush of air. A huge black and white eagle plunged out of the sky towards the colonel. Glancing upwards, he cringed and raised his arms to protect himself. To no avail. Squawking loudly, the great bird drove its talons into his shoulders. The man screamed. His knees buckled, but the broad wings beat the air—I felt the breezes on my face—and he did not fall. The great yellow beak struck again and again at his face.

"Help me! Help me!" he shouted, but the men in suits backed away.

His hands went up to cover his eyes. The great bird lifted a foot from his shoulder and slid the talons into his neck. Still thrusting at his face—which distracted him, I realized later—it ripped from his ear to his shoulder a red chunk trailing what looked like a big string of spaghetti.

Croaking exultantly and clutching the dripping chunk, it flapped its wings faster and rose past the curved facade of the hotel. A man beside a limousine fired a pistol at the fast-moving mass of feathers and talons, and I heard a crack as the bullet struck a window high on the hotel's facade.

I looked back at the colonel. Red jets spurted from his neck. He staggered in a little dance looking oblivious. The men in suits stood frozen as his blood arced into a widening pool on the pavement. Red ran down from gashes in his cheeks. He looked at his bleeding hands, held one of them to his mouth, and spit out blood. The spurts from his neck weakened.

I was so close that I could have gone to the man and pressed my handkerchief against the gash in his neck, but I didn't and would be glad I hadn't when I realized that if I had, a bodyguard might have thought I was attacking him and shot me.

The colonel collapsed onto the red and gray pavement. He seemed at last to realize he was bleeding out. A hand went to his neck too late. But what could he or anyone of us have done after the eagle carried off so much of his carotid artery? His hand dropped to the pavement as more blood oozed from his neck.

"That was María," Sara said softly in Spanish.

A crowd of men in suits, drivers, bodyguards, and brown uniforms from inside the hotel gathered around the body. Sara and Old Pablo collected up her wares and vanished casually down the sidewalk. I took the hint and casually hurried to my room to look downwards at men in uniform photographing the body. Several firemen drove up in a truck and carted it off, as firemen did with bodies on the streets of Guatemala City. Two hours later I ate lunch in the hotel restaurant, noticing that there and in the lobby everyone was acting was though nothing has happened.

I'd done with touring and lay on my bed. Scenes of the man's bloody death played and replayed through my mind. That night a dream terrified me but vanished as I awoke.

The next morning, I felt great relief as my plane took off. The flights to and from Miami were reassuringly uneventful. Emma greeted me with a warm hug as I walked from the ramp in Newark after a bumpy landing.

With her long black hair splashing on her tan shoulders and the strap of her sleeveless blue sundress, she looked wonderful.

"I'm so relieved," she exclaimed as she took my hand and pulled me towards the wide corridor that bustled with hurrying people like an enclosed city sidewalk. "There's an empty boarding area right down here where you can tell me all about it. Did you see Sara and Old Pablo?"

"Both mornings."

"Perfect!"

"Are you cold." The terminal's air conditioning made it, as usual, frigid. "I have a sweater in my carry-on."

"I'm fine. Here we are. What happened?"

I related my meetings with Sara and Old Pablo. Tears rolled down her cheeks as I told her about the village and María. Suddenly she clung to me and sobbed against my shoulder. "I knew she was dead," she said after a few minutes. "This makes it real."

We put our heads together so we could both listen to the cassette recorder. "That's really them," she said as she heard their voices. "Oh, my poor, brave sister! I had no idea she was so strong…. Our poor parents!" She was weeping again. "I hope she's still alive… but I don't think so."

She drew back as the tape erupted with the sounds of the eagle attacking and men shouting. "What's that?"

"The most terrifying thing I've ever seen. A huge eagle plunged out of the sky and killed an army officer not ten feeet from where I stood. I'm thankful it wasn't me she attacked."

"My God! She?"

"She was too big to be a male. Sara said the dead man was the colonel who gave your village its terrible choice. She thinks the eagle was María."

"Is that all she said about it?"

"We didn't have time to talk. She and Old Pablo packed up and left quickly. So did I. I didn't want the police to question me. I'm sure they didn't either."

"If Sara's right about the eagle, María is surely dead."

"Not likely. Dead people don't come back as birds."

"You're so *norteamericano*. There's more going on than you realize."

"We do have cultural differences," I said lightly. "Shall we find baggage claim?"

She took my arm and off we walked, dodging the speedy people—new venue, same problem. Before boarding the bus to my car, we ate supper in a not-bad TGIF. Sitting across the little table, I filled her in on my stay in Costa Rica and how much she might enjoy the Pacific surf now that she knows how to swim. She told me the doings at the office, which weren't many. Before I dropped her off at her apartment, she said she'd been thinking about an adventure we might consider. She hoped to finish her research and tell me about it by Monday. Adventure? Research? I could hardly wait.

Chapter 28

Like many Manhattan activities, litigation slows down during the summer, and on Monday morning there wasn't much on my desk that demanded attention. I had a trial scheduled for early October between companies that weren't likely to settle; but there'd be few witnesses. After jury selection, the trial should take only a day or two, and I needn't start preparing before Labor Day. Which was arriving next weekend. One o'clock came slowly. Emma and I ordered our lunches, and I looked across the table expectantly. She reached into her purse, which she seldom carried, and placed between us a tattered L. L. Bean catalogue.

"Have you ever camped in a tent?"

"Two or three times in Costa Rica. Never here."

"Have you ever been to Vermont?"

"Not yet. It's on my list."

"I hear its mountains look a lot like Guatemala except no volcanoes." She blushed. "I was wondering whether you'd like to go tent-camping there."

"What a lovely idea! That would be delightful!"

Her blush deepened. "Vermont's small but long. Some friends at church told me there's a really nice campground called Winhall Brook that's not very far into it."

"Have you picked out a tent in that catalogue?"

She flipped to a page and turned it around to show me. "That one," she said, pointing to the biggest of several tents. "It's quite expensive, but if we split it, it won't cost so much."

"And I suppose Bean sells propane stoves and battery-operated lamps and sleeping bags and some sort of mattress to go under them." She smiled and nodded. "When do you want this adventure?"

"How about next weekend or the weekend after?"

The sweetheart! I was starting to feel adventurous already. "Next weekend is Labor Day, which would give us three days, but the campground may be full and I don't know whether Bean can get us the stuff that fast. I'll call and ask the campground if they still have a decent tent site. If they do, I'll ask Bean to expedite the shipping."

The woman on the phone told me there were a few free sites quite remote from the bathhouse and toilets. "That's fine," I said. Knowing how tents heat up in the sun, I asked for the shadiest site. The woman said we might want to bring bathing suits since the brook that runs through the campground was quite warm.

The package from Bean awaited in the lobby when I returned home from work on Thursday. As I drove up to Emma's building early Saturday morning, she was standing on the sidewalk with her suitcase beside her and in her hand a paper bag holding the PB&J's she'd made for lunch. The urban sprawl along the north shore of Long Island Sound amazed her; and after the turn in New Haven from I-95 to I-91, she enjoyed the hills and greenery, especially in the rather modest Holyoke Range of mountains in Massachusetts. Leaving the Interstate in Brattleboro, we stopped at a supermarket, bought food for the rest of the weekend, and headed northwest into the mountainous heart of Vermont. This was new territory for me too, and quite beautiful. The Green Mountains are neither tall nor rocky, but I found them—I searched for the word—*comfortable*. Not comfortable, of course, if you are lost on one at two a.m. and thirty below, but that wouldn't be us.

We checked in at the campground, found our tent site, which would soon be shaded by nearby trees, unloaded our gear onto the picnic table—every site had a picnic table—and spread out the tent on the flattest part of the grass. I had usually been the one to explain stuff to Emma, but we were both beginners at erecting this modern lightweight tent that was a big improvement on the canvas Peace Corp tent I'd camped in before. We worked well together though we had to keep checking the instructions. At the center, the tent was high enough for Emma to stand upright. But not me.

"Let's explore," she said, "and take our bathing suits in case we want to swim."

As we set off down the dirt road to the bathhouse, I was holding a shopping bag with our bathing suits and towels in one hand and Emma's hand in the other. Though no one had taken a site near ours, we were soon passing one tent after another. Couples were sitting outside, children were playing, and beside a big tent people pranced in a lively game of volleyball. After using the toilets in the bathhouse, we followed the sound of laughter through a grove to the stream in which two families were splashing around. The water ran no deeper than my waist.

"That looks like fun," said Emma. "Shall we try it?"

When she emerged from her side of the bathhouse, she was wearing a modest but fetching one-piece black bathing suit with a little skirt on it. I wanted to hug her again, but didn't. We swam with leisurely strokes against the warm current, staying abreast of the same rocks and trees on the shore, and finally left the water on the same muddy path. We changed in the bathhouse, and back at the tent, spread our wet suits on the hood of the car to dry. Emma had suggested laying them on the roof, but I was afraid we'd forget about them the next time we drove someplace.

"You must be tired," she said. "Shall we take a little nap?"

"Now that you mention it…"

We unrolled our sleeping bags side by side on the fabric floor without bothering to blow up the mattress. It was warm enough inside the tent to lie on top of them in our summer clothes. We leaned towards each other on our elbows for a little kiss, and I must have fallen right to sleep. The next thing I knew, I was alone and Emma was bustling about the table outside. She must have unzipped and zipped the mosquito netting without waking me, spread the oilcloth tablecloth, filled the plastic water bag at the faucet by the dirt road, and screwed the LP bottle to the Coleman stove. I put on my shoes and worked the zipper. At its buzz, she turned and watched me crawl out.

"Are you rested?"

"I think so. How can I help?"

"Open the clams." Our entrée was to be spaghetti with minced clam sauce. "Take the grapes down to the faucet and rinse them. Get out the lamp—I think it'll be dusk before we finish. And uncork the wine. I won't boil the water until we've had our appetizers." Which were unsalted peanuts, crackers, and Vermont sharp cheddar.

"It's wonderful to be back on the land," she said, as we put aside our empty spaghetti plates and turned to a bunch of red grapes and the zucchini bread she'd baked in Manhattan. She reached across the table and took one of my hands in both of hers. "As the light fades, we can be anywhere we want. Look at what's left of the red in the sky. You and I are sitting with my parents and María, poor brave María, in front of the family hut, and I'm translating your English into Mam and back again so you and they can start to know each other. They've arranged to spend the night at friends' so we can have the hut to ourselves—like here tonight."

We squeezed hands and stood up. She put the forks and dishes into a big pot and poured water on them while I closed the stove and unscrewed the LP hose. I picked up the lamp and followed her crawling into the tent, then zipped the opaque flap shut, letting the bug net hang loose inside.

"Would you switch off the lamp? I want it to be as dark as it is in my family's hut."

We faced each other on our knees pressing our bodies gently together, our hands roaming each other's backs, her hands reaching my buttocks before mine reached hers. Backing off a bit, she unbuttoned my shirt and pushed it off my shoulders. I started to lift her shirt and was momentarily perplexed to feel her hands on mine gently stopping me.

"There's something I need to tell you," she said with a slight quaver. "My nipples aren't normal. They're all massive scars from the cigarette burns."

She caught her breath as though she feared how I'd take it now that she'd said it. "I'm so sorry," I said. "Do they hurt?"

"Not any more. But they don't look very nice."

"It doesn't matter. I want to kiss them."

She gave a little gasp and released my hands. I lifted her shirt off her upstretched arms and bent down and kissed each nipple slowly, and straightened up and hugged her to me, loving the warmth of her breasts against my belly.

We separated again and she undid my belt and button and zipper. It was a bit of a trick to push my pants and underpants past my erection, but she managed.

"I brought condoms," I said, "just in case."

"That's not necessary. I started taking the pill before you returned, just in case."

Naked now in the dark, we continued to explore each other's bodies.

"That's where they put the electricity on me." I withdrew my hand. This was the first time I'd heard her say that electric shocks were part of her torture. "That's all right," she said. "It doesn't hurt now."

Later she would not remember mentioning the electricity. I gently returned my hand. We wouldn't need the K-Y jelly I'd brought just in case.

"Let me be on top," she said and in a moment she was. It felt wonderful to hold her and slide inside her, and soon my whole body felt wonderful longer and stronger than I ever remember.

"Oh, Charlie, thank you, thank you. I've been so afraid the rapes would make me hate it. I don't. I like it. A lot."

"I'm afraid I came too quickly for you to get much out of it."

"I loved it just now, I still love it, and"—in the darkness I could hear the smile in her voice—"the night is young."

After the second time, which was better for her and just as strong for me, we tried to sleep in each other's arms, but couldn't get comfortable. So she lay prone and I lay against her with a leg over her warm legs and an arm across her back. Soon she was breathing the regular breaths of sleep.

Ever the lawyer, I kept on thinking. Part of how good it felt must have been because I wanted her so much for so long and had had nothing but lunch with my woman friend in Costa Rica. Part, though, must have been because I cherished her, missed her when we were apart, and, face it Charlie, you're probably falling in love.

She had taken the initiative in each step that led to my lying across her warm, naked, trusting body: the camping trip, the tent, supper, the undressing, asking to be on top, which told me she was ready. Reversing the initiatives was unusual for me but also fine. Woman on top is not my favorite position, but when she requested it, it flashed on me that she didn't need another man pressing her down—for which she would bless me when I mentioned it to her the next day. We may both have known instinctively that, as a psychologist named Tina would confirm years later, it is important for a survivor of rape to be in control after the rapists have ripped away all her control. Control may be too strong a word for a mating that was as mutual as ours was, but, whatever the term, she made me happy and I seemed to make her happy. With that thought, I, too, fell asleep.

Some time after midnight, the mutual need to pee made us unzip the tent flap and crawl outside. It surprised me how much cooler it was. Mosquitoes bit her once and me twice, I won't say where. Back inside, we made love again and slept as before. The next I knew, gray light filled the tent and Emma's brown eyes were looking into mine. "*Buenos dias*," I murmured.

"When I roll over, you'll see my nipples." She sounded anxious.

"I don't have to. I can look away while you put your shirt on."

"If they're going to gross you out, I want to know it now."

Atop her comely breasts, the ragged red scar tissue was less obtrusive than I had expected. I leaned over and kissed them as I had last night.

"Oh, Charlie, I'm so relieved. Again! You're such a sweetheart." She hugged me to her, and my need to pee took second place.

Afterwards, we held each other until our bladders forced us to put on some clothes and crawl outside. The sky was clear, the sun had not reached the lawn nearby, and none of the other campers were in sight. We got our sweaters from the car against the morning chill and relieved ourselves a short way into the nearby woods, our second urination as a couple, though the first one, being in the dark, hardly counted.

We spread the tablecloth and covered it with plates, bowls, mugs, spoons, knives, paper towel napkins, a box of raisin to sweeten the Cheerios, bottles of orange juice, skim milk, and blueberry jam from our cooler. Emma toasted bread in the frying pan while I got the coffee perking on the Coleman's other burner. Finally we laid sections of yesterday's *New York Times* on the wet benches and sat on them across from each other for our first breakfast as lovers.

"Did you sleep all right," she asked, "without the mattress?"

"Never better. How about you?"

"Like a baby. Almost like in the hut. I'm so relieved we got past my nipples."

"Not a problem. I'm just terribly sorry for what they did to you."

"You know, if they hadn't mistaken me for a subversive, I'd probably still be working in San Salvador, still waiting till it's safe to go home."

"You miss home a lot, don't you," I said without a question in my voice.

A long moment passed while she poured herself another cup of coffee.

"It's like there are two halves of me. Half yearns to go to the people I love and the life I left. I've felt waves of grief since you told me María is probably dead. Grieving for her is only a week old. My yearning to go home feels almost like grief, but as the years have passed, it's gotten smaller and comes to my mind less often."

She stopped speaking and lowered her gaze to her coffee mug. After several minutes I said, "What about your other half?"

"That's the side that's in the present. I found San Salvador exciting—so much to see and learn. Texas was different but also a lot to experience. New York is even more exciting. There's no library in my village, no movie rentals, and except for the Bibles that can get you killed, hardly anybody owns a book."

"Maybe when the war's over, you can go for a long visit and see if you want to stay there."

"I wish we could visit right now. I've seen so much of your life, I'd like to show you mine." Our eyes met, and she was smiling. "But since we can't do that, let's use the facilities and go for a walk."

That's what we did, about a two-mile round trip to the main road and back, past a few houses and meadows of swaying grass that awaited the summer's second haying. After a swim in the river and lunch and more time in the tent, we took a drive north beside one green mountain after another, through South Londonderry and Londonderry and Weston to an Episcopal church called Saint Andrew's, because we'd been told we mustn't miss the choir's vespers. The church's minister had fallen in love with that service while he was studying at the General Theological Seminary in New York City, so included it here in Vermont. It would be at 5:30 in a simple stone chapel and anyone could attend. Near the chapel were a lake, a parking lot, and a shop that we visited before the service. Emma tore into the books on display, opening one after another and putting them carefully back, except that we bought one on Latin American liberation theology and another on the Sanctuary Movement after she'd asked me to look at them.

At the service, the audience wore summer clothes and most of the women's heads were not covered, a relief to Emma, who put the blue bandana she'd brought back in a pocket of her jeans. The choir emerged from behind a partition of rough-hewn planks up front, about a dozen men and women of varying ages in black and gray robes. Two of them carried guitars. Except for their robes, I thought, they might have been a non-threatening law firm. The minister, who wore jeans and a sports shirt, read to us, which was fine, but mostly the choir sang simple, often profound folk songs of a spiritual bent. Members of the audience who seemed to be church regulars joined them in the choruses.

Afterwards Emma and I agreed that we must come to these vespers again. We dined heartily at a restaurant called DJ's in the town of Ludlow a short drive over the north end of Terrible Mountain—its real name, you can find it on a Vermont road map. By the time we returned to the campground, it was nearly dark, and still no other campers near our tent. We passed the night much like the first one and spent a quiet morning reading our new books rather than the partly finished ones we'd brought, in our foldup chairs in the shade near the tent.

As we were striking the tent that afternoon and jamming it into its stuff sack, Emma said, "This has been the nicest weekend I can remember. Shall we do it again soon?"

Wary as I am of trying to recreate an idyll, I agreed at once. We stopped in the camp's office to ask for a tent site for the weekend after next.

"Most of the good sites are gone," said the woman on duty. "The leaf peepers are coming in droves."

Emma and I looked at each other. "How does next weekend look?" said Emma. I smiled and nodded to the woman. "Actually it's better," she said. "You can have the same site if you like it."

The Labor Day traffic south was not awful, and as our time for parting drew near, Emma said, "Before you drop me off, would you like to show me your apartment?"

I had been wanting to invite her there but was waiting to see if she'd take this initiative too. The next morning I dropped her at her place in time to change her clothes and reach the office on time, then parked the car in the garage I rented. Would we have missed our weekend's adventure if she had not worried that her minor disfigurements might repulse me if I saw them before we'd lain together all night in the dark? More than likely we'd have made love in my apartment with the lights on and the scar tissue wouldn't have mattered except to make me sorry again for what she'd endured.

But the venue of our consummation mattered. Maybe someday we'd have discovered the joy of camping in Vermont and all that followed, but maybe not, and surely not so soon. Emma's elaborate and probably needless precaution that Labor Day weekend would have a greater effect on our lives than we could have guessed as I past her desk with a hearty, "Good morning, Emma." Her blushing smile warmed my heart.

Chapter 29

I sat behind my desk with the most recent harvest of Charlie's sperms inside me but not likely to start a baby I wasn't ready for. What would the staff I was greeting think, I wondered, if they knew we'd spent the weekend together? I supposed Mr. Sigourney and Ms. Sisson would be fine with it. They were exceptional people, had put me into this job, and heard my Sanctuary talk. But the United States is so class-ridden and racist, I had heard in San Salvador and observed since then, that I'm sure many of my friendly fellow workers would hope our weekend was merely an exalted white partner having a fling with a lowly receptionist of color, sort of like Thomas Jefferson humping Sally Hemings except they produced six kids. Was it that? I thought better of Charlie than to think so. We had so much more between us than a two-night stand that any man and woman can walk away from. We liked each other, we got along so well, and I didn't think we'd rushed it. Sure, we had cultural differences, but they hadn't seemed to matter, not yet anyway. We spent Wednesday night together and paid the price at the 5:00 a.m. alarm.

By the way, "person of color" is so ridiculous. Everyone is of one color or another. Maybe some whites think white is not a color, but whites are not white.

Yellow and orange leaves among the greenery decked the trees on Saturday morning as we crossed from Massachusetts into Vermont. Three tents stood within sight of ours, but not within earshot except when the kids at one of them ran around shouting. We set up on the same spot by the trees, zipped our sleeping bags together into one big one, and left the air mattress in the car. Much earlier than necessary, we drove to Saint Andrew's in order to dig back into the books on offer in the gift shop and relax by the pond. To our surprise, several rows of cars covered the parking lot. Curious to see what was going on, we pulled back one of the thick wooden double doors of the stone chapel and found the seats nearly full and a short, sturdy man up front who, to my amazement, looked like a Maya. He was speaking in Spanish while the minister, again in jeans and a sports shirt, translated. The subject was the horrors going on in Guatemala! Even though the man did not have a bandana across his face, this was a Sanctuary talk! As the audience rose to leave, Charlie and I hurried through them towards the Maya.

"May I speak with you?" I asked him in Spanish.

"Si, señorita," he said with a broad smile.

Taking a chance, I spoke a few words in Mam. He replied in Mam! To my delight, he and I rattled on in Mam while Charlie and the minister, whose name was John Gensel, chatted and watched us carry on in the now empty chapel. The Maya, who had taken the name Enrique Canek, his wife Sophia, and their children had fled from a town near Quetzaltenango that I had heard about but never visited. Like me, they had passed through the Southside Presbyterian Church in Tucson, and the Chicago Religious Task Force had placed them with the congregation of Saint A's four years ago. Charlie and I had planned to have supper at DJ's again, but Enrique insisted we join his family after vespers in the converted barn near the church where the congregation was housing them.

It was a charming home—a weathered gray building with more windows than a working barn would have—with a lawn and little pond outside and a flower garden forming a many-colored apron below the many-paned main window. Inside, Enrique introduced us to Sophia, their five children, and their black and white dog, Tikal. Sadness and delight swept through me as I beheld Sophia clad in Mayan *trajé*—a long multicolored wraparound *corte* or skirt, a billowy white *huipil* or blouse with colorful designs sewn across it, and her hair wrapped in a colorfully woven sash—the first *trajé* besides my own I'd seen since leaving home.

"It's wonderful to see your clothing," I told her, "but it makes me homesick."

"I don't wear it for show," she replied gently. "This is who I am."

I found myself weeping tears of joy as feelings for my family and village swept through me. "I know how you must feel," she said in Mam, hugging me as I sobbed. "I, too, long for home."

"These mountains remind me of our highlands, even though they're not the same."

"They remind me too. We're lucky the people in Chicago sent us to Vermont."

Their children attended a local school and spoke the English of *norteamericanos*. Back home, Enrique had been one of eighteen members of a civic improvement group that engaged in projects like widening the road to their town so that trucks instead of carts could carry their potato crops to market, but the Guatemalan army had convinced itself that Maya who showed leadership were a threat. Of those eighteen young men, Enrique was the only known survivor, and he only because late one night in Guatemala City, a priest had hidden him in the Maryknoll House and shouted through the door to the secret police who were after him, "No subversive in here. Go away and let me sleep."

Dinner at the Caneks was a special treat: chicken tamales made with masa harina corn flour and richly seasoned salsa wrapped in banana leaves they had somehow found. There were enough for Charlie and me, a real touch of home except the salsa tasted different and was not too hot for Charlie. Then a long, delightful evening in all three languages, while their son played gently on his guitar. Before we left, they invited us to spend Columbus Day weekend with them.

We reached the tent late, but not too late for what I was enjoying more and more. Before I dropped off to sleep with Charlie lying half across me again—I'd never guessed that flesh against flesh could feel so safe—I reflected on the evening's touches of home. I think I'm in love with him, I thought, and right now I want us to stay together forever, but I can't believe he'll be willing to give up Manhattan to spend the rest of his life raising corn, beans, and children in a village whose amenities are close to Stone Age.

But now that I've seen parts of the wide world, shall I ever want to go back for more than a visit with a return ticket in my suitcase? If I feel this way now, what about whenever the war finally ends and it's safe to go home? The war had been going on, more or less, for more than twenty years with no end in sight. Enrique and Sophia were determined to return—their town was physically more advanced than my village—but I think their kids wanted to stay here. Vermont was all the youngest ones had known. Would Charlie join me for a visit so we can see if it still suits me and could possibly suit him? It wouldn't be the Peace Corps, and he'd have to make many more adjustments than not having an air mattress. I seemed to be assuming we'd still be together whenever the war ended, yet fearful that we couldn't last. This was a lot to sleep on, so I slept.

Chapter 30

During the four weeks between our drives to Vermont, Emma moved into my apartment, not a complex operation because everything she owned filled only four suitcases, but a big deal for both of us. We'd been seeing less of each other lately because I had to prepare for the upcoming trial. The five a.m. alarm needed to get her home in time for work had quickly grown old. Most of all, we wanted to be together and missed each other when we weren't. All the same, we arranged with her roommates that she would pay her share of the rent for several more months just in case.

While Emma was unpacking, she suddenly took one of her suitcases into the bathroom and shut the door. A few minutes later she emerged wearing the many-colored skirt she had woven in her teens, the blouse on which she had embroidered colorful flowers, and her hair wrapped in an equally colorful sash she had woven—her most precious possessions. She had carried them from her village to San Salvador, while escaping through Guatemala and Mexico, and ever since. As she pirouetted before me, she could have been Sophia's daughter. My darling partner! I hugged her and we wept.

October brought more warm colors and cold nights to Vermont. Columbus Day weekend with the Caneks was another delight. Emma marveled at the reds, yellows, and oranges that decked the mountainsides—as though Vermont had donned Mayan *trajé*, she said. She'd never seen foliage like this in her village and only an all-yellow version in Texas. I had to admit that the foliage blanketing these slopes beat the displays I'd grown up with in the hills of Ithaca. We attended Sunday Eucharist with Enrique and Sophia in St. Andrew's big gray barn, which was packed. Half the license plates in the parking lot were out-of-state. In the Caneks' ample home, the guttural sounds of Mam flowed in a constant stream. I felt a tad excluded as Emma rattled on with Enrique, Sophia, and their oldest daughter Jiliana, though she turned from time to time to tell me what they were talking about, especially the abominable stuff the army was doing to their people. Since sound traveled unimpeded throughout the converted barn, Emma and I had to be very quiet after bedtime, so we both discovered the joy of doing it slowly. Back when Annie and I visited my parents, we had simply abstained.

Jiliana, who was a mature sixteen, and Emma hit it off, and their friendship would deepen that winter as we would spend more time with the Caneks and learn to snowshoe, no great trick, and begin to downhill ski on nearby Okemo Mountain's bunny slope.

It had been my custom since moving to Manhattan to spend Thanksgiving weekends with my parents in Ithaca, a custom that Annie had had to tolerate for only two years. My brother Mike and his wife Gretchen made it when they could, but since they lived in Oregon, that wasn't often. My father Patrick taught astronomy at Cornell—the renowned Carl Sagan was one of his colleagues and Frank Drake of the SETI project was another. My mother Elinor taught senior English at Ithaca High. Indeed, reading the books she assigned and participating in her classroom discussions may have been the best part of my formal education. I asked her once why she didn't share what she knew about books at our dinner table. "I have to confess," she said, "it takes the stimulus of twenty young minds to turn on my faucet. You and Mike didn't quite do it. I expected you'd hear my best when you were seniors. Maybe you remember the times I read to you before you learned to read to yourselves." That was probably the most defensive I ever heard her.

The October evening after Jenny Erdman and I won a verdict in our jury trial, I asked Emma, "How would you like to spend Thanksgiving weekend with my parents?"

"I have mixed feelings about Thanksgiving, given what white folks did to Native Americans after the first one, but personally I have much to be thankful for, and I'd love to meet them and see where you grew up."

After dinner, I dialed their home. After Mom and I ascertained that everyone was well, I said, "I'm hoping to spend Thanksgiving weekend with you."

"We'd be disappointed if you didn't. I was expecting you'd ask sooner."

"I'm sorry. I just finished a jury trial. You know how that goes." True of course, but I'd also delayed calling because I wasn't sure how to tell them about Emma.

"I do. Did you win?"

"I did. Would it be all right if I bring a friend?"

"Of course. I hope he's interesting. What's his name?"

"Emma Diaz."

With hardly a pause, "I see. Is it serious?"

"We're living together."

"Then I hope it's serious. It must be if you want us to meet her. I'm sure you're being careful after the debacle with Annie. Now I've got to meet her. I'm suddenly dying of curiosity."

"Don't come on too strong, Mom. Don't scare her."

"Who, me? She'll probably be scared enough as it is. I'll be gentle and so will your father. I'll see to that."

Emma had stopped putting the dishes in the washer so she could listen to my side of the conversation. "How did it go?"

"No problem. She's dying to meet you and promises not to scare you."

"It's funny what scares people, and funny that funny means humorous and odd, though humor isn't odd, at least not for us."

I loved her active mind even when it sometimes verged on corn, and corn is a Mayan staple. She'd gotten me doing it.

In mid-November we learned that six Jesuit priests and two of their staff had been shot dead at the *Universidad Centroamericana*. "The bastards!" Emma fumed. She knew at once who the perps must have been. "The absolute bastards! I wonder whether the CIA advised them that murdering these priests would be a good idea." In bed later I felt her weeping.

Early Thanksgiving morning, we rolled along New York's Route 17, stopping for a late breakfast at the opulent Roscoe Diner. The leaves had fallen except for a few brown ones clinging to the oak trees, but Emma still enjoyed the scenery. She was eager to see the house I grew up in, high on the same hill as Cornell, with a clear view of Lake Cayuga far below. My mother prepared the classic dinner, turkey, well-seasoned stuffing, mashed potatoes with gravy, creamed onions, sweet potatoes on which she'd melted several marshmallows, real cranberry sauce, and mince or pumpkin pie or both if anyone was still hungry. I enjoyed Mom and Dad trying to be casual as they grilled Emma.

"Manhattan must be quite a change from your village in Guatemala," said Mom.

"It is, but I got there by degrees, first in San Salvador, then around Fort Worth."

"Still, New York's an impossible place to live, especially to raise children in. I hope Charlie doesn't want to live there forever."

"So do I," said Emma. Startled, I'd have to ask her what she meant.

Dad, as usual, was gentler, and he took the occasion to tell Emma about the heavens. She was fascinated, as was I, while he explained that stars explode at the end of their lives, creating and scattering the stuff that formed the Earth, the rocks, the air, oceans, our bodies, everything.

"There was nothing in the beginning," Dad said, "except a lot of hydrogen and some helium. Their own gravity pulled clouds of the stuff into balls, and when the balls grew big enough, they ignited into nuclear fires that burn fiercely for millions or even billions of years. They are the Sun and all the other stars. Eventually they burn out, not with a whimper, but with a mighty bang that shoots the heavier stuff they've created into space. Some of it came together as the hard balls that are Mercury, Venus, Earth, and Mars, and the huge gas balls of Jupiter, Neptune, and Uranus."

"Do other stars have planets?" Emma asked.

"We think so."

"And the Sun's planets came from other stars?"

"Right. The Sun hasn't blown up yet."

"When will it?"

"Not in our lifetime or for thousands of generations if we don't nuke ourselves into oblivion." This prompted Emma to ask more questions. After the meal, Dad showed her photos of the heavens while Mom and I did the dishes.

"I love her mind," Mom said. "She wants to know about everything. She's quite a find. I see you two get along."

"So far, so good." I told Mom about Emma being tortured and the risks she took and was still taking by speaking out in public against the Terror, though I did not mention the minor risk she'd asked me to take during my vacation.

"What an admirable young woman! Maybe you'll think she's the one for you, but you're still in your honeymoon phase. You'll have to see how you feel about each other after the glow wears off. She's certainly an improvement over Annie."

"The only problem I see—it's a big one—is that she yearns to return to her village, and I'm pretty sure I couldn't live there."

"Your children might develop sounder values there than here, but apart from that, I don't blame you. I couldn't live in primitive conditions and neither could your father."

If Mom hadn't liked Annie from the start, I wished she'd said so when it might have helped. Annie was a decent human being but very much a product of her upbringing in Fairfield County in the gold-plated panhandle of Connecticut. She donated money to charities but felt entitled to have nice things, meaning expensive things that I could barely afford even on my Manhattan lawyer's salary. She was a creature of the culture that the real world of Costa Rica had pulled me out of. Partly out of at least. Our similar ethnic heritages were zero help. After we married, I felt increasingly the clash between living the values I'd felt so good about in the Peace Corps and the lifestyle that meant so much to her and I was beginning to feel trapped in. I had explained all this to Mom and Dad soon after Annie and I split. I didn't mention our sexual incompatibility.

Driving back from Ithaca on Sunday afternoon, I said, "Well, they certainly approve of you, and they like you too. I'd say the weekend was what we *norteamericanos* call a success."

"I like them too. They're good people and so interesting. I have to start reading some of the books your mother told me about. And your father! My forebears were avid astronomers. They got it partly right and partly wrong, but the stuff your father told me is amazing. We must buy Carl Sagan's book *Cosmos*. Oh, Charlie, I hope we stay together, honeymoon phase or not."

"That's how I feel," I said. She snuggled against me as far as her seatbelt allowed, and we drove in silence.

I had told her Mom's comment about the honeymoon phase, and we'd agreed it was probably sound. I sensed that Christmas with the Caneks might clarify her inner conflict about returning to her village. If she chose the village, would I seriously consider going with her? And what would we do with ourselves in Manhattan until the civil war ended? Marry and make babies and bring *them* to that primitive life? Emma and I could always solve the problem by splitting up. I certainly didn't want that solution and hoped she didn't either.

I didn't have the heart to tell her about another comment Mom had made: "Right now I'm as taken with her as you seem to be, but I'm sure you know there must be large cultural differences between you. Marriage between people of the same backgrounds is hard enough. Emma's such a fine person that you may tie yourself into an impossible situation even more easily than you did with Annie."

My head knew Mom was right. My heart said, So what! I didn't want to think about the problem, much less talk about it with Emma. Maybe her determination to return to her village would save us, painfully but sensibly, from the impossible situation. Time would tell. For now, I couldn't be happier with her.

Chapter 31

Charlie wasn't trying to talk me out of my desire to return to my village. That's part of what endeared him to me. Many men, I believe, would expect me to abandon my dream and subordinate myself to their life in Manhattan—or else they would abandon me. But much as Charlie may have wanted me to stay here with him—I hoped he did—I trusted that he saw it had to be my decision. Was I right, or had he simply not gotten around to pressing me? One evening as we sipped our wine at dinner and watched the sun go down over New Jersey, I put a question I'd been hesitating to ask.

"When the war ends, how would you feel about joining me on a visit to my village?"

"A visit on which you might decide to stay there?"

"If the war ended while I was in Texas, I'd surely have gone back, and maybe lived to regret it. Now I'm not sure. Much as I love my family and friends, I feel less likely to want that life again, especially if you weren't willing to live there with me, which I'm not sure you would be."

"A week or two's visit is the best way to find out. This is the only serious issue I see between us. I keep waiting for our vast cultural differences to rise up, but so far I don't see any that matter. I'll definitely join you and give it a try. Besides I'd like to meet your parents and see where you grew up. Like you did for me."

I had not meant to test him, but I had. I felt relieved and cheerful. I couldn't ask for more than that he give it a try. I realized that I, too, needed to try it. My beloved María and dear Frida were gone. Would that make a difference? There was Ana, but I'd met many people like her in the U.S. and felt I only related to them on the surface.

"There's a movie called *Witness* that came out two or three years ago." It irritated me that Charlie was changing the subject until I saw he wasn't. "Harrison Ford is a streetwise Philadelphia detective who has to spend time in a primitive and demanding community of Amish farmers. Kelly McGillis lives in the community, and she and Ford fall in love. By the end of the movie, I was hoping he'd give up his life in the city and live with her among the Amish."

"He'd be giving up a lot. Why don't we rent the movie and see if I agree."

We visited the local Blockbuster and watched it the next night.

"I agree, Charlie. He'd have had better life staying with her."

"The humorist W. C. Fields wanted his gravestone to say, 'Better here than in Philadelphia.'"

"Oh, Charlie!" I enjoyed the distances his mind often leapt.

"Of course she might have grown to like Philly if they took an apartment together," he said as he started to rewind the film.

I went to the Bible, which I'd brought from Texas, along with Strunk and White's *Elements of Style* that Jonathan had given me, and found the passage in Genesis that had struck me during my evenings at the Rodríguezes'. I recalled it after our discussion last night, and now I read it to him. "'Therefore shall a man leave his father and his mother, and shall cleave unto his wife, and they shall be one flesh.' It's written for men, but I'm sure it goes for women too. I feel you and I are already one flesh, and it's up to us, not some dead Scripture writer, to decide whether we ought to stay that way."

"Agreed. And what we ought to do right now is eat supper."

"Agreed. And the night is still young."

Just as Charlie didn't press me to squelch my desire to go home, I never mentioned to him that if he married me, that would end my daily dread of being arrested, deported, and forced into the fatal corridor at the Aurora Airport. That would be the excruciating end of Emma Brenda. The world-famous peace activist Rigoberta Menchú, who would win the Nobel Peace Prize in 1992, was disappeared at that airport only last year, and it took an international hue and cry to get her freed. I was only a minor activist and didn't any expect a hue and cry. But I refused to pressure Charlie by playing the safety card, and I wouldn't ask him for the marriage of convenience that some aliens use. No, I'd not marry him unless we meant to spend the rest of our lives together. Right now I felt I did, and hoped he felt the same; but I knew it was still too early to trust our feelings, especially because he had once had the same feelings for Annie.

During the drive back from his parents', I had asked him why he and Annie split. He gave me the same explanation he'd given his family, except he told me but not them that soon after they'd married, Annie stopped wanting to do it with him. He was sorry then and glad now she'd shut him out before they made a baby. She realized that sex mattered a lot for him, but neither of them wanted him screwing other women while he was married to her, so they had what's called an amicable divorce. Because she was young and able, they agreed on no alimony.

"I'm sorry you had to go through all that," I'd told him as we sat stuck in the holiday traffic on the Tappan Zee Bridge, "but glad she freed you for me."

"Me too. You're a nicer person. You have better values. I like you much better."

How nice to hear! As the car inched forward, I reached up and tousled his hair. How long, I wondered, before we can trust our feelings for each other? And feelings were only part of it. Could I spend the rest of my life in his country? Could he in mine? If we decided to live here, I trusted he would accept the social and business price that a white man pays for having a non-white wife. Yes, I was sure he'd accept the price. Wasn't I?

"By the way, what is your ethnicity?"

"White, I guess. The biggest part of me is English. The best part's Irish."

"That's something else we have in common. How long did your biggest part oppress your best part?"

"Actually about seven hundred years."

"The Spanish speakers have done it to my people for only five hundred years, and it's still happening."

"It's still happening to my people too if you count the Catholics living in the Six Counties of the north. My Uncle Charles calls them the Occupied Territory."

Charlie paid the toll at the Tarrytown end of the bridge, and we were able to drive somewhat faster. This was only a few miles from where we'd visited Sister Darlene at Maryknoll and I'd introduced Charlie to her. She and I had written letters back and forth while I was in Texas and she was serving in Kenya, and I had taken the train from New York to see her while she was briefly in the States.

Christmas at the Caneks was another delight. Enrique and the children had built a crèche scene in the center of a miniature Mayan village in a corner of their common room. According to a custom I didn't know about, the baby Jesus in the crib was the biggest figure, Mary and Joseph were the next biggest, and the shepherds and wise men were smaller. As I gazed at the village, a wave of homesickness surged through me, and I turned my face away from the others.

On Christmas Eve the Caneks had a dozen local friends in for dinner, which again featured tamales and salsa wrapped in banana leaves. The secret of Enrique's salsa, he told me, was coriander. The locals I remember best were an elderly woman named Maríanna McGuffin, who served as a sort of grandmother for the children and drove Enrique and Sophia to their speaking dates, and a middle-aged woman, Nancy Bell, who was a justice of the peace but was too warm and natural to seem like one.

On Christmas morning we joined the Caneks and several hundred other people for a 5:00 a.m. service in Saint A's barn, followed by a sumptuous potluck breakfast where Reverend Gensel and the choir mingled with the attendees in their dining room and twin parlors behind the stone chapel. I had pleasant little chats with several of the locals.

Driving back to the City Charlie said, "You know, I'm really beginning to like Vermont, the mountains, the pace of life, the people I've met so far."

"I was just thinking the same things." I paused. "Are we doing anything for New Year's Eve?"

"Not yet. What do you have in mind?"

"It's another three-day weekend. Why don't we explore up north, maybe check out Montpelier and Burlington?"

"And not see the Caneks or ski?"

"Right. These Maya aren't the only reason I like Vermont. They've asked us back for the last weekend in January. We can ski then."

We bought a tourist book for Vermont, and the next Saturday morning I studied it, putting paper clips on the interesting pages, while Charlie drove us through the boring parts of Connecticut. Instead of leaving I-91 at Rockingham to reach the Caneks, we continued northwards, passing close to massive Mount Ascutney beside the Connecticut River, and turned left at White River Junction onto I-89, which took us through the mountains. An hour later we entered Montpelier, the state capital, a neat little city that serves excellent food and has fine bookstores. It impressed Charlie to see that the State House backs right up to a wooded hillside. Further along in Waterbury, we made the stop that several people in the office told us we must, at the big Ben & Jerry's factory for bowls of Cherry Garcia ice cream. The area gave us fine views of Camel's Hump, which I was told is the most dramatic mountain in Vermont. To me, though, it's peak looks less like the hump of a camel than the fin of a shark. I guess it's a sort of Rorschach test where people see what they want to. Charlie thinks it looks like the beak of a bird.

Half an hour later we were in Burlington and found the B&B where we'd reserved a room. Then we walked and walked—along the pedestrian Church Street Mall, the long sidewalks down to Lake Champlain, back up the hill on a different street to slake our thirst at a brew-pub, and back down Church Street for a fine dinner at Leunig's Bistro.

"This is a really nice city," Charlie said.

"It's the nicest-looking city I've seen in America, or actually anywhere."

On Sunday we explored local roads to the east, often spotting Camel's Hump against the distant sky, and to the north as far as the picturesque little city of St. Albans. "I don't want to go any closer to Canada," I told Charlie, "in case the Border Patrol stops this car with a white guy and *latina*-looking woman in it."

"Now that you mention it, you're right." I don't think my peril had occurred to him. He had never thought like a fugitive, I suppose, and I hoped he never had to.

By the time we headed south on Monday, I won't say we had fallen in love with Vermont, but our affection for it was blossoming in the snow.

A Saturday morning or two later, I was reading *My Antonia*, which Charlie's mother had recommended, and Charlie had finished the *Times* and turned to the *National Catholic Reporter*.

"Here's a review I think you'll find interesting," he said. "The book is called *María's Courage*. It's by an anonymous author and claims to be narrated by a quetzal. It tells how a young Maya named María saves her village from being massacred."

"You're joking!" I rushed across the room and took the paper from his outstretched hand. I raced through the review, then read it slowly. What it said of the plot—not a lot—matched what Old Pablo and Sarah had told Charlie about María's and Germán's heroism!

"It' sounds like María's story," I said, "but I cannot believe that one bird, no matter how smart, heard hours of conversation in Mam, flew to Tucson, and dictated a hundred and fifty pages in Spanish. That's what the review says the book claims. He calls it a good example of Latin American magic realism for readers who find *One Hundred Years of Solitude* too long a slog. Not a word in the review about U.S. complicity in the terror, though that's the part that should interest U.S. readers the most."

"It's not hard to believe a bird dictated it," said Charlie, oozing smugness as he sometimes did. "It's impossible."

"You *gringos* think you know so much. Then the world surprises you. But it's *very* hard to believe. Let's phone the bookstore and see if they have it."

They didn't, so Charlie called Scribner's and they did. On the bus down Broadway, we debated whether to buy one copy or two. We decided on two, but Scribner's had only one. During the walk from the store on Fifth Avenue to Broadway, I could hardly wait to dive into it, but my fear of speedy pedestrians was such that I didn't open it until we were sitting in the bus.

Back in the apartment, we ate a hasty lunch and Charlie read his current novel while I read *Bird* studiously, remarking from time to time to Charlie: "The author certainly knows my village… I was still living there the awful day that Luis disappeared. I was one of María's loved ones who tried to comfort her. The author certainly got that part right…got Ana's wedding fiesta right, I was there for all three of them. There's a bit about me going to San Salvador during the famine, and it uses my real name. I'm glad to see María and Ana became friends again though they still squabbled. I'm certain the book is not the concoction of some hotshot American who never left Park Slope."

Then the danger the book created dawned on me.

"I have to ask you not to tell anybody about this book because my real name is in it." I paused. "I'm not sure how much *Emma* protects my family now that the secret police can read the whole story here—as I'm sure they will or have already."

"All the same," he assured me, "I don't think they'd connect a suspected subversive named Brenda in San Salvador with the Emma who denounced them in Texas and here. You'll have to use Brenda if you decide to apply for citizenship, but I agree you're best being Emma for now."

Towards time for wine, I put the book down. "It's heartbreaking. It absolutely breaks my heart. It makes me want to shoot the whole fucking army. I absolutely understand why the eagle killed the colonel." Charlie's look of incredulity told me he still didn't believe the eagle was María. "But there's one huge hole in the book."

"Oh?"

"Didn't Sara and Old Pablo tell you Frida was part of the group that decided to shoot Germán?"

"I think so. Let's check the tape."

We did, and there it was. Frida was part of the group, and she left the village when María did and hadn't been heard of since.

"I'm not ruling out the bird," I said, though I probably was but didn't want to give Charlie the satisfaction, "but I think what happened is that Frida was determined to tell the story, and she made her way to Tucson or Brownsville or San Ysidro"—three of the main points where refugees crossed the Border in those days—"and dictated the book to a bilingual author whom the Church or the Sanctuary Movement probably put her in touch with. To protect her family, she wrote herself out of the story and switched in the bird, which she seems to have enjoyed inventing. She may indeed have walked past the smoking ruin of the village described at the outset—she often roamed away from our village, and I'm guessing she went with María and Sara to the GAM demonstration and the discussion with the nuns that evening. She must have enjoyed making up the part about shitting in the sergeant's ear."

"This is amazing," Charlie said. "I think you're right that she's the author—a hero who will always be unsung unless she steps forward after the war."

"I truly hope her book makes a difference, but you know how Americans are about admitting their war crimes, much less denouncing them."

Charlie and I had another great weekend of fellowship with the Caneks and skiing on Okemo on the last weekend in January and again two weekends later, which happened to be the weekend before Valentine's Day, which had nothing to do with what I had decided to tell Charlie and myself. We were driving south through snow-covered northern Massachusetts when I came out with it.

"There are two things I want to talk about, Charlie. The first is that I can never go back and live in my village again. Visit yes, but never stay."

"Are you sure?"

"I am." I gave him the reasons I'd been mulling over during the last few months. "And there's one more. It's not only that I've been missing those people and places. I've been missing a wonderful part of my life that ended on the day I climbed into Padre López's car. My parents may be almost the same, but the village has probably changed, and I've certainly changed. I can't recapture the past and would only be disappointed if I tried. I'd have to start a new life, and with María and Frida gone, I have less reason to try. I really like living here, and I'd want to stay even if you and I were to split up."

"Are you proposing?"

"I hadn't intended to? At least not yet. What do think?"

"Number one, I think it's a really stupid custom for the man to say will you marry me and the woman says yes or no. It's the biggest decision of their lives, and they don't discuss it? How foolish! Unless the woman is sure she doesn't want the man."

"I love you with all my heart, and I want to marry you." There, I'd said it.

"I love you too, and I want us to marry. Maybe next weekend we can pick out an engagement ring." The conversation had gone much farther than I'd expected. I was aglow. How exciting! But would I be sure tomorrow?

"You're making me incredibly happy, Charlie, but what would you think of living with our decision for a little while before we make it public?"

"Agreed. You've just made me so happy I guess I'm a little impetuous."

How does a couple celebrate their engagement? Primal instinct, I suppose, made me reach over and rub his trousers where I thought his penis was. Feeling it respond, I put my hand back in my lap and said, "Don't speed up, Charlie. The evening is young."

"The evening is young." Or, "the night is young." "Just in case." It's neat that we're developing our own clichés, a modest start, I thought, but our relationship is young.

Back at the apartment we sealed our engagement. Then he went to the bookcase, still wearing nothing, and pulled out a thick book called *You Can't Go Home Again* by Thomas Wolfe, a name his mother had mentioned.

"He was a great author according to my mother, though few people read him anymore." Charlie sat down on the bed. "I haven't read the whole book yet, but tell me if these words apply to you, quote: 'You can't go back home to your family, back home to your childhood…back home to places in the country, back home to the old forms and systems of things which once seemed everlasting but which are changing all the time—back home to the escapes of Time and Memory.'"

"That's pretty close. I'm guessing Mr. Wolfe tried to go home from someplace and it didn't work out."

"So I understand."

As if we hadn't done enough deciding for one day, Charlie said during dinner, "You mentioned in the car that you wanted to discuss two things."

"Right. Do you want to have children?"

"Definitely."

"How many?"

"Three or four. I haven't considered the number."

"Three or four sounds good. Would you like to raise them here on Riverside Drive or in Brooklyn or Queens, or in a suburb, or maybe in a place like Vermont?"

"You've done a lot of thinking. Vermont is definitely worth considering. I have no connections there. I wonder how I'd develop a decent law practice."

"But you're a courtroom lawyer. It's my observation that Jenny Erdman is the only lawyer besides you at S&S who likes that kind of work. You've told me that trying a case is like staging a play while you are writing the script and so is your opponent. I saw how grueling it was even for that trial in October. Maybe Vermont has a law firm in needs someone to go to court so the rest of them can sit safely in their offices."

"Definitely worth looking into. I'll check the directory tomorrow. Just in case."

"Since I'm going to stay in the U.S., it's time I get a high school education.

There must be a way study in the evening for a GED."

The more we talked about moving to Vermont, the more the idea grew on us. The key reason we could afford to consider it: neither of us cared about earning more money than it took to live in modest comfort, educate our children, and have enough left over for books and occasional travel. Charlie updated his resumé and studied the law directory write-ups of several firms in Burlington and Montpelier.

One Saturday morning in early April we went down to the diamond district on West 44th Street to find an engagement ring. The displays glittered under the lights of the shops, and I tried to discern how a diamond differed from a similarly cut zircon or piece of glass. The greatest difference I could see was the price.

"You know, Charlie," I said on the sidewalk outside the third shop, "the workmanship on some of these rings is exquisite, but I never saw a diamond ring on a woman in my village. A fair number of married women I've seen in Texas and New York wear only a wedding band. The price of one of these trinkets can buy us round trips to Guatemala and back and quite a few camping trips in Canada."

"Won't an engagement ring help you feel at home in a strange land?"

"You help me feel at home. So do Sister Darlene, most people at work, my dear congregation in Fort Worth, and all the other good Americans I know. I guess I had to see these sparkling arrays to realize how little the custom touches me. I truly appreciate that you'll buy me one, but I'll soon be wearing the ring that matters and so will you."

"Now that you mention it, there's a feminist angle. The engagement ring tells the world that the woman is spoken for. The man is equally spoken for, but he seldom wears an engagement ring."

"He could."

"If I did, I'd feel like an asshole."

"But the woman is supposed to feel, 'Look at me, somebody desires what I have on offer.' All the more reason I don't want one."

Having settled the question, we took a walk around Times Square, impervious to the assaults of the huge sales pitches on the walls, before riding a bus home for lunch.

Charlie and I bought the flights to Guatemala that I mentioned on the sidewalk, not to visit my village—that would still be too dangerous—but to do business with the U.S. Embassy. The trip would be dangerous, but the State Department gave us no choice. Before I could get a green card or become a citizen—I wanted dual citizenship—I needed to leave the country, obtain the proper papers at a U.S. embassy or consulate, and enter the country legally. Any embassy or consulate would do. This struck both of us as being reasonable and not so hard: we'd drive to the consulate in Montreal. But out of what looked like cruel spite, the State Department required me and Charlie, who said with no hesitation that he'd accompany me, to use the embassy in Guatemala City. They assured us we'd be safe because Rigoberta Menchú had safely come and gone, but they fail to say that she did so on a second trip but had been disappeared at the airport on her first trip.

We decided to go during our August vacations and, working backwards, to get married on the second Saturday of June. I sent word asking Aunt Sara and Old Pablo, who had become my uncle by marriage, to meet us at the Camino Real if they could. They sent word that they'd try.

Charlie and I sealed our commitment to Vermont by deciding to be married there. Sophia and Enrique said they would be honored to have the ceremony on their lawn, weather permitting. Nancy Bell, who was a justice of the peace, agreed to officiate and very kindly met with us over Memorial Day weekend to create the ceremony. She showed us the vows of several couples she'd married, to help us compose our own.

It was a sunny, warm Vermont morning with enough breeze to blow the black flies away. Charlie's brother Mike had flown with his wife Gretchen to Rochester, New York, picked up their parents in Ithaca, and driven to Weston. Now Mike stood beside Charlie as his best man. Felipé, serving as my stand-in father, walked me down the short aisle between a small audience who were sitting on folding chairs on the grass near the pond. Young Jiliana stood beside me as my maid of honor while Nancy united Charlie and me in holy matrimony. The choir of Saint A's, who filled nearly half the chairs, stood and sang a hauntingly lovely song that was part of their repertoire:

> *Wherever you go, I shall go.*
> *Wherever you live, so shall I live.*
> *Your people will be my people,*
> *And your God will be my God too.*
>
> *Wherever you die, I shall die.*
> *And there shall I be buried beside you.*
> *We will be together forever;*
> *And our love will be the gift of our lives.*

Tears of joy streamed down my cheeks and onto my *huipil* as the choir's rich harmony told our story to the guests and the woods and mountains around us. I hoped against hope that the lyrics, which seemed so appropriate today, would still seem so after Charlie and I visited my village, whenever that would occur.

We had warned Jiliana and Mike to look unruffled when Nancy called me Brenda during the service. If people in the audience asked whether they'd misheard, we'd tell them they hadn't and why we'd like them to forget *Brenda*. Charlie's mother was the only one who asked. After we told her, she said this was one more reason she was sorry for all the horror I had gone through. I think she was realizing, too, that her Charlie was sharing the burdens of my being a fugitive from *Latino* death squads and the American *migra*.

We didn't worry her about our upcoming trip to Guatemala City. It had kept me awake several nights. The fatal corridor in the Aurora Airport was the first and biggest fear I had had if I were arrested in the U.S. and deported. Now it seemed inevitable that I'd have to pass through it. Charlie was determined to stick with me, whether or not it pissed off the authorities to see a blond *gringo* in that corridor. I dearly hoped he could.

Sophia, Maríanna McGuffin, Nancy Bell, and two more women from the community had put together a lunch of sandwiches, a large bowl of freshly picked strawberries, a cake, and a bowl of fruit punch. For the toasts, nearly everybody turned to cans of Guinness in honor Charlie's Anglo-Irish heritage and strong *guaro* from Enrique's private stock to honor mine. A folk group, The Turkey Mountain Window Smashers, whom Maríanna McGuffin had hired, played their jubilant music during the reception.

Charlie and I had puzzled over what to do about our friends at the office, his other New York friends, and mine at the Riverside Church. We hadn't wanted to not invite them, but few if any would make the long drive to Vermont, and we didn't want our invitation to be simply a way of asking for a gift. So we decided to invite only Mr. Sigourney and Ms. Sisson, out of respect and because they'd probably give us a gift anyway. Maybe we'd throw a party in a restaurant for our City friends.

We made an appointment to see Ms. Sisson in her office. "That's wonderful," she said when we told her our newsour news. "I congratulate you both. You are very fortunate to have found each other."

As to attending the ceremony in Vermont, she thanked us and said, "I'll have to talk to Calvin of course, but I don't think we'll be able to make it." Slight pause. "I don't imagine many of your friends will either." Another pause. "Forgive me for thinking aloud. How would it be if Calvin and I have a reception for you in our apartment?"

Charlie and I looked at each other. We knew they had a large apartment on Fifth Avenue overlooking Central Park. He saw a yes in my nod, and said, "That's very generous of you. We would be delighted."

Her next remark jarred me: "I've been so proud of you, Emma, for the way you've been speaking out for your people, and I've understood why it's been best for the rest of the office not to know your story. But as I understand it, once you've married a citizen, you'll be safe from deportation. How would you feel about taking a few minutes at the reception to tell people what you told us at church about your ordeal?"

"It's not that straightforward anymore," I said. "I still need to go get clearance from the U.S. Embassy in Guatemala to enter the country legally. They should give it, but if they decide not to, there's not much I can do. So I'd be happy to tell everybody my story after I'm safely back."

"How terrible! You'll be in danger down there, won't you. I had no idea!"

"We'll be going during our August vacations," Charlie said. "If the embassy refuses us, we'll go to the Canadian embassy and tell them her life is in danger. As it will be." I was so glad to hear him say *us* and *we*.

"My God!" said Ms. Sisson. "I feel guilty for being so safe."

"You're not guilty," I said. "You've taken an imperiled refugee into your office and you have taken the trouble to learn our reality. I thank you and Mr. Sigourney from the bottom of my heart."

Ms. Sisson stood up from her desk, walked around it, and gave me a big hug. Then she turned and hugged Charlie. "I'm so happy for you both. Calvin and I will be praying for you while you're in Guatemala."

"Thank you," Charlie said. "That means a lot." He paused and raised a subject I hadn't expected. "There's one more thing I should mention. Emma and I think we're going to move to Vermont. It's not imminent, but it's pretty definite."

"I appreciate your telling me." It was her turn to pause. "May I ask whether you plan to have children?"

"Yes. That's definite."

"Then I think you're doing the right thing. If Calvin and I had it to do over, we might very well do the same. Please let us know if there's anything we can do to help you find a job there. We'll hate to lose you. We'll write excellent references for both of you of course."

I was inwardly breathing a sigh of relief at how well she was taking all this. She hadn't finished.

"Do you think Jenny Erdman is ready to fill your shoes in court?"

"She handled three witnesses very well at the trial last fall, and I've sent her out to take depositions on her own. She's five years out"—out of law school—"and tried a number of cases during her two years in the U.S. Attorney's Office. She'll find it a challenge—I did at first—but I believe she'll do well."

"Is she easy to work with?"

"Very. She can think outside the box and turn setbacks to her advantage—a natural litigator. We sometimes disagree, and she knows when to stop pushing."

"She sounds like more of a treasure than I'd realized. Besides, you're not gone yet." She turned to me. "We'll miss you too." Pause. "Charlie's farewell lunch, whenever it comes, may be a good time for you to tell the office your history."

"That sounds good to me."

Out in the hall, I said, "This is the first time I've seen two lawyers do business. Is it always so economical?

"Hardly ever."

"I was impressed at how easily you rattled off Jenny's resumé."

"A good lawyer learns to speak before he thinks."

I'd have to ask him later whether he meant it.

Chapter 32

As our departure approached, Emma and I took the same precautions and contacted the same people as I had when I visited Guatemala the previous August. We each carried a letter like the ones I'd carried before on the gold-embossed letterhead of the United States Senate and signed by our Senator Daniel Patrick Moynihan. It was meant to impress any secret police who detained us and stopped to look at it. It was in English and said essentially nothing: "Dear Mr. and Mrs. Marlow: Thank you for informing me of your trip to Guatemala on August 13, 1989. Please do not hesitate to tell me if I can be of any further service. Very truly yours." We got this letter, and mine from Moynihan last year, because one of my partners had worked on his staff.

Last year I was scarcely in danger. This year the danger was real. The Salvadoran secret police had doubtless told their Guatemalan counterparts that they had interrogated a Mayan suspect and she had fled the country. If they figured out that the Emma who was denouncing them in Texas and New York was Brenda Tuyuc, so much the worse. Unbeknownst to us, 1989 had seen renewed attacks on Americans in Guatemala.

We flew down on a Sunday so as to give the embassy a full work week if they needed it to deal with Brenda. Again I reserved at the Camino Real, thinking it a relatively safe place and handy for meeting Sara and Old Pablo, not knowing that a small bomb—obviously a message to someone inside— would explode in front of it a month later. As we left the plane at the Aurora Airport, I remained determined to walk arm-in-arm with Brenda, which I'd been calling her since we took off from Newark, when we had to pass through the corridor for Guatemalans only; but to our great relief, they'd changed the system and everyone walked through the same corridor. Even though Brenda's only experience in Guatemala City had been to change buses on the way to El Salvador five years ago, she was overjoyed to feel her homeland beneath her feet, hugging my arm more for joy than safety as we crossed the sidewalk to a dilapidated cab. The Guatemalan sampler dinner in the hotel did not overwhelm her. "What do these *ladinos* know about Mayan food!" she muttered.

None of the brown uniforms at the hotel seemed to recognize me from the year before, nor I them, and we passed the night without incident. Around three a.m. I awoke to see Brenda standing the window and gazing across the city.

The sunny next morning we took a cab down the broad, busy Avenida Reforma to the U. S. Embassy. That gray monolith testified to the reality of the civil war and local feelings about the United States. Along the sidewalk stood massive concrete flowerpots with green bushes rising from them, obviously meant to stop a truck bomber. I wondered if they could. A high fence topped with iron spikes spread across the wide front steps, and outside it stood several *latino*-looking men in blue Wackenhut uniforms holding short-barrel shotguns—a sad contrast to the U.S. Marine in full dress uniform that I'd seen guarding our embassy in Costa Rica, but as I remarked to Brenda, these local guards were less likely to provoke a drive-by shooting.

You didn't enter the embassy by the big front door at the top of the steps but had to walk around the corner, line up outside an entrance on the side of the building, and go through a metal detector inside a security hut. The man in line ahead of us pulled out a black automatic pistol and checked it with a guard before entering the detector.

The room we entered in the embassy and an adjoining room were locked off from the rest of the building like an abscess in its side. The first room contained a square of folding chairs arranged as if for watching a movie, but actually for sitting in until we were called to one of the solid glass windows with a space underneath for passing papers, like a ticket window at a movie theater. When we were finally called to a window, an immaculate young man named William Silkworth told us through a voice transmitter that Brenda needed to see a certain doctor for a physical this afternoon and return in two days for her papers, which, he added, would probably be ready by then if she passed the medical tests. Probably! If she passed! The address and phone number of the Canadian Embassy were in my wallet, just in case.

I don't recall what the second room in the embassy was for except that behind its big glass window, huge color photos of President George H. W. Bush and Vice President Dan Quayle smiled down on us. I wondered for the umpteenth time what would happen if Bush died and ignorant, lightweight Quayle became the leader of the free world. Brenda wondered whether they'd lose those smiles if they came here and saw what they were inflicting on her people. A travel advisory for Guatemala faced us from a bulletin board between the rooms. All the more reason to get the hell away as soon as possible.

As we emerged from the hotel on equally sunny Tuesday morning, there were Sara with her wares spread across the pavement and Old Pablo lounging nearby. Brenda and I had agreed to be casual and discreet. To no avail. On seeing her beloved aunt, Brenda rushed into her arms and Old Pablo came over and wrapped his arms around both of them. The three laughed, wept, and rattled on in Mam. A nearby brown uniform and I exchanged smiles.

The three of them continued in Mam, both naturally and so as not to share with the brown uniform. After a few minutes I went over to him and told him frankly that my wife lived in New York and had not seen her beloved aunt and uncle for several years. If he knew the rest of the truth about the four of us, which I thought possible, he didn't let on. He simply replied that it's hard when families have to separate though probably not as hard as when his ancestors came here from Spain and never saw their families again. I thought but did not say that mine came from the North Sea islands, the price we all paid for a new start in the New World, too bad we had befouled the land with so much blood of the original owners. From the man's features, I guessed that he had ancestors among those owners as well as from Spain.

"Those two are regulars here," he said. "Does your wife come from their village?"

"Yes," I said, hiding my alarm as I would at a nasty turn in a trial. But maybe his question was natural and innocent. "She's planning to buy a bunch of their wares," I said, "to show off to our friends in New York."

Which she did, two bundles, which we carried up to our room. Not much had changed in the village, she said. Ernesto and Lourdes had finally married. We were sitting in chairs facing our huge window—the city fascinated Brenda in the daylight too—and I was playing music loudly on the radio in case the room was bugged, though I should have waited to debrief her out on the sidewalk. Nothing had been heard of Frida. Yes, Frida had definitely been part of the fatal debate and was the first one to agree with María that they had to sacrifice Germán. Brenda had not told Sara or Old Pablo about the *María's Courage* book so as not to worry them, but their account of events that occurred after she left the village matched the account in the book. Except for Frida.

"Do they know how the army responded to the death of the colonel?" I asked.

"This is terrible." Anger darkened Brenda's voice. "The army didn't say anything at first. Then they said he died in an auto accident, but didn't say when or where. They shot a lot of eagles! And they replaced the colonel with a colonel who was even worse!"

"So the avenging eagle did more harm than good."

"I'm afraid so. My poor, dear sister!"

I didn't challenge her about the eagle's being María. Didn't I assume it too, at least for a moment, when I called it *avenging*?

"On the remote chance it was María, it's too bad she didn't foresee how the army would probably react," I said.

"Would you have foreseen seen it?" Brenda snapped, and I realized too late that I should not have criticized her sister.

Except for visiting the doctor, who certified Brenda's good health, we stayed close to the hotel. The food in the dining room was pleasant though not cheap. On Wednesday morning, I joined the conversation on the hotel patio, with Brenda translating my Spanish and Sara's Mam. Brenda asked them to tell her parents that we would visit the village as soon as we could, and they understood.

At the embassy that afternoon, Silkworth slid under the window a visa for Brenda and a maroon file envelope, sealed with scotch tape and official imprints in the pale red ink that American post offices use. Eureka! The papers we came for! No more fear that Brenda would be deported and tortured to death!

We walked at an exuberant clip up the *avenida* to the hotel. Fierce-looking men holding shotguns stood in front of several shops we passed. Apparently it cost the shop owners less to hire them than to buy theft insurance. One after another, they smiled and returned our greetings when we said, "*Buenas tardes.*"

We felt greatly relieved, yet on Thursday morning when the door closed on our plane and the pilot told the flight attendants to prepare for take-off, Brenda felt sad. She was clutching the Embassy's maroon envelope with both arms and pressing her forehead against the small plastic window to watch the capital city of her homeland grow smaller and glimpse the towering *Volcán Pacaya* to the south, into whose crater many of her countrymen had been thrown from helicopters supplied by her new homeland.

Late that Tuesday afternoon, two bombs had gone off in front of the small Peace Brigades house in another part of Guatemala City, sending shards of window glass knifing across the desks of the volunteers inside. No one was cut or killed only because they had just sat down to supper behind a partition that divided the office from the kitchenette. News of the bombing did not appear in the *Prensa Libre* that we read at breakfast Wednesday and Thursday, and we would not learn of it until Brenda talked with her Sanctuary friends in New York.

Chapter 33

Even with the Embassy's blessing inside the maroon envelope and, at last, my green card that wasn't green, I could not become an American citizen until Charlie and I had been married for two years. The inconvenience made sense as the government's way of sifting out "marriages of convenience." What made no sense, but made me angry, was the gasoline my new government kept pouring on the fires in Guatemala and El Salvador. My evenings at *Universidad Centroamericana* had nearly convinced me that the U.S. had joined in shedding all this blood in order to stop Communism, and that Communism in these lands did not mean a creaky economic system, or a threat that the Soviet Union would take over. No indeed. Communism meant anything that Uncle Sam didn't like. In this case, Communism meant that the elected government's refusal to pay the United Fruit Company of Boston its inflated price for some land it wasn't using.

When I asked Jonathan in Texas whether this was true, he said probably, but what made him angry was the many occasions when his beloved country climbed into bed, as he put it, with totalitarian people around the world. A scholar named Jeane Kirkpatrick had concocted a silly distinction, which the Reagan people found convenient to adopt, between authoritarians and totalitarians. It was okay for Uncle Sam to have intercourse with the former, but the latter were bad people.

When I told all this to Charlie, he dug out one of his books and showed me a quote that has stayed with me by a *New York Times* writer named Harrison Salisbury: "There is little difference to the man to whose testicles the electrodes are applied whether his torturer is 'totalitarian' or 'authoritarian.'" I shuddered and said the same would hold true for a woman too. A question flashed through my mind: Had the men clipped an electrode onto me?

"I'd think you'd remember if they did," said Charlie, "but if you don't, you don't."

I couldn't remember and promptly put the question from my mind.

The weeks passed swiftly back in Manhattan, and soon I was hanging more topcoats in the closet. Life with Charlie was an adventure and a joy.

We spent Labor Day Weekend, which we considered our first anniversary, at the same campground and on the same tent site by the woods. The law firms that Charlie sent his c.v. to and phoned in Burlington and Montpelier liked his qualifications and were sorry they couldn't consider hiring him, except for one, Gifford & Foster, a six-lawyer firm in Burlington that was swamped with work and needed a trial person who was admitted to the New York bar. They arranged to interview him the Friday before Columbus Day weekend and invited us both to a cookout at one of the partner's houses the next day.

The cookout meant that the lawyers and their spouses would be checking me out and I'd better not screw up Charlie's chances of being hired. Either I would be sweet and shy and evasive when asked the inevitable questions, or I'd come out with my story and risk Charlie's chances. He and I quickly agreed I'd come out with it. They were sure to learn it sooner or later and, like Charlie and my nipples, best to know now if it turned them off.

Charlie explained my story to Jack Foster, who was hosting the cookout. He didn't see a problem. The firm sometimes did pro bono work for illegals who came in from Canada, and I was well on my way to becoming a citizen. Indeed, he hoped I'd be willing to tell everyone my story. Willing I was for Charlie's sake. I didn't want to, but we saw no choice.

During the cocktail hour on the Fosters' back lawn—Charlie and I nursed one bottle each of Catamount IPA, the best *cerveza* I'd ever tasted—I answered frankly about my village and jobs but once or twice ducked a question by saying, "I'm supposed to talk about that after we eat." Which I did. Jack Foster was sitting next to me at the middle of a long table covered with white paper, After the apple pie, Jack, as he'd asked me to call him, stood up and said, "Charlie's wife Brenda has had some experiences that I've asked her to tell you about." He sat down and looked at me. I guessed that was my cue. I wiped the hamburger shine off my chin and stood up and gave a short version of my Sanctuary talk. At the end, the people clapped. Which felt good but didn't tell me whether my story or complexion rubbed anyone the wrong way.

Jack stood up again. "I hope you've all met Charlie or will before we finish. He and Brenda have decided to leave Manhattan and move to God's country. We're going to try to help them. I've asked him to give us a short bio. Charlie?"

My husband pushed back his chair, stood on the grass, and sounded more like Ithaca than Manhattan. I knew that's how he liked himself best. Again applause. I thought he was frank and charming and hoped the others did too.

Driving back to the motel, we rehashed the party. "How do you think it went?" Charlie asked.

"I didn't see any problems. Everybody seemed welcoming."

"People sometimes seem it when they don't mean it. After your talk, I heard two people tell you how brave you are. Two other people told me the same."

"That's kind of embarrassing. I didn't take a big decision to give those talks. They just seemed like the best thing to do. I never felt brave about it, just sometimes scared."

"Or about the chances you kept taking that you'd be sent south and tortured to death? I suspect you didn't give it much thought because you're brave and caring. Most people in your position wouldn't have done it."

"I guess not. Most don't. They attract as little attention as possible, and I don't blame them. Anyway I'm glad I'm doing it, and I'm glad you're glad."

"How many guys can honestly say they admire their wife?"

I felt myself blushing and changed the subject. "There's something I noticed during your talk."

"When I stood up, you saw my fly was open."

"No, Silly! It was your manner. In the office you have a Manhattan manner. Around me and our friends, you're more relaxed. I've thought of it as your Ithaca manner ever since we went there. You like yourself better when you're in it, and I saw you were in it when you spoke to those people just now."

"You may know me better than I know myself. Why didn't you tell me about my Ithaca manner sooner?"

"Who knows? Maybe it was still fuzzy in my mind. But this evening it really struck me. These are your kind of people, Charlie. You were yourself with them, whether they offer you a job or not. There's nothing wrong with the way you are in the City, but it's not your happiest self. If I'm right this is big. Moving to Vermont isn't just for me. You'll be your happiest too."

Long pause. "Maybe you're right. I wonder whether I would have figured it out if you hadn't told me. I never thought the move is just for you. It'll make *us* happy."

The next morning, the woman behind the desk at the motel told us they don't serve breakfast—our mistake for assuming they did—and recommended a diner across the road and up a short hill. We ordered pancakes, with Vermont Grade B maple syrup of course. From our booth we could see Camel's Hump at quite distant but still dramatic.

"When we move here," I said, "why don't we find a house that faces that mountain?"

We thought it likely that Gifford & Foster's cookout meant they considered Charlies competent to meet their immediate need and maybe stay on afterwards. But did we pass the personality test?

"If they don't offer you the job," I said in the car driving home, "I suppose we'll never know whether we messed up or it was just my tan skin and flat nose."

"Unless you said something awful that I don't know about, I don't think we did anything that would alienate a client, which would be their main concern. And if they can't accept a lawyer who has a Native American wife, best we leave them in the dust."

"Worst case would be if they hire you for an immediate need, then dump you."

"I could live with it. If they take me on, I'm going to keep my feelers out and my resumé current unless and until they take me into the firm."

Neither Charlie nor I did very well with the suspense. We liked the people we met at the party and hoped Charlie's professional future would lie with them. The next Thursday Jack Foster phoned with an offer he could accept. The Friday after Thanksgiving we found a very nice house we could afford on a hillside outside the little city of Waterbury. It was half an hour from Burlington, five minutes from Ben & Jerry's, and faced the sunsets and the profile of the mountain we felt unaccountably drawn to.

Between those happy events came the terrible news that Padre Ignacio Ellacuría, five other Jesuit priests, and two of their housekeepers had been shot to death on the campus of the *Universidad* in San Salvador. Both governments claimed, of course, that the FMLN guerrillas did it, but I was sure it was the army, and Charlie accepted my judgment. Events would soon prove me right.

The U.S. then played an ugly role in the aftermath. The Jesuits' cleaning woman, Lucía Barrera de Cerna, had seen men in the uniforms of government soldiers while she heard the last shouts of the priests and the shots that killed them. The Spanish and French ambassadors, fearing for her safety, arranged for her to go into hiding with Jesuits in the United States. But as she landed in Miami, FBI agents and a Salvadoran intelligence officer seized her and held her incommunicado for six days while they interrogated her until she recanted and said she hadn't seen anything on the fatal night. But upon being released, she returned to her original story and explained that her interrogators had repeatedly accused her of lying and threatened to send her back to El Salvador, where she knew that if she did not tell it their way she would most likely be killed,. Soon, ballistics analyses, confessions by guilty soldiers, and other evidence proved that Lucía had been truthful the first time and U.S. and Salvadoran officials had forced her to lie.

Charlie, I was happy to see, was even more outraged than I was by what the FBI did to Cerna. "They fucking kidnapped her," he said, "and threatened to kill her. She knew they'd send her to her death if she didn't tell their lie, and they knew she knew it, even though they fucking denied it!"

The Jesuits' murderers were members of the Atlacatl Battalion, which the U.S. had created at its School of the Americas in 1980 and trained, equipped, and advised ever since. This same U.S. pet battalion had also murdered more than eight hundred civilians in 1981 at a town called El Mozote. Both governments denied that their troops committed that massacre too. Charlie was impressed by how much of this sort of information I had retained from my evenings at the *Universidad,* and, of course, he understood what he called the righteous anger and the motivation that my torturers had instilled in me.

Since Charlie had a pile of work to clean up before he left S&S, I did most of the packing for Vermont, filling my four suitcases plus a lot of cardboard cartons that we got from the local liquor store.

We had been able to spend Thanksgiving weekend house-hunting in Vermont upon Charlie's promise to his parents that we'd spend Christmas with them. The whole of Christmas week was free because S&S gave Charlie his farewell lunch the Friday before, and he was not to start the new job until Tuesday, January 2nd. At the lunch, Jenny Erdman, who was succeeding Charlie as the S&S litigator, asked us enthusiastically about the new life we'd be having up north. Ms. Sisson reminded me to tell my Sanctuary story. I did, though did not say when I got the green card that made me legal at S&S. And no mention of the murder of the priests and housekeepers, which the media had reported only briefly, nor of the kidnapping of Lucía Barrera de Cerna, which the media ignored and my Riverside friends told me about. Much as I wanted to tell these people, many of them friends by now, about these crimes, Charlie and I had agreed that his farewell lunch was not the time or place. So I would never tell them, if that mattered in the grand scheme.

Chapter 34

Our new surroundings quickly taught us, as all our weekend visits had not, that Vermont weather can change your plans. When it snows in Manhattan, you put your head down and walk to the subway, and the snow quickly turns black and goes away. But when a blizzard sweeps through Vermont, you cancel your plans and stay home. The road crews quickly free you, but the snow on the meadows and beneath the trees stays a beautiful white until April when islands of ground begin to appear. In Texas I had learned that hard water and ice are not the same thing; in Vermont I learned that winter's greatest peril is black ice, which isn't black and you may not know it's there until your car slides out of control. We bought skis—no more standing in line for rentals—and enjoyed them on the nearby mountains to the south of us, several times at Sugarbush and Glen Ellen and once at Mad River Glen, whose bumper sticker brags "Ski it if you can."

Spring brings Mud Season when flatlanders (which we so recently were) don't invade, and we Vermonters get our state back. The snow melts, the rains come, the ground remains frozen underneath, and dirt roads turn to pudding. The ruts sling the car from side to side as you power forward. We decided not to try any more dirt roads than necessary during Mud Season, until we traded in the car for an SUV with four-wheel drive. First, though, I learned to drive in Charlie's stick-shift sedan, which I did that summer more slowly than I'd expected. Charlie was patient with me, and we had only a few near misses.

During the next twenty years, we settled in as a mostly typical American family. Charlie's job at Gifford & Foster worked out well, and they made him a partner. I obtained a Vermont driver's license and graduated with honors from Champlain College after four years of driving with him to my classes in Burlington while he went on to his office. Then I got a job teaching Spanish at Burlington High School, and we still commuted together. During summer vacations we'd camp for two or three weeks at one or another of the splendid campgrounds in Quebec or on Cape Breton Island. This was only possible because my green card would let me back into Vermont before I became a U.S. citizen.

That happened in 1991. I was sworn in, along with eleven other immigrants, in a ceremony in the federal court in Burlington. It didn't seem to bother anyone that I was retaining my Guatemalan citizenship; dual citizenship was legal, and somehow I felt more secure having it. We recited the Oath of Allegiance in a chorus. The judge stepped down from his perch, congratulated us and welcomed us one by one while shaking our hands. Everybody including him fussed over me because I was obviously pregnant. I found myself weeping, as did several of the other new Americans. In spite of my feelings about U.S. misconduct, I was proud to become a citizen of this great nation.

I may have mentioned that some of us Maya look oriental. Several times while I was walking in Burlington, a person told me to go back to China. The first time it hurt. Later it pissed me off, but outwardly I ignored it. A putdown even from a boor is not fun. One spring afternoon as I was walking towards Charlie's office on the Church Street promenade and even more obviously pregnant, an elderly man in a gray suit gestured towards my bulging belly and said, "Aren't there enough Chinks in the world already?"

"Why don't you go fuck yourself?" I replied. He started to say something but didn't, and we both walked on. I had never said that to anyone before and haven't since. I hoped he wasn't a client of Charlie's firm.

"Good for you," Charlie said when I told him. "You must have the same fire as María, but you hide it better."

Our precious Mary Elizabeth was born in June of 1991, seven pounds, one ounce. Though we named her for my sister, we decided to call her Liz. I knew that saying María or even Mary all the time would hurt.

Amanda, the midwife, and Charlie had just helped me back onto the bed in the birthing room and jacked me up so I was almost sitting. Amanda laid my precious little Liz across me. She was so warm. My breasts were so full. I guided her tiny mouth to the remnant of my left nipple hoping against hope I could still pass milk. She began to suck. She sucked harder and harder. She squirmed and began to cry.

"Her mouth has a good latch, but the milk does not always come at once." Amanda's tone was reassuring, but time passed and Liz kept crying. We tried the other nipple. No milk there either. Amanda fetched a bottle, and I held it to Liz, who sucked rapidly while Amanda placed warm compresses on both my breasts and gently massaged them. That felt good, but I was failing my daughter. Even though I knew it wasn't my body's fault, I wept, hoping my tears didn't upset Liz. Charlie stroked my head and muttered curses at the men who cauterized me. After a time, Amanda fetched the hospital's lactation specialist, who examined my nipples.

"The scar tissue is blocking the ducts," he said, as we had feared it might. "Whoever burned you knew what he was doing—quite a thorough job. I wonder who taught him." His professional appreciation was not what I needed to hear just then. He continued, "Later we'll see if surgery can free them."

Bravo for the torturers who thwarted a non-existent Communist threat by preventing an infant born five years later from receiving this most primal love and assurance! I held Liz against one bare breast or the other while holding the bottle and vowed to give her as many kinds of love as I could. As non-violent as I was, if it had been within my power to cut off the torturers' *cojones*, I would have done so. The fire inside me that Charlie mentioned I suppose, or just normal anger.

Well after my breasts calmed down and stopped making milk, we consulted a surgeon. He ran scans and seemed thorough and told us the milk ducts were sealed for good and couldn't be replaced or bypassed. So my temporary disappointment turned into a part of my life. We didn't say much in the car driving home from his office. That night we did not make love and I kept from weeping until Charlie was asleep. It hurt him when he saw me upset.

With the new responsibility came new joy. Charlie insisted on taking his turn with the 2:00 a.m. feeding even though he had to go to work in the morning, while I got to care for our adorable, demanding little soul for much of the day. Fortunately, Champlain College provided excellent baby care while its students were in class or study hall. Camping in the summer, it felt so refreshing to return to the land and relive our first nights together in the tent, though we would have to defer the latter when Liz got to be two years old. When the boys came along, we bought a bigger tent.

The winter after Liz was born, peace came to El Salvador, ending twelve years of a civil war that killed around 75,000 people, most of them murdered by the security forces, as I had believed right along and a truth commission would later confirm. It angered Charlie and me to hear on the news that all these people "died" in the war. Not so! Children, men, and women in their prime don't simply "die." The security forces slaughtered most of them, many by torture, and they tortured thousand more, many worse than me. I thanked God and Señor Rodríguez that I got off as lightly as I did. Charlie and I wondered whether we would ever know how the señor happened to enter the chamber and rescue me, and what became of him and his family. Eventually we would.

When our precious Herman and Peter came along two years after Liz, I was prepared, but my inability to nurse them still made me feel like a failure, and I wept again. Thank God for tears! We named them Herman for my childhood friend who gave his life to save my village and Peter for my father.

We had been lucky to find in Amanda a midwife who knew how to help me give birth in the manner of my people, by squatting on a mat so gravity could help make it relatively easy. I learned later that a hard delivery can awaken past trauma, and I might have been screaming in the hospital, instead of only weeping over my failure to nurse.

My parents, Pedro and Rosa Tuyuc, and I had been sending letters to each other ever since I reached the U.S. Ernesto would write to me in Spanish what they asked him to in Mam and translate the letters I wrote in Spanish because I couldn't write Mam and he couldn't read it. During the summer of the year Liz was born, we skipped camping and, incredibly and joyously, brought my parents to Vermont for a two-week visit, the first time we had seen each other in eight years, thanks in good part to our Senator Jim Jeffords who kindly arranged for their visas. Neither of them had ever traveled more than a day's walk from our village, but Padre López accompanied them all the way onto their seats on the flight from Guatemala City. Charlie and I met them at Miami International, flying down the day before in case of delays, so they wouldn't have to change planes by themselves. At our house they quickly adjusted to the indoor plumbing.

We drove them up Mt. Ascutney and the Okemo ski mountain, took them for a ferryboat ride across Lake Champlain and back, had lunch on the busy outdoor deck of the Long Trail brewery beside the Ottauquechee River—Papa quickly discovered the joys of Vermont microbrews, Mama not so much—and gave them a little taste of Austria with dinner at the Trapp Family Lodge. One of the Sunday afternoons, some close friends had a small lawn party for them. They enjoyed the hamburgers but declined the hotdogs. Some days we just hung out at home and sat on our deck to watch the sun go down and the sky redden behind Camel's Hump. Little Liz took to them instantly; she was the part of Vermont they enjoyed the best. We caught each other up on much that had happened to us and the village since I left, but I did not tell them I had been tortured.

The visit was ending. Mama and Papa were sitting with Charlie and me at a small table in front of a tropical juice bar in Miami International. We were nearly oblivious of the humanity rushing their wheelies past us in both directions. We knew the words we were exchanging would be our last for a long time, maybe forever. Half-finished purple smoothies were on the table in front of Charlie and Papa, orange smoothies in front of Mama and me. Tears were running down Papa's cheeks as he put his wrinkled brown hand on Mama's shoulder. She was sobbing as she spoke.

"First it was María. She is dead. Now it's you. You are gone. The darkness of war has plucked the roses from my life. Thank God, Brenda, you are alive and healthy and have born a child. Perhaps you will bear more."

The three of us were speaking in Mam as we did throughout the visit. Charlie was used to my telling him most of what we said.

"This visit, seeing how you live," Mama continued "has convinced us of what we did not believe before. You will not return. Charlie is a good man, but I don't think he could live our life."

"I don't want to hurt you, but I don't think I could either. I loved it growing up. You were wonderful parents and María was my best friend. But I just don't think I could live there anymore."

"I know," Mama said. Papa nodded.

Suddenly I was not as sure as they were that I could no longer find contentment in the life I grew up in. "We'll come and visit as soon as we can after the war ends."

"Him too?" Mama said. Papa looked equally doubtful.

"Him too. You said he's a good man. He is."

We finished our smoothies and walked through the throng to the security gate. As we hugged goodbye, three of us were weeping and I saw tears on Charlie's cheeks.

Could I return to village life? If I did, would Charlie possibly join me? If he couldn't or wouldn't, could I bring myself to leave him? If we split, would I try to take Liz? By the time we picked her up from the sitter in Vermont and I carried her through the front door of our cozy home, I had stopped asking myself these questions.

Charlie and I kept up with our Mayan friends Enrique and Sophia, thus keeping me in touch with my roots, even though the drive to their house takes an hour and a half. Charlie incorporated a small non-profit, which they created and dubbed the International Mayan League/USA. Its purpose was to educate people about the history, culture, and present plight of the Maya of Guatemala. Charlie agreed to serve as its corporate secretary and do its legal work, which wasn't much, pro bono, meaning unpaid. He did this for me and my people as well as for the Caneks and his sense of right and wrong.

Our friendship with the Caneks led Charlie and me to spend a weekend with an American hero, and me to meet a soulmate. Enrique and Sophia, who were highly regarded in the Central America solidarity community, invited Sister Dianna Ortiz, a missionary from Kentucky who was horribly tortured in Guatemala six weeks after our trip there in 1989, to go on a speaking tour around Vermont, to venues in Burlington, Montpelier, Brattleboro, and Saint Andrew's Church. It was our privilege to drive them, Charlie and I in front and Sophia, Enrique, and this slender, gentle, indomitable survivor sitting behind us.

That Friday evening Dianna spoke at the bottom of a curved amphitheater at the University of Vermont. Though I had nothing to do with somebody's failure to properly publicize the event, I felt embarrassed that only nineteen people scattered themselves around the seats after she had traveled all this way and told a story that obviously pained her. Dianna responded by trying to make me feel better.

"It wasn't your fault. They were very attentive and asked good questions." Then the words I'll always remember, "I'll speak any time, any place there's any chance of saving a single life in Guatemala."

The next afternoon the audience comfortably filled a cheery church basement in Montpelier. As the evening before, the audience kept absolutely silent while Dianna was retelling and, we could sense, reliving the horrors that three men had inflicted on her. What struck me most, besides her courage, was her certainty that a large man who entered the chamber, ordered the torturers to leave, helped her to dress, and drove her away was an American. All the while he spoke awful Spanish, until she finally shamed him into using English. He said he was fighting Communism and was driving her to the American Embassy. Not trusting him, she fled from his car when it got stuck in traffic.

They burned her with cigarettes many times and raped her many times too, a perk, I suppose, of being a male torturer. Could the American who entered her torture chamber and mine be the same person? How many interrogators who spoke bad Spanish did the CIA have down there?

After our hosts treated us to a potluck dinner at the church, we made the short drive home, and Dianna and I stayed up talking in the brightly lighted living room—she liked brightly lighted rooms at night—after Charlie and the Caneks had gone off to bed. I felt so comforted talking with this gentle woman even when the subject was as mundane as her experience teaching Mayan children in a town not far across the mountains from my village. Besides teaching, she and two other nuns had been helping the townsfolk to reorganize themselves after the army had come in and executed the town's leaders. Apparently towns without leaders are easier for the army to control. This may have been why she was tortured, or maybe it was just to send a message to American missionaries to stop helping us Maya.

"You know, I was tortured too," I finally said.

"No one told me, but I was almost certain you were."

"I feel very close to you even though we just met."

"I feel close to you too. Survivors often do. We're sort of a secret society that shouldn't exist, but since we do, it's good when we can support each other."

"I never felt a kinship like this before. It's more comforting than I'd ever thought I needed."

"If you ever want to talk," she said, "I'm just a phone call away."

Though we went on until after midnight, we did not discuss the particulars of our tortures. In the years to come, I would think of phoning her, but I never did. Just knowing she was there for me gave me a comfort I hadn't known I needed.

The next day was a grim cloudy gray, and none of us said much during the long drive south to the city of Brattleboro on the Connecticut River. The program was in a cheery church basement with an audience much like the one in Montpelier, and this afternoon there were three warm-up speakers before Dianna. During the second talk, she got up from the table facing the audience and left the room. She'd used the toilet when we arrived, and this was less than half an hour later. Ten minutes passed, then fifteen. She knew where the restroom was. She couldn't be lost. I got up and went to look for her.

And found her sitting on a step the half way up the short flight between the room full of people and the door to the parking lot. There was no expression on her face. She seemed to be somewhere else. What to do? I had read in a book by a Salvadoran survivor named America Sosa, "We were taught to resist torture. Members of the Christian communities taught us that when all our strength and identity were gone, we should think of beauty. We had a mental exercise to think not of family or children but of beauty."

I asked Dianna to come outside. We walked across the parking lot, which stood on the lip of an embankment. The broad river flowed below, and a mountain studded with granite outcroppings rose from the far bank. The gray sky muted the beauty, but it was the best I could offer. After a few minutes she seemed to return from wherever she had been, and we walked back inside to the speakers' table.

She gave her talk as though nothing had happened, and again the people listened in absolute silence. As Charlie drove us away afterwards, I told her that she should feel absolutely free to cancel her appearance at Saint

Andrew's. Sophia and Enrique agreed, but she wouldn't hear of it. After supper in the parish hall, she was the center of a gentle conversation with fellow diners sitting around her in comfortable chairs of the church's well-lit parlor.

I felt sad saying goodbye to Dianna in the Caneks' driveway the next morning. I wanted so much to spend more time with this gentle, brave, determined woman who was giving so much of herself to seek justice and relief for my people. She felt like a friend I had known all my life. Before leaving, she told me that the weekend taught her not to tell her story so often in that short a time. The memory of her sitting on the stairs taught me that a beast inside a survivor can spring forth at any moment. Inside me? I didn't think so.

Charlie continued to enjoy practicing law in Vermont. Now and then I translated in the asylum case when a refugee who came in from Canada spoke only Spanish or Mam. The summer after Sister Dianna's tour, Charlie's parents bravely took our children for two weeks while we made a two-day drive to Forillon Park at the east end of the Gaspé Peninsula, where we hiked and biked and sat in folding chairs and read. While dining at the picnic table, we sometimes spotted minke whales arch their backs from the water near the magnificent cliffs that march along the bay to the tip of the land. Or drove past a tall white lighthouse to nearby Cap-des-Rosiers (Cape of the Roses) for bouillabaisse at Restaurant Chez Mona. I missed our kids and looked forward to the summer they'd be old enough to bring camping here. Charlie agreed with me how important it is, for him and them as well as me, to return to the land and sleep close to the earth. As so many of my people still sleep every night.

Chapter 35

I was lying awake on a mat in my parents' hut. The darkness was total, the blackest I have experienced in thirteen years because a hut in the highlands grows blacker than a tent in a street-lighted campground. My parents' regular breathing told me they were sleeping. This was my seventh night in my childhood home and wonderful to be here, yet I felt an awkwardness that I hadn't expected. My rusty Mam amused my old friends who were now adults. In spite of talking now and then with the Caneks and occasionally translating in court, I found rapid Mam hard to follow. During my childhood, María had slept beside me. This week it was Charlie, breathing regularly now too. He was adjusting well, or at least not griping, about the simple living that was his ancestors' lot a few centuries ago in Ireland. He had been as filled with questions about life here as I was about Manhattan,

A long-overdue though imperfect peace had come to Guatemala in the final days of 1996. All these years after I left home, it finally became safe for me to return. But I was an American citizen and glad of it. All the same, my anticipation heightened as the day approached to deliver our children to Charlie's parents and fly south. My joy at seeing my family and friends was tinged with sadness as my heart felt what my mind knew, that life had gone on for them too and theirs was no longer the world of 1984. Aunt Sara had changed less than I expected. Old Pablo was no longer the Elected Representative, and it seemed a little odd at first that, having married Auntie, he was now Uncle Pablo. It was good to see Ana and Byron and their children, though as the days passed, we ran out of things to talk about. She was still very sweet but asked little about my life since leaving.

It warmed my heart to see Lourdes and Ernesto as the happy parents of her two nearly grown children and two more that he fathered with her. Also to see Charlie hit it off with him. He had learned to speak, read, and write Spanish, and was checking out the documents in Spanish that *ladinos* occasionally asked villagers to sign, as I had once planned to do. He told me that the loss of María had moved him to become fluent in the language of the people who cost him so dearly. So he should learn English, too, I thought.

He told us that *María's Courage* was translated into Spanish before it was disappeared in the U.S. He had a copy and said it got everything exactly right about the fatal day—including things he'd forgotten until it reminded him of them—except that it left out Frida. He could not understand why she was missing unless she had pretended to be the quetzal and left herself out to protect her family—just as Charlie and I surmised.

Charlie and I meet Padre López on the grassy plot with the trees and rock where María had waited for Luis, and Germán gave his life. The padre was balder and thinner and, of course, older than I remembered as he toiled up the path from the road. Sweat beaded his scalp, and he was panting as he greeted me and grabbed Charlie in an *abrazo*.

I peered down at the road to see whether he had the same car he had driven me in. I saw it but couldn't tell. "It's the same," he said, still slightly out of breath, "much repaired and with two bullet holes, rusty now, that someone put in the hood."

It was a warm sunny afternoon much like the one when María gazed at the road waiting for Luis. We sat on stools on the grass around the rock. While Charlie and Padre López got acquainted, I kept glancing into the branches overhead. A quetzal can't possibly be perched there! The breeze parted the greenery and I thought I caught a flash of scarlet. As the men's conversation continued, I glanced up now and then, but the breeze had slackened and the leaves did not part again. Even if there was a quetzal up there, that didn't mean that Frida did not write the book.

The padre turned to me. "You're not the girl I put on a bus in Quetzaltenango. I'm happy to see the woman you've become."

"I'm so happy you still visit our village."

"I made a point of it. I want to tell you how much I admire you for speaking in *El Norte* against the Terror. That took courage. You were doing the Lord's work."

"It was the least I could do." My cheeks flushed. How did he know what I did?

"Most refugees didn't do it, and I don't blame them. You're a lucky man, Charlie, to have such a brave and caring wife."

"I know," he said, and I saw it was his turn to blush.

"I suppose you've wondered how Señor Rodríguez happened to rescue you from the secret police."

"Many times. I think it was a miracle that he showed up in time to stop another assault and maybe save my life."

"It may have been a miracle but not the kind you think. After peace came to El Salvador, Padre Quiñones told me the story. It seems that the Señor had a broader outlook than most of the ruling class because he'd been educated at Yale College in *El Norte* and took a graduate degree at the London School of Economics. He also took his Christianity more seriously than most of the elite. As you know, he often brought his family to Padre Quinones's church while many of his colleagues were playing polo or splashing around with their kids in a swimming pool.

"He obviously could not stop the war or the torturing, but he managed to make El Salvador slightly less barbaric than Guatemala by convincing the junta that Guatemalans were foolish—not barbaric, but foolish—to kill everyone they tortured. Granted that both juntas used torture, not so much to extract information as to terrorize the people into being passive. The Guatemalans relied solely on dropping mutilated bodies where they'd be seen, but, he told the junta, it would be more effective to create terror in two ways, both by displaying mutilated bodies—which he knew he could not prevent—and by allowing some victims to survive and tell everybody their terrible stories. Who knows whether his two-message system created more terror, but it saved many lives."

"So the bottom line was, it was the lesser of two evils," Charlie says. "Some killed and some merely tortured is better than everyone tortured to death."

"Certainly," said the priest.

I shuddered but saw they're right. "How did he find the chamber and save me?"

"It wasn't only you he saved. His day's work was to drive to the army base in the morning, watch people being tortured through a one-way mirror, and every now and then—not too often, or he might endanger his family and himself—he would step in and save the victim's life. Suppose the secret police kidnapped a hundred people. His system allowed fifty to survive. But his own interventions raised the number to fifty-five. He knew that if he intervened too often, they'd probably stop him from intervening at all—or worse. So he passed many days watching tortures and not stopping any of them. Then he'd drive home in the evening as though he'd spent the day at the office, and everything would be as normal as you saw it while you worked there. Only Señora Rodríguez knew about his terrifying dreams and the years he awoke in the night screaming or weeping."

"The poor, brave man. So they were going to kill me." I feel Charlie reach over and rub my back.

"That's not clear, but he wasn't going to risk it."

"My God! So maybe it *was* a miracle that saved me. One good man in an evil system, and the price he paid! What became of him?"

"The murder of the Jesuit priests upset the whole family. Several months after peace arrived, they moved to Spain."

"Interesting," says Charlie, "that they stuck it out through the murders of seventy-five thousand civilians but six murdered priests drove them off."

"The murdered priests may have been the last straw. If he'd left too soon, he couldn't have saved me."

"I think you're both right," said the padre. "He and his wife hated what their country had become. Imagine, if you can, the U.S. turning fascist! They had been discussing for several years whether to move to Spain, where the right-wing violence had, they hoped, ended for good. The Jesuits' murders tipped the balance, but they felt they couldn't move as long as Señor still had the ability to save some lives in the torture chamber. The war ended, the state closed the torture chamber, and off they went."

"What about the tall, blond CIA guy?" Charlie asked. "Did he know what Rodríguez was up to?

"He did, and he was okay with it. What was a few lives more or less as long as the terror succeeded? The two of them became friends and sometimes ate lunch together."

"My God!" I said.

"The CIA man didn't like the tortures, but they were part of his job," the padre continued. "After he went in and wrote out his questions, he'd stop looking through the mirror and read a newspaper or something until the next suspect was brought in."

"Then he didn't watch everything they did to me." I didn't want to say *raped* to a priest. "That's something, I suppose."

"I'd like to kill the bastards!" Charlie said and the padre nodded. "How did Padre Quiñones learn all this?"

"The very question I put to him. Indeed, I went further. I asked him if by any chance the Seal of the Confessional had suffered a little break. He stared at me for a long moment and said, 'The Lord works in mysterious ways.'"

So burning my nipples made sense from the standpoint of terrorizing the public, except that I inadvertently thwarted the terrorists and their CIA advisers by not telling anyone about it except Charlie, the midwife and surgeon, and our children when I decided they were old enough to understand.

"Do you know what happened to the man who drove me from Padre Quinones's church to Guatemala City?" I asked. "Do you know if he survived the war?

"That was terrible," Padre López replied. "but not because of you. He continued taking risks, and about a year after he got you out of El Salvador, they kidnapped him and his wife and their two children. They were never seen again. If the secret police followed their usual practice, he and probably his wife were tortured to death, their eleven-year-old girl was killed so she couldn't be a witness, and the two-year-old boy is being raised by a Salvadoran officer's family or an unsuspecting couple who adopted him in *El Norte.*"

"My God!"

"The bastards!" said Charlie.

Before we walk the padre into the village, I paid him back with interest for all the money he spent sending me to El Salvador and taking my parents to and from the airport. He said he'd use it for people in need.

My parents and Aunt Sara and Uncle Pablo wept when we parted a few days later. I tried to be as cheerful as possible through my tears, but deep inside I felt I might never see them again. At least we'd keep exchanging letters, those pitiful tokens that would bind us across the miles and years until death did us part.

The next year the Archdiocese of Guatemala released a 1,400-page truth commission report on the Terror. It called it *Guatemala: Nunca Mas!*, which means Never Again! That April in the happily crowded National Cathedral, mainly tall, white bishops presented copies of the report to mainly short, brown, colorfully clad Mayas, including Rigoberta Menchú. Among the principal speakers was a courageous man named Bishop Juan Gerardi Conedera, who had headed the team that compiled the report. Two days later a cabal of soldiers smashed Bishop Gerardi's head with a chunk of concrete so totally that he had to be identified by the ring on his finger.

The Church's report gives a precise, historic, and heart-rending account of the human rights violations suffered by 54,000 victims, most of them my people. It exposed years of U.S. official and media misinformation and vindicated what we human rights activists had been saying all along. It found that the security forces committed 88% of the crimes against those 54,000 souls, the guerrillas 7%, and persons unknown 5%. Of the 22,500 civilian killings it considered—about ten percent of the total—it found that the military murdered 90% and the guerrillas 6%. The bodies of 30% of murder victims showed marks of torture. The report said nothing about the role of my new homeland.

I knew the slaughter had been very one-sided but not that much. My heart broke anew and I mourned this martyred bishop and the 200,000 dead, most of them harmless Maya like my family and friends and me, who were simply trying to lead their lives and not starve or hurt anybody. The report shocked Charlie too. It hurt him to see my grief.

A United Nations truth commission was working on their own report. A member of their team told a friend from the Riverside Church, who told me, that the army was putting enormous pressure on them to attribute the crimes more or less equally between the military and the guerrillas—just as both governments and the responsible U.S. media had been doing for years. But in February of 1999, the UN team, uncowed by the still-prevailing terror and the murder of Bishop Gerardi, issued *Guatemala: The Memory of Silence*, which attributed 93% of the 42,000 crimes it considered to the military and only 3% to the guerrillas. It recorded 669 massacres, 626 of them (also 93%) committed by the security forces. Some 83% of the 42,000 victims it studied—a modest cross-section of all victims—were Maya, while the rest were *ladinos*. The report concluded that the army had deliberately targeted and destroyed Mayan parts of the departments of Huehuetenango and Quiché, not very far from my village, in what amounted to "acts of genocide."

Unlike the Church's report, which did not discuss foreign intervention, the UN report blasted the United States for its complicity in these horrendous crimes. No surprise here of course, but it was nice to see it repeated on such good authority.

Again the U.S. media paid little or no heed to this hard-won statement of truth that gave the lie to their years of reporting. The next month though, to our great surprise, President Bill Clinton announced that U.S. "support for military and intelligence units which engaged in violence and widespread repression was wrong, and the United States must not repeat that mistake."

Bravo! What an extraordinary admission for a U.S. President to make! Yet what a feeble admission of helping to torture uncounted thousands and murder two hundred thousand, most of whom looked like me! Most Americans who heard that Clinton said this—precious few, I suppose—could not have had the foggiest notion of what he was talking about. Thank you, responsible media! Responsible for the public's ignorance!

Though Clinton's words were grossly inadequate for the bloody horrors my adopted country had wrought upon my people, what U.S. President has ever admitted even this much? It was almost an apology! Charlie reminded me that ten years ago, after a U.S. warship had accidentally killed nearly three hundred people by shooting their Iranian airliner into the Persian Gulf, Vice President George H. W. Bush declared that he would never apologize for the U.S. no matter what the facts were. Apologies obviously don't bring anybody back to life or reattach sliced-off body parts, but I thought they help the humanity of both the survivors and the perpetrators. Charlie agreed.

One Saturday morning in November, the trees outside were bare, and we could see more of the mountains from our picture window than when clouds of greenery cut the view. A fire danced behind the glass doors of the woodstove, and the children were playing in the fallen leaves in the yard beyond the deck. Liz was showing the boys how to rake the leaves into a heap and jump into it. Two years younger, they were still her little brothers.

Charlie and I were finishing up our copies of Orbis Books' shortened English version of *Guatemala: Never Again! The Official Report of the Human Rights Office, Archdiocese of Guatemala.* The book had taken its place beside *María's Courage;* Sister Dianna's *The Blindfold's Eyes: My Journey from Torture to Truth;* Jean-Marie Simon's *Guatemala: Eternal Spring, Eternal Tyranny;* and Jennifer Harbury's *Searching for Everardo: A Story of Love, War, and the CIA in Guatemala* as the most significant books in my life. Charlie and I had decided we each needed a copy of the Archdiocese's report, and they arrived last Monday from Amazon, which we were still buying books from. Every evening after the kids were in bed, we consumed it, I with many tears and much rage, and Charlie with unintelligible angry mutterings. We had agreed not to discuss it along the way so we'd finish sooner. He finished first and was reading the *New York Review of Books* when I closed my copy.

"This is the most disgusting stuff I've ever read," I said, "also some of the most painful, soldiers burning my people to death or slicing them up—hands, breasts, testicles—while they're still alive. My God, how can one person do that to another!"

"Reminds us how thin the veil of civilization is, doesn't it," he replied.

"Listen to this," I said. "I know you've read it, but listen to this by somebody who hid and survived! 'They killed the men, shot them in the head, and then burned the bodies. They shut the women and children up in a school, threw grenades at them, and burned their bodies. Young women were raped, then tortured and killed. I saw a river of water, but it wasn't water—it was the melted fat from the bodies that were being burned.' The young women who were raped before being burned up could have been Maria and Frida and Ana...."

"Our guys trained and advised that army," Charlie interjected. "I hope they didn't train and advise them to do a whole lot of this stuff."

"At least your guys tolerated it! At least they didn't talk them out of it!" I snapped, and continued, "The book is so immediate for me! It shows me what could easily have happened to my family and friends and the whole village if María and Germán hadn't sacrificed themselves."

"María sacrificed herself?"

"She probably didn't think of it like that, but that's how it turned out. She wouldn't have joined the guerrillas if the army hadn't forced her to kill Germán."

"Probably not. Too bad the Church didn't say what the UN said about American complicity."

"Anyone who's been paying attention knows about it. Telling people about it was one of the main points of Sanctuary. My church in Texas told me avoid it, but Jonathan and the other gringos gave them an ear full."

"I think you told me that. I was thinking about the village the quetzal saw before he flew to your village."

"Or Frida probably saw during her ramblings."

"They were only murdered. Not tortured or burned alive. The soldiers stopped at gang-raping those three women, and didn't mutilate or kill them afterwards. What a world we live in when only being murdered passes for good luck!"

"If these tragedies had not occurred, I'd probably still be living in my village and you'd probably be in Manhattan with goodness knows what woman."

"You amaze me with your ability to see the glass half full."

"I'd better call the children for lunch. I don't feel like eating."

That winter we started the twins on skis with the help of their big sister, who'd been on them for two years. In the summer we packed ourselves into the SUV for the two-day drive along the south shore of the St. Lawrence to Forillon Park. The trip was lots of fun mostly. A highlight was taking a tour boat along the cliffs, where we watched thousands of birds nesting on the jags of the vertical face, seals playing in the wash along the rocky base, and two whales that were much bigger than the minkes we sometimes saw from the picnic table. I think the birds bored the boys.

In Washington, DC, in 1998, Sister Dianna Ortiz founded a project she called the Torture Abolition and Survivors Support Coalition International, TASSC for short. It's mission: "To end the practice of torture wherever it occurs and to empower survivors, their families and communities wherever they are." And that's what they tried to do in many ways, a truly uphill struggle against prevailing American attitudes. It was a valiant effort but tiny, given that an estimated half million survivors of torture live in the U.S.

Every year Dianna and her TASSC teammates gathered fifty to a hundred of us survivors from around the world to take comfort in our solidarity, deal with our problems, lobby members of Congress—or more often their staffers—and hold a twenty-four-hour vigil in Lafayette Park across the street from the White House on or near June 26, which the United Nations designated the "International Day in Support of Victims of Torture." When the UN established the day, Kofi Annan, its Secretary General, declared in words that move me every time I read them, "This is a day on which we pay our respects to those who have endured the unimaginable. This is an occasion for the world to speak up against the unspeakable."

During the next several years, Charlie and I attended these vigils. He helped with the logistics of feeding and housing us survivors and shepherding us through the DC Metro. (Incidentally, we say "survivors" because it's more empowering than "victims," and empowering is what we need.) I joined the other survivors for intimate conversations in a big room where non-survivors were excluded except for two therapists who specialized in treating survivors. Though I had long been sure that the effects of my torture were behind me, these gatherings gave me an enormous feeling of being whole. I always felt that my batteries were being recharged.

Charlie and I were shocked and saddened and insulted by the attack of 9/11, 2001. Most Americans seemed to feel violated, and in a sense we were, but heretical as Charlie and I may sound, we felt, too, that some chickens had come home to roost. When we reflected on the violent U.S. meddlings abroad—three thousand American dead on 9/11 versus two hundred thousand Guatemalans and seventy-five thousand Salvadorans, for instance—it was easy to see that the Saudis and Egyptians who flew the airliners into the Twin Towers and Pentagon could just as well have been Salvadorans and Guatemalans or Chileans or Indonesians or Iranians or Bolivians or you name it.

"But you must never tell anyone, even our closest friends, that this is how we feel," Charlie said on the deck that evening while the children were inside doing their homework. "Most Americans feel so damn exceptional—tribal—that our friends and, God forbid, my partners and clients might very well be offended if we told them."

"But shouldn't we be honest with them?" I asked, maybe cluelessly.

"What good would it do? Most of them probably don't even realize they value three thousand American lives more than a hundred thousand Maya. They're nice people. Why piss them off with stuff they won't want to hear?"

"And that won't do any good."

Charlie was right. We decided not even to share these feelings with our children, so as not to burden them with keeping our heresy from their chums.

Perversely, the 2004 scandal of the Abu Ghraib torture photos nourished the love affair that millions of Americans have with torture—a love affair based, as far as I can tell, on ignorance plus their gut feeling that it works plus false propaganda. Most of them don't seem to know, for instance, that FBI and other veteran interrogators use kindness and deception to get more accurate information more quickly than torture usually gets.

Shame on the nation that has tortured thousands of Iraqis, many of them admittedly innocent, and then walked away without helping them to recover, leaving them to live damaged lives, many of them in much worse shape than I ever was.

One day at a TASSC gathering, Charlie asked one of the therapists how many of her clients were as deeply affected by their tortures as Sister Dianna was. "All of them," she replied. The next day he asked the other therapist the same question and received the same answer.

"I'm sure that's true for their clientele, though it surprises me," I replied when he told me, "but it can't be true for survivors like me who never needed therapy." With what expertise or bravado, I wondered later, did I brush off the possible legacy of my torture?

Chapter 36

The curved crest of Camel's Hump rose against a blood red sky like the beak of a great predatory bird. I was sitting beside Brenda and Liz on the couch on our deck. The evening was warm and filled with the sounds of August. A trio of citronella candles flickered in green glass cups on the table among Brenda's mug of coffee, mine of tea, and Liz's bottle of mineral water. Across the table, a pair of plastic chairs awaited the boys, who were finishing up the dinner dishes. The three of us sat in silence.

The flaming sky took me back to the evening twenty years ago when I sat alone in my apartment watching the sky turn red over New Jersey and weighing the pros and cons of taking a small risk to satisfy the curiosity—and maybe win the favor—of an attractive receptionist who was becoming a close friend. The blood red above the mountain took me, too, to the horrible death of an evil man a few feet from where I stood in Guatemala City—a scene I usually brushed from my mind.

I liked Vermont's mountains, too, because they reminded Brenda of the home she had to leave. She had adjusted to the Vermont winters with a speed that surprised me, and appreciated at once the beauty of the lumpy, snow-covered land on frigid sunny days. As I learned to ski, so did she. She loved, too, the bushes of violets that deck the byways of Vermont in May. This view of Camel's Hump had all but compelled us to buy this home. A few weeks ago, the five of us had hiked up it, an easy climb for our teenage children, less so for us. Sitting on the rocky peak, we tore into the PB&J's that Brenda had made and gazed at the Champlain Valley below and the Adirondacks beyond.

These years with Brenda and our burgeoning children, though not without hassles, were the best I've ever spent. After Enrique and Sophia returned to Guatemala, Brenda was probably the only person in Vermont who spoke Mam, Spanish, and English; and occasionally the government or a defense lawyer called on her to translate for an asylum seeker who had crossed from Canada. She also volunteered with the Vermont Human Rights Commission in Montpelier. I enjoyed the law more than I had in Manhattan—mainly because of the people it involved me with—and did what I could at the

Vermont chapter of the American Civil Liberties Union. I also took pro bono a fair number of criminal and immigration cases. Twice I was the lawyer and Brenda the translator for the same refugee. I had believed that she, too, was fulfilled and happy with our life, but one evening last June as we were sitting out here and the children were inside doing their homework, she said she felt there was a piece of business that she needed to attend to.

"I've never told you or the children the details of my torture."

"I thought you did."

"Only the generalities. In the Sanctuary talks too. Not that I was trying to evade. I just thought I'd said enough. But the memory has been pacing around in my mind like a caged beast. It wants out. I need to tell you and the kids, though I'm not sure why." She paused. "Actually I dread telling you. I thought the beast was dead, but it's only been sleeping."

Several times since, she brought it up, then put it off. But tomorrow we'd be driving Liz south to start her freshman year at Mount Holyoke College in Massachusetts, so this evening was Brenda's last chance until Thanksgiving if, as she insisted, the whole family was going to hear it. During our supper of takeout pepperoni pizza capped with cherry pie, we sat around the table in the brightly lit kitchen and talked it over.

"Are you really sure you want to, Mom?" said Liz, who looks like her mother but is a few inches taller. She had read Sister Dianna's *The Blind-fold's Eyes* which warned her (and me) that detailing the ordeal might propel Brenda into reliving it.

"You don't have to do it if it's going to hurt you," said Herman, who didn't read much but was the most attuned to his mother's feelings. At sixteen, the twins were nearly as tall as I am and look Anglo-Irish too.

"Do it if you have to, Mom," said Peter, who was on the wrestling and tennis teams and still managed to get good grades, "but don't do it for us. We know enough already. We've seen your burn scars."

"I second everything they're saying." I felt she was really going to go through with it. The youngsters probably did too, and it warmed my heart to hear them trying to protect her from herself. I sensed that she wanted her loved ones with her for what she feared she was letting herself in for. "It's often best to let sleeping dogs lie," I said.

"The trouble is, the beast isn't sleeping. It's straining at its cage. I'm more afraid to keep it in than let it out." She added more calmly, "Probably no big deal after it's had its fun."

We tried, we failed, she was going ahead. I wasn't sure she had post-trau-matic stress disorder, but she sometimes showed the symptoms—I'd looked them up—nightmares, flashbacks, easily startled, still somewhat distrust-ful. At least she liked sex and didn't go into rages. When we were alone, I sometimes felt she was somewhere else. As our years passed, she seemed to lock whatever-it-was into the back of her mind and usually be the alert, sunny person I loved so much. Now she wanted the five of us to face the beast—I would have called it her demons—together. For all these years, I speculated, she had avoided consulting a therapist because she knew that talking with one would mean telling a stranger what she was about to tell us, and she hadn't felt the need to put herself through it. If you let sleeping beasts lie, they won't bite. Or so we had thought.

Brenda and I had been leading reasonably normal, middle-class lives during these years, but I sensed, too, that her terrible day in El Salvador had lurked behind us and maybe a bit between us. As she uncages it now, would it shrivel in the light? Or was she about to open a Pandora's box that wouldn't close?

"Look at that silhouette of Camel's Hump," I said to distract her or may-be myself. "Doesn't it look like the beak of a predatory bird?"

"You've said that before," she replied a bit irritably. "I don't see it."

"Neither do I," said Liz. "It looks to me like a recumbent George Wash-ington."

Brenda turned to me. "Do you suppose that being so close when the eagle killed the colonel traumatized you into seeing something in the mountain that isn't there?"

"No." I paused. "Well, maybe a little. I do think it looks like a beak."

The churning throb of the dishwasher rumbled through the open kitch-en window. Moments later the boys emerged and sat facing us across the flickering candles. The crimson sky had nearly faded into black behind them. Brenda half turned her body against the arm of the couch and faced the four of us.

"Here goes," she said and drew a deep breath. "You know that secret po-licemen named Max and Jorgé grabbed me off a street in San Salvador. They drove me to a torture chamber on an army base, and they beat me, burned me with cigarettes, and raped me while they interrogated me for informa-tion I didn't have."

We nodded.

"That's how I've thought about it and talked about it for more than twen-ty years—when I thought about it at all. But during the past few months, the details have reared up in my brain, in nightmares, and even while I'm awake"—this is more than she'd ever told me—"They scare me. I shudder.

For better or worse, I've felt the need to tell you, my dearest ones, and myself what really happened. I'll begin where they hauled me out of the car."

The past became present in the August night.

"In the doorway they stop and blindfold me. This is a good sign. If they're going to kill me, why would they care what I see? They lead me into a cold room and sit me on a colder metal chair. 'Don't get up,' one said. 'Don't move around or you'll hurt yourself on the furniture.'

"They turn out the light and leave. I push up the blindfold and see nothing. I stand up and move carefully around the room. It is small and doesn't have any furniture at all except the chair. So they lied about furniture. I find the chair and sit. I'm shivering in my shorts and cotton blouse. I feel fear. I don't know what they're going to do to me but I know what they usually do to women. Will they really rape to me? I am totally in their power. What must I endure? I doubt God, but it can't hurt to pray. 'If you're there, God, please help me.'

"Time passes and passes. The men return and switch on the light—one bulb hanging from the ceiling. They tie on the blindfold again and lead me through several corridors, I think. They slide off the blindfold. We are in a sort of office. I see a desk and several metal chairs like the one I was sitting in. It's warm in here. Max sits at the desk in an armchair. I see a pen and a pad of paper. There's a big mirror on the wall behind Max. Jorgé sits me in the chair in front of the desk and stands behind me. I notice a mattress stands rolled up in a corner, gray, white, uncovered, and filthy. Maybe it's where the foul smell is coming from.

"'We know all about you,' says Max. 'We know that Padre Quiñones helped you come here from Guatemala. We know you worked for the Rodríguez family and are working for insurance people who may not know you're a subversive. We know you spend many evenings at the *Universidad*. So you must answer our questions truthfully because if you lie, we'll know it.'

"Bam! Jorgé slaps the back of my head. That hurt! My eyes blur. Pain and anger surge through me. Is this what happens if I lie? The slap really pisses me off. Any idea I have of cooperating, even a tiny bit, vanishes. They ask me many questions about Father Ignacio Ellacuría and the other priests at the *Universidad*. I say I'm not religious. I never talked to any priest or heard any of the priests at the university, only Padre Quiñones when I went to church with the Rodríguezes. Bam! Jorgé slaps my head. It hurts.

"'If you're not religious, why did you go to church?' Max says.

"'To get out of the house. To see other people. I wanted to learn about your country.' Bam!

"A tall blond man comes into the room. His skin is much lighter than the other men's. The torturers greet him like an old friend. 'Bienvenido, Tio Mike!' He doesn't say anything. He writes on a little pad and tears off the pages. The men read them to me. Questions in bad Spanish. They sound like he's been listening and watching through the mirror. Jorgé doesn't hit me now. My throat is parched. I ask for water. The men pay no attention.

"The fair-skinned man leaves. Jorgé stands me up and spins me around. He rips open my blouse. Buttons pop off. He unhooks my bra and roughly pushes the clothes off my arms. I stand naked from the waist up. My face goes hot with shame. Is the blond man watching through the mirror? Jorgé pushes me back into the chair. He lights a cigarette, takes a couple of puffs, and moves behind me again. Max asks a question he'd asked before. A great pain stabs my shoulder. I shriek. Now it is horrible pain one place and another. Each burn hurts like fury. I shriek and shriek. Jorgé comes around. He lights a new cigarette. He holds the tip to my nipples again and again. O, God, this hurts! How can they stand my shrieking? The stink of burnt flesh fills my nose. On and on goes the knives of pain. Oh please, God, make it end!

"The men stop the questions. Jorgé crushes a cigarette on the floor under his boot. He yanks me to my feet."

Brenda stood up. She was breathing fast. She faced the four of us but looked past us. I glanced at the boys. Horror was on their faces. Tears ran down their cheeks. Liz was weeping and moaning. I was furious and I wept. Brenda paused as if to collect herself and resumed. Her voice quavered. I wasn't sure she knew we're there.

"He is undoing my shorts and pushing it and my panties down my legs. He sits me back in the chair and pulls them off my feet. I am naked. My back and breasts are on fire. Max has rolled out the mattress on the floor." She shuddered. "It's covered with filthy blotches and stinks worse than they do. I am trembling. I try to stop sobbing but can't. The burns are on fire all over my back and front and shoulders! I hate being naked like this. What they're about to do fills me with fear.

"Max pulls me out of the chair. I jerk an arm free. Jorgé's hands grab me from behind. He pins my arms to my sides and lifts me up. I kick the air. Max pulls the chair away."

Her sobs grew louder. She was panting.

"No! No! No!

"Jorgé carries me. I kick my heels on his legs. He throws me down on the stinking mattress. It is damp and smells of sweat and urine. I try to roll off.

He is behind my head and pins my shoulders down. I try to kick. Max forces my legs apart and lays his stinking shirt on top of me. He is very heavy. Something pokes between my hips.

"'Lie still,' he says. 'Make it easy for both of us. It will only take a few minutes.'

"'No!' I scream. 'No!'

"He arches up and thrusts into me. O, God, that hurts! Virgin no more. I scream and scream." She is screaming out her words. Horror twists our children's faces and I suppose mine. "His hand covers my mouth. I turn my head. He mustn't smother me! I stop screaming so he won't. Uh, uh, uh, uh, he grunts. Each push scrapes my flaming back against the mattress and my flaming chest against him. Faster and faster. He sighs and pants. He must be finished. His weight squashes me.

"Max gets off. Jorgé gets on. Heavy too. He pushes more. The burns scrape. Then Max again. I try not to scream. I moan. I weep. Max takes longer than he did the first time, more pushes. God, they hurt!"

Liz, Herman, Peter and I watched as our dear companion suffered before our eyes. I was screaming inside myself. She had left us and was lying on the mattress even as she stood before us. Her fists pounded the air. "No! No!" She sobbed and shook. Gradually her screams subsided and she stood at the end of the couch panting in the candlelight. Maybe she had come back to us. But no. "Then it's Jorgé's turn again...."

"You don't have to continue," I said. She didn't hear me. Liz and I looked at each other and back at Brenda. I wished the evening was over or hadn't begun.

"He is off me. I lie sobbing. I smell blood in the stench. I shake. I shudder. I am cold but don't want to move. I lie there while they fiddle with something with wires on it. I don't pay attention. All I want is to lie still and rest and hope the pain in my nipples and front and shoulders and back and crotch will subside.

"Maybe I doze. Jorgé is behind me holding my wrist above my head again. Max is on his knees between my legs. One grubby hand parts my hair, which is stiff—with blood I suppose. Something bites into my most sensitive part. Oh, my God! No!"

Scream after scream issued from Brenda's perspiring face in the quiet August night. Her body convulsed again and again. She was oblivious of us. I saw Max's grimy hand biting an alligator clip onto the tender nub in the woman I cherish. I longed to kill him. Rage mixed with my ache for her. I had never been violent, but now I fumed to smash these men to pieces. In spite of myself, I was glad the nearest neighbors were too far down the hill to hear the screams. Were we wrong to let the children watch this? She wanted them to know what the men did to her, but I doubt she expected they'd watch her live it.

After what seems like a long time, her screams subsided. She stood panting in the candlelight. She looked down at her shirt and shorts, drenched with sweat, and tugged at them as if to make sure she wasn't naked.

Liz and I stepped towards her while the boys sat frozen. I wanted to hug her, and I think Liz did too. As we come towards her, she shrank back.

"No! No!" she screamed as if we, too, were torturers. She cringed against the wall between the sofa and the doorway and held up her hands to fend us off. "Don't touch me!" she screamed. "Don't come near me!"

She looked hard at us and seemed to return to the moment. We stood, she panting, Liz weeping, and I beside myself. The boys went to her. Much taller than she, they hugged her to themselves. She let them.

"What happened? Why is my shirt all wet?" She looked from one to another of us. "The last thing I remember is, one of the men was burning me with his cigarette."

"It was terrible," Liz said. "You were there. You screamed your head off. We can't ever let this happen again."

"So that's why I sound hoarse."

Then nobody said anything. The five of us sat in silence, none of us touching yet very close. The night was calm. Katydids chattered quietly beyond the light. Tears glistened on all our faces. The moon was nearly full. The curved peak of Camel's Hump stood black against the radiant sky. I had no idea whether reviving her long ago agony had brought her relief. Maybe the opposite. Would she relive it tomorrow?

At last she broke the silence. "I can't remember what happened just now except it was horrible, a nightmare that I could not wake up from. I had no idea how much is still inside me. No idea at all." A long pause, and she shook her head. "All these years I've felt so normal. The people in Texas may have been right. Maybe I need therapy."

"My God," said Liz softly. Tears glistened on her cheeks in the candlelight. "It was one thing to read about torture in Sister Dianna's book, but to watch it happen! To my mother! To feel your fear and almost your agony! To watch you live it!"

The boys remained silent. After a while, Herman blew out the candles, and we went inside. Liz climbed the stairs to finish her packing. The boys went up to their room.

In the small hours Brenda woke up screaming, her first nightmare in several months, the first time in several years that she'd awakened screaming. I guessed the cage was open and her beast roamed free. Would she be Brenda in the morning?

Chapter 37

During breakfast, Peter and Herman were unusually quiet. We stuffed the back of the SUV and half the back seat with Liz's things. There was no room for the boys to go even if they'd wanted to. During the drive Brenda and Liz rattled on, leaving me at the wheel alone with my thoughts, which were mostly that the years with Liz at home had passed quickly, and was there more I might have done with her and the boys, and was I going to be able to settle a case where my client was in the wrong? Already I was beginning to feel the pangs of missing my daughter. When thoughts of last night intruded, I pushed them back. Liz and the boys would tell me later that this morning they had wanted to talk with Brenda about her meltdown but were afraid they'd touch it off again. That hadn't occurred to me as the reason I avoided the subject. Was I in denial that the horrible evening had occurred, that I was helpless to protect my wife from her past?

We carried all Liz's stuff up to her room, which had a cheerful view across the campus, and exchanged pleasantries with the girl who would be her roommate. Then the hard goodbyes. On the drive home, Brenda was silent and I was supposing that, no longer protected by chattering with Liz, she too was feeling the pain of missing her and avoiding the memory of last night.

"You know, Charlie," she said as we left Massachusetts for Vermont, "this morning begins the end of a wonderful part of our lives. It seemed long sometimes, but right now it's like it lasted only a moment. Our household is no longer whole. Liz will visit us from college for holidays and maybe a few summers. Soon it's the boys' turn. When they're back, they'll expect the freedom they have at college. We'll try to adjust."

"Good luck with that!" I said.

The towns of southeastern Vermont passed slowly by, unseen except as white names on the green exit signs. We reached White River Junction and looped onto I-89.

"I *do* need therapy," Brenda said. "At least I'll give it a try. I don't want to put any of us through *that* again."

I felt relieved that she'd brought up the scene the rest of us had been avoiding—the eight-hundred-pound gorilla in the car—and even more re-lieved that she had not slipped back into her denial and would try therapy.

It stunned me that for twenty years I'd believed we were happily mar-ried—I certainly had been—and had no idea about the ferocity within her. Occasionally it woke from its sleep like a hibernating bear, and she'd scream at night and I'd talk to her until she was okay, or she'd seem to be to be somewhere else, but I'd never put the signals together. Was she as happy as we both thought she was? I had no idea. Was I too insensitive, too absorbed in my own concerns? Too contented in my own denial of her plight? Prob-ably, but I wasn't sure what I could have done before her beast awoke. They were good years for me, and mostly for her I think.

The green and rock-faced hills slipped past and the occasional village below us. We crossed the White River and crossed it again. Soon we were back in our home with Peter and Herman, without Liz, and with Brenda the same though not the same.

Chapter 38

I'm told that no one is the same after torture. The September evening when the beast broke forth convinced me at long last that this was true for me. Therapy every week during the next five years did not banish it but helped me to live with it. Well that it did. It's not uncommon for people who survive torture to kill themselves, even after twenty of thirty years. Did I ever consider suicide? Hasn't everyone? But, thank God, I haven't come close to doing it.

Yes, thank God. Charlie told me that as I relived the torture, I kept calling on God. Soon afterwards I faced reality and became a believer. How else can anyone explain how our lives, with all their faults and blessings, came into being except through the will and power of a Creator? But God obviously does not prevent all evil. That's where I went wrong. I'd thought that if God existed, He would protect me. But then He didn't. Did He have a hand in creating my luck, good and bad? In this life, I'll never know. Did He prevent my torture? Obviously not. He didn't prevent Jesus's torture either. I wish I had talked with Padre Quiñones about faith in a time of war.

It was my good luck that Señor and Señora Rodríguez and Mr. Sigourney and Ms. Sisson managed to be both rich and good people at the same time. Was it just an accident that all four of them were also people of faith? I'm glad I still have my curiosity about life. Without it, I doubt I'd have found God.

I completed twenty years of teaching a year after I finished therapy, or more accurately, finished my regular sessions with Tina, the therapist. Even though I loved working with my students, I retired and went to work for New England Survivors of Torture and Trauma in Burlington. Hundreds of thousands of survivors of politically-motivated torture—some say more than a million—live in the U.S, and unfortunately, most of them live (or don't) without therapy. I had known since meeting Sister Dianna that we survivors have a unique rapport, and I wished I had devoted myself years earlier to helping every one of them I could. Did some part of me sense that doing so would arouse my beast? For twenty years I kidded myself—call it *denial* if you will—that I'd gotten over the trauma all by myself, in spite of the signs that I hadn't. Not until the beast sprang forth did I admit it existed. I'm glad, though, that Charlie didn't pushed me to find Tina before I saw I had to.

And not until I'd been in therapy for four years did I appreciate a series of articles about CIA-assisted torture in Honduras that reporters named Gary Cohn and Ginger Thompson wrote in *The Baltimore Sun* and one of my friends at the Riverside Church had sent me copies of during my 1995 summer vacation. Skimming through them back then, I'd thought something like "how terrible" and "so it happened in Honduras too, why am I not surprised." I put them aside and didn't bother to mention them to Charlie, but I didn't throw them out.

When I happened to mention them to Tina, she said, "Why don't you read them here? I'll read a book and won't charge you for my time."

"Why?" I asked. We had already discussed the fact that many thousands were tortured like I was in El Salvador and Guatemala, some more, some less.

"So we can both see how you respond now that you've been confronting your beast."

"Why can't I read them at home and tell you later how it went?" I realized as I spoke that this was a dumb question, but after ignoring them for years I suddenly didn't want to wait to read them.

"So you'll scream at *me*, if it comes to that, though I don't think it will. I want to see how you react."

A week later I sat in my usual chair in Tina's office with the articles on my lap and, on a table beside me, a glass of unsweetened ice tea to which I added maple syrup as I did at home. Instead of her pad and pen, Tina held a copy of *The Davinci Code*. "I'm behind in my reading," she said.

The CIA and the Honduran army, the *Sun* reported, set up a torture unit called Battalion 3-16 and flew in torturers from Argentina's dirty war to help train it. CIA men, whom the local torturers greeted warmly as "Mr. Bill" and "Mr. Mike," entered the chamber and wrote out questions in bad Spanish for the poor souls who were in their power, just like Tio Mike at my ordeal. I wondered as I read, why doesn't the CIA teach them better Spanish?

Then came a part I found hard. Battalion 3-16 captured a young woman named Ines Consuelo Murillo. She was probably around my age then, and she actually was a guerrilla. They beat her, of course, and stripped her. It doesn't say they raped her, but they fondled her and threatened to rape her if she fell asleep. Some nights they kept pouring ice water on her to keep her awake. Once, they forced her head into a barrel of water until she went limp. They attached electrodes to her breasts and genitals. "It was so frightening," she said, "the way my body would shake when they shocked me. They put rags in my throat so I would not scream. But I screamed so loud, sometimes it sounded like an animal. I would even scare myself."

My family told me that my screams scared them. As I read, I felt I was in her place. I didn't scream though. I wept.

"Are you all right?" Tina asked.

"I think so," I sniffled.

"Do you want to stop?"

I didn't. I wanted to keep reading every word about Ms. Murillo, awful as it was. They tortured her much longer and more creatively than they did me, but she survived through a family connection and became a human rights worker. She told the reporters, "Sometimes, I wish I could go away and work on a boat in the middle of the ocean. I speak not for myself, but for those who cannot speak."

Which exactly why I gave all those Sanctuary talks. Except for her words in an old newspaper, I barely knew this woman; yet I felt we were sisters. I knew what she was feeling, and I wept for her.

Cohn and Thompson asked a repentant torturer about a survivor who had said, "The first jolt of electricity was so bad I just wanted to die."

"They always asked to be killed," the ex-torturer replied. "Torture is worse than death." Had I asked Max and Jorgé to kill me? I don't remember. The articles don't say whether Ms. Murillo asked to be killed. I would not be surprised if we both did.

"I sort of lost it again, didn't I?" I said as I laid down the papers. It embarrassed me to weep in front of Tina, though I suppose she was used to her patients weeping and I had wept in front of her during the first year or two of therapy.

"You acted like a normal human being the night you screamed your head off, and today you acted like a normal human being whose compassion for a stranger overcame your terror. Congratulations! Tell me the details about Murillo."

It was telling the details that had set me off the night I screamed, but now I only wept. When I finished, she said. "That's horrible. I feel badly for that woman. But you'll notice my eyes are dry. I imagine Charlie's will be dry when you tell him about this afternoon. But you wept as you read, and more as you told me about her. Her ordeal touched you more deeply than it did me or will Charlie. That's how you survive horror, and that's how the rest of us survive it. I'm so pleased for you. But we aren't done yet."

Tina and I stayed in touch, as she invited me to after we finished a year later. I told her I was sorry I hadn't helped other survivors sooner. "That's a generous thought," she replied, "but I'm not sure you were ready to counsel others before the terror broke through and you faced your own reality."

Had I really not been ready, or was Tina letting me off the hook? I saw no point in asking her. A question I did ask and she answered: Shouldn't the closeness I felt to Sister Dianna have tipped me off to the beast inside me?

"Logically probably yes, but you were in denial."

"I guess I was, though it's not very flattering to admit it."

"Don't knock denial," she said. "It gets a bad rap because it often causes trouble, but it often protects us too. We didn't evolve it for nothing, though part of my job is to help people like you to outgrow it."

That was Tina. Don't ask her a question if you don't want the answer. But it felt good to hear her say I'd outgrown my denial. I'm sure she knew it would.

Speaking of denial, I feel that the therapy helped me to get rid of more than my denying that the torture had scarred my mind as permanently as my nipples. Before being tortured, I faced *everything* a lot like María— though I'm not sure I would have grilled Ana about sex the way the book says María did. She never told me she'd badgered Ana about that, and I got a kick out of picturing the scene. After the torture, I was a bit more like Ana. When I asked Charlie to meet Sara in Guatemala City to satisfy my curiosity, for instance, I denied the risk I was asking him to take for me—the small risk that he'd be tortured like Sister Dianna or killed like Father Rother!

"Not to worry," he said when I confessed this to him. "It was a worthwhile adventure. It made me realize I was falling in love with you."

"Did you see I was selfish and inconsiderate of the man I was starting to love?"

"I don't think you were. A sensible fear of the paranoid army kept you from your home. You suffered a gruesome ordeal and moved to one strange place after another, always in fear. You knew you were risking deportation and death each time you denounced the horror. No wonder you were desperate to know about your loved ones."

That was Charlie, generous as usual, always arguing my case. Accepting the beast freed me in ways I had not known I was not free until the awful evening when it ravished me again. I had been angry with Ana for abandoning María after Luis was killed, but now I realize that people like Ana can't help denying bad stuff—as I did for twenty years—and I no longer fault them for it. But denying the bad stuff means missing part of life. If I see it all, I can live it fully. *Curiosity*, until death do us part! As death nearly did.

Speaking of denial, I'm nearly certain that Charlie's close brush with the eagle's bloody ripping of the colonel marked him more deeply than he admits even now. Not that he seemed different after than before. Maybe he would have thought the rocky nob on Camel's Hump looks like a bird's beak even without his touch of trauma. Be that as it may, we both felt mysteriously drawn to the mountain. We loved to sit on the deck and watch the sun set behind it. I once asked him whether he feels that María's spirit hovers on the peak. "Oh, no, not at all," he protested too quickly.

"If her spirit hovers anywhere," I said a few minutes later, "I suppose it's over my village. When I was a girl, Padre López taught us that Christianity promises us an afterlife. I almost believe it now, and I hope I'll find María there—the real María, not some killer eagle. We'll hug each other if spirits can hug, and I hope she'll tell me she's proud of me for speaking out for our people. I'm certainly proud of her."

"I'm proud of both of you," said Charlie. We went inside and climbed the stairs.

Epilogue

The years sped up after I melted down and began therapy. Charlie and I continued to camp in Canada with such of our children whose jobs and preferences allowed us to snare them. We never did sleep on the air mattress we bought so long ago. Early on, we bought a sponge rubber roll-up that felt like the mat I'd slept on growing up, and before I nodded off in the tent, I'd imagine I was lying beside Charlie in the family hut. This may have been a remnant of my longing to go home, and as the longing faded, I kept the image as a warm reminder of my origins close to the earth. Charlie enjoyed that closeness too—for those two weeks a year.

The September evening when the beast seized me marked our children deeply. We feared at first that having them there had been a dumb mistake; but they told us later that, hard as it was to watch me suffer, they were glad we'd included them. I believe it helped to motivate them towards leading lives of service. In a way I don't understand, sharing my agony with them bound the family closer together.

Actually, the next summer we snagged all three children for a four-week camping trip across the country to Seattle, down the coast to San Francisco, and back east by a more southerly route, taking in many national parks—Yosemite, Glacier, the Grand Canyon, and more, the horns of the freight trains wailing through the night in Flagstaff, visiting Oglala Lakota College near Badlands Park, and a long conversation with a Navajo family in their hogan at the edge of Monument Valley. Even in the big van, it was a tight fit for us, our equipment, and clothes. I slept in our three-person tent, sometimes with Charlie and sometimes with Liz. The boys were always in the six-person tent, and the nights Liz joined them, they all changed their clothes inside their sleeping bags. There are limits on togetherness for full-grown teenagers, but otherwise it was a warm family experience across this vast, magnificent land. It may seem strange that I love America after having its sins carved into my mind and flesh, and this summer driving through the landscape where white men had decimated people like me, but I do. The 9/11 attack made me realize I felt this love, and driving across its varied vastness confirmed it. Nearly all the

Americans I know are good people. Like nearly all the Maya.

After college, Liz spent two years in the Peace Corps in Guatemala and managed to visit my village. She went on to Cornell Law School and off to San Diego to work as a badly needed immigration lawyer. So she traced several of her father's footsteps and showed she'd inherited my anger at injustice. God gave us anger for a reason, and if controlled, it can improve what we do. It does for me, and I've seen it help Charlie in court. Here is part of a letter Liz sent us in 2019:

> Especially awful has been the media's failure to call by its proper name President Trump's "separating" of children from their parents at the Border. The proper name is not *separating*. It's *kidnapping*. It's a terribly destructive crime whether the person who carries off the child is a thug in blue jeans or in a U.S. uniform. Obviously the children and parents suffer just as much trauma no matter what clothes the perp is wearing. Many of these kids will probably never get over it. Some have died in federal custody, and it looks as though hundreds will not see, or be hugged by, their parents ever again. While Democrats dither about whether to impeach our career criminal President, I hope they will have the *cojones* to charge him with the high crime of kidnapping—but I won't hold my breath.
>
> What do you suppose, Mother, the chances are that these thousands of traumatized kids will ever receive the healing therapy that they need and you received? The other day I learned that some sadistic border agents tell the kids the lie that their parents are happy to be rid of them and don't want them back! I'm so glad that you and Dad decided to stay in America and give me the chance to do what I can against these disgusting officials. If I'd lived in your village, I could have done nothing.

Charlie and I were so proud of her. She wrote towards the end of the letter that from time to time she has an opportunity "to hug to some of these kidnapped kids. Someone has to."

One warm evening before Liz began her work in San Diego, we were all sitting on the porch much as we were the night I melted down. While the candles flickered, she told us that by representing refugees, she felt she would follow my stand against U.S.-abetted violence and media silence, except that I risked my life and legal work usually doesn't. It pissed her off, she said, that it was a big deal for an official or a talking head to admit that hundreds of thousands of people were fleeing Guatemala, El Salvador, and

Honduras because rampaging gang violence, extortion, and sexual assaults have made them one of the most dangerous places on Earth.

"And that's the most that anybody who gets listened to will admit," Liz fumed. "Not one Goddamn word about the mass murders, the tortures, army sweeps, and death squads that El Norte taught, supplied, advised, encouraged, and prolonged! That's what destroyed the rule of law in those countries! Which is the main reason so many people get murdered there or flee here! We disappeared their rule of law!"

"You tell 'em, Lizzie!" Even now Peter still sometimes teased her.

"Don't forget their violent drug trade driven by our demand," said Herman.

"'We have met the enemy and he is us,'" Charlie recited, "but we won't admit it."

I loved Liz's passion. She rarely swore. María could have said what she just said. "At least our village has been spared so far," I added mildly, "because it's not worth robbing."

"Our village got spared when the army was wiping out hundreds of others," Liz said with fervor, "thanks to Aunt María."

Liz had honed her high school Spanish in the Peace Corps like her Dad, but the boys don't speak it, and none of the children speak Mam. The boys went through college at the University of Vermont, living in dorms the first two years because all of us wanted them to have that experience, and commuting with Charlie and me the last two years because it was cheaper and by then they had many friends among their classmates to hang out with. An unexpected bonus was the pleasure we all took in discussing their courses in the car. I think the discussions improved their grades, and I know Charlie and I learned a lot. After graduating they, too, followed their Dad's footsteps into the law, as classmates at Vermont Law School, in Royalton fifty minutes down the turnpike from our house. We all agreed they would live at home, given the costs of all this education. Their hours commuting in the car brought them closer together than they'd been growing up or driving to college with us parents.

After graduating, each of them chose to serve others, Herman by becoming a career public defender, because doing that job well (or not) matters so much to so many people, and Peter by becoming a career prosecutor for exactly the same reason. Unlike some of his colleagues, Peter chooses to make his job tougher by putting justice ahead of winning convictions. Is the person before him a smartass who needs a few years in prison, he says, or a kid who made a mistake and could use another chance?

In all these years I have never learned what became of Frida. Charlie, Ernesto, and I are certain that she wrote *María's Courage*. If she were still alive, I believe she would have gotten in touch with her family after peace came, but as far as I know, she hasn't, so I fear she is dead. Liz talked with her parents when she visited the village, with Ernesto translating. They haven't known whether to hope or grieve for her, so they have done both, two more casualties of the war.

By including *María's Courage* in this book, I intend to honor both María and Frida and thwart the CIA or whoever it was that whisked it off the U.S. market. If anyone tries to disappear this book, my publisher has sworn to keep on printing it. "Let them try," he said. "I'll enjoy the profits." In Guatemala during the so-called civil war, the government would have killed him.

Sometime during my therapy, I wondered whether Old Pablo has suffered aftereffects of the tortures that Frida describes in her book—besides having his hair turn white. If he has, he hides them well. For many years, so did I.

When people say you make your own luck, they usually mean good luck. By studying Spanish in my teens, I brought on the unexpected chance to ease my family's hunger during a famine. By visiting the *Universidad* to satisfy my curiosity about El Salvador's civil war, I brought on the bad luck that I may have been foolish to risk. But much of my luck was simply luck. As were many of the chances and choices that got Charlie and me together. I've noticed that many couples find each other through random chances and choices. As we Americans say, go figure.

Among the huge number of people who have been tortured in recent years, I consider myself very fortunate: I survived. I was in Max and Jorgé's hands for fewer than eight hours, not the weeks, months, or even years that many people endure it. The rapes did not impregnate me or destroy my sexual desire or alienate the man I love. I haven't killed myself and don't expect to. I did not let my hatred for those men or my fantasies of revenge plague me for very long, and eventually I nearly forgot them. Not to criticize my valiant sister, but her revenge on the evil colonel didn't work out very well.

Fortunately for my family and friends, I've never had the fits of rage that plague some people who have PTSD. Except for snapping at Charlie and the kids now and then and telling that asshole in Burlington to fuck off. There, I've said it, I do have post-traumatic stress disorder. But Tina says the term is not accurate. It isn't post, it remains present. It isn't a disorder, it's a normal reaction of a person in abnormal conditions. She says that the reason I don't express much rage may be that I never had much anger inside me to begin with.

At some point, I told Tina how lucky I felt to enjoy sex with Charlie in spite of the rapes. "It was more than luck," she said. "The tenderness he showed you and his instinct to let you control your first encounter let you feel safe enough to be the woman you are. Without feeling safe, you might well have felt raped again."

Her words startled me. "You mean if he'd taken the initiative the way men usually do, then maybe I'd have had bad sex or no sex at all for all these years." I paused as her words sank in further. "And maybe no marriage and no children?"

"These are possibilities," she replied, "but who knows what would have happened? You're a resilient woman, and you apparently were in love with him before the first sexual encounter. If you hadn't liked it, you might have started therapy years sooner, and we'd have had another issue to work on. Mights that didn't happen. Your husband's gentleness with you is one more reason for appreciating him. And a lesson for me. I'd thought of trial lawyers as having aggressive personalities unable to be gentle. Shame on me for stereotyping."

So, one more reason to treasure that first night in the tent, I thought. Remembering it, I felt my face grow hot.

"Incidentally," she added without apparently noticing my blush, "you'd be surprised how many women take the initiative the first time."

How do you know that, I wondered but did not ask.

Though my nipples remain rather grotesque, they don't hurt. My family accepts them and didn't want plastic surgery to create a new version. Apart from nightmares that grew less frequent and my reluctance to trust people that faded too, I lived what seemed like a normal life for twenty years before the beast popped up. Then Charlie and I were able to afford the lengthy therapy that helped me about as much as therapy can. Now my occasional bouts of depression have stopped and I think I'm almost normal. I am so grateful to have been able to love my husband more deeply than I ever thought I could love a man, and I've usually liked doing it with him. I suspect that loving him and becoming engaged with the world through Sanctuary were a sort of pretherapy therapy.

A good many people who trust in torture don't seem to believe the obvious truth of our Founding Fathers that *all* people are created equal. So these naive pro-torture people consider us their inferiors or less than human. I believe they fail to grasp that the pain and humiliation they inflict piss us off and fortify our determination to give them zero information or false information. They don't credit us with having the same human spirit that they have. So dumb!

Speaking of inferiors, I have been fortunate, too, in having encountered fairly little of the racist discrimination that so many white Americans inflict in so many ways on us non-whites. I never heard Charlie show any racism—which I looked for in him and everyone else I met in this country. He never doubted that I was his equal. Nor did I ever doubt that he was my equal.

The cultural differences between Charlie and me that he and his mother feared a lot and I feared a little never amounted to much. If anything, he and I have constantly seen how similar we are as human beings. Shakespeare had Shylock say about Jews, "If you prick us, do we not bleed? If you tickle us, do we not laugh? And if you wrong us, do we not revenge?" The same goes for us Maya, for Texas rednecks, Vermont liberals, and Manhattan lawyers.

Poignant for me are the long-gone people who spent much of their lives hoping that, *Someday I'll move back to the old sod*—Englishmen passing their prime under the sun of colonial India and Irishmen in the torrid silver mines of Virginia City, Nevada, yearning to return home. How desolate they must have felt when they finally did return and found that their homelands had become foreign countries. I had the same yearning during my years in El Salvador and Fort Worth and first months in New York City; but the yearning began to fade after I met Charlie, and I think it would have faded, though more slowly, if I hadn't met him. Many refugees I've known came to the U.S. fully intending to return home, but their intentions faded as the years passed and they settled into their new lives. If U.S. aid had not prolonged those wars, more refugees would probably have gone home.

When we visited my village in 1997, I realized that it had changed and I had changed, and it would have been a mistake to try to live there again. I was pleased to find myself certain—taking it for granted, actually—that *coming home* meant returning to the town and mountains where Charlie and I were living our lives and enjoying our friends and raising our children.

If a best friend is someone you can talk with about everything, Charlie and I have been best friends almost since that first summer when I risked being deported by trusting him with the truth about my past. I didn't become my own best friend, though, until years later when my therapy wiped away my years of denial. So, call us lucky that the beast finally subjected Charlie, the kids, and me to the horrible hour that opened my way to deepening our marriage, tightening the bonds of our family, and loving myself.

I cannot believe that Charlie and I are about to become grandparents for the fourth time, one child each for the boys and the second on the way for Liz! Looking back, it's hard to believe that I could have spoken out for my people to so many Americans who had no idea what their government and mine were inflicting, or become a citizen myself and enjoyed so many opportunities that I never would have had in my lovely little Mayan village. None of this would have happened if I had not been tortured and forced to flee for my life. I am indeed a fortunate survivor.

Author's Note

— Francisco Goldman, on PBS's *Fresh Air*, May 11, 2021

While the Mayan villagers portrayed in this book are fictitious, I believe they are typical of many who lived in the western highlands of Guatemala during the 1980s, where the violence that surrounded them was all too real. The army admitted destroying 440 of their villages.

Rigoberta Menchú, the winner of the 1992 Nobel Peace Prize, described in her book *I, Rigoberta Menchú, An Indian Woman in Guatemala* (Verso, 1984) the Mayan life and rituals portrayed here. The vow that María says with Ana and the prayer that she says with Ernesto come from that book. A Maya living in Vermont as portrayed in *Brenda's Luck*, graciously showed me how to prepare the corn for tortillas and tamales. Lourdes and Brenda squat while giving birth; it is customary for Mayan women thus to let gravity assist their labors.

Rosalina Tuyuc, a Maya whose surname I borrowed for the sisters' family, is a brave and honored human rights activist. After losing her husband to the Terror, she founded in 1988 the National Association of Guatemalan Widows (CONAVIGUA). In 1995 she was elected a Deputy in the Guatemalan Congress, where she served as its Vice President during her four-year term.

The march of the GAM, the murder of its leaders, and the other grim events that help to shape María's outlook happened as described in Chapter 9. Part of what fictitious Sister Justine tells María that evening resembles remarks by Maryknoll missioner Sister Bernice Kita in her book *What Prize Awaits Us* (Orbis Books, 1989), except that the teachers' strike mentioned there actually occurred in 1989. Prof. Phillip Berryman's *Liberation The-ology* (Pantheon Books, 1987) explains Christian base communities like the one in Chapter 19. Sister Beatriz Zapata, CSJ, who led many groups of Americans through Guatemala and appears in *Brenda's Luck,* assured me that Mayan subsistence farmers tend to be better informed politically than most Americans are.

The awful choice that our villagers must make in *María's Courage* was suggested by an incident that Jean-Marie Simon reported in her remarkable *Guatemala: Eternal Spring, Eternal Tyranny* (W. W. Norton, 1987). Father Fernando Bermúdez described a similar incident in *Death and Resurrection in Guatemala* (Orbis Books, 1986); a veteran of the Guatemalan army told me that a number of such incidents occurred. It has not been disclosed whether the U.S. advisors who worked with the Guatemalan army originated the tactic of giving villagers this fatal choice, or agreed with its using it, or acquiesced, or ineffectively objected.

My veteran friend also witnessed a torture like Old Pablo's third. I heard of Old Pablo's second—waterboarding, which was much in our post-9/11 news—from a veteran of the U.S. Special Forces that taught it to soldiers of Central America circa the 1970's. Old Pablo's first was common in Guatemala.

At the end of Chapter 20, Ernesto cries out, "The horror! The horror!" Towards the end of Joseph Conrad's classic novella, *Heart of Darkness,* the dying Mr. Kurtz, a perpetrator of horror circa 1890 in Belgium's misnamed Congo Free State, utters the same exclamations. The fictional narrator of that work calls himself Charlie Marlow. The perspective in Conrad's story is that of colonialists exercising power; here the perspective belongs to people on the receiving end of the current version of that power.

Brenda is modeled in good part (not the painful or romantic parts) on a trilingual Mayan friend who became a U.S. citizen and asked me not to mention her name. Mam was her first language. On entering China one time to attend a conference, she endured a stiff interrogation by officials who thought from her face that she must be a Tibetan. Quite a few attendees took her for Chinese; on hearing her English, they had trouble believing she came from Guatemala. Besides being there as an observer, she also led a workshop. A *ladina* member of the Guatemala delegation could not believe that anyone so accomplished could be an *india.*

My Mayan friend, who reviewed *Brenda's Luck (Maria's Courage* raised too many painful memories for her), wants readers to know that her people are still being oppressed, forgotten, and taken advantage of.

While I knew a number of Salvadorans and Guatemalans who were tortured by U.S.–advised security forces, it was an American woman, Delores Barbeau, M.D., who had been repeatedly tortured by the U.S.–backed forces of Bolivia, who generously shepherded me through Brenda's' ordeal related in Chapter 36. These survivors are a major reason I wrote this book. Though Brenda Tuyuc Marlow was luckier than most of them, I hope the book represents them fairly.

Regarding Luis's death and Brenda's survival: During their respective civil wars, the Guatemalan security forces killed virtually all their prisoners, often by torture, while those forces in El Salvador kept a good number alive. Whether there was a Señor Rodríguez who advocated the latter practice and personally stopped a number of tortures, I have no idea. There is much testimony, though, that Americans participated in these "enhanced interrogations." To the extent that the tortures sought information as a biproduct of instilling terror, it made sense for the CIA to participate as Brenda and Srta. Murillo describe in the book.

Brenda's experiences with the Sanctuary Movement are based on what my wife Nancy and I learned and did during our Quaker Meeting's participation in the movement. Sister Beatriz Zapata, Sister Judy Stephens, Reverend John Fife, Maríanne Fife, Reverend William Sloane Coffin, Reverend Michael McConnell, the Canek family (not their real names), Maríanna McGuffin, and Nancy Bell are real people who participated in the movement. I call the older Mayan sister *Brenda* for a Salvadoran refugee whose courage and dedication to her people I have long admired. I call a nun whom Brenda befriended *Darlene* in memory of Sister Darlene Nicgorski, who was a hero of the movement. I can conceive that some people attending Reverend Coffin's Riverside Church had the information and lines of communication that I attribute to Brenda's friends there. I did the legal jobs for the International Mayan League/USA that I attribute to Charlie. A Maryknoll priest saved Enrique Canek's life exactly as described in Chapter 29; the priest was a Maryknoll missioner who was one of the leaders of the search for Sister Dianna Ortiz when she was kidnapped and tortured in November 1989.

Early in 1991 as the Sanctuary Movement was fading away, the Immigration and Naturalization Service (INS) belatedly settled a major lawsuit that the American Baptist Churches and several others had brought against it for wrongfully denying asylum to desperately deserving applicants.[1] Under the settlement, the INS agreed to retry, under legally correct standards this time, 150,000 asylum cases, involving several hundred thousand refugees,

---

1 American Baptist Churches v. Thornburgh, 760 F. Supp. 796 (N. D. Cal. 1991).

or as many as had evaded or survived deportation back to the terror.

The brief disappearance of Rigoberta Menchú and the bombing at the Peace Brigades office occurred as described in Chapter 32. The later bomb, outside the Camino Real, exploded the night before an undocumented Guatemalan friend named Adriana Portillo-Bartow, her two daughters, her American husband Jeff Bartow, a gringo named Sidney Hollander, and I arrived in the process of her and her girls becoming free from the constant danger of being deported to the death squads and also becoming U.S. citizens. Adriana's father, her two older daughters, and other family members had been disappeared in Guatemala in 1981 and have not been seen since. She and her two younger girls fled Guatemala, were crossed into Arizona by Sister Beatriz Zapata and another woman, joined Sanctuary, and denounced the violence from a church in Fort Worth and a synagogue in Chicago. Our days in Guatemala City were much like Brenda's and Charlie's, including the visits to the U.S. Embassy and William R. Silkworth, near the start of his career in the State Department. These events are described in greater length in my as-yet-unpublished book *Sisters in the Storm: Life and Death on the Receiving End of U.S. Power.*

Like Brenda in Chapter 33, Adriana and her girls still had to wait two years to become citizens. The murders of the Jesuit priests and the F.B.I.'s kidnapping and coercion of Lucía Barrera de Cerna happened as Brenda describes them.

Sister Dianna Ortiz's speaking tour around Vermont occurred much as Brenda describes it in Chapter 34 except that it was not Charlie but me who drove, and not Brenda but me who stood with Sister Dianna by the river. Torture survivor América Sosa wrote the words that Brenda attributes to her. After Dianna's painful talk to the tiny audience in Burlington, she told me, as she tells Brenda, "I'll speak any time, any place there's any chance of saving a single life in Guatemala."

The truth commission reports of the Archdiocese and UN and President Clinton's admission of complicity were as reported in Chapter 35. I assisted at a number of Dianna's June gatherings of survivors of torture in Washington and had the exchanges with two therapists who specialized in treating survivors of torture that I attribute to Charlie, namely, that all their clients were as deeply affected by their tortures as Dianna was. Sister Dianna died of cancer in 2021 at the age of sixty-two. For Nancy, me, and many others, she was a saint.

Re Brenda's curiosity: Jennifer Harbury (cited in Chapter 35), who probably did more than anyone else during the 1990s to inform the public about

U.S. support for the terror in Guatemala, told me that her Mayan guerrilla husband, who also came from a remote village, "wanted to know about absolutely everything. It was quite amazing." The same was true of a brave guerrilla named Emma whom I drove around Vermont for a few days and whose name Brenda took at first in the U.S. Emma was a *ladina* from a city but had spent the previous fifteen or so years in the forests and quizzed me intensely.

Chapter 38 summarizes the 1995 *Baltimore Sun* articles about U.S.–abetted tortures in Honduras as reporters Gary Cohn and Ginger Thompson wrote them.

Epilogue: The 9/11 attack first made Brenda realize that she loved America. That attack had the same effect on a Guatemalan refugee friend.

Martyr update: In the early 1980's, U.S.–advised security forces murdered Monsignor Oscar Romero of El Salvador and Father Stanley Rother, an American missionary in Guatemala. The former was beatified in 2015 and canonized in 2018, making him Saint Oscar Romero; millions of us had called him Saint decades sooner. The latter was beatified in 2017; he is now Blessed Stanley Rother.

For the people of Guatemala, the resplendent green and scarlet quetzal is the symbol, not only of freedom, but of life triumphing over death. For Guatemalans as for Americans, the eagle may stand for freedom or savagery, as we choose or allow.

Malcolm Bell
Randolph Center, Vermont

Acknowledgments

I heartily thank these generous people for their contributions to creating this novel:

Richard Dougherty, Gail Mott, Margaret Swedish, Christine Christopher, Pat Davis, Suzanne McLone, Rev. John Fife, my brother Richard, and my cousin Laura for their encouragement and constructive suggestions.

Sister Judy Stephens for her most fitting epigraph about the Sanctuary Movement.

Dr. Delores Barbeau for reliving her multiple tortures in Bolivia to help me portray Brenda's.

Professor Emerita Karen M. Fondacaro of the University of Vermont for reviewing the book from her perspective as a clinical psychologist who has worked with survivors of torture from over thirty countries.

Kitty Werner for her artistry, expertise, and patience in creating the book's apt and powerful cover, and shepherding me through this, my first self-publishing venture. Were it not for her, this novel would still be only a file on my MacBook.

And as always, my wife Nancy Bell for remaining my number one inspiration and critic.

About the Author

Malcolm Bell grew up in Brooklyn, served in the U.S. Army, and practiced law in Manhattan before the state and federal courts of New York. He wrote *The Turkey Shoot: Tracking the Attica Cover-up* (Grove Press 1985), reissued as *The Attica Turkey Shoot: Carnage, Cover-up and the Pursuit of Justice,* (Skyhorse Publishing, 2017, paperback 2022) which tells of being a New York State prosecutor who was assigned to indict police for the murders and other violent felonies they committed during the 1971 Attica prison riot, then was blocked from finishing the job.

In 1986 he became active in the Sanctuary Movement and broke the law to stand with illegal refugees fleeing the state-led, U.S.-backed terror in Guatemala and El Salvador. He spent three years on the national steering committee of the Alliance of Sanctuary Communities. During 1995–2012, he was a contributing editor and book reviewer for *Interconnect,* a quarterly of the U.S.–Latin America solidarity community. From 1991 until 2016 he was a director and the corporate secretary of the International Mayan League/USA. Today he lives with his wife Nancy among the Green Mountains of Vermont, where he continues to write.

www.ingramcontent.com/pod-product-compliance
Lightning Source LLC
Chambersburg PA
CBHW020103310726
48970CB00002B/458